ABOUT THE AUTHOR

Philip Trotter lives in Cornwall with his wife and two children. Having travelled extensively around Asia, particularly the countries of what used to be known as Indochina, he became fascinated with the history of each and cherished the idea of writing fictional novels set around the major historical, political and military events of the region. While not writing, Philip enjoys walking, especially along the beautiful Cornish coastline, mulling over the future adventures of Ned Rivers...among other things.

PHILIP TROTTER

INTO THE FIRE

NINE
ELMS

Into the Fire

First published in 2021 by
Nine Elms Books
Unit 6B
Clapham North Arts Centre
26–32 Voltaire Road
London SW4 6DH
Email: info@nineelmsbooks.co.uk
nineelmsbooks.co.uk

ISBN: 978-1-910533-56-7
Epub: 978-1-910533-57-4

Typesetting: Dominic Horsfall
Cover design, Vietnam map: 01Eleven
Saigon map: Rebekah Glockling

Set in Borgia Pro.
Printed in the UK.

To my Dad,
who inspired my love of history.

Author's Note

In covering the scenes of this book, I have tried to stick as close as possible to actual history. But by inserting a fictional protagonist, I have occasionally had to divert from true fact in order to embellish the narrative. Ned Rivers, my invented lead character, strays dangerously close at times to real individuals who lived through the maelstrom of Saigon during the second half of 1963. Never more so, in fact, than to Malcolm Browne, the bureau chief of the Associated Press in Saigon who captured the famous images of Thich Quang Duc's self-immolation, and went on to win World Press Photo of the Year 1963 for it.

I want to make clear from the outset that the credit for such an outstanding photograph of such an emotive moment in history belongs to Browne and not Ned. Browne, who sadly passed away in August 2012, was the only Western journalist invited to this event with the presence of mind to arrive with a working camera. He deserves full recognition for the photograph that changed a nation one hot day in June 1963.

I don't like authors banging on before their work can be read, but I would like to mention a couple of people who encouraged me to persevere with this, my first novel. Doon Wake was the first to read my completed manuscript, and as a teacher of many years, I trusted her opinion. When she reported back that it met the base criteria that I had set to allow others to read it, I circulated my work to a few choice others. Thank you, Simon Gravestock, Harry Dodds, and my sister, Victoria Thomas, for being my guinea pigs, and for your constructive criticisms. Particularly my dear sibling's: after learning that she'd enjoyed the story, I asked if the quality of the writing was good enough to share with her book club. She said 'no'. This honesty made me realise that self-publishing was not an option; I needed a professional publisher to elevate the manuscript to the exacting standards of her club. With the help of my agent, Harry Bucknall, I persuaded Anthony Weldon of Nine Elms Books to take a chance on me, and with Dominic Horsfall's extraordinary editing skills, we have, I hope, produced a book that you, the reader, will enjoy.

Finally, thanks must go to my wife, Louise, and children, Reuben and Xanthe, for their encouragement and patience. Indeed, this venture would never have started had I not asked my son, who suffers with dyslexia, if he had ever finished reading an entire book. Aged fifteen at the time, I was shocked to discover he hadn't. But he joked that if I wrote one, he would read it from front to back. The spark was lit, the idea grew, and a book was born.

Over to you, Reuben...

Philip Trotter
June 2021

VIETNAM SPLIT AT THE 17TH PARALLEL

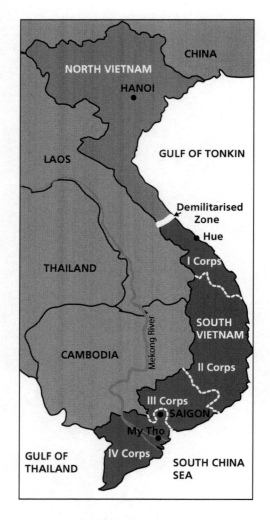

*Including locations of
South Vietnam's army corps*

CENTRAL SAIGON

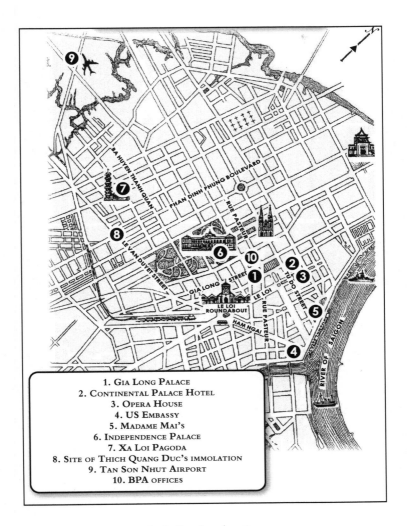

1. GIA LONG PALACE
2. CONTINENTAL PALACE HOTEL
3. OPERA HOUSE
4. US EMBASSY
5. MADAME MAI'S
6. INDEPENDENCE PALACE
7. XA LOI PAGODA
8. SITE OF THICH QUANG DUC'S IMMOLATION
9. TAN SON NHUT AIRPORT
10. BPA OFFICES

Including key locations

Part I: Tinder

EARLY SUMMER, 1963

1

The battered blue cyclo and its elderly driver manoeuvred carefully through the crowded street, trying to avoid fellow travellers. Mopeds and scooters competed to make headway in the confusion, their underpowered two-stroke engines whining like a hive of disturbed honeybees on a warm afternoon. Occasionally, a lone car would break the equilibrium and, spying a gap, lurch past the cyclo, horn blazing, to gain a few crucial extra yards.

In the front seat of the bicycle taxi sat a man – though still a boy to his mother – captivated by the chaotic scenes around him. Ned Rivers looked again at the note he'd been given:

Be at the corner of Phan Dinh Phung Boulevard and Le Van Duyet Street at midday tomorrow. Something important will happen.

A look of irritation crossed the nineteen-year-old's face as he studied the cryptic message, forming premature lines around his blue eyes.

Ned had only been in South Vietnam for two weeks, but already he'd realised how different its capital was to the cities from his childhood, both in America and Britain. Saigon intrigued him: the people, their culture, their work ethic. He remained confounded and amazed in equal measure at how adeptly the Vietnamese balanced their livelihoods on their bicycles, often loaded to the hilt with wares of all descriptions. Yesterday, he'd seen a man cycling down the iconic Rue Pasteur with a six-foot sheet of glass horizontally strapped to the back. Nobody seemed to object to the apparent danger; people just calmly moved aside and waved him on his way. Later, he saw another man with so many coils of plastic pipe fastened to his bike that it was now the size of a small truck. How he'd been able to ride it without tipping over, Ned could only wonder.

He continued to watch the commotion around him with interest, his face grimacing in shock as a Honda motorbike drove past with a live pig secured across the back, squealing in distress. Finally, without incident, his cyclo arrived at the desired location. He climbed out and looked around expectantly, searching for a clue as to why he'd been directed here, wondering what was going to happen that could be so important.

In truth, he had no idea and cared even less. He'd been given the note the day before by his new bureau chief, Mel Johnson. She'd thrust it into his hands on his return to the office, after he'd wasted the day chasing phantom stories of Viet Cong activity in Can Tho, a small town deep in the Mekong Delta.

"Ned, I want you to deal with this tip-off. I get notes like this the whole time. Nothing ever comes of them, but you've got no other plans for tomorrow, have you?"

He hadn't been sure if this was a question or a statement, but by the time he'd looked up from scanning the message, she'd already turned her back and walked away.

He'd been hoping to get back down to the delta and carry on his search for the illusory Viet Cong. In the short time he'd been at his new bureau, several reports had filtered back to Saigon about VC movements and attacks in the region, but as a photographer he'd discovered very little to photograph – apart from some blood on the road one day, but it hadn't made for a very interesting picture.

Nor, in fact, had anything else since he'd arrived in the country, at least in the sense of making it into a newspaper. He'd still been a photographer's assistant in London at the time of the Battle of Ap Bac, infamous to the few correspondents stationed in Saigon as the first time the Viet Cong had stood their ground and fought, though still largely unknown to anyone in the outside world, especially in the United States where the bulk of his work was most likely to be seen. Let's face it, he thought, very few Americans had even heard of Vietnam, fewer still would be able to point to it on a map. But at least it had shown the Viet Cong were real, even if, for Ned, they remained tantalisingly elusive.

He still hadn't adjusted to his surroundings since arriving in Saigon, especially the oppressive heat and sweat-inducing humidity, and the further he ventured from his office, the more profound the differences with his last bureau in London became. Ned hadn't requested Saigon specifically, but having nagged his bosses at the Bellanger Press Agency for a transfer abroad, he'd willingly accepted the offer of Vietnam. He'd hated the London bureau with its tedious hierarchy and constant paperwork, and yearned for a small office where he could be free to do what he wanted most: take photographs. Infinitely preferable, he'd decided, to making the teas, acting as darkroom assistant, and all the other hundreds of menial jobs he'd been forced to do by his many superiors.

Standing as instructed at the corner of Phan Dinh Phung Boulevard and Le Van Duyet Street, he reflected on how he'd never have been allowed out in London by himself. He looked around expectantly but decided that nothing seemed unusual. The traffic was flowing as normal, chaotic in comparison to the polite order of London, but routine for Saigon. The pedestrians appeared unperturbed. He thrust his hands into his pockets and wondered again why Mel had thought this more important than sending him back to the Mekong Delta.

As he lingered there trying to identify the reason for his presence on the street corner, he couldn't help but notice how much he stood out from those around him. At six foot two inches tall, he towered above the average Vietnamese person, his mop of blond curls in stark contrast to the straight black hair possessed by everyone else. At school in America, he'd been known as 'Beanie' – short for beanstalk – as he'd always been tall and thin. That, however, was before he'd been forced to relocate to England with his mother at the age of twelve, where a new moniker had given him his first taste of British irony – 'Stubby'. He'd hated both names, and the boys in his run-down East London school had soon learnt that the kid from America was prepared to fight to preserve his reputation.

He let his gaze wander further along the streets and noticed he was opposite the Cambodian Embassy. He wondered if that was important. It occupied one corner of the crossroads, with an Esso filling station on another, but otherwise the remaining buildings were nondescript concrete structures with little character. He guessed they were shops, though he couldn't tell what they sold as he hadn't yet begun to master the Vietnamese language, particularly its written form with all the diacritic markers.

Fruit sellers lined the roads leading into the junction, each selling numerous varieties, not all of which Ned recognised. Sadly, the inviting aroma from their produce fought with the caustic fumes from the traffic, especially the large trucks with their deep, throbbing diesel engines. But when he did catch the sweet smell of a mangosteen or papaya wafting across on the warm breeze, he smiled inwardly at the pleasure of the scent.

Ned studied the fruit seller nearest to him out the corner of his eye; he didn't want to be caught staring. She was sitting on her haunches gossiping with her neighbour and wore a strange leopard-print cotton top with matching trousers, barefooted but grinning frequently. Protecting her from the sun was a traditional conical hat made from palm leaves tied around her chin with a fetching piece of pink silk. It hadn't taken Ned long to notice how striking the women in Vietnam were; with their straight black hair and fresh complexions, they all seemed so happy. He wondered why some of the poorest people he'd encountered always looked the most content and concluded that perhaps inner peace was not connected to wealth. This deduction pleased him, because he wouldn't have described himself as a philosophical kind of person. No, Ned Rivers was definitely more of a doer than a thinker.

His rambling observations were interrupted by the sounds of soft chanting. He looked up Phan Dinh Phung Boulevard – a small, innocuous street in contrast to its grand title – to see a procession of Buddhist monks walking slowly down the road in two columns. Dressed in their distinctive saffron-coloured robes, they chanted to a drumbeat as they marched, the melancholic rhythm increasing in volume with each step closer. As the parade approached, Ned could see banners held aloft by the marchers. He was surprised to find some were in English, their protesting slogans bemoaning President Diem and his unjust treatment of Buddhists. Ned knew of course that the communist Viet Cong were fighting to oust the South Vietnamese leader and his government, but he'd had no idea the Buddhists didn't like him either. He wondered if the two causes were somehow linked.

The heavy traffic showed deference to the marchers by slowing or pulling over to the side as the procession walked by. Quickly, Ned remembered why he was there. Removing his hands from his pockets, he began readying his cameras. He'd brought his two favourite cameras with him from London: a Nikon F with interchangeable lenses and a small Leica M3 with a fixed 50 mm lens at f/1.4, great for shooting in low light levels. Crucially, he checked that both cameras had film in, but his nervousness caused him to drop the Nikon's lens cap. Bending down, he fumbled for it on the ground before looking up to see how close the marchers were. They were still walking toward the crossroads, but as they reached the leading edge of the junction, the left column of monks split left while the right column went right. Instinctively, Ned started to take photographs, trying to capture the scene accurately; though since he wasn't sure exactly what this was supposed to be, he eventually stopped and watched the display instead.

With the traffic having come to a complete standstill, the two lines of monks walked around the outside of the crossroads and met at the far side by the Esso petrol station. They continued to chant while the warm breeze picked at their light cotton robes. An inner line of monks made their way inside the outer ring, creating a second tier of chanting figures, followed by a third and a fourth. This unfolding piece of theatre fascinated the passers-by gathering to watch, and within moments the pavements had become overcrowded. Ned wondered why the monks would want to block a busy crossroads, but acknowledged this event was obviously what the note had referred to and began taking pictures once more. The air of expectation was palpable, and even through the monks' chanting he could tell the mood was sombre. He finished his first roll of film in the Nikon, praying as he replaced it that he'd captured at least one decent image out of the twenty-four shots taken.

Hundreds of monks had now entered the junction, and as many passers-by and motorists had stopped to watch, leaving Ned struggling to get a clear shot. He moved to his right and found a small concrete wall to climb onto, affording him a better view. As he continued to take pictures, the monks collectively sat down and crossed their legs; only those carrying lit joss sticks remained standing, the smell of the joss surpassing even the fumes of the now stationary traffic. Ned noticed the circle of Buddhists was not complete; a gap had been left at the entrance to the street from which they'd come. The onlookers were growing in number, some even climbing onto the roof of the filling station to watch. The commotion had attracted the attention of a few policemen, but they observed the spectacle from a distance, choosing not to intervene.

Ned was busy photographing the hordes of spectators when he spotted another Westerner in his viewfinder standing among the packed crowds. The man was leaning forward, trying to observe what was happening while scribbling in a notebook. As Ned scanned the crowd for other Western journalists, he saw a light grey four-door Austin driving carefully through the gap left by the encircling monks. It drew slowly to a halt, not in the centre of the circle but off to one side. An elderly priest emerged from the passenger door, while out the back sprang a much younger, more agile monk. Both with saffron outer robes and shaven heads, the old man and his young colleague looked identical; only in age could they be told apart. Together, they walked calmly but with purpose to the centre of the crossroads. The younger monk carried a brown cushion, which he placed on the ground before helping his companion down onto it. With a serene look on his face, the elderly monk arranged himself into the cross-legged, meditative lotus position. It was only when he was settled that Ned saw another monk emerge from the driver's side of the car, also dressed in a saffron robe with a shaven head. This Austin model had its luggage compartment under the bonnet; the third monk walked around to open it, revealing a five-gallon fuel container made from heavy-duty white plastic, which he lifted out with caution. Unscrewing the lid, he strode over to his elderly colleague seated in the centre of the crossroads.

A hush descended on the bystanders, and even the chanting from the other monks sounded less enthusiastic. Ned was mesmerised by what was happening before him, but with a jolt realised he couldn't just stand and watch; here at last was a scene worth capturing. He raised his Nikon to his left eye and began shooting, occasionally lowering the camera and changing the aperture setting to ensure a variety of different exposures. This was a trick he'd learnt a year earlier after taking some photos of a jewellery shop robbery he'd happened to witness; only when he'd developed the film had he discovered all the shots had been overexposed. Not a single picture had made it into the local paper.

The monk with the fuel container stood above the elder and slowly, almost ritually, began to pour the petrol over him, though avoiding his head, which Ned had recently learnt was the holiest part of the body according to the Buddhist faith. The crowd let out a collective gasp, and even Ned, despite his journalistic cool, felt his stomach muscles tighten as he finally understood the full meaning behind the note. The monk only stopped pouring when the elderly priest was completely drenched, small trickles of liquid beginning to flow out from him toward the ring of his colleagues. Both assistants turned to face the seated figure, bowed their whole upper bodies, and retreated back toward the car. The crossroads fell silent except for the sustained chanting of a few older, more experienced monks; but the younger ones stared in wide-eyed horror at what seemed to be about to occur. Ned couldn't believe what he was witnessing either. His breaths were ragged and his mind appeared to have gone into slow motion. The urge to look away was strong, but his brain spurred him on. *Don't stop. Keep clicking. This is what you're here for.*

Everything was still. No one moved. Ned watched as the petrol-soaked monk, now alone, carefully unfurled his hands to reveal a box of matches. Unbelievably slowly, he took one out, hesitated a few seconds, and then struck it. Like a tsunami sucking water from the shore, the air seemed to rush inward before the petrol caught, and – *WOOOFF* – exploded outward in flames. It was difficult to see the monk at the centre since his robes blended perfectly with the orange of the fire; but it was clear he hadn't flinched. In fact, he stayed perfectly still as the flames engulfed him completely.

There was stunned silence; by now, even the older monks had ceased their chanting. Only the sound of the flames as they billowed around the body could be heard. A thick plume of acrid black smoke rose from the seated figure, who remained totally motionless, his head held high and proud. Those surrounding the flaming body bowed their heads and put their hands together in salute to their elder. The original assistant walked forward to stand before the burning figure, knelt down and prostrated his upper body, touching his forehead to the ground in a final act of respect.

The priest's clothes had been the first things to catch fire, quickly shrivelling in the heat. The flames were now reaching six foot in height as they continued to emanate oily black smoke into the blue sky. The smell of joss had been replaced by the noxious odour of burning petrol, and moments later burning flesh. The monk's face and hands began to go black. In contrast to the reverence shown by his comrades, the other onlookers reacted with horror. As audible as the gasp after the first flames had caught, Ned could now clearly hear people sobbing and crying in distress. He too was aghast, but he forced himself to photograph the scene as dispassionately as possible. Checking the light levels, changing the aperture and refocusing the camera lens helped take his mind off the sight of a man burning before his eyes, withering in the flames. In his heart, he felt the urge to rush forward and help somehow, but his head stopped him. Although still just a rookie, he understood his role was that of an observer, not a participant.

The flames continued to swirl around and consume the body for another minute before finally the figure slowly toppled backward and twisted onto its side. The monk's body had withered and blackened under the intense heat, and lay there, still engulfed by fire. It was impossible to tell at what point the man had actually died since he hadn't moved from the moment the flames had first erupted around him to the moment he'd keeled over backward. He hadn't screamed or whimpered or made any other noise during his immolation; simply sat there in deep meditation, seemingly at peace.

After the body collapsed, the surrounding monks leant forward and prostrated themselves on the ground in similar fashion to the young assistant, who was still positioned before the charred remains of his esteemed colleague. For Ned, the whole scene was captivating, however shocking. He continued to shoot, changing the film in his Nikon regularly, even though at this point the flames were decreasing in intensity. He was aware of more movement around the periphery now. A fire truck had arrived, but its passage was blocked by the sheer number of people present. More white-uniformed police appeared, but, unable to do anything, they too stood in awkward silence outside the circle of monks.

Only when the fire had diminished, leaving nothing but small fingers of flame licking at the charred remains, did the young assistant stand and walk back to the car. The doors were still open and the bonnet up. He leant into the back seat and removed a woollen blanket, similar in colour to the saffron robes all the monks wore. He returned to the elderly priest's body and, with the help of a colleague, unfurled the blanket and placed it over the vestiges, extinguishing the last of the flames in the process. A simple coffin appeared and was brought alongside the smoking corpse. The young man and his helper carefully lifted the body into it, but the rigid, blackened limbs prevented them from closing the lid.

At that moment, a Buddhist protester began shouting through a loudspeaker at the gathered crowd, now numbering in the hundreds. "A Buddhist priest burns himself to death, a Buddhist priest becomes a martyr!" he cried over and over in both Vietnamese and English. It dawned on Ned that the monks had always wanted this incident to be reported in the international media, hence why he and other journalists had been tipped off, and why so many of the banners and slogans were in English. He also knew that, finally, he'd taken a photograph worthy of being published.

Due to the nature of the event he'd just witnessed, he felt strangely subdued, but equally recognised the importance of acting fast and getting his films back to the BPA offices for onward transmission. He gathered his belongings, making certain the eight rolls of film he'd used were safely secured in the pockets of his sleeveless photographer's jacket, and only then noticed his Leica camera was still nestled in the chest compartment; in all the drama, he'd completely forgotten to use it. He prayed his Nikon had worked fine, and this wouldn't be a repeat of the jewellery shop debacle.

Ned pushed through the milling crowds out onto Phan Dinh Phung Boulevard. He could walk back to the office, but a cyclo would be quicker, even though the closure of the crossroads had caused a huge jam on the surrounding streets. Luckily, he didn't have to wait long before one pedalled up beside him.

"Where you go, sir?" the elderly man with a wispy grey beard called out eagerly, keen to get Ned's business before another driver arrived with a competing offer.

"BPA offices on Rue Pasteur, and as quick as you can!" Ned demanded, launching himself into the front seat. He wasn't sure what the protocol was now he'd finally taken a newsworthy photograph, but his instincts were telling him to rush back and let Mel know what had occurred.

"Did you see monk fire himself?" asked the cyclo driver in surprisingly good English.

"Yes, it was horrible. Did you?"

"No," replied the driver, "but if Buddhist monk burn for protest, you know trouble coming."

Not keen to get into a conversation with the old man, Ned kept silent. His thoughts were still with the scenes he'd just witnessed. How could the monk have just sat there without screaming in pain? Some sort of trance? He tried to imagine the agony of being engulfed in flames and burnt alive. It made him shudder, and he felt the muscles tighten in his stomach once more. He looked down to find his hands shaking in his lap and prayed they hadn't been doing so while taking the photographs. In that moment, Ned knew his posting to Saigon was going to be very different to anything he'd experienced before, and he mentally reprimanded himself to toughen up. As he fought to control the trembling with some deep breaths, he pondered as to what on earth the government could have done to make someone kill himself in such a horrific way.

The cyclo driver, every bit as good as a London cabbie, continued to manoeuvre his bicycle taxi down the little streets and back alleys, deftly avoiding the congested main roads, before emerging in front of the BPA offices. Ned passed him some piastre notes and rushed inside.

The Saigon bureau was nothing like the bustling, hectic offices of the London branch from which he'd come. There was just a single open space with two or three small rooms at the back, all occupying the ground floor of a larger office block.

Mel was the only person in there. She'd obviously just got back from 'the field'; still wearing her muddy camouflage trousers and army-issue boots, her petite frame and gentle features challenged the stereotypical image of masculine field reporters. She looked up in surprise at the horror on Ned's face.

"What happened?" she demanded.

"Oh my God, it was horrible!" said Ned, the words tumbling out of his mouth.

"Okay, slow down, tell me everything."

"I went to the corner of Phan Dinh Phung Boulevard and Le Van Duyet Street, like the note said. When I got there, nothing strange was happening, everyone around me looked normal. But after twenty minutes wondering if I'd been taken to the wrong crossroads, hundreds of monks started parading down the street in their robes." Ned continued to tell the whole story, careful not to omit any details. Mel may be a lady, he told himself, but he was sure she'd seen worse.

Indeed, she didn't flinch once at the idea of a man burning himself alive.

"So did you get any photos?"

This was all she wanted to know. Ned hadn't worked Mel out at all. Although she was technically his boss, she hadn't exactly bossed him around yet. Her aloofness to him in particular had made him wonder if he'd managed to upset her in some way. She seemed cheery and happy with their other colleagues, but Ned felt she treated him dismissively. Perhaps she didn't see him as an American like everyone else in the bureau. He hadn't had a female boss before, but he knew he'd have to win her approval if he was to make a success of this career move.

"Yes, I took hundreds," replied Ned, unloading all the films in their little black canisters from his jacket. As soon as he'd thrown them down on the desk, he quickly shoved his hands into his trouser pockets to conceal the fact they were still shaking. "I just hope to God they're good. I don't know about you, but I've never watched someone burn to death up close before, and I sure as hell don't want to experience it again!"

"No, I'm sure," said Mel with distracted empathy, "but we have to get these over to New York. Were there any other Western journalists or photographers there?" She'd launched into full business mode.

"Yes, I saw one other. A tall man, but he was scribbling in a notebook rather than taking pictures," Ned replied nervously, never having seen Mel so focused before.

"Okay, we need to get these films out to Tokyo as quickly as possible. It's the closest BPA office where the pictures can be photo-wired through to New York. Our telegraph office here is just too slow and unreliable in an emergency."

Ned guessed she was talking rhetorically, so remained silent.

"Get yourself over to the airport and find a pigeon. Quickly!" she barked.

Ned gathered up his films and stuffed them in a large envelope.

"You'd better take my car," said Mel, throwing him the keys. "It's just outside on the street. But get back here as soon as you've got the film away. You'll need to run through the whole incident again so I can file a report."

Within thirty minutes, Ned had found his way to Tan Son Nhut Airport, where, with a small inducement, he found himself a willing passenger to take his package on the next flight out of Saigon to Tokyo.

The photographs began their fifteen-hour journey across the globe. Arriving at Tokyo Airport approximately seven hours after the immolation, Ned's 'pigeon' was met by a BPA employee, who retrieved the films and took them back to his offices. As a regional hub, the Tokyo bureau was substantially larger than the tiny one in Saigon. The films were developed, printed and photo-wired on to San Francisco, taking two and a half hours to travel the five thousand miles under the Pacific Ocean, and a further two hours to be relayed on to BPA's head office in New York. Here, the best images were selected and wired out to all the newspaper companies around the world subscribed to BPA's service, which were then free to use whichever pictures and stories they chose.

Back in Saigon, his precious package safely away, Ned Rivers took a moment to reflect on the extraordinary day he'd just had, little suspecting how much his life was about to change.

2

WEDNESDAY 12ᵀᴴ JUNE 1963

The crisis was nearing its zenith and the President was exasperated. Why couldn't his officials behave like normal people, he wondered as he stepped out the door from his private apartment. The walk to the Oval Office in the West Wing took only a few minutes, along corridors and down staircases with sumptuous carpets and walls adorned with oil paintings of military victories stretching back nearly two hundred years. He normally enjoyed looking at these as he went past, imagining how he'd have reacted in Roosevelt's or Lincoln's or even Washington's shoes. But not this morning.

This morning he was agitated, downright angry in fact. He descended to the ground floor and decided to pass along the outside colonnade toward the West Wing. What sort of country was he leading, he wondered, when one of its governors, a Democrat at that, could be so intolerant? And in front of the nation's media too. The President knew he'd risked a constitutional crisis by ordering Alabama's National Guard to forcibly remove their governor from the entrance to the university buildings. But who the hell did George Wallace think he was, trying to physically block two students from entering the university to register just because they were black? Christ, it was a hundred years since the Civil War and the emancipation of the slaves! With a start, he suddenly remembered the centenary of the Battle of Gettysburg, the most horrific event in the whole conflict, was only three weeks away.

The President was equally annoyed with his Deputy Attorney General, whom he'd sent down to Alabama to ensure this kind of situation was avoided in the first place. God, he was dreading the morning headlines. The most influential newspapers were all based in the North and vociferously against any form of racial prejudice demonstrated by southern state officials. They'd all come down hard on the incident at Foster Auditorium, and the President knew he wouldn't escape their withering criticism either.

The marine guard saluted as his commander-in-chief reached the door to his outer office, opened it and walked in.

"Good morning, Mr President," said Evelyn Lincoln, his personal secretary of ten years, seated at her desk as usual, ready for his arrival. "How are you this fine day?"

"Yes, fine...fine, thank you, Evelyn," the President replied without a smile. But he could see Evelyn didn't believe him. The worry lines above her eyes, reflecting his own anxiety, seemed more pronounced than at any time since the missile crisis of last fall. "Evelyn, can you get the Attorney General on the phone please?"

He walked into the Oval Office and sat purposefully down at his desk, fiddling with the cuffs of his shirt as he made himself comfortable. A moment later, the phone rang.

"Mr President, I have the Attorney General for you."

"Thank you, Evelyn, put him through." The line went silent for a moment before he heard the sound of his brother's voice.

"Morning, Jack. What do you want?" it said in the abrupt manner only brothers could use between themselves.

"Morning, Bobby. I need to speak to you about Alabama," said the President as Evelyn entered and shut the door silently behind her. As he began to discuss the day's issue with his brother, Evelyn began arranging the morning papers on the desk in front of him, before moving over to the coffee table between the two sofas in the centre of the office to pick up a stray coffee cup left there from the previous night. With the phone still held to his left ear, the President leant forward and turned the papers around to face him, using his right hand to unfold the top one.

"JESUS CHRIST!" he suddenly exclaimed, kicking his chair back as he jumped to his feet.

"What the hell's the matter?" demanded the Attorney General down the phone. Evelyn too had jumped in surprise at the outburst. The President silently apologised to her with a simple wave, which she acknowledged by putting her own hand to her heart with a breath, as if to say: *You nearly gave me a heart attack*.

"Bobby, have you seen this morning's papers? They're not what we expected."

Staring up at John F. Kennedy, the thirty-fifth President of the United States of America, was a grisly photograph of a burning monk sitting serenely in an upright position, his charred body totally engulfed in flames, and above him a cloud of black smoke.

"Not yet," replied his brother. "Is it Wallace…?"

But already the President had lost interest in the problems of Alabama. "Bobby, I'll call you back later. Vietnam just took centre stage!" He put the phone down and looked again at the front page of the uppermost newspaper. Below the shocking photograph was the highly understated headline:

VIETNAM:

BUDDHIST CRISIS TAKES TURN FOR WORSE

Kennedy sat back down, his face gaunt, and began to read:

In central Saigon yesterday, Buddhist monk Thich Quang Duc set fire to himself in an act of protest against the Diem government. Surrounded by four hundred monks and as many passers-by, Thich Quang Duc, a leading priest at the nearby Xa Loi Pagoda, self-immolated in the middle of a busy intersection in downtown Saigon, only two blocks away from the presidential palace.

This shocking spectacle was in protest at South Vietnamese President Ngo Dinh Diem's discriminatory religious policies. President Diem and the leading figures in his government are Roman Catholics, in contrast to an estimated 80% of South Vietnamese who are Buddhists. Tension between Buddhists and the ruling Catholics has been building since President Diem came to power nearly nine years ago, but the issue came to a head in May this year when the government ordered provincial officials to prohibit the flying of religious flags on 'Vesak', the birthday of the founder of Buddhism, Gautama Buddha. Vesak is a major celebration in the Buddhist religious calendar, normally celebrated with much flag-waving.

The prohibition came a week after the government encouraged Vatican flags to be flown for the 25th anniversary of Ngo Dinh Thuc becoming Archbishop of Hue, the former royal capital. Ngo Dinh Thuc is not only the highest Roman Catholic cleric in South Vietnam but also President Diem's elder brother, and had requested that his brother outlaw the flying of Buddhist flags. The prohibition at such an important religious ceremony provoked uproar from the majority Buddhists, and on May 8th, several thousand Buddhist supporters demonstrated in Hue. Police ruthlessly broke up the demonstration by throwing grenades and firing into the protesters, which caused a stampede leaving nine dead. Two of the dead were children run over by armoured personnel carriers belonging to the police.

Despite clear evidence to the contrary, President Diem blamed the deaths on the Viet Cong and other communist groups. This angered Buddhist campaigners, and by the end of May, the protests had spread to Saigon, where another mass rally was held.

Thich Quang Duc's self-immolation is the latest protest against the government's religious policies, and the horrific nature of his death will certainly cause concern in Washington, given the United States' position as a keen ally and sponsor of President Diem and the South Vietnamese government.

Kennedy sat back and stared again at the picture of the burning monk, recognising the damage it would do to the reputation of President Diem's government and, by association, his own. He knew from his own election victory the power of pictures, in his case television rather than newspapers. Opening the paper, he wasn't surprised to find spread across pages two and three a sequence of photographs showing the drama unfolding, each more shocking than the one before. Underneath the last image, in small type, he read the caption: *Photographs by Ned Rivers of BPA.*

Never heard of him, thought Kennedy as he reclined in his chair, crossed his arms and considered his response. Instinctively, he knew he'd have to review his policies on Vietnam; he couldn't be seen to sit back and do nothing in response to an ally so extreme that Buddhist monks had taken to self-immolation as a form of protest. He checked all the other newspapers Evelyn had left on his desk. Apart from the *New York Times*, they all ran with the same haunting image splashed across the front page.

"Evelyn, can you organise a meeting for as soon as possible? I need to see the Secretary of State, the Secretary of Defense and my chief of staff."

It was early evening before the high-ranking officials of the American government had gathered on the two sofas in the middle of the Oval Office to discuss the 'Buddhist Crisis', as news reporters had begun calling it throughout the day's coverage on the wireless.

President Kennedy opened the informal gathering. "Good evening, gentlemen. I assume you've all seen today's papers and the photograph dominating the front pages. I understand the same picture has been published around the world, with considerable impact. What we need to decide is: does this change anything, or should we not be concerned with such brutality?"

"The story also led the news bulletins, Mr President," chipped in the chief of staff. "Our press office has gone crazy with journalists wanting to know our reaction to the burning monk."

Kennedy took a sip of the coffee Evelyn had just handed him and fixed the man with a stare. "Well, I reacted pretty badly too when I first saw the picture this morning. What are we telling the press?"

Before his chief of staff could reply, the Secretary of State butted in. "I thought we were helping Diem fight the Viet Cong, not the damn Buddhists."

Dean Rusk was only a little older than Kennedy, but his balding pate made him look many years his senior. The President knew the man shared the view of many in his State Department: that Ngo Dinh Diem was autocratic, nepotistic, egotistic and much more interested in holding onto power than beating the communist insurgency.

Rusk continued. "That picture symbolises everything wrong with our support for Diem. We've sent over ten thousand military advisors at huge expense to train his forces and keep his country from falling into the hands of the communists; and he goes and picks a fight with innocent monks!"

Kennedy looked across to his Secretary of Defense, Robert McNamara. "Robert, do you share that view?"

"Mr President, you have to understand Diem's view of the situation. He believes the Buddhists have been infiltrated by the communists, so they are the enemy."

"Believe that and you'll believe anything," interrupted Rusk with a raising of his bushy eyebrows. "He's a Catholic and he hates Buddhists. Pure and simple."

The chief of staff looked up from his notebook. "Well, maybe. But if he keeps persecuting the Buddhists, he's going to be alienating eighty percent of his population...and that's never a good move for a leader."

Rusk and McNamara were sat together on one sofa facing the President and his chief of staff on the other. It was how Kennedy liked to host his smaller, more informal meetings, considering it the best way to find solutions to the problems of the day. And there was always a problem.

"Robert, what reports have you been getting from your commanders on the ground as to how effective the South Vietnamese army have been lately?" asked the President, trying to move the discussion on.

"Mr President, my commanders in Vietnam, especially General Harkins, tell me the war will soon be won. Because of our support, the ARVN are better led, better equipped, and greater in numbers than the communists. Harkins reassures me the Viet Cong will be beaten sometime next year."

Rusk rolled his eyes. "At the same time, I'm being told that, since their defeat at Ap Bac at the beginning of the year, Diem's instructed his generals not to confront the Viet Cong when they're gathered in large numbers, as he doesn't want a high casualty rate." As he spoke, he picked up the copy of the *Washington Post* from the coffee table and pointed to the photograph on the front page. "This is who Diem considers the enemy: the monks. He's already given up fighting the communists, and now, thanks to a single picture appearing in every paper across the country, every American can see it too. Soon, they'll be asking us why we're spending their money to prop up a government that persecutes monks. Yesterday, barely any Americans had heard of Vietnam. Tomorrow, everyone's going to be an expert."

President Kennedy frowned. "Yes, that's exactly why I called this meeting. This one photograph has, in a single click, shifted the public's attention from Alabama to Saigon."

He became silent, staring down at his notes as he considered his options. In deference, the others remained quiet too until Rusk broke the lull.

"I know the Defense Department are feeling upbeat, but I think we need to threaten to withdraw economic aid from South Vietnam. We should remind Diem it's given on the understanding that it's to be used to help his people and not to persecute them. While military aid is for fighting the Viet Cong and not the Buddhists. And if he breaks this understanding, then we'll stop both."

The conversation continued for another thirty minutes, to-ing and fro-ing between the State Department's view that Diem was a liability and the Defense Department's position that a little patience was all that was needed. But the President knew he had to come to a quick decision. He was expected at a local Democrat fundraiser in an hour and wanted some time with his wife in their private apartment beforehand.

"Well, it strikes me," he said, now in a vehement mood, "that if we're going to keep on aiding the South Vietnamese government and supplying them with our equipment and advisors, then we should have a say in who they're goddamn fighting...and it's not the Buddhists!" The President paused to consider his next statement before continuing. "Secretary of State, I want you to contact our Ambassador in Saigon. What's he called...Nolting? Get him to put a proverbial bomb under Diem and instruct him to desist from his persecution of the Buddhists and get back to fighting the communists. Tell Nolting to pass on my personal concern at the situation. Make it clear I do not support his fight with the Buddhists, and I want it ended! He has to make a deal with them, or else we'll start cutting back our economic support."

Inside, Kennedy felt better for having offloaded his anger. He hoped he could rely on his Secretary of State to resolve this issue as a priority.

"Diem needs to know that if he continues, there will be consequences," he concluded, standing up and bringing the meeting to a close.

3

THURSDAY 13ᵀᴴ JUNE 1963

With Saigon eleven hours ahead of Washington, Ned was paying his cyclo driver for taxiing him to work just as President Kennedy was wrapping up his evening meeting. The journey had been fraught with all the normal dangers of Saigon's roads; this morning had consisted in almost being hit by a brightly coloured bus with little care for whom or what was in front of it. Ned was thinking his commute really shouldn't be the most dangerous part of his working day as he pushed open the front door and stepped into the offices of the Saigon bureau of Bellanger Press Agency.

Inside, he was greeted by spontaneous applause. Ned was...perplexed, and even looked back to see who might have been walking in after him. But it was meant for him. Mel and the other members that made up the small band of intrepid BPA operatives stood with large grins and clapped enthusiastically. Mel was closest, with her desk nearest the door, and to her right were Harry Roberts and Joseph Coleman. Ned had only met Harry and Joseph on one occasion but liked them both. Harry covered the whole of South-East Asia and had been reporting on the civil war in Laos for most of the previous month, while Joseph was embedded with South Vietnam's

1st Infantry Division based near Hue, responsible for guarding the so-called demilitarised zone, the border areas with North Vietnam.

Mel walked out from behind her desk and put her arm around Ned's shoulders. "You have no idea what you've done, have you?"

"No, I'm very confused. Why are you all clapping? What's happened?" He felt like he'd just woken up and his mind couldn't fathom the reality. And seeing Mel smile at him only made it stranger.

"Your photos of Thich Quang Duc have gone global," replied Mel.

"Thich Quang who?" asked Ned, scrunching his face in confusion.

"Thich Quang Duc – the monk who set himself on fire two days ago. Your pictures of him are a hit. Listen to this message I got wired from New York." Mel reached across to her desk and grabbed a piece of paper to read it aloud: *Please congratulate Ned Rivers on his photos of Thich Quang Duc. Appeared in approx. 145 separate newspapers across globe. All over front pages in America. Most used photo this year. Executive floor here in NYC very happy. End.* So, excellent news – well done, Ned!"

Ned wasn't sure how to react to the congratulatory telegram, and so, with a weak smile and a shrug of his shoulders, simply stood there embarrassed. "Thank you. I'm shocked. I'm surprised. Really?"

Mel sat on the edge of her desk. "In the twelve months I've been in this office, I've never known a message like it from New York. The most used photograph this year, that's quite a feat. You should be proud. You might even be in line for a Pulitzer!"

"Sure, Mel!" said Ned, laughing. "Junior photographers don't win Pulitzers. I was lucky, that's all. There were no other photographers there."

"Well, lucky you may be, but we need a bit of that if we're going to compete with the other agencies. Remember, we're the minnows around here. But now you've set the height of your bar, New York'll be expecting more great pictures from you! Okay, come on now, work to be done."

Mel moved around behind her desk to pick up her jacket and protective helmet before turning back to Ned.

"There was an attack on a provincial police station last night by the Viet Cong in the delta." She let the statement hang in the air before continuing. "Why don't you join me and we'll go see how bad it was?"

Ned was even more amazed than at the thought of a Pulitzer Prize. "What? You want me to go with you…down to the delta…today?"

Mel had already reached the door to the street. "Well, don't look so surprised, you earned it. Come on, I don't bite."

Ned pulled himself together and chuckled. "No, of course not." Picking up his cameras, he set off after his boss. "At least, I hope not," he added, more to himself than anyone else.

President Ngo Dinh Diem was walking along the corridor that led around the outside of the first floor of his Saigon residence, enjoying the cool of the morning when his brother Nhu caught up to him.

"Who the hell is Ned Rivers?"

Diem knew his brother would be angry. He had been ever since they'd first heard about the bonze setting himself on fire two days earlier. The man was always angry, even when in a good mood. Diem carried on toward his office, several aides following in his footsteps. He enjoyed following the black and white marble-tiled corridor surrounding the Gia Long Palace that allowed him to look out onto the streets of Saigon below, enchanted by the wide tree-lined boulevards designed by late-nineteenth-century French town planners. Even though he was originally from Hue, a thousand kilometres to the north, he still thought this was a beautiful city.

The Gia Long Palace was a two-storey colonial mansion built in 1885 to house the French Governor of Cochinchina, the southern third of Vietnam during the colonial period. It was a large, rectangular building, Baroque in style, combining French colonial architecture with the practicalities of traditional Indochinese design. It had an impressive facade with large columns interspersed along the front, affording it an air of grandeur, completed by a large, ornate portico. Corridors ran along the outer edges of the first floor on all four sides, giving access to the interior rooms through large French doors. On the exterior wall were louver-shuttered spaces facing outwards from the building.

The Gia Long Palace hadn't started out as Diem's residence. Upon first becoming Prime Minister of South Vietnam in 1954, he'd lived at the Norodom Palace, former home of the French Governor-General of all Indochina. A year later, when he'd become President after deposing Emperor Bao Dai, he'd renamed it Independence Palace. It was less than a mile away from where he stood now but had been badly damaged in an assassination attempt twelve months earlier. Two Vietnamese air force pilots had decided to drop their bombs on him in the palace instead of on the Viet Cong in the countryside. He'd survived the attempt on his life, but the bombs had caused massive damage to the building, and so President Diem had decided to have the whole thing demolished and start again rather than repair the damaged wing. While it was being rebuilt, he'd requisitioned the Gia Long Palace as his residence and moved his administrative offices here too, along with his most trusted official, his brother Nhu, and Nhu's wife.

Arriving at the large French doors to his office, President Diem decided the Gia Long Palace wasn't such a bad place to live and work.

"Who is Ned Rivers?" shouted his brother again. "He's working with the monks, I can tell you that much!"

"Nhu, sit down and calm down," responded Diem as he sat down imperiously behind his desk. He'd chosen a corner room on the first floor for his office so he could look out both the front and side windows. The room had a high ceiling with a large wooden fan lazily circulating the air.

Nhu hurriedly sat down but ignored the second instruction, launching instead into a tirade without pause for breath. "I've just heard he was there at that bonze's bonfire and captured it on film. His pictures are all over the front pages of the American newspapers."

"Yes, so I understand," replied Diem in a more measured tone. "It's a great pity his photographs have made our fight with the Buddhists public. You can be sure we'll be hearing from the Americans at some point soon." He searched for a packet of cigarettes in his jacket pocket and dug out his favourite French Gauloises with no filter. He took one out and lit it. "He was obviously told about the stunt in advance. We need to find out how involved he is with the Buddhists."

Nhu leant forward. "The Buddhists are making us look foolish. We have to stop this. They're getting more radical and taking ever more extreme actions." His spittle flew in all directions as he spoke.

"So deal with it," demanded Diem, slapping his hand down on the desk. He knew he shouldn't get angry with his brother. Nhu did an excellent job of running the secret police and keeping his enemies subdued. It was just that sometimes he didn't want to know what the man got up to in the name of 'security'; he just wanted him to do it.

"We should just ban the whole Buddhist religion and force everyone to become Roman Catholics," said Nhu facetiously. "That would solve everything."

"Don't be so damn stupid, Nhu," snapped Diem. "We have to come up with an effective way of shutting this Buddhist rebellion down and stamping out their protests. We have to stop them using the likes of this Rivers man to shout their battle cry to the world. It makes me angry to think we let these Western journalists into our country and all they do is stir up revolution against us. They're the ones we should get rid of!"

"*Ngài*, I have US Ambassador Nolting on the line for you," interrupted one of Diem's secretaries after quietly knocking and entering.

"See? I knew it wouldn't take the Americans long before wanting to lecture us!"

"Well, you'd better take the call," said Nhu. "We need their money and military hardware. We can't afford to antagonise them too much."

Picking up the phone, the President let the last of the smoke from his Gauloise escape his mouth and nodded in agreement, however annoying this fact was to him.

"Ambassador Nolting, how lovely to hear from you. To what do I owe the pleasure?" said Diem in his most diplomatic English, doing his best to sound reassuring and friendly. He was talking to the representative of his most important ally after all.

"Good morning, Mr President," came the voice of the Ambassador down the phone. "Secretary of State Rusk has personally requested that I call you to communicate the American government's displeasure at your attacks on the Buddhists…"

"I have not authorised any attacks on the Buddhists, Mr Ambassador," replied Diem with a little more force in his voice, irritated that Nolting had not even taken the trouble to engage in respectful small talk before coming to the point. So uncouth, so American. "If they decide to set themselves on fire, that is their choice. My government did not force him."

"We're not accusing you of lighting the match on Thick Quang Duck," said Nolting, "but you can't deny you're in a battle with them. The American government's view is that, if we're going to supply you with our military advisors and hardware, we should at least have a say in whom you use it on. And we don't want it used on the Buddhists!"

Diem noted the Ambassador's hopeless pronunciation of the monk's name. "Mr Ambassador, we are not using your advisors or your hardware against the Buddhists."

"Mr President," answered Nolting, sounding a little less assured. "You may not be fighting the Buddhists with the weapons we supplied you, but every time you attack them, it reflects badly on us."

"Well, if you kept a closer eye on your press, perhaps that photograph wouldn't have been published in the first place," responded Diem, hoping his anger had come through clearly in the harsh tone of his voice.

"We may not always like what the American press write in the newspapers, Mr President, but the government would never stop them writing it…"

"More fool you," interrupted the President. There was a silence on the line as he waited for what he knew would be the crux of the call.

"President Diem, should you continue to persecute the Buddhists rather than fight the Viet Cong, the United States government will have no choice but to restrict the level of *economic* aid sent to South Vietnam. You have been warned."

President Diem slammed the phone down, "How dare he speak to me like that?" he shouted. "He's nothing but an…"

"Idiot!" said Nhu, finishing his brother's sentence. "What do the Americans know about these Buddhists? Don't they realise they're all communists?"

"Nhu, just sort it out. I have enough to deal with without the Buddhists causing me extra problems. Find out who their leader is, their strategy, and their connection with the Western press. And find out more about this Ned Rivers person, we don't want any more of his photographs turning the world against us."

A shriek from the outer office alerted the President to the sudden arrival of his brother's wife, who came bursting into the room, almost breaking the large teak door in the process.

"I've just been stopped outside by a journalist asking me about some photographs of that burning monk causing such a stir in America. How dare these Buddhist bonzes protest against us!" Madame Nhu shouted, clearly distressed. Her anti-Buddhist opinions were famously as strong as her hatred of Western journalists, whom she saw as responsible for propagating anti-Diem sentiment. And in the Gia Long Palace, her opinions were taken seriously. Very few, if any, of her brother-in-law's ministers dared argue with her on government policy.

"What did you say to him?" asked her husband.

"I told him I'd be delighted if all the Buddhist monks were to barbeque themselves. Let them burn and we'll clap our hands. The more, the better, and the foreign journalists could join them for all I cared."

The President examined his sister-in-law, imagining the consequences of ever crossing this small, immaculately dressed lady who brought with her the force of a small nuclear explosion. He stood up to usher Nhu and his wife out of his office.

"We are dealing with it, Madame Nhu." Despite their close relationship, he, like everybody else, always addressed her in this way. "Your husband will bring them all under control, including the American media. And very soon, I'm sure," he concluded with a pointed look at Nhu before closing the doors behind them.

Nhu strode quickly along the upstairs corridor of the Gia Long Palace toward his own office. His wife had already stomped off, presumably to find another Western journalist to harangue. It was clear whom he had to speak to, however: the same person he always turned to when their position as South Vietnam's leading family was under threat.

Nhu's office was on the same floor as his brother's, but on the other side of the palace. He slammed the tall wooden door shut behind him and reached for the phone on his desk. He knew the number off the top of his head and dialled it quickly.

"I want to speak with Colonel Tung," he said into the receiver.

Colonel Tung was head of South Vietnam's special forces – of which one division was the secret police – and answered directly to Nhu. Tung had made it his personal mission to set up secret police branches in every province and every city of South Vietnam, using predominantly Catholic supporters, and they were a force to be reckoned with. Controlling every aspect of state security, from investigating to detaining and usually executing any political rivals to the President and his government, Tung oversaw a fearsome security apparatus, and this was Nhu's preferred way of keeping his brother and himself in power.

"Tung, we have a problem," said Nhu. "When Thich Quang Duc killed himself on Tuesday morning, there was an American photographer called Ned Rivers who photographed the whole damn thing. Apparently, his pictures are splashed across the world's newspapers, making us look very callous."

"Yes, *ngài*," replied Tung respectfully. "I saw the picture in yesterday's *Paris Herald Tribune*. They were very vitriolic about us."

"Yes, well, we need to put an end to these types of headlines. The Americans are threatening to stop their military aid." This was a lie, but Nhu knew the withdrawal of American military – and not just economic – support would be more of a threat to the communist-hating Tung. "We need to end this Buddhist revolt quickly and ensure they can't continue to use the Western media in their propaganda against us."

"Yes, *ngài*. I agree…"

Nhu cut in, already knowing full well his man agreed with him. "What I want to know is: who is leading this Buddhist revolt? What's their strategy? What are their links with the foreign press corps? And what involvement does this Ned Rivers have in promulgating their lies? Find out and let me know."

"Yes, *ngài*," said Tung. The line had already gone dead.

Ned was pleased Mel had asked him to accompany her down to the Mekong Delta; it meant he got to travel in her VW Beetle, an old car, but far more convenient and comfortable than any public bus, his normal method of travel outside Saigon. Usually, these were so full that there was rarely a place to sit. On his first journey down to the delta, he'd tried to move an old lady's rope cage full of chickens she'd placed on a spare seat, but he'd accidentally opened the cage door instead and the chickens had forced their way out, creating a huge commotion of squawking and flying feathers. Along with several other passengers, he'd managed to recapture the birds, but not before being shouted at by their owner. Ned's face had turned puce in humiliation; and still she hadn't moved them to allow him the spare seat. No, he thought to himself from the VW's passenger seat, this was a much better way to travel.

"As long as we travel in daylight," Mel interrupted his thoughts, "then we should be safe enough. The Viet Cong only attack at night."

"Not at Ap Bac," replied Ned.

"Well, that's true enough, but that was the first and only time they chose to stay and fight rather than melt back into the countryside once the government troops arrived."

"Were you there?" asked Ned, knowing full well she had been, but keen to hear her take on the battle.

With the windows down, Mel was having trouble controlling her long dark hair, which was blowing all over the place. "Yeah, I was there. I was lucky – one of my American military contacts tipped me off in advance. When I first arrived in Vietnam about a year ago, I was told to get to know a guy called John Paul Vann. He was the senior US military advisor helping General Cao, who was the commander of South Vietnam's 7th Infantry Division based down here in the delta."

Ned watched out the window as the built-up area of Saigon began to give way to fields and open spaces. "Is John Paul Vann still around?"

"No, he left back in March; he was fed up with the way the South Vietnamese and American commanders are fighting the war against the Viet Cong. I think Ap Bac might've been the final straw."

"So was it his fault the Viet Cong won the battle?"

Mel had to brake as she came up behind a slow-moving truck belching out black diesel fumes. The truck, like most of them, was overloaded with canvas bags piled up high on the roof and tilting wildly to the left, looking as if it might topple over at any moment.

"No, not at all. He was the one urging General Cao to fight with as much force as possible, but Cao was resisting because President Diem had threatened to demote any commander who loses too many troops on the battlefield. You see, Diem thinks the army is there to protect him against coups rather than fight the communists. Fighting the Viet Cong's a secondary consideration. And the 7th Infantry Division is the closest one to Saigon, so the one most responsible for his protection. And he's very paranoid, especially after last year's attempt."

Ned was still watching the truck, wondering if and when it would tip over. "So were you there for the actual battle at Ap Bac?"

The road straightened out, allowing Mel to overtake. "Well, I missed the beginning, but I arrived in time to see most of it. Vann had given me a tip-off at a New Year's Eve party at the US Embassy that there was going to be a big operation down here, near My Tho. So two days later, I travelled down this exact road. You couldn't exactly miss it; I'd only been driving an hour when I heard the sound of gunfire. I parked the car on the side of the road, grabbed my jacket and helmet from the back seat and set off. I only had the noise of battle to guide me across a bunch of paddy fields, but I could see the fighting about one klick ahead."

"Klick?"

"A klick, come on, keep up, a klick is a kilometre," chided Mel. Ned tried not to show his embarrassment at this display of ignorance. "Bent over double and virtually crawling on my hands and knees, I moved through the mud toward the government troops. They were less than a *klick* away from a line of trees, and that's where the Viet Cong were holed up. When I got there, there was total confusion. I could see four helicopters crashed in the paddy fields midway between the government troops and the VC. There were quite a few soldiers around the helicopters, most of them dead, but some still alive. Nobody was doing anything to help them. General Cao wasn't there, so none of the officers wanted to take control or make a decision. An American advisor was shouting and screaming at a South Vietnamese officer who commanded some armoured personnel carriers, but he was refusing to listen to an American or take his APCs to the crashed choppers to rescue any survivors."

"It sounds chaotic."

"Yeah, it was. I stayed with the South Vietnamese troops all day and they did nothing – absolutely nothing – to try and defeat the Viet Cong, despite having four times the number of men and considerably better weapons. They didn't even try to rescue the injured pilots of the downed choppers. Eventually, a new attack helicopter came along to mount a rescue, but that was shot out the sky as well. Useless, fucking useless they were. Later in the afternoon, the APC commander must have gotten an order from someone higher up the chain because he moved a few of his vehicles forward and got within firing distance of the Viet Cong. And you know what happened?"

Ned shook his head.

"About eight Viet Cong guys ran out of the cover of the woods, threw some grenades at the APCs, and then scarpered back into the trees, all before the South Vietnamese could fire a single shot."

"Then what?"

"Oh, the grenades exploded, the APC commanders panicked and turned their vehicles around and fled for the South Vietnamese lines. And that was it. Apart from some napalm bombs being dropped on the hamlet of Ap Bac instead of on the Viet Cong positions in the treeline, nothing else happened. I stayed all night with the South Vietnamese troops, and by dawn the next day the Viet Cong had gone, retreated and taken everything with them. Apart from some signs of blood in their foxholes, we found no evidence the army had killed a single guerrilla."

With Saigon now several miles behind them, Ned gazed out distractedly at the little villages they were passing through, nothing but a small collection of thatched huts scattered randomly across the flat countryside stretching out before them. "Not much of a battle then."

"No, not like a World War Two battle, but mark my words, the Viet Cong will take strength from their win. They won't melt away quite as quick now when they come up against South Vietnamese soldiers."

"That must have been a bit of a scoop for you – were you the only Western journalist to see the battle?"

"Well, I was the only one there to see any shots being fired," said Mel as she manoeuvred her VW around another pile of corn spread evenly across half the carriageway, drying on the sun-soaked road. "Although I missed the main fight earlier in the morning when the initial assault was mounted and the helicopters were shot down. A few other journalists from AP and UPI turned up later in the afternoon and stayed until the following morning, so I didn't have a complete scoop, but my reports did make it into some of the big papers back home. Not as big as your photo though, that was amazing. Strange how it takes the death of a monk to bring this anonymous little war to the attention of the American people – instead of a battle."

Ned was warming to Mel now she seemed to be showing him a little more respect and confiding in him as a peer. She was older than him, mid-twenties probably, and petite, but he began to appreciate what a tough cookie she was, and how dedicated she was to the job. It must have taken courage to stay out in the field knowing there was a company of Viet Cong just a few hundred yards away. He was excited to spend the day with her, and keen to prove himself as a photographer, not just in the city, but out in the field too.

As they sped down Highway 4 to My Tho, the nearest provincial capital to Saigon, he watched out the open window as the countryside passed by. Although they were on the main road from Saigon to the Mekong Delta, Vietnam's most southern region, where the mighty Mekong River split into several channels as it powered its way to the South China Sea, the road was nothing more than a tarmacked farm track, just wide enough for two vehicles to pass each other. It ran along an embankment, on either side of which, about six feet below, stood paddy fields full of rice plants neatly arranged in rows, swaying gently in the breeze. It was still early morning, but already the heat was rising, with mirages making the road ahead fizzle and blur, while out in the fields wisps of mist still hovered above the water. The local villagers were working away in them, the women bent double as they tended the rice crops. They looked up as the VW sped past, but it was impossible to see their faces, cast as they were in shadow from the big conical hats they wore to protect against the fierce sun.

Mel slowed as they came up behind an old wooden cart with large wooden wheels pulled by two lumbering water buffalo, huge horns curling in on themselves, their extended ears shivering and vibrating to keep the flies from settling. Spurring them on was an elderly man wearing a green canvas hat and a big grin, his crooked, rotting teeth not seeming to bother him at all. Mel overtook and carried on.

Arriving at the headquarters of the 57th Transportation Company in My Tho, they swept into the compound and immediately found Major Don McAlistair of the US Marines in conversation with a senior ARVN infantry officer.

"Hey, y'all!" he shouted in a southern drawl when he saw who was stepping out from the car. "How you doin', Mel? You ain't been to see us for a while. Come to check up on us?"

The 57th Transportation Company's main role in the delta was to fly ARVN infantry soldiers into search and destroy missions to hunt for the elusive enemy. The company consisted of thirty CH-21 Shawnee helicopters flown by a few dozen US pilots and backed up by a strong contingent of mechanics and other ground crew. Major McAlistair was stationed in their barracks, but his main role consisted in mentoring a battalion of ARVN soldiers from the 7th Infantry Division.

"Hello, Don," said Mel, smiling happily and reaching up to kiss him on each cheek. "We were wondering if we could catch a ride and tag along on your next mission?"

"You sure can, Mel. And perfect timin'! We're fixin' for one now, we'll be loadin' up the bananas in a minute, so you're welcome to join." The CH-21 was a twin-rotor helicopter with a bent fuselage, often referred to affectionately as a 'flying banana' by those who loved them for their shape.

"This is Ned Rivers, our new photographer just in from England. He's a bit of a city boy, all he's found to photograph so far is a monk in downtown Saigon, so I wanted to bring him down here and show him the real countryside."

"Howdy, Ned," said McAlistair, shaking his hand. "You come to the right place if you wanna see the countryside.

Now, when Mel says 'monk' – was that your picture of the fella burnin' himself that's kickin' up the stink back home?"

"Yes, it was, but I'd rather not have to go through that again," replied Ned modestly.

"Well, you certainly focused everyone's attention on what's happenin' over here, which I guess is a good thing. Now we gotta kick ass and show our folks back home how we deal with commie shit!" The major gave Ned a slap on the shoulder and Ned managed a weak smile in return before looking down at his boots, unsure how to take the gung-ho American.

"Great!" said Mel. "Is this search and destroy mission connected to the police station attack from last night?"

"Sure is. We reckon they've gone to ground in a nearby village called Tan Hien, 'bout fifteen klicks to the east. They'll be headin' back to their camps in the Plain o' Reeds, so we're tryin' to cut 'em off before they get there."

"Plain of Reeds?" asked Ned.

Major McAlistair smiled, which Ned assumed was in response to his ignorance of the surrounding countryside. "Plain o' Reeds is an area 'bout two and a half thousand square miles over toward the Cambodian border, Junior. Basically, a huge swamp, so it's almost impossible to find their camps."

Ned and Mel watched as six 'flying bananas' were loaded up with two platoons from the 7th Infantry Division, about seventy men in total, including two US advisors, among them Major McAlistair. The major had explained half the helicopters would fly to the east of the village to block off any retreat to the Plain of Reeds, while the other half would fly west with the aim of flushing the Viet Cong out toward the soldiers from 2nd Platoon. Ned and Mel would accompany the mission in one of the 'flushing' helicopters.

It was just past 10.00 am, later than normal, when the six helicopters took off. This was Ned's first trip in a 'flying banana' and his first mission with the ARVN, so he was nervous. Not that anyone would guess judging by the grin he was desperately trying to suppress; his enthusiasm to repeat his recent success was etched across his face. Not having had a female reporter join them before, especially not a *tây*, as Westerners were known in Vietnamese, the soldiers were polite and welcoming. Most of the twelve or so men in their helicopter were crammed in, standing and gripping onto the webbing strung floor to ceiling. On one side were some fold-down canvas seats, which one soldier lowered for Mel and Ned to sit on. Ned chose to remain standing, keen to show solidarity with the troops. Mel had no such compunction and promptly took the proffered seat.

As usual, Ned was wearing his photographer's waistcoat with its array of zippable compartments, his small Leica in the chest pocket, and his Nikon F slung around his neck with his trusted 50 mm lens attached to the front. He always chose a 50 mm lens for it as he felt this was the closest focal plane to the human eye and so produced pictures similar to how the scene would actually have looked in reality. It was not, however, considered a telephoto lens, so the photographer needed to be close to the subject to take engaging photos.

While Ned was checking both his cameras had film in, the door gunner was checking his 7.62 mm machine gun. The tension was evident, even among the experienced 7th Infantry Division soldiers. In Ned's opinion, the only person who looked relaxed was Mel. The revving of the engines was the first indication of imminent take-off. As the twin blades rotated at an ever-increasing pace, the vibrations transferred to the fuselage and those inside. Ned felt the back of the helicopter lift off first, followed eventually by the front. The noise was incredible; as it climbed into the sky, the pulsating throb of the engines burst through Ned's inner ear almost to the point of pain. As one of the last to have climbed in, he found himself standing close to the gunner in the open doorway. Through the opening, he could see the countryside speeding away fast below him, a patchwork containing every shade of green imaginable, including the water in the rivers and canals. The land was flat and uniform, mostly paddy fields, but interspersed with small river tributaries and canals feeding into the main Mekong channel. On either side of these waterways were thick groves of palm, banana and bamboo trees, their fronds waving dramatically as the helicopters passed low overhead, causing havoc with their downdraught. Occasionally, just for a moment, Ned would see a small traditional wooden boat filled with fruit or vegetables being rowed sedately through the waters by a local villager standing on a platform in the stern and pushing the two oars in a scissor-stroke action to garner forward momentum. The helicopters swept over small villages and hamlets, nothing more than a collection of little huts with thatch roofs. Ned expected children to come running out to see what was clattering by, but noticed how people quickly ran inside instead, seemingly terrified by the arrival of troops.

There was another helicopter off to Ned's right, its rotors a blur as it snaked through the morning mist. Suddenly, without warning, he watched its front swing up aggressively, causing the back end to drop down, landing swiftly on its two rear wheels, the flimsy framework holding the back axle in place bending violently under the force. Ned was shaken out of his reverie as his own helicopter unexpectedly plunged downwards, leaving his stomach in his mouth. In a similar manoeuvre, their front lurched upwards, forcing the back end down, a moment before he felt the heavy thud as they hit the ground. The back of the helicopter jumped up from the hard impact and then realigned to land flatly on all three wheels.

Immediately, an ARVN lieutenant started screaming at his men to exit the helicopter and take up a safe-zone firing position. Ned was caught up in the rush for the door and brusquely thrown from the helicopter. Luckily, he landed on his feet but then stumbled forward onto his knees. Close by were the soldiers he'd travelled with, jumping out around him. He tried to get his bearings and find some form of cover, when he heard a whistling sound close to his ear. Instinctively, he fell forward into the dirt, his stomach landing on his Nikon, which winded him painfully. As he lay on the ground, hurting and muddled, he tried to work through his confusion. His brain jolted into reality as he realised the very precarious position he was in. The noise was intense as the ARVN troops fired back at whoever was shooting at them. With a stab of panic, Ned worked out the cause of the whistling noise as another bullet streaked over him. He forced himself to lay as flat as possible in the dirt and looked over to the soldier on his left, seemingly frozen in a similar position. With growing alarm, Ned diagnosed the cause of the trooper's stillness, shocked by the sight of so much blood bubbling from the man's neck and pooling around his head. Ned looked up, realising he had to find some form of cover. He could see ARVN soldiers moving forward, crouching, firing and moving forward again. He decided they must be pushing the insurgents back, so this was his moment to run for it. He spotted an old wooden cart about twenty yards in front of him. After one final look to check for any immediate danger, he scrambled to his feet, crouching low, and ran for cover.

The cart had been left at the edge of the main track leading into the village. It had obviously been there a long time as tall weeds had grown up through the wooden spokes of the wheels. Away from his perilous starting position, he felt safer, and remembered why he was there. He grabbed the Nikon and brought it to his eye. Blackness. Confusion.

Come on, Ned, pull yourself together! he admonished himself, realising he hadn't taken the lens cap off. *Keep calm, think it through, get the basics right.*

The sound of firing was getting fainter and seemed to be coming from a bit further off. He looked out from behind the cart to make sure he wasn't about to be overrun by Viet Cong, before taking out his light meter and adjusting the settings on his Nikon: f/5.6 with a 1/50 shutter speed would be a good place to start, he resolved, setting the dials and removing the cap. He brought the camera up to his right eye and used it to peer over the top of the cart. Twisting the focus ring, he searched for signs of movement or activity, but couldn't find any.

Covered in a sheen of sweet, not all of it attributable to the intense humidity, he was still searching moments later when he heard a familiar voice behind him: "What are you doing hiding down there? You get any good photos?"

Startled, Ned turned around to find Mel standing quite calmly out in the open.

"Um, er, I'm not sure," Ned replied, feeling now was not the time to admit he hadn't taken a single shot. It was only then he noticed the firing had ceased. He could hear the American advisors shouting at the ARVN soldiers, but there was no more shooting.

"You better not be wasting my time, Ned. Come on, let's go see what happened!" And with that, Mel strolled off in the direction of the shouting as if on a Sunday walk. Ned caught up with her as she ambled into the village of Tan Hien, heart still pounding from his near-death experience.

"Are you okay?" he asked hoarsely.

"Yeah, I'm fine," she replied, looking around the village as if sightseeing in Yellowstone National Park rather than standing in a warzone where bullets had been flying only moments before.

Ned looked past Mel to see the ARVN soldiers milling around next to a young man from the village, who was sitting on the ground with two rifles pointing down at him. Mel found Major McAlistair and asked what was happening.

"I think we caught 'em with their pants down, though we did have a bit of a warm reception on landin'. The first chopper only just touched down when we came under fire. We reckon there was only one or two o' the bastards firin' at us, but they vanished back into the village by the time the third had landed. I think they got one of ours from the second chopper, but otherwise it looks like we're unscathed. We captured this guy." McAlistair pointed to the dejected villager on the ground. "But it doesn't look like he was involved. We're waitin' to hear if 2nd Platoon on the other side of the village had contact yet. I ain't heard no firin'."

Mel and Ned watched as the ARVN soldiers searched the village, but they found no evidence of any Viet Cong activity, nor could they locate the gunmen, who, as was their habit, had melted away into the adjoining countryside. Once it was apparent there were no more Viet Cong hiding, 2nd Platoon entered the village from the east and joined up with the troops Mel and Ned had travelled in with. Ned took the opportunity to photograph the soldiers searching the place and the interrogation of the captured villager, but knew none of his pictures would be worthy of publication.

The two platoons stayed for about an hour in the village before collecting the body of their ill-fated colleague from the landing site and travelling back to the headquarters of the 57th Transportation Company, where everyone disembarked. Don McAlistair invited Ned and Mel into the officers' mess for lunch, but they declined, using deadlines as a pretext to head back to Saigon.

Halfway back along Highway 4, Ned felt the compulsion to own up. "Mel, I don't think I'll have any photos to support your article on this morning's mission. I didn't manage to capture any of the firefight. I had my face planted in the dirt for most of it, and by the time I got into position and started looking for a subject, the fighting had stopped. I didn't react quick enough."

There was a pause as Mel glanced away from the road to fix him with a stern look. "Ned, you've got to be quicker if you want the good shots, and you've got to be in there among the action."

"I know," said Ned. "I'm obviously better at photographing people who want to kill themselves rather than people who want to kill me!"

Mel laughed at the weak joke and the tension in the car broke. "Ah, don't worry about it. The first time I had bullets flying around my head, I was flat on the floor in a heartbeat too. But now I always look to see where my point of safety is, so I know where to take cover if shooting breaks out. Take it as a lesson."

Having come clean, Ned was relieved to see Mel didn't appear to hold it against him; in fact, she seemed quite relaxed about the situation. He was still trying to figure her out. Despite her diminutive stature and well-manicured appearance, he decided she must have an inner strength as hard as nails. She hadn't been the least bit fazed earlier in the day about walking in the open with bullets flying, nor it seemed about sleeping close to a company of VC communists during the Battle of Ap Bac. Ned was in awe of her nerves of steel and wondered where she'd learnt to remain so calm in such dangerous situations. It made him realise there was so much he still didn't know about her. How had she ended up running a press bureau in Saigon, for instance? He didn't even know how long she'd been out here. What was her background? Was she married? Did she have a boyfriend?

Whatever her story, at least she was softening to him. And as they motored back along Highway 4, he was happy enough with that.

4

MONDAY 17TH JUNE 1963

Ned had arrived in Saigon with very few thoughts as to what dangers a war photographer might encounter. In fact, up until being shot at four days earlier, he hadn't really considered himself a war photographer at all, just a photographer in a dangerous place.

He'd spent the weekend questioning whether he'd be able to meet Mel's high expectations and make a success of the job, especially after his near-death experience.

By Friday evening, he was wondering if his success with the photos of Thich Quang Duc had been purely down to luck; after all, he'd been the only journalist to turn up with a camera. Apart from that one, albeit significant incident, he was conscious of the fact he'd had little success photographing anything else even remotely newsworthy.

By Saturday evening, he was considering whether he was brave enough to be a war photographer at all. But talking the shooting incident through with three experienced Western journalists in the ground-floor bar of the Continental Palace Hotel on Tu Do Street helped him put the episode in some perspective, and after several beers, he'd managed to shrug the event off.

By Sunday evening, he'd given himself a lecture, reminding himself no one else was going to help him succeed. He had to do it all on his own.

So, as Ned Rivers arrived for the start of his third week in Saigon, he recognised the need to demonstrate his success hadn't been a one-off, and he was both brave and capable enough of capturing more photographs worthy of the world's front pages.

As he walked into the office, he found Mel talking to a young Vietnamese woman he hadn't seen before, and wondered who she was. Mel saw him and called him over.

"Ned, I want you to meet Bich, our latest recruit. She was waiting around to see me last Thursday after we got back from the delta. She asked for a job, and it suddenly occurred to me, with the office becoming busier, we need someone to help manage it...and us. So I've offered Bich the role of office manager. She's starting today."

As Ned stepped forward to greet her, he was struck by how beautiful she was, especially her eyes. These were jade green in colour, rare for a Vietnamese person. She looked almost angelic. But she was slow to smile, and when she finally did, it wasn't with her eyes and looked forced.

"Hello," he said, shaking her small hand, conscious not to squeeze it too hard. She shook his in return, but Ned felt uncomfortable at how she looked him in the eye a second or two longer than he felt was normal, giving him the distinct impression that, for some reason, she was judging him.

The moment over, Ned turned his attention back to Mel, hoping she'd accompany him back down to the delta in search of more photo opportunities. He desperately wanted the chance to show her he wasn't scared of the potential danger. He still felt embarrassed by his performance the previous week on the search and destroy mission and knew he could do better.

Mel picked up a piece of paper from her desk. "New York wired me a telegram last night. They say the Buddhist crisis is big news in America since your photo of Duc was first published. They've asked us to follow up and find out more about the monks. New York think this'll be a long-running story and want to make sure we're one step ahead of the other agencies."

"So what do you want me to do?" asked Ned, trying to hide the disappointment in his voice. Monks weren't as exciting as Viet Cong guerrillas, despite his recent experience.

"Find out where the monks are based and go get me some photos. Oh, and I got you a translator and driver. He's waiting for you outside. He's called Pham."

Outside the front door to the bureau on Rue Pasteur, Ned found a young Vietnamese guy dressed in a white shirt over grey slacks leaning up against the side of a Citroen 2CV. On closer inspection, Ned decided the car must have seen better days – the beige paintwork was peeling away and the wheel arches were corroding with rust. The whole thing was covered in dust and dirt, leading Ned to conclude it must only get washed when the monsoon rains came around each summer.

"Hi, you must be Pham?"

Pham stood upright and shook Ned's proffered hand. "Yes, I am Pham. Are you Mr Rivers?"

"Yeah, that's me. Mel tells me you're going to drive and act as a translator."

"Yes, okay. Miss Johnson tells me to drive you wherever you want to go," replied Pham with a grin that suggested he was a relaxed and friendly sort of person. About twenty-five years old, give or take, with straight black hair parted to one side, Ned decided he could be a useful addition.

"Right, Pham. Mel tells me to photograph some monks. Do you know where I can find some?"

With a nod and another smile, Pham indicated for Ned to climb in. Ned opened the passenger door and was alarmed to find a large rust hole in the floor where his feet would normally go.

"Don't worry about the hole – put your feet either side of it," Pham said with a chuckle.

Ned carefully sat down in the passenger seat, placing one foot on each side of the opening as instructed, and tested the strength of what was left of the footwell. He wondered where Mel had found this guy, and if letting him drive him around Saigon was wise.

"So you know where we can find some Buddhist monks?"

"Well, the biggest pagoda is Xa Loi on Ba Huyen Thanh Quan Street. I'm sure there are lots of monks there. It's about six blocks from here, as you Americans would say."

"Ah well, I wouldn't know about that," said Ned. "I'm from England."

"But you sound American."

"I might sound it, but I feel more English. My dad's American and my mum's English. They met when he was stationed in England during the war. They got married, had me, and after the war we moved to America near my father's family in upstate New York. I spent the next twelve years there. My mother didn't really settle in the States and eventually my parents split up and I returned to London with her, where I've lived for the past seven years. The only good thing is that I have dual British and American nationality. So to an American I sound English, but to an Englishman I sound American."

"Oh, so you're not proper American. I'm proper Vietnamese. Southerner, not northerner," Pham said, pointing to himself proudly. He laughed and leant forward to start the car, but before Ned could question the comment, he noticed there were two ignition points, each with a key in it. As Pham turned these one after the other, Ned was surprised to hear two different engines starting, one in the back and one in the front. He turned to his driver enquiringly.

Pham grinned again as he explained. "You look surprised my car has two engines? This is a special 2CV made for the French colonies in North Africa. Too many cars broke down in the desert, so Citroen invented a 2CV with two engines; if one breaks down, the other is a back-up. They called it the 2CV Sahara and a few were exported to Indochina. Even though it's not in great condition, it's mine and I love it."

"Back home, the four-by-fours are ex-army jeeps and Land Rovers, but I've never heard of a four-wheel-drive 2CV before." Ned was pleased the two of them had found a common interest and hoped this could be the start of a good working relationship.

Pham crunched the car into gear and set off through the teeming streets of Saigon toward Xa Loi Pagoda. Rue Pasteur was especially busy this morning, Ned reflected as he studied the scene around him. He enjoyed the strong French connections that remained in modern-day Saigon. Not just the architecture, which would doubtless last for generations, but the cultural aspects too. He examined his surroundings out the window, appreciating the fact South Vietnam was not trying to erase all signs of French colonisation, unlike in the North. The North was the land of the Viet Minh, the Vietnamese nationalist fighters led by Ho Chi Minh. It was they who'd routed the French at the Battle of Dien Bien Phu nearly a decade before. The ensuing peace agreement had split Vietnam in two along the 17th parallel. From what Ned had heard, North Vietnam was far keener to remove the memory of French occupation than the South. The streets down here were still full of Citroens and Peugeots and Renaults. Ned wasn't sure what they drove up North, but he found Saigon to be a beautiful city with its tree-lined boulevards and street café culture, exactly how he imagined Paris to be.

As Pham turned right at a junction, Ned recognised with a jolt where he was. The Esso fuel station alerted him to the fact they were driving through the crossroads where Thich Quang Duc had burnt himself alive less than a week ago. It all looked so normal now. The fruit sellers were still trading from their stalls, the motorbikes and cyclists still swarmed like ants on a mission, and beautiful Vietnamese ladies strolled gracefully down the pavements. Ned stared out the window, his mind whirling as he recalled the dark memories of that day. He was still visualising the blackened body of the monk lying at a twisted angle when Pham parked the beige 2CV Sahara on a side street a couple of minutes later.

"Okay, *ngài*, we're here."

Ned looked at Pham quizzically. "*Ngài*, what does that mean?"

"*Ngài* means 'sir' in Vietnamese."

Ned looked at Pham for a moment, guessing his driver was older than him, and suddenly felt awkward. "Well, I'm not having you call me 'sir', that's ridiculous. That's one of the reasons I escaped London. Can't you just call me 'Ned'? I see us as being equal partners."

Pham beamed again. "Okay, I'll call you 'Mr Ned'. Deal?"

Ned put out his hand and they shook on it.

Together, they walked around the corner and down to Xa Loi Pagoda. It wasn't difficult to find. Set back from the pavement was an ornate gatehouse with intricate iron grill gates set in between two large stone pillars. The gatehouse itself was larger than most houses in Saigon and looked to Ned like the photos he'd seen in books of Chinese buildings with tiled roofs set in several layers, each smaller than the one above, the corners curling up to a point. Strung across the front of the gatehouse was a large banner with hand-painted Vietnamese letters.

"What does that say?" asked Ned, pointing up at it.

"It's a protest banner against President Diem and the government," said Pham.

Ned wanted more than just a protest sign but decided to take a photograph anyway. As he took the lens cap off his camera, he considered what a bright, beautifully lit morning it was, meaning he could afford to choose a high f-number for his aperture to give him greater depth of focus across the scene.

Behind the gatehouse, through the main gates, Ned could see a courtyard shaded from the sun by tall palm trees with masses of green fronds swaying in the gentle breeze. Off the courtyard was the great hall of the pagoda sitting high on concrete pillars, accessible up a set of concrete steps; and to the left of the hall the bell tower, a seven-storey structure with another Chinese-style roof protruding out at each layer. The whole site was surrounded by a tall, rendered wall.

The front gates were locked shut, so Ned chose to take a few stock pictures of the main entrance and the bell tower from the street, without consideration for the two silhouetted figures sat thirty yards up the road in their car.

Ned walked along the edge of the site to see if there was another way in. Finding little sign, he turned to Pham and said disappointedly, "Well, there's not much happening here. Is there another pagoda we could try?"

"We could wait a bit longer and see if a monk comes? Or maybe we go and get a bowl of *phở* and come back later?"

"*Phở*," enquired Ned. "What's that?"

"*Phở* is our favourite food in Vietnam. It's noodle soup made from chicken or beef mixed with green vegetables and spices. There are many street vendors so it's easy to find. It's very popular, especially in the mornings. Come, there are vendors up there by the junction – look. Let me introduce you to *phở*."

They walked up the street – past the two gentlemen in their car reading that morning's *Times of Vietnam* – and on to the crossroads, where a collection of street vendors had set up their mobile stalls. Ned looked at each in turn to see what they were selling. The nearest was a little old lady, who gave him a big grin from under her worn and dirty conical hat, revealing her remaining teeth, badly stained a reddish-black colour from constant chewing of betel nut. Pham explained how chewing betel nut was an important part of Vietnamese culture; made from the areca nut wrapped in a betel leaf, it was a mild stimulant, hence its popularity. It didn't take Ned long to realise the downside: it completely rotted the teeth and left the lips bright red, as if wearing inappropriate lipstick.

The old lady was sitting on an upturned crate, crouched over her two cooking woks, which, Pham explained, would have been carried here on the ends of a bamboo pole, and were now bubbling with hot oil. The woks were perched on top of cookers, similar to mid-sized stoneware flowerpots, each with several air vents and filled with red-hot charcoal. Ned looked at the deep-fried objects being cooked, trying to determine their origin, and took a step back in disgust when he realised they were whole frogs, legs included.

He turned to the next vendor, a middle-aged man wearing a grubby, open cotton shirt and blue bucket hat, standing behind his cyclo. The front passenger seat had been converted into a portable food stall complete with canvas awning above the display counter. He was selling exotic fruits like pomelo and *nhãn* fruit, commonly known as 'dragon's eye' because of the black pip surrounded by soft edible flesh that revealed itself once peeled. There were also baskets of mangosteen, rambutan, star apple, as well as durian hanging off the sides – huge, spiky fruits with orange flesh and a very strong odour that Ned took an exception to.

"God, those stink as bad as the gutters!" he exclaimed, trying politely to mask his disgust.

"Yes, but the fruit is delicious. Come, Mr Ned, here is some *phở*," said Pham, pointing to a third vendor.

Behind a mobile kitchen on wheels stood a pretty girl, no more than twenty years old. In front of her were laid out three steaming cooking pots, one containing beef broth, the second chicken broth, and the third boiling water, each sitting on a charcoal heater to keep them hot. Pham asked her for two bowls of beef *phở*.

The girl picked up some noodles and put them in a large, perforated metal ladle, which she dunked into the boiling water for about thirty seconds. Once drained, she separated the noodles into two china bowls and sprinkled some finely chopped basil, coriander and spring onion on top. Next, using the same ladle as before, she placed thin slices of raw beef into the hot broth to cook for about twenty seconds before adding them into the bowls. Finally, with a delicate touch, she added the broth. The liquid was clear but contained cinnamon and star anise and had been boiled for several hours with the meat and bones from a cow to give it flavour. According to Pham, the chicken broth would have had a whole chicken added during the cooking process instead of beef. In front of the vendor stood a collection of little wooden stools scattered loosely around some tables, so small, Ned thought, they could have come from the local primary school. He pulled a blue stool out from underneath a table and, with great dexterity, manoeuvred his six-foot-two-inch frame into it, leaving Pham in fits of giggles. A pair of chopsticks each in hand, they finally tucked into their *phở*.

"What do you think?" asked Pham.

"It's tasty," said Ned. "It's not as spicy as I thought it might be."

As they ate their *phở*, they chatted amiably, giving Ned the opportunity to get to know his driver a little better.

"Where are you from, Pham?"

Pham finished his mouthful of *phở* before replying. "Here in Saigon. I've always lived here."

"Are you married?" Ned asked. "And what do you normally do? I mean, how come you ended up at BPA as my translator? And where did you learn such good English?"

"So many questions!" Pham appeared surprised but pleased. "Okay. I live with my mum still. My dad died when I was a teenager, and after school I was sent to the Saigon Institute of Languages, where I studied English. I finished this spring, so I thought I'd find a temporary job as a translator until I decide what I want to do. Lucky for me, Miss Johnson hired me."

"Lucky for me too! But what happened to your dad?"

Pham studied his *phở* for a moment before looking back at Ned. "He was murdered by communists. He worked as a civil servant at the Ministry of Interior, and one day, as he walked out the building with some colleagues, someone threw a grenade, which exploded and killed him. It was the ministry that paid for me to study English."

Ned looked away, feeling awkward that he'd asked. "I'm sorry."

"Don't worry, it was several years ago." Pham paused before changing the subject. "Anyway, why are we looking for monks today, Mr Ned?"

"I'm not too sure. Personally, I wanted to go and find the Viet Cong, but apparently my New York office wants me to photograph monks instead."

"What happens to your photographs once you've taken them?"

Before he could answer, Ned suddenly noticed some orange-robed figures, eight of them, walking in a line from the direction of the Xa Loi Pagoda. At the front and just ahead was a younger monk, who struck a small cymbal that chimed exquisitely. Ned picked up his camera and focused the rangefinder on them as they walked along the road, each holding a metal bowl. There were four ladies standing on the street corner; when the monks reached them, the ladies sank to their knees, lifted their hands and pressed their palms together in prayer. As the monks lifted the lid on their alms bowls, each lady transferred some sticky rice into it from bowls they'd placed on the ground by their sides. After the last one had delivered her offering, the ladies remained kneeling in prayer while the monks gave a brief chant and then turned to cross the road in single file.

The monks were barefooted and held their alms bowls in both hands close to their robed chests. Ned spotted that, except for the young monk out front with the cymbal, the first in line seemed to be the eldest, with each appearing younger the further down they were. As they approached the frog vendor, another lady dropped to her knees and proceeded to give each of them some food. When the last monk had placed the lid back on his alms bowl, the group chanted a small prayer and continued on their way in Ned and Pham's direction. As the eldest reached their table, he unexpectedly leant over and passed a note toward Ned. Despite his surprise, Ned had the sense to take it, and instantly the monk straightened back up and moved on. The procession continued down the road before turning right onto a side street and disappearing from view.

"What did he give you?" asked Pham, looking with surprise at Ned's hands.

Ned looked at the piece of plain white paper, which had been folded several times. There was nothing written on the outside. He began to carefully unfold it, almost as if expecting a venomous bug to jump out at any second. Unfurling the last corner, he could see it was a message written in pencil in very ostentatious curvy handwriting. It was almost illegible.

"What does it say?" asked Pham impatiently.

Ned read it aloud slowly, trying to decipher the words as he did so. "*Meet me. We need to talk. Midday tomorrow at Esso garage where Thich Quang Duc died. Come alone. Be careful, you are being followed...* What!" he exclaimed, alarmed at this turn of events.

He looked around, trying to identify who might be following him. But nobody seemed suspicious, everybody was just getting on with their lives. He even looked at the old lady with betel-stained teeth.

No, don't be stupid, he admonished himself.

Later in the afternoon, the heat of the day still intense, Ned and Pham returned to the office and informed Mel of the strange developments.

"Do you think they mistook you for someone else?" asked Mel, placing the note down on her desk, having read it through three times.

"No, they seemed to know who I was, didn't they, Pham?"

Pham confirmed with a nod of his head, exhibiting a shyness Ned hadn't detected in him up to now.

"Well, what do you think they want from you?"

"I don't know. You've read the note, it just says I should meet them, it doesn't say why." Ned pulled up a chair and sat across the desk from Mel, who studied the note again, looking for clues.

"And what's this bit about you being followed?"

Bich, sitting at Joseph's desk nearby, picked up some files and banged them on the desktop to straighten them out, then looked over to Ned. "You seen anyone following you or watching you?"

Ned looked over in surprise. He hadn't expected her to include herself in the conversation. He put his hand through his hair and met her gaze as he considered the question. "No. I haven't spotted anything unusual. Well, actually…everything looks unusual to me, but I haven't spotted anything more unusual than usual. If you see what I mean."

Bich smiled her unsmiling smile again but said nothing further and returned to her files without asking any more questions. Ned turned his attention back to Mel, who leant forward, placing her elbows on the desk and pushing her hands together, as if in prayer.

"Well, you'd better go meet them and find out what they want. And keep an eye out for anyone who might be tailing you."

Although excited by the mission unfolding before him, the idea of being secretly observed nagged at Ned, leaving him mystified and, if truth be told, a little scared.

5

Ned did as the note instructed and at 12.00 pm was standing alone at the Esso garage on the corner of the crossroads where, exactly a week earlier, almost to the minute, Thich Quang Duc had calmly but purposefully set not only himself alight, but also the tidy relationship between South Vietnam and its greatest ally, the United States.

Ned was keen to find out who it was he was meeting here at what had become such a symbolic location. The Esso garage was small, nothing more than a forecourt with a single pump and a shack at the back covered by a roof of corrugated iron. He stood by the decaying structure feeling conspicuous, searching for a follower, a watcher, but he couldn't see anyone.

He'd almost given up waiting when at last 'they' appeared. The first Ned knew of their presence was from a whistle behind him. He turned to see a flash of familiar orange disappearing along a weed-infested path that ran alongside the shack. Ned walked cautiously down the path and saw the orange-robed figure vanish again behind the building. When he turned the corner himself, he found two monks there, each scanning the surroundings for any potential trouble. They were both young, in their twenties most likely, and wore the same Buddhist robes with brown sandals. Their facial features were so similar they looked like twins, or at least brothers, and the only way to tell them apart visually was by the prominent mole one had to the right of his mouth.

"Are you alone?" the latter asked Ned.

"Yes," responded Ned. "But who are you?"

The two monks looked at each other, as if seeking reassurance it was safe to continue.

"My name is Tran Dinh Ba," continued the one with the mole in excellent English, "and this is my brother Dai. We are from the Xa Loi Pagoda and we wanted to talk to you, Mr Rivers, and ask for your help."

"And how exactly do you know who I am?" Ned asked warily. "We saw you outside the Xa Loi Pagoda yesterday and recognised you as the photographer at Thich Quang Duc's immolation. There was only one Western photographer there, despite us sending the note to many organisations, so we guessed it must be you. And if you weren't Mr Ned Rivers, you wouldn't have known where to meet us. We monks aren't stupid, you know." Ba tapped his forehead with his index finger, a hint of a smile on his face.

Ned was trying to keep up but felt unnerved by the clandestine conditions of the meeting.

"After recognising you yesterday," continued Dai, speaking for the first time, "we set up an alms round to follow you and deliver the note."

"Okay," responded Ned tentatively, "say I am Ned Rivers. What do you want with me?"

"Your photograph of Thich Quang Duc has been printed in newspapers all over the world, you've already helped us. You see, President Diem and his government are all Roman Catholics, and they're trying to destroy the Buddhist faith in this country. We have to stand up to them. They're too strong for us, so we can't hope to beat them without help from outside.

Thich Quang Duc's selfless act helped, but it was your photograph that brought his death to the world's attention. And with the world on our side, we may be able to stop President Diem from persecuting us into extinction."

"Go on," said Ned, unsure if he was understanding correctly. Their English was very good, but they both spoke with strong accents, making it difficult to understand each word clearly.

"We need your help to keep showing the world what Diem is doing to us," said Ba, continuing to search the space around them as if a rush of policemen might suddenly appear from around the corner at any moment.

"So you want me to take more photos of you guys burning yourselves to death to get them published around the world?"

Dai's eyes narrowed and Ned knew he'd overstepped a mark.

"No one else will be killing themselves just for your camera, Mr Rivers. But I can assure you there'll be more to capture that will make the world support us in our fight. And we would like you to be there when these things happen."

"I'm sure you would," replied Ned as he studied the more earnest of the pair, "but I'm not here to help you. My job is to photograph events wherever they occur." He thought back to his experience in the Mekong Delta with Mel and decided search and destroy missions to remote villages in helicopters with the ARVN must surely offer greater opportunities than monasteries. But then he remembered, for now, his all-important bosses in New York were specifically requesting material on the rebellious monks.

"We know you have a job to do Mr Rivers, but are you really willing to turn your back on this persecution and ignore our fight?" barked Dai suddenly, his eyes glowering.

Ned was taken aback by this forcefulness – from a Buddhist monk of all people. "No, of course I care about your struggles..." he said rather lamely. "It's just there's other things to photograph in this country right now." He paused to think the situation through again. It was a monk, after all, that had afforded him his best success to date. "Really, it's up to my bureau chief what I cover. But if you guys can provide me with photo opportunities that the newspapers will run with, then I'm sure I'll be there with my camera."

"Thank you, Mr Rivers," said Dai, letting out a large breath of air. "In that case, we'd like to invite you to the Xa Loi Pagoda tomorrow to photograph Thich Quang Duc's funeral. It will be a big event, with lots to photograph. No violence, very peaceful. And we'll introduce you to more of us involved in the fight against Diem's government. Be there at 8.00 am, the front gates will be open, come up to the great hall."

As he finished speaking, he turned his head and gave one last scan of the space before giving a quick bow and striding away down the path away from the Esso garage, his brother following two paces behind.

Ned watched them go, wondering why the need for such caution, and then remembered he'd meant to ask the monks who it could be that was following him.

6

The area around Xa Loi Pagoda was packed on the morning of Thich Quang Duc's funeral. Ned guessed a few thousand had turned up to honour the priest; mostly Buddhist monks in their saffron robes, but also Buddhist nuns, students and hundreds of everyday Saigonese come to show their respects. Ned ambled through the crowds taking photographs of anyone who looked interesting and photogenic. Since the occasion was peaceful, even joyous, no one seemed to mind having their picture taken.

"Pham, what are these costumes the ladies are wearing?" asked Ned, having noticed that many of the women in the crowd were dressed in bright-coloured silk outfits, tightly fitting around the upper body from the neck to the waist, but free-flowing around the legs. Each was characterised by a split up the side from ankle to hip, revealing tight silk trousers or a full-length skirt underneath, mostly in white, but sometimes in the same colour as the dress.

Pham turned around and scanned the crowd. "Ah, those are *áo dài*. They're considered the national costume of Vietnam."

Ned stopped to take a photograph of two beautifully dressed ladies in their traditional *áo dài*. "They certainly make for a colourful scene. Pity they won't show as well in black and white." Ned thanked the ladies and went in search of his next photograph, Pham following closely behind. They'd arrived early, so had had plenty of time to enjoy the festive mood of the crowd. There was no focus to the throng yet; everyone was simply milling around waiting for the ceremony to begin.

Mel had informed Ned she would also be covering the funeral, and expected other Western journalists to be there too, including David Halberstam from the *New York Times*, Neil Sheehan from United Press International and Peter Arnett from the Associated Press. Ned was busy photographing a gaggle of students when Mel found him and Pham.

"Hey!" she shouted in greeting so her voice could be heard above the general hubbub. "What a huge turnout."

"Isn't it just? I've never seen so many people in one place before. I guess it shows the support the Buddhists have among the people here. I don't suppose the government will like this one bit."

"Yeah, you're right. Let's hope it doesn't descend into the same mess as the Vesak celebration in Hue last month."

"I got the impression from Tran Dinh Ba and Tran Dinh Dai – the monks I met yesterday – that they thought today would pass off peaceably, but we'll have to wait and see."

"I'd like to meet these guys," said Mel. "If you find them among this lot, can you introduce them to me?"

"Yeah, sure. I just need to take some more general photos to try and capture the size of the crowd, then I was going to go inside and find them. We're meant to meet at 8.00 am. Why don't Pham and I meet you by the main gates in twenty minutes?"

"Yeah, that's fine," replied Mel before walking off in search of other press colleagues.

Ned and Pham walked up Ba Huyen Thanh Quan Street, toward the junction, close to where they'd eaten *phở* two days previously. The street was filling with even more people, but up by the junction the crowds had thinned, and this allowed Ned to find a good place to take some photographs looking down the road toward the pagoda. He could see the seven-storey bell tower toward the end of the street, but in front of it, occupying every available inch of space, were the thousands come to offer their support. It would be impossible to drive down the road; a route could never be cleared.

The overriding theme of the scene was orange, but the ladies in their best *áo dài* added to the bright kaleidoscope Ned could see through his viewfinder. He climbed up onto a half-wall belonging to a neighbouring property to find some height, but it still wasn't enough.

Looking around for a better vantage point, Ned suddenly heard a squeal of tyres as a four-door Renault Frégate screeched around the corner and stopped abruptly right in front of him. Out of the black saloon car jumped three men wearing black leather trench coats. One grabbed Pham and bundled him into the back of the vehicle; the other two strode toward Ned, who was still standing on the wall, utterly bewildered as to what was happening, and wondering why anyone would want to wear a trench coat in this heat. He'd remained frozen in shock as Pham had been pushed into the car, but seeing the two Vietnamese men moving toward him, he realised his dangerous predicament and started running away down the wall. He wasn't sure who they were, but he guessed they weren't here to offer him a lift.

The wall was very thin, only just wider than one of his feet, so he couldn't run very fast. His pursuers – one tall, one short with an acne-scarred face, both with slick-backed hair – were able to catch up with ease. As they reached him, the taller of the pair stretched out to grab his leg. Instinctively, Ned kicked him in the side of the head, and seized the opportunity as the man fell back in pain to jump down onto the road and make his escape.

Landing with bent knees like a parachutist to cushion the impact, he sprang up and looked left and right to decide which way to run. In that moment, he saw both men lunge forward and grab hold of him. The taller man, seemingly recovered, clutched Ned's right arm, while his smaller companion with the pockmarked face managed to grip onto his photographer's jacket. With his free left hand, Ned tried to swing around and punch the taller assailant, but it was a difficult manoeuvre with little power behind it, so the blow was deflected. The act of spinning around had dislodged the smaller man's hold on his jacket, however, giving Ned one last chance to break the other's grip on his arm. He went in for another punch, aiming for where he'd kicked him before in the hope it was still sore. This time, the blow connected, and the attacker spontaneously let go. Feeling himself come free, Ned made a break, but the smaller man, having anticipated the move, went low and grabbed his legs, preventing him from going anywhere. His larger friend, evidently unimpressed at being kicked and punched in the head, took a step back and, with a short jabbing motion, hit Ned in the stomach. Although not a full swing, it contained enough power to make Ned double up in pain.

With the wind knocked out of him, he found himself being dragged across to the shiny black saloon car and bundled into the back alongside Pham, who also appeared frozen in shock. The smaller attacker jumped in the back with them, while the other ran around to the front passenger seat next to the driver. As soon as the doors were closed, the car reversed out of the crowded street and drove at speed toward the outskirts of the city. Very few in the crowd had witnessed what had happened; of those who had, none could have done anything to prevent it.

Still wheezing, Ned couldn't believe he'd just been abducted, if that indeed was what was happening. Why would anyone kidnap him? He was nearly penniless and his parents not much richer. The two men sitting in the front were talking heatedly to each other in Vietnamese, as if having an argument. The taller man in the passenger seat was rubbing his cheek to check for blood where Ned had kicked and punched him, but Ned could see he hadn't broken the skin.

He looked across at Pham and mouthed, *"You okay?"* Pham nodded his head unconvincingly, still seeming dazed. Ned tried a smile of reassurance, then turned to their assailants.

"Why have you abducted us?" he asked finally.

No answer. All three men kept looking straight ahead.

Ned turned to Pham desperately. "Pham, ask them who they are and why they've taken us." He listened as Pham nodded and spoke to all three in Vietnamese.

The two in front remained silent, but the smaller man with the acne scars replied in English, "Not abducted – arrested. Now, shut up!"

Ned looked at Pham and raised his eyebrows quizzically, mouthing silently, *"Arrested for what?"* Pham shrugged his shoulders in reply, but neither dared speak.

Jesus, what was going on? What had he done to be arrested? He convinced himself it was obviously a mistake and he'd soon be released once they realised their error. He studied his three captors. They didn't exactly look like policemen. Where were their uniforms?

He didn't have too long to dwell on his situation, however, as the car soon turned off the street and drove under an arch into a courtyard, where two more black Renaults Frégate were parked up alongside some more ominous-looking army trucks.

From the outside, Ned thought the building looked like any other in Saigon, but once through the arch he realised it was far from normal. The courtyard was paved and surrounded by a single three-storey building with a flat roof. On each floor were lines of windows, partially obscured behind thick, vertical iron bars, revealing the building's true function. The arch was the only feature that broke the symmetry; set within it were solid wooden gates topped with barbed wire that slammed shut behind the Renault.

Ned and Pham were hauled from the car and taken inside. There was a small hallway beyond the entrance with several smaller rooms off it, some with open doors, through which Ned could see men working behind desks. Instead of being taken into an office, however, he found himself pushed roughly through a metal-grilled door, which had been unlocked and opened by a guard, and along a corridor, then shoved unceremoniously inside a cell. Pham too was pushed in after him, and the iron door slammed shut.

Ned took a moment to appraise their cell, which didn't take long as there wasn't much to it: flaking white walls and a ceiling dotted with holes where the plaster had crumbled away. The floor was plain concrete covered in dark, unsettling stains. Opposite the door was a window, and in the middle of the room stood a simple wooden table with two wooden chairs.

"Shit, Pham! What have we done wrong? Why have they arrested us?"

Pham looked apologetic but didn't say anything.

"The monk who gave me that message the other day said I was being followed. But why would anyone follow me? Where do they think I'm going to lead them?" Ned murmured, more to himself than Pham, who'd taken a seat in one of the chairs. Ned went and stood by the window, looking out to see if there were any answers hidden in the courtyard. Realising Pham hadn't said anything since they'd arrived, he looked down at him with frustration. "Well, come on, Pham! You're my interpreter and guide, what's going on?"

"I don't know, Mr Ned, but we have to be careful. These people might be Mat Vu."

"Mat Vu – who are they?"

"Secret police. In South Vietnam, they're known as 'Mat Vu'," explained Pham.

"Secret police," hissed Ned in amazement. "What the hell do they want with me?" And then something occurred to him. "Is it you they've arrested and I'm just caught in the middle? Have you done something wrong?"

"No, I've done nothing wrong. I don't know why they've arrested us, it must be a mistake. Don't worry, Mr Ned, I'll sort it out. Maybe they meant to arrest someone else instead," said Pham unconvincingly. He sat in his chair staring at the natural patina of the wooden tabletop, evidently concerned by the turn of events.

"Have you ever been arrested before?" asked Ned, still staring out the window into the courtyard.

"No, never. Being arrested in Vietnam is not good, you might not be released." As an afterthought, Pham asked, "Have you, Mr Ned?"

"No. But I nearly was."

"What happened?"

Ned paused, watching a bird hopping about in the courtyard, looking for anything to eat. He wondered if he should tell Pham the story but concluded there was nothing else to do in this squalid little cell.

"When I was thirteen, I was hanging out with some friends in an old shell of a house. It'd been bombed during the Second World War. Not all the houses bombed in London during the war have been repaired yet, you see. We were messing around and we came across an unexploded bomb in the cellar. One of my friends decided it would be fun to try and explode it, you know, the kind of stupid idea kids have. So we set up this platform above the bomb and placed some bricks on it. The idea was, if the bricks fell on the bomb, then that would be enough to detonate it."

Pham sat a bit more upright in his chair as he listened to the story. "Weren't you scared of being blown up? I could never do that; I don't like dangerous things."

"No," Ned laughed, "we weren't scared, we were young! We tied a rope round the leg of the platform and took the other end outside across the street. We were taking shelter round the side of another house when the police arrived unexpectedly. My friends all ran, but I was left holding the rope. The police asked what I was doing and I had to lie to them. I told them I'd been walking along when some strange boys said I should pull on this rope. Well, they didn't believe me, so they followed the rope inside the building, and a few minutes later they all came scrambling out again, quick as they could."

"Is that when they arrested you? In this country, they'd think you're Viet Cong and shoot you if you tried to make an explosion in a town."

Ned looked back to where the bird had been hopping, but it had gone now, and the courtyard was still and empty. "Yeah, I was arrested, but eventually they let me go. I don't think they knew what to charge me with. They told my mum though and she went crazy at me. They made me watch the bomb disposal men do a controlled explosion. They were only trying to destroy the detonator, but they blew the main charge by accident and it blew the whole house down. They'd even taken the precaution of covering the bomb with hundreds of sandbags. I got in a lot of trouble, but in my opinion I did them a favour. The house had to be destroyed anyway."

Pham looked at his watch and groaned before rubbing his face and turning back to Ned. "Did your mother hit you? Mine would; she didn't like me misbehaving and always hit me if I did anything wrong."

"No, she didn't hit me, but she hated my friends after that. She said they were nothing but trouble. She wanted to make sure they couldn't influence me, so when I turned sixteen, she looked for a way to get me to leave school. I wasn't very good at school anyway, never enjoyed reading or studying. My teachers called me lazy, except my art teacher who said I had a visual mind. That's probably why I ended up in photography. One of our neighbours worked at BPA as a dark room technician, so he persuaded them to take me on as an assistant. I was developing film and printing photos, stuff like that, and one day they asked if I wanted to go out on a job with the photographer. I'd been badgering them to let me, pretty much since I'd started. It was a huge anti-nuclear march in London and there was loads to photograph: banners, people, faces, the police, the marchers. It was cold and wet, thinking back on it, but I loved it. Turned out my pictures got used by the papers more than the actual photographer's, so they promoted me to junior photographer, which was great. But after that, the senior photographer hated my guts. I did two years in London, and then BPA moved me out here. And my first event out here was the burning monk and my pictures went global."

Talking had almost made Ned forget where he was. Before he could continue, the cell door suddenly swung open with a nasty screech and a guard walked in holding a clipboard. He looked straight at Ned and demanded, in a loud and aggressive manner, his name. Ned stared back at the guard, unsure what to say. Should he be helpful and friendly? Or was it better to be angry and indignant? Before he could decide on the best course of action, Pham interrupted his thoughts.

"You'd better answer, Mr Ned, no point making them angry."

Ned considered the situation as he moved his gaze from Pham to the small, hostile guard.

"Ned Rivers," he replied haughtily. The guard gave him a hard stare, but Ned pressed on. "Why have I been arrested? What am I supposed to have done wrong?"

The guard ignored the question, turning instead to Pham and barking in Vietnamese, presumably to ask his name too.

"Vien Che Pham."

The guard scribbled down the information and left the room without another word, locking the door shut behind him.

Ned dropped down in the second chair across the table from Pham but didn't pursue their conversation. Pham had begun to look bored, whether from his story or how long they'd been in the cell, Ned wasn't sure. He put his hands behind his head, stretched out his legs and wondered how long much longer they'd be held before the Mat Vu realised they'd arrested the wrong people.

The hours dragged by inside the cell, the humidity growing unbearable. Ned was covered in a film of sweat and conversation had dried up completely. He found himself sitting in his chair, picking at a splinter of wood he'd worked free from the side of the table and musing as to just how peculiar the last week had become. Watching a man burn himself to death, being shot at it in the delta, clandestine meetings, and now arrested by the secret police, apparently – though for what, he didn't know.

For the umpteenth time, he shifted in his chair, trying to eke out some comfort from something inherently uncomfortable. Eventually, he gave up and went and stood by the window...again. A single lightbulb dangling from the ceiling had been on all day, so it was only now he noticed how dark it had become outside. The courtyard was illuminated by spotlights, but above the flat roof of the building Ned could see the deep dark blue sky confirming night had fallen. He checked his watch and saw it was 7.45 pm. That meant they'd been locked up for nearly twelve hours already. He swept his dirty blond mop of hair away from his forehead, feeling how sticky it had become in the heat, and looked across at Pham, who was still sitting in his chair fiddling with a shirt button that was now hanging by a thread. He didn't look up.

Hearing the noise of tyres outside, Ned returned his gaze to the window to find a shiny black Citroen sweeping into the courtyard and park up alongside the military trucks. A chauffeur jumped out the driver's seat and opened the rear passenger door.

"Uh oh, looks like someone important's just arrived."

The occupant emerged slowly. He was tall and slim, aged about forty, Ned reckoned, and dressed in a formal white military jacket and trousers, with a swagger stick tucked under his arm. The jacket was covered in gold braid with epaulettes on the shoulders, five lines of service ribbons illustrating in shorthand his importance. His thick black hair was slicked back in the style of a Hollywood actor and shone with confidence, while his little pencil moustache was perfectly trimmed, conveying a certain menace. In fact, everything about him communicated danger. He and his small entourage walked across the courtyard, only to vanish out of sight as they entered the building.

Ten minutes later, the iron door to the cell opened and the same small guard who'd taken their names walked in carrying another wooden chair, which he placed on the far side of the table from them.

"Sit down," he shouted across to Ned, who was still standing by the window.

"Why?" said Ned defiantly. "You haven't even told us why we've been locked up in here all day."

"Sit down, before I call more guards and force you," replied the guard slowly and calmly.

Ned considered his options and decided he didn't like the man's composure. It made him think of a stream running through a mountain meadow, gentle and sedate, but all it would take was a summer thunderstorm to turn it into a fuming, raging torrent.

As he sat down in the chair next to Pham, he was surprised to see his friend give him a disdainful look and whisper, "Don't make these guys angry. Our only chance of leaving here is if you answer their questions."

Before Ned had a chance to reply, the small guard stood rigidly to attention, and the pencil-moustached officer strode into the room, filling the space with his presence. He stared momentarily at Ned, then wandered over to the window to peer out. Ned, ignoring Pham's advice, stood and asked again why they were being held. Without hesitation, the officer swung round and thwacked Ned on the side of his head with his swagger stick.

"Sit down!"

Ned shrieked with pain and immediately fell back, realising his outburst had been a mistake. He sat as instructed and faced front, rubbing the side of his head and staring at the guard as hard as he could to convey his anger.

"Are you Ned Rivers?" asked the officer as if nothing had happened.

Ned's indignation got the better of him. "Why do you want to know?"

Thwack came the swagger stick again.

"I asked if you were Ned Rivers. I will take your insolence as a yes. And do you work for Bellanger Press Agency?"

"Yes, I'm sure you already know I do." Ned flinched in anticipation of another hit, but none came.

"Tell me, Mr Rivers, what were you doing taking photographs of Thich Quang Duc burning himself to death last week?"

"It's my job."

The tall, suave officer examined his swagger stick as if searching for the smallest imperfection in the polished wood. "How did you know to be there when he set himself alight?"

"A note was dropped into my offices the day before informing us of the event and saying we should be there."

"So you hadn't spoken to any monks before the barbecue party?"

Ned recognised the use of the word 'barbecue' from an interview given by President Diem's sister-in-law, the notorious Madame Nhu, to the English-language *Times of Vietnam*, which was famously little more than a government mouthpiece. She'd been particularly scathing of Thich Quang Duc, explicitly stating she would clap every time a 'bonze' wanted to 'barbecue' themselves. Ned had found this distasteful to say the least.

"I asked if you had spoken to any monks before the barbecue party?"

"No."

"Then why do I have photographs of you meeting a pair of monks at the exact spot that stupid, publicity-hungry Buddhist killed himself?"

Ned hesitated, recognising now he really had been followed, but immediately felt another thwack across the side of his head, not hard enough to injure, but hard enough to hurt.

"I asked you a question!" shouted the officer, his pencil moustache curling at the ends as his face contorted in anger.

"I met them after Thich Quang Duc's death, not before!"

"And what did the monks say to you?"

"They thanked me for taking the photographs and getting them published all over the world." Ned hoped he wasn't getting the brothers into trouble. Although dazed and in pain, he decided he'd have to keep his answers as vague as possible to ensure he wasn't inadvertently signing someone's death warrant.

"They thanked you, did they? So are you helping the monks organise a rebellion against the President?"

"I most certainly am not," said Ned, appalled by the accusation.

"Then what were you doing at the Xa Loi Pagoda this morning?" shouted the officer, his voice growing ever shriller.

"I was there to photograph the funeral."

Thwack. "You're a spy, here to foment revolution and bring down the government. Aren't you?" *Thwack* went the swagger stick again.

Ned grabbed his head with both hands to protect himself. "I'm not a spy!" he cried. *Thwack.*

"You're a spy and an agitator. How are you planning to overthrow the government?"

Pham chose this moment to speak up, addressing the officer directly in Vietnamese. To Ned's relief, the thwacking stopped, but he had no idea what was being said. He listened as the conversation to-ed and fro-ed, quietly nursing the side of his still smarting head.

This time, after a short discussion, the officer struck Pham across the side of his head, but then tucked the swagger stick back under his arm and nodded to the guard to open the door. The officer marched out the cell without looking back, followed by the guard.

Still struggling to work out exactly what was happening, Ned turned to Pham, who was clutching his head in his hands from the pain.

"What did you say to make him stop hitting me with that bloody stick?"

"I told him you couldn't be a spy," said Pham without looking up. "You can't bring the government down."

"Thanks," Ned said soberly. And as an afterthought: "How did you do that?"

"Because I said you'd only recently arrived in Saigon and you don't know anything about anything, especially not Saigon politics. Then I told him you only do what your boss tells you, and she definitely didn't tell you to create a revolution."

"How come he believed you?"

Now Pham laughed, looking sheepish. "I said, look at him. He's only a young boy, does he look like a spy? He was just doing his job, that doesn't make him a revolutionary."

Ned couldn't help laughing. "Did he believe you?"

"I hope so."

"Why did he hit you with his stick then?"

"I don't know. Maybe frustration. He wanted you to be a spy or a revolutionary or something, but I calmly explained you weren't. All you did was your job," said Pham wearily.

Ned paused a moment. "Thank you," he said again softly.

For the next few minutes, Ned sat and watched a cockroach scuttling along the floor. He checked his watch again and was surprised to find it was already 8.35 pm. No wonder his stomach was rumbling; he hadn't eaten anything since last night. A wave of nausea washed over him as he realised he hadn't drunk any water since leaving for the pagoda either. He'd used up his supply of adrenalin and now he felt exhausted. For fuck's sake, how much longer did he have to wait in here? He was tired and hungry and just wanted to go back to his apartment.

He was still watching the cockroach, which had now been joined by several others, wondering where they were all coming from, when the cell door opened again and the guard beckoned them out.

"Come with me," he instructed.

Cautiously, Ned and Pham got to their feet and were led out of the cell, back down the corridor and through the iron-grilled gate into the hallway, where Ned, to his great relief, was handed back his cameras that had been confiscated earlier in the day. With high expectations of their imminent release, Ned followed the guard out into the courtyard and on toward the main entrance. The guard spoke to the gatekeeper, who opened one gate a mere sliver.

"Go, go!" was all the guard said, gesturing sharply toward the opening. Ned didn't wait for him to change his mind and rushed through the gap out into the street, followed closely by Pham. The large wooden gate shut behind them with an audible thud.

Ned turned back and looked at the forbidding entrance topped with barbed wire, thanking his lucky god in acknowledgement at what a close shave he'd had today. He guessed many prisoners never got to see this side of the gates again once they'd been brought through them. With Pham beside him, he began the long walk back to the centre of town feeling exhausted and emotional, relieved to be free, but thoroughly bewildered by the events of the day.

7

Ned arrived at the office on Rue Pasteur moments after Pham had pulled up outside. His car being his pride and joy, Pham had gone straight to the Xa Loi Pagoda to retrieve it following their release the night before. They walked into the office together, Ned wondering if he'd receive any sympathy from Mel for the events of the previous day. He suspected she wasn't the type to empathise, but he wasn't expecting what followed.

"Goddammit, where the hell have you been?" came an angry shout as soon as they walked through the door.

Ned and Pham immediately stopped in their tracks as if they'd hit an invisible wall.

Mel was standing behind her desk with her hands clasped tightly to her hips. "I waited all morning for you to show up yesterday and did you bother? Did you, hell!"

Ned tried to interject but the accusations only worsened as her rage flowed thick and fast like the mighty Mekong River in flood. Disobedience, disloyalty, lack of respect, lack of care – all were thrown at him in the torrent of allegations. Ned had guessed Mel might have a temper; now he was on the sharp end, he knew for sure. 'Pissed' was how his American colleagues would describe her mood when the story of that morning was gossiped about later among the foreign press corps.

But, like many with a short fuse, she eventually calmed down enough to listen to Ned's side of the story, and, with Pham's help, he described their arrest and interrogation. The red marks, still visible across the side of his head, helped persuade her of his innocence and the authenticity of their story. So by mid-morning, Mel had been sufficiently placated as to withdraw her threat of sending Ned back to London; by lunch, she'd relaxed enough to sit down next to him and discuss the events of the previous day.

"So what did I miss yesterday?" asked Ned tentatively.

"Well, a long goddamn walk for one. I waited for you by the main gates, but when you didn't come, I got more and more angry. After twenty minutes, I heard chanting start from inside the compound, and a few minutes later this long string of monks in pairs came out and walked through the crowds, making this sort of long snake. When the last monk passed, the crowds joined in on the end, making the snake stretch even further. Thich Quang Duc's casket was at the front being held up by some of the younger monks."

"But where was the funeral held? I assumed it would be at the pagoda."

"You and me both. It turned out to be ten miles out to the cemetery. Three and a half hours of walking."

"And then what happened?" asked Ned.

"To be honest, it was pretty interesting," started Mel, beginning to smile as she recounted the story. "There were about three hundred monks and nuns, and about a thousand other people. There'd been more at the beginning, but I think a lot of people peeled off and went home. They certainly didn't all make it to the cemetery. I walked all the way there behind the monks. All I could hear was this muffled chanting like the sound of summer thunder rumbling away in the distance. By the time I got there, the monks had formed this big circle round an unlit pyre with the casket placed on top. I won't bore you with the details, but believe me, there was a huge amount of prayers, more chanting, and prostrating monks. The pyre was lit, even more chanting, more prayers and more prostrating, but you know what the extraordinary thing was? When they collected his ashes after, they found his heart buried in them. It hadn't burnt. One of the elder monks held it in the air and there was silence. Everybody stared in wonder, and then somebody started clapping, and suddenly everyone was applauding as if some divine miracle had happened."

"Wow. And what did they do with it?"

Mel paused to accept a cup of strong black coffee that Bich had brought in from the kitchen before continuing. "I assume it's gone back to Xa Loi. I didn't hang around much longer. Lots of people were drifting away, clearly the funeral was over, so I found a motorbike taxi and came back here. I knew I had to get it written up and across to New York before the wire office shut. It's just a pity there were no photographs to accompany my copy." She gave Ned a pointed look. He couldn't tell if she was ribbing him or not.

"Believe me, Mel, I'd rather have walked the ten miles with you than spend the day in a cell with Pham."

Mel didn't respond. In the awkward silence, Ned looked across at Bich, who was standing nearby trying to bring the office's chaotic filing system into some sort of order. It hadn't escaped Ned's notice she'd made Mel a coffee but not him, and he wondered, not for the first time, how best he could break the ice with her.

Mel stood up and walked across to the overflowing cabinet Bich was trying to sort, removed a file and returned to her desk. She flicked through its contents, and then, removing a photograph, showed it to Ned.

"Is this who interviewed you yesterday?"

"Interviewed? It was more like a violent interrogation, Mel!" exclaimed Ned as he took the photo and studied it. "Yeah, that's him. So it really was *the* Colonel Tung?"

"The one and the same. Evil bastard by all accounts."

Ned glanced up to find Bich watching Mel. As soon as she became aware of Ned observing her, she quickly returned to her work with the files.

"What troubles me is that he's set his sights on journalists now," said Mel, staring down the photograph. "It won't do us any good to get ourselves embroiled in a prolonged argument with him or the secret police."

"Couldn't agree more. I've already discovered what happens in an argument with him and his swagger stick."

Ned wasn't sure she'd heard him given how intently she was studying the picture; but then she suddenly looked up with a wry smile. "Oh, stop moaning. What doesn't kill you makes you stronger."

Ned chortled in response but didn't say anything.

"Well, we can't let him beat us, can we?" Mel said with determination, standing abruptly and almost knocking over her coffee. "The best response would be for you and Pham to get your asses back over to Xa Loi and carry on photographing the monks."

Ned recognised the suggestion for the order it was and quickly went off to find Pham. On this occasion, he didn't care about being followed by the secret police. He was still more scared of Mel's unpredictable character than anything they could do to him. And if the boss wanted him to integrate with the monks of Xa Loi, then that's what he'd do.

"Thanks again, Pham," said Ned back in the car as they navigated through the chaos caused by the many two-wheeled vehicles around them.

"What for?"

"You saved my arse for the second time in two days. Without you backing up my story, I'm not sure Mel would've believed me. You're like a trouble-buster. Pham – the man who can talk his way out of any situation."

"Pham the trouble-buster. I like that name."

On their arrival at the front entrance to the pagoda, Ned and Pham discovered the little side gate open. They went through and found a young monk sweeping leaves in the courtyard. Pham let him know they'd come to see Tran Dinh Ba and Tran Dinh Ba Dai, and they were directed up to the great hall to wait while the monk went to inform the brothers of their arrival. Pham pointed out two vividly coloured concrete staircases painted in red and yellow leading up to the great hall and indicated they should use the left-hand set by the sign saying *Chỉ dành cho Nam*, explaining the other side was reserved for women. At the top, Pham opened the main doors and they walked through into the hall.

Before them was a large, open, rectangular space dominated at the far end by a raised stage set back from a proscenium arch. Here, a huge statue of Gautama Buddha sat in the meditation position atop a lotus leaf. A large sun disc hung behind the statue on the back wall framing the Buddha's head. In front of the stage stood a simple wooden altar, a shrine with wooden carvings across the front, and vases of bright flowers in different shades of yellow, orange and red on top. Interspersed among the bright floral array were candlesticks similar to those Ned had seen on church altars back in England.

He moved further into the hall and looked about him. A series of pillars ran down each side of the room decorated with long, vertical Buddhist flags composed of rectangular blocks of colour: blue, yellow, red, white and orange. The hall was brightly lit by windows on both sides, some of which contained red, blue and yellow sheets of glass allowing the sun to stream through and dapple the room in coloured light. The space was bare of furniture and had a simple tiled floor for the faithful to kneel and pray upon. Ned took a moment to take it all in – the space, the light, the colours – and liked what he saw. He immediately felt at peace, recognising this as a place of calmness and serenity.

There was nobody in the hall and it echoed to their foot-steps. Along the sides of the galleried walls ran a series of wooden friezes depicting the life of Buddha, each of which Ned studied in turn with interest. On reaching the last one, which featured Buddha lying on his side entering nirvana, he heard footsteps, and turned to see Tran Dinh Ba and his brother Dai coming into the hall. They both beamed with pleasure when they recognised Ned.

"Ah, Mr Rivers, you came!" said Ba in greeting. "Thank you. But I thought you were going to come to Thich Quang Duc's funeral yesterday?"

Ned studied the smiling monks, warming to their easy nature and outward projection of friendliness. They created a scene of such welcome, it made him wonder if this was how it felt to enter nirvana.

"I did come," said Ned, "but as I was taking photos of the crowd, Pham and I were arrested by the secret police."

To Ned's surprise, Ba laughed delightedly in response to something Ned had, until that point, considered rather serious.

"Yes, we all heard about that, didn't we, Dai? Nothing is secret around here. We did warn you about being followed!"

Despite his initial indignation, Ned failed to suppress a grin in the face of Ba's gentle mocking. The shaven-headed monk's light-hearted take on the situation put Ned at ease, removing some of the tension from the previous day's events.

"Yes, I suppose you did. But you didn't warn me we'd be arrested and held in a squalid little cell all day!"

"Well, you missed a good funeral. Many people were there and we cremated him…again," said Ba with a dark-humoured smile. Ned couldn't help but laugh with him and instantly felt a rapport with these small-statured monks, one he'd rarely felt with anyone on first meeting.

"I was sorry to miss it. I can promise I'd much rather have spent the day with you guys compared to being locked in a fetid cell and beaten up by Colonel Tung."

"You met Colonel Tung?" asked Dai, raising his eyebrows.

"Not met in a nice way. He interrogated Pham and me, and beat us with his stick. He claimed I was helping you guys foment a rebellion against the government. Can you believe it?" Ned showed the brothers the red marks he knew were still visible on the side of his head. Both brothers took a step forward to examine them.

"We're sorry you had to experience this, but we did try to warn you," said Dai, more sombre in tone than his brother, as he walked across to the altar and sat down on the floor before it, beckoning the others to join him. "How did you know someone was following me?" asked Ned as he, Ba and Pham all knelt down together. "I haven't seen anything suspicious. Well, except for being arrested."

Ba adjusted position on the floor, ensuring he kept his feet pointing backward. "We saw them. When you tried to get into the pagoda on Monday, there were two members of the Mat Vu sitting in a car watching you."

Ned looked at Ba quizzically for a moment. "Can you explain to me what the hell is going on? I mean, why exactly did Thich Quang Duc kill himself? And why do the secret police think I'm trying to organise a revolution just because I took a photograph?"

"Because they are paranoid, Mr Rivers," Dai shot back plainly.

"Dai, perhaps you should give Mr Rivers a quick lesson on the religious conflict in South Vietnam," commented Ba.

Dai looked across to Ba as if to say, '*Why me?*', but then turned back to Ned and Pham.

"I'll keep it simple. Essentially, the Catholics in this country think they are better than us Buddhists. They hate us. Unfortunately, all the important people in South Vietnam are Catholics. The heads of the military, the government, the civil service – all Catholics. They hold all the power and we do not. To defend our faith from their discrimination, we have to demonstrate and motivate our supporters to show our anger. Thich Quang Duc simply took it one step further."

"So that's why you hate President Diem so much?"

Ba looked across at his brother. "Dai, another one for you to answer."

Dai looked around as if afraid someone might be listening, but after a pause resumed speaking. "President Diem is a bad man, just like his brother Nhu. And his sister-in-law, Madame Nhu – now, she is really evil."

"Why do you consider them evil?"

"They only became Catholics to get the best jobs when the French were in control. Now the French are gone, they act as if they're the new colonial power. But they forget we Buddhists outnumber them greatly, so now we're reminding them."

"But how exactly do they discriminate against you?"

"In lots of ways. You know in the countryside where the Viet Cong are terrorising everyone? The government will only provide weapons to protect your village if it's a Catholic village. They don't give any weapons to Buddhist villages; they leave them to be attacked by the Viet Cong. They don't do anything to help Buddhist communities, the government only spends money on Catholic communities. Have you heard of *corvée*?"

"No, what's *corvée*?"

"*Corvée* is when you have to do unpaid public works for the government, like helping build a road. It's an old French system, but the French stopped it after their revolution two hundred years ago. In Vietnam, we still have to do it, but not if you belong to the Catholic Church. It's all very unfair, they treat us like slaves. If you want to be promoted and you're a Buddhist, you have to convert to Catholicism; otherwise, no promotion. The government makes sure all the contracts go to Catholic companies. Tax, land ownership, business favours – they're all biased in favour of the Catholics. We're not even allowed to wave our flags. It's all deeply unfair, Mr Rivers, and that's why we're so angry."

Ned felt for the monks. He was beginning to understand the depth of their discontent and why they were so annoyed with the government. He knew what it was like to be picked on by those more powerful, albeit on a much smaller scale. Besides the sarcastic nicknames about his height when he was young, he'd also had to endure being called 'Septic', cockney rhyming slang for 'Yank'. He'd hated being the only American in his school and quickly learnt that fighting back, like the monks, was indeed the best form of defence.

Ned and Pham stayed at the pagoda until the sun began to dip toward the horizon, having enjoyed an afternoon of drinking tea, taking photographs, and talking about Buddhism and the threat it faced from the government. Ned found the two brothers to be genial hosts and was beginning to observe the marked difference in their characters, despite their physical resemblance. Ba was the more humorous one, more likely to make light of a situation or tell a joke; whereas Dai was more serious and keen to explain their problems or the history behind their argument in greater detail. Ba was more extrovert, Dai more introverted; Ba the doer, Dai the thinker.

In the days following their reunion in the Xa Loi great hall, Ba and Dai introduced Ned and Pham to more of the pagoda's leading monks, and Ned was authorised to photograph anything and anyone he wanted. Mel too started accompanying them to talk with the monks, especially once she realised their plight was earning the most column inches in the newspapers back home. Ned was learning that, as a written journalist, she experienced as much satisfaction in having a story published as he did with his photographs. The latter were getting increasing attention too, though he had yet to recreate his front-page success.

He also saw how good a nose Mel had for what editors back in America wanted, demonstrating how she'd managed to become a bureau chief at such a young age. She even admitted to Ned how, initially, she'd only started joining him at the pagoda when she'd recognised how big a story it was becoming and wanted a front-row seat of the action. But Ned also noticed how the more she came, the more she seemed to believe in the monks' cause, and, like Ned, was growing determined to help them achieve their objectives.

Together, they sent back thousands of words of copy explaining the situation from the Buddhists' point of view along with many photographs to illustrate the point. Ned and Mel were finding they complemented each other in their way of working too; they'd both bought into the monks' plight and shared a desire to help them. Now Ned actually looked forward to spending the day with his boss and felt she was finally treating him as her equal. And their time with Ba and Dai was always well spent, especially as more and more monks flocked into Xa Loi every day, and the tension in the capital grew increasingly palpable.

The only concern nibbling away in the back of Ned's mind was just how the government would respond to this mounting pressure.

8

SATURDAY 29TH JUNE 1963

S aigon had been basking in the sun for most of the day with temperatures in the high thirties and humidity levels to match, but now in the late afternoon a wisp of wind was the first clue that change was in the air. Ned didn't spot this to begin with as he relaxed in one of the many bars along Le Loi, having discovered one of the joys of living in Saigon was sitting out in the street with a cold beer at the end of the day watching the girls walk by. He'd been appreciating the pleasure even more in the ten days since his arrest and the subsequent bawling out by Mel. Maybe it was because he knew how close he'd come to being unceremoniously kicked out of the country, and not just by the secret police.

Ingratiating himself with the monks and, more importantly, back into his boss's good books had clearly worked wonders, because Mel had invited him to her house that evening for a party she was holding. Ned had figured out Mel liked to be at the centre of the social scene in Saigon, and with the number of news organisations sending foreign correspondents out to South Vietnam increasing every week, she'd obviously decided it was time for one of her renowned evenings, where he'd heard she partied as hard as she worked.

The noise of a parasol clattering to the ground interrupted his thoughts, making him realise the wisp of wind had turned stronger. Even the pedestrians were walking that little bit faster than five minutes earlier. Soon, more parasols around him were blowing over in the wind and the awning on the front of the bar was rattling with excitement. Ned wondered where this energy had come from and turned to look down the street. Looming in from the right, he could see an enormous dark grey cloud enveloping the eastern side of Saigon, so heavy with moisture it was rolling along the ground rather than floating in the sky. The gusting wind whipped up by this giant front was throwing up swirling whirlpools of dust and rubbish and sending them careering down the street like a wizard's spell. The locals evidently knew what was about to happen: cyclo drivers parked up and ran for shelter; street vendors hurriedly covered their wares with large plastic sheets; and pedestrians simply ran, hoping to reach where they were going before the cloud dropped its heavy contents upon them. Ned could only sit and watch as this metaphor for Vietnam's problems bore slowly down, marvelling at the almost black and white scene before him. To his left was a beautiful day with hot sunshine; to his right was the blackest, most malevolent cloud he'd ever seen. With the wind now truly fierce, he knew he should take refuge, but the cloud was too awe-inspiring and gripped his attention. He sat transfixed until it finally passed above him and burst. And then came the rain.

The door of the bar and safety were only ten paces away, but he was already drenched by the time he reached it. The raindrops were the size of peas and each one hit with an unexpected force that exploded all over him. One moment, sunny day; the next, a storm of such power and magnitude that the roads had soon become rivers while the blocked downpipes brought forth waterfalls from the gutters. Ned stood and beheld this transformation from within the doorway of the bar.

He didn't believe it was possible for the rain to fall any faster or the storm to be any fiercer; the force was truly unbelievable.

He ordered another beer and watched some children who'd stripped off their clothes and were playing excitedly in the cascades of water gushing over the side of the buildings. A Frenchman who'd taken refuge in the same bar introduced himself as Jérôme and told Ned that, although this might be the first big downpour of the year, he should expect several more of this scale over the next few months. "That's why it's called the rainy season!" he laughed. They chatted amiably for another fifteen minutes until the storm started to lose some of its power. Within another five, the cloud had moved on and the sun was shining again. And soon after, the soaked ground began steaming with the heat of the sun evaporating the moisture. Ned had another beer with Jérôme before making his excuses, bade him farewell, and left for Mel's party.

Most of the street drainage system was blocked, so he was met with several inches of water as he stepped out onto the road. The flood had built up and overflowed onto the pavements, and the uppermost layer of water contained a toxic mixture of rubbish, grime, rotting fruit and dead rats. Not surprisingly, Ned chose to take a cyclo out to Mel's house rather than walk.

Yet now the storm had passed, Saigon felt revitalised and reinvigorated. The humidity had gone, replaced by a refreshing breeze, and the decaying, contaminated smells of the city had given way to the sweeter scent of the blossoming flowers. People were smiling again, excited by the first storm of the year. A salubrious, cleansing mist seemed to rise from the street as Ned's cyclo meandered toward Mel's house, which was located out in one of Saigon's smarter suburbs, only a mile and a half or so from the centre of town.

There were nearly twenty people there already when Ned pushed through the gate into Mel's garden. They must have sheltered in the house while the storm passed since everyone looked remarkably dry. Ned was immediately impressed and decided his boss had been lucky to find such a house to rent. He suspected ten years ago, the area would probably have been popular with French expats, but guessed there weren't so many of those around these days. He assumed Mel's current neighbours would be US military officers or diplomats from the growing American Embassy – and very few would be Vietnamese.

The back yard was more like a patio than a garden. It was about the size of a tennis court and surrounded by a seven-foot wall rendered in white with iron railings running along the top. Trees were scattered around the edge: palm, banyan, and red phoenix bulging with colourful red flowers. Interspersed among them were frangipani plants with their delightful yellow and white flowers, bougainvillea and other fragrant shrubs. To those present, it must have been a refreshing change from the sticky, squalid smell of central Saigon, and everyone that night appeared transformed, eager to enjoy the evening suffused in the perfumed aroma surrounding them. Garden lights had been strung up through the trees, and in the corner near the house stood a table bar with big tubs of iced water and chilling beers.

Mel was talking to two gentlemen as Ned appeared, and she beckoned him over to meet them.

"Wow...Mel, you look amazing in your party clothes!" he said as he got a closer look at her figure-hugging, sleeveless canary-yellow dress. He was already feeling a little tipsy between the heat and the drinks he'd enjoyed with Jérôme but hoped it wasn't apparent.

"Oh shush," she replied. "What are you saying? I'm not attractive in my field gear? I thought I looked very fetching in my army-issue boots."

"No, no, I didn't mean that," Ned garbled back, realising the pit he'd just put both his feet into in his semi-inebriated state. "I'm just saying you look great tonight." His face reddened and he hoped he'd pulled at least one foot out the hole.

"I agree," said one of the gentlemen. "But if you do turn up to work on Monday wearing only your army-issue boots, you will give me a call and let me know, Mel, won't you?" This provoked a burst of laughter from the four of them, helping to relax the mood.

"Ned, meet David Halberstam. He works for the *New York Times* and he's been out here almost as long as me. And this is Neil Sheehan," said Mel, indicating the other man. "He heads the United Press International office out here."

Ned shook hands with both men, recognising Halberstam as the other Western journalist he'd spotted on the day of Thich Quang Duc's self-immolation.

"Congratulations on your photograph," said Sheehan. "It was a big hit."

Halberstam, who stood a couple of inches taller than even Ned's six foot two and spoke with a New York accent, also complimented Ned on the photograph's success.

"I noticed the *New York Times* was the only main paper not to feature it on their front cover," Ned responded. "Too grisly for your editor, I heard."

"Well, of course they didn't!" replied Halberstam boisterously. "They had my account of the immolation, why would they need a photograph as well?"

"Typical New Yorker!" laughed Mel. "Where do you hide your modesty?"

Halberstam looked across at Mel. "Mind you, I heard Kennedy wasn't very pleased with my version of events. Then again, he's never very pleased with any of my stories. He thinks I'm responsible for everything that's gone wrong with American policy out here."

"Aren't you?" joked Ned, having already been made aware of Halberstam's reputation.

"Hey, I'm just the writer, like you're just the photographer. It's Diem and his brother Nhu they're really pissed at. It's just the messenger always gets the blame."

Ned laughed, happy to be in the company of like-minded people. Having been arrested and interrogated by Colonel Tung before nearly being sent home by Mel in disgrace, he'd certainly felt the pressure since relocating from London. An evening of relaxed conversation mixed with sharp humour felt as necessary as a pressure-relief valve on a faulty boiler.

"Jeez, speaking of," said Mel. "Did you see Madame Nhu's interview in the *Times of Vietnam* the other day? Claiming Western journalists are trying to bring down her brother-in-law."

"She's a fruitcake, that one," interjected Sheehan. "Even worse than Nhu himself. They're so paranoid about everyone plotting against them." He took a swig from his bottle of beer.

"I'm not sure it's paranoia," said Mel. "I think there really are coups being plotted to overthrow Diem the whole time."

"Yeah, I must hear about at least one a day. Maybe we should start calling them the *coup du jour*," laughed Halberstam.

The four of them carried on chatting as they moved toward the bar in search of more beer. Mel picked a can of 33 Beer out from one of the tubs of iced water. "*Ba Muoi Ba*, anyone?"

The talk moved onto the Buddhist crisis, how the monks were resisting with their weekly demonstrations after prayers each Sunday morning, the chances they had of bringing down the government (very little was the general consensus), and all things political. Ned enjoyed the conversation immensely. Although he'd always thought of himself as non-political and more of an observer, he was beginning to realise how fascinating it all became when he was a player himself involved in the affairs of the day. He was also enjoying the chance to relax and meet new people. He found if he stayed by the bar, people would naturally gravitate toward him when their drink needed refreshing. *One for them, one for me* became his rule as he took on the unofficial responsibilities of the chirpy barman. Although he knew very few of the resident press corps in Saigon, they all knew him by reputation; everybody was keen to meet him and quick to congratulate him on his success with *those* pictures.

As the evening went on, he watched Mel network around her guests, laughing and chatting excitedly, and admired her for it. He liked her vitality and was surprised to find himself complimenting her in his mind. Was it her visual appeal in the tight yellow dress or just the amount of beer he'd consumed? To think she'd nearly sacked him just a few short days ago!

"Jeez, can't you limeys handle your beer?" interrupted a smiling Mel as she strolled up to the bar. "You look miles away."

"Hi Mel!" exclaimed Ned, a little louder than anticipated, embarrassed to be caught daydreaming. "No, I was just thinking about Ba and Dai and the monks for some reason. Another beer?" He fumbled in the ice bucket and brought out another can for her, which she accepted.

"You got to stop thinking about work the whole time. Sometimes it's good to just let your hair down and be naughty," she said with a wink, before disappearing back into the throng with her drink.

Ned watched her go, pulling himself up with a start when he realised he was staring at her behind.

Later in the evening, Neil Sheehan asked Ned about the incident with the secret police. It seemed word of the arrest had spread around the small community of Western journalists. Most ascribed it to the fact Ned's photograph of Thich Quang Duc must have angered Nhu in his role as political leader of the Mat Vu.

"I heard you were personally interrogated by Colonel Tung himself?" Sheehan wasn't as tall as Ned but the intensity in his eyes gave a clue as to why he was head of the second largest press agency in Saigon.

"I didn't realise it at the time, but it turns out I was. I knew he had to be senior from what he was wearing."

"Is he as unpleasant as his reputation leads us to believe?"

"Well, he wasn't very pleasant to me. He kept on hitting me with his swagger stick. For some reason, he was convinced I'm orchestrating a revolution against them."

"One photograph, eh – that's all it takes to piss these guys off. You're lucky you got out; I've heard most people who get picked up by the secret police disappear."

Ned and Sheehan continued their conversation about the fearsome secret police and how Nhu had corrupted them for his own needs, inevitably leading back to the Buddhist monks and their anti-government protests.

"Are you going to tomorrow's protest?" asked Sheehan.

"Yes, but I don't think it'll be very big. They're saving that for the following week. Next Sunday – July 7th – is the ninth anniversary of Diem becoming Prime Minister, and I've heard the monks are organising a huge protest straight after prayers."

"Yes, I heard that too. Anyway, might see you tomorrow, it's time I went home."

Ned noticed the party was thinning out. There were pockets of people still talking, but a lot had already left. He looked at his watch and realised it was after midnight, but he was still having a good time, and so walked back to the bar for another beer. But after searching the coolers and under the table for spares, he discovered there were none left, though he did find a bottle of Jameson Irish whiskey secreted away below.

He was busy pouring himself a glass when he suddenly heard a voice from behind: "So you're the new hotshot photographer at BPA, are ya?"

Ned turned to find a scruffy urchin of a man swaying toward him with a can of 33 Beer in one hand and a joint in the other. He was dressed in jeans and a ripped T-shirt, about five foot nine, broad-chested, with a week's worth of stubble on his face and a long scar above his left eye.

"Yes, that's me, though I wouldn't exactly describe myself as hotshot," replied Ned modestly.

"I've been watching you strutting around here all night like a peacock, just 'cause you struck it lucky on your first assignment!"

Ned assumed at first the guy must be joking but began to realise perhaps he wasn't. "Fortune smiled on me, that's all," he replied with a smile, hoping to defuse the situation.

"Fortune, huh – but you still think you're a pro now, don't ya?"

Ned's anger was rising; he didn't like this guy or the way he was being spoken to. "Leave it out, I just said I'm no hotshot."

"That was meant to be my job. Mel pretty much promised it to me, and then she tells me she's being sent a goddamn limey out of London instead."

Ned put the bottle of whiskey down and carefully screwed the cap back on before pulling his shoulders back, standing tall, and trying to look as imperious as possible. "Yeah, well, maybe she realised what a gobshite you are and changed her mind."

The man took a pull on his joint and let the smoke out slowly, fixing his eyes on Ned as best he could in his drunken state. "She didn't change her mind – you were forced on her by the New York office. What does a freaking limey know about war anyway? You had to be bailed out twice by us Americans."

"Oh, sod off, my dad was an American soldier, so don't give me that bullshit!"

"Yeah, well, you're still a goddamn limey in my books. You may have my job, but I bet you suck as a photographer."

This was one insult too far for Ned, who pulled his arm back and bunched his fist, ready to strike. But as his antagonist took a step backward in response, the man stumbled and lost his balance. As he fell, he reached out for something to support him and found the bar table, which promptly fell over on top of him, ice buckets and all, creating enough noise to make everyone turn to see what the commotion was. The drunk lay on the floor for a moment covered in empty beer bottles, before scrambling to his feet and launching himself at Ned. The alcohol had dulled Ned's responsiveness, so he was too slow to move out the way and took the full force of the charge. The drunk knocked into him like an angry bull, knocking Ned into the air and back down painfully onto his back. Although the fall winded him, it also sobered him up, alerting him to the danger of this man, who now stood before him, arms raised and fists clenched like a boxer, waiting for Ned to get back on his feet.

"Come on, you limey sonofabitch!"

Ned stood, eyed the man up, and instinctively felt on home ground. He hadn't enjoyed boxing at school, but if a tough inner-city education taught you anything, it was how to look after yourself in a fight. The drunk came on quickly once more, ready to throw a right-handed punch. Time seemed to slow down for Ned, the charge almost in slow motion. He held his position until the last moment before moving his head out the way, ensuring the drunk lost his balance again as the momentum tipped him forward; Ned swivelled and punched him on the side of the face, sending him sprawling into a frangipani bush. His opponent stood and charged again, the red mist having clearly descended. Ned was ready to dodge sideways, but as he did, the attacker swapped his drive from right hand to left, which met Ned's ducking head, sending him backward, though not enough to make him fall.

The blow had caught Ned above his left eye, slitting the skin and causing blood to drip down his face. The pair stood face to face, assessing each other and generally communicating their mutual dislike before the drunk charged again. Ned was ready this time and stepped neatly aside, leaving his foot out and causing the aggressor to trip, stumble and lose balance a third time. With a helping hand to the back from Ned, he went crashing to the ground and hit his head on the upturned table, knocking himself out instantly.

Ned stood over him breathing deeply. Using his right hand to wipe away the sweat and blood on his forehead, he looked around and was embarrassed to discover the guests had all stopped their conversations and were staring at him in disbelief. As one or two started making their way in for a closer look, Mel burst through the side door of the house and bellowed, "What the hell's going on here?"

Ned stood motionless without a word and gave her a blank stare, wondering exactly that question himself.

"I go inside for two minutes and you start fighting. What's going on?"

"I'm not sure. I was pouring myself a drink when this arsehole started hurling insults at me, and then he ran at me and knocked me to the ground."

"Why?"

"I don't know, Mel. Like I said, he just came at me."

Mel looked down at the man on the ground, who at that moment started moving again and let out a soft groan.

"David, help Danny up, would you?" she said to the big New Yorker, who was still at the party.

"Come on, O'Connell," said Halberstam as he bent down and gently helped the man into a sitting position. After a few seconds, he appeared to have fully regained consciousness and stared up at Ned with eyes full of hatred. Suddenly, he jumped up and tried one last time to land a good punch. The shot connected with Ned's cheek, though without any power.

"Stop it!" shouted Mel toward him. "What the hell do you think you're doing?"

The man named O'Connell grunted in reply and continued staring at Ned like an erect king cobra about to strike. Ned glared back, but it was O'Connell who blinked first, turned, and headed for the garden gate.

"To hell with you all!" he shouted in one last act of drunken bravado as he left. The remaining guests watched him go in silence until a broad New York voice broke the spell.

"Well, that was exciting. What other entertainment have you got for us tonight, Mel?"

"Shut it, David!" Mel looked around at the stragglers in the garden. "Party's over for tonight, people, come on, beat it!"

While those still present shouted their thanks to Mel as they made to leave, Ned bent and picked up the overturned table, feeling he should at least stay and help tidy up the mess he'd created. After the last guest had left, he saw Mel approach. She still seemed angry, but then stopped and looked at his forehead.

"You've got a cut above your eye. Come on inside, I'll get you cleaned up."

Ned followed Mel into the house and inspected his surroundings. The floor was mosaic tile, the walls were painted creamy white, and contrasting against them was the dark wood of the windows and doors. The furniture was oriental in design and appeared hand-crafted from teak. The soft furnishings were in different shades of white, making the space feel authentic rather than contemporary.

Mel caught Ned looking around. "Yeah, I know it's a bit traditional, but I like it. Lie down on the sofa while I fetch a cloth."

She reappeared a few moments later with a blue flannel and a bowl of warm water. Sitting down on the edge of the sofa beside him, she gently started mopping up the blood, first from around his eye and then from the rest of his face.

"You're going to have a bit of a shiner there tomorrow," said Mel, indicating his left eye. She stood up and fetched a fresh flannel she'd run under cold water. "Here, hold this to it, it should take the swelling down a bit."

As Ned took the cloth and held it in place, Mel disappeared outside, to return a few moments later with two glasses and the bottle of Jameson.

"At least this wasn't broken during the fight," she said, taking back her position on the edge of the sofa next to Ned and pouring some whiskey into each glass. "What was it all about then?"

"Nothing, he was just a drunken arsehole."

"Something must have started it." Having each drained their glasses in one swig, Mel topped them up as she waited for a reply.

"Well, he did accuse me of stealing his job," said Ned, looking enquiringly at Mel. "He said you'd complained to him you didn't have a choice, and that New York had decided to 'send a limey'."

"Yeah, sorry," replied Mel awkwardly, "that might've been what I said. But I really didn't want Danny O'Connell to work for us and using you as an excuse was the easiest option. Danny might be a good photographer but he's a loose cannon."

"Thanks for the advance warning, I worked that one out for myself."

Mel chuckled in response.

"So *were* you annoyed when the New York office told you I was being sent out here?"

"To be brutally honest, yes. We'd been using Danny on a freelance basis, which wasn't perfect, but it was working. I didn't want the hassle of another staff member to babysit. And yeah, when I found out you were a limey, that didn't exactly help change my mind."

"Thanks, Mel, nice to feel welcome."

"But hey, it all changed once you arrived. I know I was dismissive and kept sending you down to the delta, but I was pissed with New York, and stubbornly I took it out on you."

Ned remained silent, watching Mel and waiting for her to compose her thoughts.

"When you arrived, I saw your enthusiasm and your determination, and I knew you'd make a good addition to the team. You may think your photo of Thich Quang Duc was down to luck, but it wasn't. That anonymous note may have been timely for you, but the point is you didn't let me down. You proved you had talent. When New York wired me a copy of the front page of the *Washington Post* – even a writer like me could see it was as powerful an image as they come. That's not luck, Ned. That's talent."

Ned could tell Mel was being sincere. Maybe the alcohol had allowed her to voice her true feelings, but he appreciated her saying it nonetheless.

"You're right though, Danny O'Connell is an asshole," said Mel. In that moment, she tenderly stroked Ned's face, looked down into his eyes and smiled at him. "I much prefer a handsome limey, especially one who knows how to fight. You may have made an enemy tonight, but you were impressive out there," she said with a twinkle in her eye.

Ned looked up at her, trying to decide if she meant what she was saying or if this was something else. Being only nineteen, he was still unsure of the signals, but, taking a chance, he lifted his head and kissed her on the lips. She didn't pull back as he'd expected. In fact, she surprised him by placing her hand behind his head and leaning down into it.

The kiss was slow and tentative to begin with, but gradually grew more intense and passionate. Ned pulled her down tightly on top of him and stroked his hands down the back of her head and delicate neck before discovering the zip on her dress, which he pulled down slowly. Slipping a hand inside, he proceeded to gently explore. He let his fingertips do the work, and only when his arm was fully stretched could he feel the soft curves at the base of her back.

In that moment, Mel broke the embrace and stood up, allowing her dress to slip smoothly down her body. Standing semi-naked before the younger man, she held out her hand.

"Come on then."

Ned stared up at her for a second, hardly daring to believe his luck, then stood and let himself be led into the bedroom, wondering how many more twists and turns the evening had in store for him.

9

Colonel Tung sat in the back of his Citroen Traction Avant watching the steady stream of bicycles and Honda C50s whipping past his stationary car. They were like a colony of ants on the march: it looked chaotic, but when studied in detail, there was organisation and a sense of structure behind the flowing masses. That was until a fool on a bicycle chose to go against the oncoming traffic, sending the well-ordered pattern into anarchic confusion and creating a cacophony of challenging horns and raised voices.

Tung sat and watched this melee unfold around him. They might be moving but he wasn't. His car was stuck in the morning rush hour on Le Van Duyet Street, and only when he lost patience and ordered his driver to plough down the middle of the road, forcing bicycles and motorbikes to swerve around him, did they begin to make headway.

He arrived at the Gia Long Palace late and in a furious mood. A military policeman in his white dress uniform met the Citroen as it pulled up under the portico. He opened the rear door and, taking a single step back, stood to attention. Colonel Tung emerged from the car, gave a brief salute to the security detail, and quickly walked up the steps and into the huge hallway. Tung was well known at the Gia Long Palace and too high-ranking to be bothered by security procedures, so without delay he was escorted up the French colonial staircase with its long sweeping curve doubling back to the first floor and along the external corridor to the Nhus' private apartment. Here, he was handed over to Nhu's private secretary, who escorted him through to the dining room. The secretary knocked weakly on the door and, with an exaggerated bow, announced the arrival of Colonel Tung.

Ngo Dinh Nhu was sitting at the breakfast table reading the *Times of Vietnam* when the head of his secret police arrived. The table was laid for two, with Madame Nhu sitting at one end and her husband at the other. There was a plate of croissants and a pot of coffee lying untouched in the middle, but Tung wasn't offered either. He remained standing while Nhu folded the newspaper and placed it on the table in front of him.

"What do you have to report, Tung?" Nhu wasn't one for politeness or small talk.

"*Ngài*, we are making further investigations into the Buddhist monks and their activities."

"Well, you're not doing very well. The *Times* has highlighted all the negative stories circulating about us in the American media," said Nhu, indicating the newspaper on the table. "They're saying the American papers have taken the side of the monks against us, calling for our so-called 'persecution' of them to stop. Now, I don't care what the American papers are saying but I do care that the Buddhists are talking freely to Western journalists and pushing their lies and deceit."

"Yes, *ngài*."

Nhu was hoping his security chief would appear more chastised, so he upped the ante. "I mean, look at this," he said, standing and picking up a different newspaper from the sideboard. "This is Monday's *Washington Post* —look at that front page."

Tung took the paper from Nhu and examined the large photograph spread across the top half of the paper of two smiling monks standing in front of a group of Buddhist protesters.

"That photograph was taken by that damn Ned Rivers man," said Nhu, "making the monks look all cute and friendly. No wonder the American public are insisting we embrace their demands. Who are those two on the front page? Have you come across them before?"

"No, *ngài*, I don't know them personally, but I'm sure they'll be known at headquarters. We're building up a strong understanding of who the ringleaders are, so we'll have them on file. But I do know that the photograph was taken at the Buddhist demonstration outside Xa Loi Pagoda last Sunday."

"Well, what are you going to do about it?" shouted Nhu, thumping the table in his frustration.

"We've planted someone inside the BPA agency and we're also following Rivers to find out who is briefing him. He and Melanie Johnson have both visited the Xa Loi Pagoda several times in the three weeks since Thich Quang Duc's death, but we've got no evidence so far to bring them in for questioning."

Tung had been watching Madame Nhu in his peripheral vision as she quietly listened in on the conversation, but she'd clearly heard enough at this point, as she stood, rested her hands on the table, and leant forward menacingly.

"Then why don't you stop these weekly demonstrations? Shut them down immediately."

Nhu swivelled to look at his wife. "We can't simply shut them down, we'd have to declare martial law. And my brother is unwilling to do that."

"To hell with martial law!" spat Madame Nhu, standing straight and waving her right hand up in the air. "Just stop the damn things from happening. And why don't you arrest Ned Rivers at the same time...and all the other American journalists? Interfering in our business – it shouldn't be allowed! Can't we just kick them out of the country?"

"No, of course we can't," said Nhu. "As usual, you come out with fatuous comments with no basis in the reality of the situation. If we kick the American journalists out of the country, then President Kennedy will promptly cancel all military and economic aid."

Tung remained still as he silently watched the pair arguing, knowing better than to interfere. He wasn't even sure which of the two he'd consider the more powerful. Nhu on paper, but his wife had the greater powers of persuasion and force of personality.

"To hell with Kennedy! I wish the damn monks would just carry on burning themselves alive instead of holding these demonstrations." And with that, Madame Nhu stood from the breakfast table and exited the room, furiously knocking the *Washington Post* off the table as she went.

"She can be very blunt sometimes," Nhu said, when the two men were alone in the room, "but she has a point. We have to bring this situation under control and stop these Buddhists poisoning our relationship with Washington. I want you to put more pressure on both the monks and the journalists."

"Yes, *ngài*."

Nhu stood up to follow his wife out the dining room, but then stopped as if appearing to remember something. "Oh, and Tung, did those two VC terrorists you captured the other day reveal anything about their organisation in Saigon?"

"No, *ngài*. They remained completely silent despite our best efforts to persuade them."

"Your specialists aren't going soft, are they?" asked Nhu. He was referring to the advanced interrogation team Tung had set up with the express purpose of extracting as much information from communist sympathisers as possible.

"Of course not, *ngài*."

"So are they still alive?"

"No, *ngài*. We put them in a helicopter, flew them over their base in the Plain of Reeds and threw them out from two thousand metres. I'm sure the VC will get the message when they find their bodies."

"Good, well done. Keep me informed with regards to the monks...and the Western journalists."

Colonel Tung took a step backward, saluted and then turned and left the room.

Ned arrived at the BPA office early that morning and was surprised to find Bich there on a Saturday. He still felt a chill whenever she was in the room but concluded she might just be shy. At least on this occasion, however, he managed to have his first direct conversation with her. She was interested to know what he thought of the Buddhists at Xa Loi, and whom he'd met apart from Ba and Dai.

They discussed the country's problems, but Bich kept on returning to the Buddhists and asking Ned's opinion on what he thought they were planning next. Ned was relieved to hear the distinctive double engine of Pham's Citroen 2CV Sahara as it pulled up outside the office. He grabbed his Nikon off Harry's desk, which he'd been using as his own for the past couple of weeks since Harry had returned to Laos, and went outside to find Pham, leaving Bich alone in the office once more.

"Ready for another day at the pagoda?" asked Ned as he climbed in beside Pham.

"Hello, Mr Ned. The question is – are you ready for another journey in my car?"

Ned smiled. Pham's humour could be very dry. "I fear for my life every time you drive me somewhere." He looked down at the footwell. "Is the hole getting bigger? There'll be nothing left of the car soon."

"Stop complaining, Mr Ned, it's good ventilation."

"That's true, and boy do we need it at the moment," replied Ned, already covered in a thin sheen of sweat. "Is July the hottest month of the year in Saigon?"

"Yes, hot today, isn't it? But not the hottest time of year. May is much hotter before the rainy season begins, but July and August are the most humid months. Don't worry, the next storm will clear the humidity."

Ned didn't reply, for as he was trying to open his half-window on the passenger door, he noticed a black Renault Frégate in his side mirror pull in behind them and sit on their tail.

"Take the next left," instructed Ned, suddenly serious in his manner. He swept his fingers through his unruly hair, pushing it back from his forehead to clear his mind and view, and better enable him to deal with this new threat. He watched in his mirror as the Frégate turned left after them.

Pham was watching in his own mirror too. "It's the same car that picked us up last month."

"They're not even attempting to be discreet anymore. Pham, what are we going to do? You're going to have to lose them."

"Don't worry, Mr Ned, leave it to me. Nobody knows this city better than me."

"Pham the trouble-buster. Here to get me out of trouble."

They both laughed nervously as Pham turned left onto Hong Thap Tu Street and carefully drove the three sides of the Independence Palace grounds so as not to arouse suspicion. As soon as they reached Rue Pasteur again, however, Pham turned left and put his foot flat on the accelerator. Both engines squealed with the demand and the little 2CV shot forward. Pham set off down the middle of the road, overtaking the cars on his side and forcing the oncoming traffic to swerve around him. Checking in his mirror, Ned could see the Frégate was still following, but a gap had opened up between them. Pham unexpectedly turned right at the next junction – the 2CV tilting at an alarming angle as it took the bend – and headed toward what Ned assumed to be a roundabout.

"They're still behind us," shouted Ned, looking out the back window.

The roundabout was more like a small town square with a fountain in the middle surrounded by houses and small shops. It was filled with large trees that blocked all but a minimal amount of sun from penetrating their outstretched branches and deserted except for a few children playing with an old tyre. The kids stopped and stared as the beige 2CV swept in and drove, wheels squealing, around three sides of the square, and departed as quickly as it had come.

Pham suddenly dived down a little side street on their left and, seeing a gap in front of a parked truck, careered into it and stopped. When the car was still, they both turned around and watched in tense silence. A few seconds later, the Renault Frégate screamed past the turning.

"I think we lost them," said Ned quietly. "I wonder why they've suddenly started following us again. What's their bloody problem?"

Pham grinned at Ned. "Don't worry, Mr Ned. With me as your driver, they'll never catch you."

"Okay, you madman, let's drive on to Xa Loi. But I'd stick to the side streets rather than the main roads."

They arrived at Xa Loi Pagoda alone without their tail picking them up again. Having parked on Ba Huyen Thanh Quan Street, they marched through the side gate and up into the great hall of the pagoda, which was empty except for a teenage monk on cleaning duty. Ned and Pham had been there enough times by now for the boy to recognise them and volunteer to go and find Ba and Dai. A short time later, the brothers arrived and greeted Ned and Pham with open arms and broad grins.

"Mr Ned, welcome back. How are you?"

"Mel's asked me to drop in and say hello. Unfortunately, she can't be here this morning, but she wondered if there was any news?"

"No, nothing's happened since last Sunday's demonstration," said Ba. "We're now preparing for the big one tomorrow: nine years since Ngo Dinh Diem came to power, so we're hoping for a big turnout."

"I've been meaning to ask you – how come he came to power nine years ago when the Republic of Vietnam's only existed for seven?"

"Now you want *me* to teach you our history?" asked Ba with raised eyebrows. "Dai, you're the scholar in our family, why don't you tell Ned?"

Dai looked happy to oblige. He explained how Ngo Dinh Diem had been made Prime Minister of all Vietnam by the Emperor Bao Dai on the 7th July 1954. But two weeks later, the country was partitioned along the 17th parallel in the Geneva Peace Accords, set up following the French defeat by the Viet Minh at Dien Bien Phu. Diem became Prime Minister of everything south of this line, while Ho Chi Minh became leader of everything north. Diem ruled the South for eighteen months as Prime Minister before ousting the Emperor in October 1955 in a rigged referendum, becoming President of the Republic of Vietnam, as the South was officially known. He'd remained the autocratic leader ever since, silencing all dissent and killing off any competition using his feared and loathed secret police.

"Okay, Dai, no more, I get it," interjected Ned in response to the unexpectedly detailed explanation. "And you reckon tomorrow's demonstration will be a big one, then?"

"Yes, Mr Ned, very big," said Ba. "You have to be there. It'll be good for photographs, you'll see!"

"Yes, I'll be there. Is it here, outside Xa Loi?"

"No, tomorrow's demonstration is at Chanatareansey Pagoda in the north of Saigon. We try to move it around so the secret police don't know where it will be held. Prayers first and then the big event. We need to tell Diem how unpopular he is, here in Saigon. And your pictures, Mr Ned, will tell the world, yes?"

"Yes, of course," Ned said absentmindedly, for he'd just spotted something strange on the altar. He walked toward the item. From a few steps away, he saw it was a glass chalice with what looked like a pumice stone inside, about the size of a mangosteen. As he leant in to examine it more closely, Ba appeared by his side.

"Be careful, that is Thich Quang Duc's heart. I'm sure you heard how it didn't burn at his cremation? It was recovered from his ashes last month. No one knows why it didn't burn like the rest of his body, but it's now a sacred relic for us all to remember the courage and selflessness of our most holy colleague. We've put it in this glass chalice to serve as a reminder of Thich Quang Duc's faith."

Ned instantly recognised a photo opportunity, the type that would pique the interest of picture editors in America. He arranged Ba and Dai to stand in front of the altar with the giant statue of Buddha in the background, the brothers holding the chalice between them. Ned was delighted to see rays of light penetrating the windows to illuminate the sides of their faces, and asked them to turn slightly toward the glass to ensure more of their faces were lit. He chose a high f-number for his aperture given the high light levels, which would maximise the depth of focus and allow the viewer to appreciate not just the monks' faces but their surroundings too.

Despite being front-page news for most of the last month, the Buddhist crisis had recently been knocked from the headlines by President Kennedy's declaration of 'Ich bin ein Berliner' at a huge rally in West Berlin in front of half a million cheering West Germans. The euphoria of the President's visit had since simmered down and strangely morphed into a story about whether he'd actually referred to himself as a 'jelly doughnut' on the basis of some misused German grammar. But Ned was keen to recapture the front pages for his monks, so spent several minutes repositioning the brothers to find the ideal shot, knowing this was the type of photograph his picture editors were crying out for.

"Come on, Mr Ned, I have something to show you," said Ba after the pictures had been taken and the chalice replaced on the altar. He led the way across the hall where some large moveable noticeboards had been positioned as screens along the side. Ba guided Ned and Pham through a small gap between two of the six-foot-high partitions. Behind was a concealed door in the wall, which opened up onto a small staircase.

"This is our secret staircase to the office area, which allows some of the priests to come and go surreptitiously during prayers without having to use the main doors," Ba explained. "Have you been down here yet? Come, I'll show you around." Together, they descended and entered a hallway. Straight ahead was a corridor with offices on either side. To the left, a set of double doors led outside toward the bell tower; to the right, two more simple, white-painted panel doors.

"Where do those go?" asked Pham.

"Well, this…" said Ba, opening the first door with a flourish and a laugh, "…is our cleaning cupboard!" Ned looked inside curiously, but it really was just a room about the size of a small bathroom with mops, buckets and brushes propped up against the walls.

"And this one," said Dai, "is a passage that leads out to Quan Pho Street, the little alley around the back. I doubt you know it unless you've visited our neighbours, USAid. This entrance is only used by our apprentice monks, who, tradition dictates, cannot use the main gates to enter the pagoda until they've finished their apprenticeships. So they use this hidden back entrance instead."

Dai shut the door, and Ba led Ned and Pham down the office corridor. Each room was filled with monks making banners for the next day's demonstration. The process was like a production line. In the first office, there were rolls of calico lined up against the walls, and long tables had been set out in the middle of the room as a workbench. Laid along these was a single piece of calico unrolled and cut to size, about six feet long and two feet wide. Around the sides, a series of monks were sewing a hem onto the banner to give it extra strength. As Ned watched, the monks, all the while chatting loudly and laughing at each other's jokes, finished the banner and rolled it up, and an elderly colleague with a limp in his left leg delivered it to the second office. Ned went with it to see what was happening in there. Again, the room was filled with monks of all ages who waved in friendly greeting upon seeing Ned and Pham enter.

"What happens in this office, Ba?"

"This is the painting department where the slogans are added to the banner."

And sure enough, as Ned and Pham watched from the door, the six-foot banner that had just been delivered was unfurled on a table and weighted at each corner. A short monk, about fifty years old with wrinkles around his eyes, gathered his pot of black paint and started to carefully inscribe his message in Vietnamese onto the bleached calico. On other tables around the room, more monks were doing the same, all showing great care in their work. Ned continued on to the third office where yet more monks were writing banners, except this time they were younger, and Ned could see the protest messages were in English:

> GET RID OF DIEM NOW
> 9 YEARS TOO MANY
> FIGHT FOR BUDDHIST RIGHTS
> EQUAL RIGHTS FOR BUDDHISTS

At that moment, an elderly monk came along the corridor wearing glasses and using a walking stick for assistance. He was slightly portly but had an air of authority about him. Behind him were three younger monks keeping a respectful distance as they followed. On recognising the man, both Ba and Dai immediately bowed their heads. The elderly monk smiled in return and asked Dai in English who their guests were.

"This is Mr Ned Rivers and his colleague Vien Che Pham, venerable leader," answered Dai. "Mr Rivers is the photographer with BPA helping us publicise our struggle with the government. It was he who took the photograph of Thich Quang Duc published all over the world."

"Hi," said Ned casually, not sure if he too was supposed to address the newcomer as 'venerable leader'.

"Hi back," replied the monk with a charming smile. "Thank you for helping us, Mr Rivers. What you are doing is very important to us, as I am sure Dai has explained. It is important that President Kennedy and the American people understand how we are persecuted by our own government."

"Well, we're trying our hardest to keep your fight with President Diem on the front pages," said Ned. And then, in a louder voice that took him by surprise, he declared, "Your fight is my fight also."

"Good, well done, keep it up. President Kennedy is the only person that Diem listens to, and that is why the American press in Saigon must come to our demonstrations and report on the injustices in this country. You and the rest of the foreign press are key to us winning our argument with Diem."

The elderly monk fixed Ned with a long, hard stare, as if searching his core for any impurity, but then broke into another broad grin and hobbled off down the corridor without another word.

"Who was that?" asked Ned, feeling oddly awestruck.

"That was our venerable leader and head of the Buddhist faith in all Vietnam, Thich Tinh Khiet. He normally lives in Hue, but since Thich Quang Duc's death, he's remained in Saigon to negotiate with President Diem for Buddhist rights," said Dai.

"How's he getting on?"

"Ah, not good. He and President Diem signed a joint communiqué last month, but since then, Diem has done nothing to honour his promises. So earlier this week, Thich Tinh Khiet spoke to us after prayers and told us we need to step up our demonstrations every Sunday, with more people and more anger. That's why you have to be there tomorrow."

Ba and Dai carried on leading Ned and Pham down the corridor, evidently excited at the honour of showing their guests around. The offices at the end contained camp beds rather than desks.

"These rooms look like dormitories?" asked Ned.

"So many monks have arrived from the countryside and small towns eager to help us with our protests that we've had to accommodate them in these offices."

"How long will they stay for?"

"Until the battle is won or lost, I suppose."

"When will you know if you've won or lost?" asked Pham in English so Ned could understand.

"When Diem is overthrown, then we've won!" answered Ba with emotion.

"And if Buddhism is made illegal, or we all have to convert to Catholicism, then we've lost," added Dai more soberly.

The sun was dipping through the horizon, projecting smudges of warm tones over the city and illuminating the western sky in brilliant hues of fuchsia, magenta and burnt orange as Pham drove Ned back down Rue Pasteur. Once back at the BPA offices, Ned climbed laboriously out of Pham's car and sauntered into the building, letting his mind think through the events of the past seven days.

He flashbacked to the previous weekend and how he and Mel had woken the morning after her party with sore heads and embarrassed expressions. They'd decided the less said the better, so risen early and attended the monks' demonstration together as work colleagues. Mel had spent the rest of the week being cold, authoritative and business-like; so he was surprised to find a message on his desk from her inviting him to supper. He was more than happy to accept, even though he'd been instructed to forget about their bedroom antics…which, of course, he hadn't.

He stopped to buy some beers en route and arrived with an empty stomach and high expectations. Mel's kitchen sorted the former and her bedroom the latter.

10

The following morning, Ned and Mel shared a cyclo to the Chanatareansey Pagoda, travelling all the way up Le Van Duyet Street toward Tan Son Nhut Airport before peeling off to the right. The gentle rolling of the cyclo echoed the comfortable, relaxed mood between its occupants. The Sunday morning traffic was sparse and calm, making it a pleasurable experience compared to the usual fume-filled journeys that characterised Saigon's streets. Together, they chatted amicably about a range of subjects, none of which included angry monks or belligerent politicians, simply enjoying each other's company in the knowledge that, upon arrival at the pagoda, relations would have to revert to normal and all intimacy would be gone.

By 9.00 am, the crowds of protesters, few of which were Buddhist monks, had already begun streaming into the square in front of the pagoda. The Sunday demonstrations may have started out as a monks-only affair, but now the Buddhist fight had been taken up by other alienated and persecuted groups; and so the square was filled with students, political activists and, for the first time, many ordinary Saigonese, all of whom had come out in support. Ned could see very few orange robes but heard the sound of prayers emanating from the pagoda itself, situated on one side of the square, confirming the monks were inside. Mel was paying the cyclo driver when Pham found them.

Ned looked around and decided to dive in among the crowd with his camera and try to find some protesters holding banners in English to ensure the photograph would have maximum effect in Western newspapers. There was plenty of choice: most of the demonstrators were holding signs of some sort, the most common being a twin-pole banner requiring two people to hold it aloft between them. In his excitement and enthusiasm for his job, Ned was running from protester to protester, banner to banner, with Pham trying to keep up beside him. Having smelt the whiff of success once before, he'd wanted more of it.

After exhausting a couple of rolls of film, he returned to where the cyclo had dropped him off in the hope of locating Mel again. More people had arrived to join the protests and, ominously, he could see a gathering of secret police dressed in their tell-tale leather jackets and pointy shoes, all staring in the same direction. Ned followed their gaze to find they were watching a huddle of seven or eight Western journalists, including Mel, standing at the corner of a small side street that led off the square some fifty yards from the closed pagoda gates.

Followed by Pham, Ned walked across the square toward them. He could see Mel was chatting with David Halberstam, Neil Sheehan and another journalist whom Ned hadn't met yet. Mel introduced the unknown as Peter Arnett, a stocky New Zealander who worked at the Associated Press.

Halberstam greeted Ned with a warm smile. "Hi there, Ned, great to see you again. How's the eye?"

"Oh, don't remind me. I feel very embarrassed by that little incident."

"Don't worry about it. Danny O'Connell always gets drunk and always picks a fight. It was just your turn last week, that's all. Anyway, you definitely came off the better. Last I heard, he scampered off to the DMZ with his tail between his legs."

Turning to Sheehan, Ned said, "I think you left at just the right moment, Neil. I seem to remember you were the last person I spoke to before Danny had a go at me."

Sheehan didn't get a chance to reply. From the other side of the gates, a drum had started beating, an amplified voice was shouting, and the pagoda gates opened. As the first row of monks walked across the threshold, the crowd let out a huge cheer and clapped them on their way. Ned didn't recognise the first few monks in front – they were clearly the young agitators most up for a fight with Diem's government; but in the second row marched Ba and Dai, both holding portable voice amplifiers. Dai was using his to shout in Vietnamese while Ba shouted in English: "Down with Diem!" "Let Madame Nhu burn and see how she likes it!" Ned could see into the courtyard beyond, where hundreds of monks were still gathered, waiting their turn to march behind their leaders. It was like a reservoir of orange water spilling through the gates. The crowd surged forward, enveloping the monks, and as a single, seething mass, they moved into the centre of the square.

From among the throng, Thich Tinh Khiet, the elderly Buddhist leader, climbed slowly and delicately onto a small platform, followed closely by two more monks who stood on either side of him. For a fearful second, Ned wondered if Khiet was about to self-immolate in similar fashion to Thich Quang Duc, but instead the priest continued to stand patiently on the platform, waiting until all his comrades had filed out of the pagoda compound. A light wind pulled at his cotton robes, but even at this time of morning humidity levels were high, so the breeze was refreshing and cooling. Ned looked up to the east where the clouds were thickening into an angry grey knot, and he knew a storm was on its way. The monks kept coming, filing out through the gates and into the square accompanied by the steady rhythm of drums and the intermittent denunciation of Diem from amplified voices. It took a further ten minutes before the pagoda compound had emptied and the orange surge had diffused slowly through the angry Saigon crowd.

Ned watched as Ba, standing in front of the platform, turned and handed his portable amplifier up to the monk on Khiet's left. The monk checked the device was switched on and passed it across to his elder. Ned moved silently through the still crowd until he was positioned in front of the platform, where he was able to get some shots of Khiet standing with his hand up waiting for silence. Ned knelt down low and photographed the venerable leader between his two young, shaven-headed assistants just in front and either side of him. Wanting a small depth of field, Ned chose a low f-number on his aperture ring. He then focused accurately on the elderly monk but used the two shaven heads to creatively frame their leader in an out-of-focus blur – still in the shot, but not dominant.

Once the general noise of the crowd had subsided, Khiet began to speak in Vietnamese. Judging by the clapping and roars of approval that erupted every so often, Ned could tell he was working his audience into a lather. He continued to take photographs, now turning to face the crowd for some spontaneous shots of angry faces and waving banners.

"What's the old man saying?" Ned asked Pham, who was standing close by.

"He's telling them this is a fight that must be won. That Diem has victimised the Buddhists more and more since becoming Prime Minister nine years ago. That all Buddhists want is equality, but all Diem is willing to offer is discrimination. He says how he met with Diem after the death of Thich Quang Duc and signed the joint communiqué, but Diem hasn't honoured their agreement. Now he's saying the Buddhist majority must rise up and march on the Gia Long Palace, and the march must begin now."

The crowd responded to Khiet's message with rapturous cheering and angry shouts. The drums started beating once more and Khiet climbed carefully down from his platform. Ned rushed back to where the other journalists were standing at the corner of the street leading off the square, from which the protesters would start their march toward the Gia Long Palace. It was only a small street and Ned could see why his colleagues had chosen to stand here: standing across the entrance and blocking the way were four rows of white-dressed police holding a baton each.

The newsmen watched eagerly as Khiet and the other leading monks walked resolutely toward the entrance to the street. As the venerable leader arrived, the police pushed out their chests, pulled back their shoulders and raised their batons as a sign of their determination not to let the monks through. Khiet stopped a yard in front of the first row of marchers and spoke quietly to the police. Ned knew he didn't want any trouble, that violence was not the way of the Buddhists, but the atmosphere was still very tense. The journalists had their notebooks open and were busy scribbling away while Ned was diligently taking photographs; so no one noticed the small posse of secret police moving in toward them.

Peter Arnett, the New Zealander from the Associated Press, was the first to be struck. Not expecting the blow, he was smashed in the nose and knocked off his feet to the ground, where other members of the secret police repeatedly kicked him while down. Arnett let out a cry for help – or maybe it was pain, Ned thought later – and tried to stand up, but his attackers continued to kick and beat him.

Ned instinctively took a step back to give himself room to photograph the scene but quickly felt his Nikon being pulled from his hands. He clung on tightly and could see a vicious-looking man with close-cropped hair and dark glasses yanking on the camera in front of him. Ned promptly punched him across the jaw. Luckily, he'd wrapped the camera strap around his left wrist so was able to use his right fist to land another punch on the side of the policeman's face, which finally persuaded the latter to release his grip.

As Ned started photographing Arnett lying on the ground with his bloody face, the other Western journalists closed ranks and took a defensive stand against the attack. Through the middle of them, he saw the six-foot-four bulk of David Halberstam reach down with his enormously long arms and pull Arnett to his feet and into safety before proceeding to swing the same arms wildly at the secret police. Standing nearly a foot taller than the average Vietnamese, he bellowed, "Get back, get back, you sons of bitches, or I'll beat the shit out of you!"

Under this onslaught, the secret police retreated, leaving behind a battered Peter Arnett and a fuming David Halberstam.

"Jesus Christ, did we just get attacked by the secret police?" asked Mel.

"Yeah, attacked and beaten," said Arnett, still in shock as to what had happened, blood smeared across his face.

"Are you okay, Peter?" asked Mel, looking at his face and checking his injuries with care.

"Yeah, yeah, I'm fine, or at least I will be once the bruising goes down. Jesus, are we now a target for Nhu? Are we really a bigger threat than the Buddhists and the commies?"

"Obviously!" exclaimed Halberstam, still breathing heavily from his exertions.

"Pham and I were actually followed yesterday by the secret police," said Ned, "but we lost them and I didn't think too much about it. But it looks like we've become a target again."

"Well, I think we need to get the US Embassy to make a formal complaint to the South Vietnamese government on our behalf," said Halberstam, looking around for support, clearly agitated by the incident. "I'll talk to John Mecklin in the Embassy press office."

While the Western journalists were discussing the dangers of being on Nhu's hit list and how they would have to be more observant from now on, Khiet was ordering his followers to retreat from the police blockade, seemingly unwilling to risk any further violence and accepting there would be no march on the Gia Long Palace today. He re-took his position on the platform and continued his denouncement of Diem's government.

Mel informed Ned she'd asked Pham to take her back to the office so she could write her report on the afternoon's turn of events, and offered to take any completed films of his with her. Ned remained in the square to watch – rather than listen, having lost his translator – as a series of extra speakers took to the platform to fill the time that the march would have occupied. After a further hour of speeches, the buoyed-up crowds were showing signs of losing their fervour for the day's demonstration, and began to thin and filter away.

The square was nearly empty when Ned, standing by the pagoda gates, found himself in conversation about the attack with a still bloodied Peter Arnett.

"You look bloody awful. You sure you're okay?"

"It'll take more than Nhu's attack dogs to hurt me. It's just that they took me unawares. I'd have flattened them in a one-to-one fight."

"Sounds like your pride is more injured than your body."

As they were discussing the incident, Ned noticed a police van drawing to a stop some twenty yards behind Arnett, out of which emerged five policemen dressed in pristine white uniforms, who advanced toward them.

"Are you Peter Arnett?" said the lead officer.

Arnett had to turn around to see who'd asked the question. "Yes, why?"

"Peter Arnett, you are under arrest," said the officer.

"Excuse me?" asked Arnett incredulously.

"You are under arrest for affray. And are you Ned Rivers?
You are under arrest too."

"You've got to be joking!" exclaimed Ned. "What have we
done to be arrested?"

"Public affray, resisting arrest and hitting a policeman."

"Does this look like I was doing the hitting?" said Arnett,
pointing at his face.

The lead officer didn't bother to reply, turning instead to
his colleagues and giving them a nod. The four policemen
rushed forward, each grabbing an arm, and frogmarched the
newsmen to the truck, where the back door was opened to
reveal a caged interior. The two Westerners were bundled into
the back and the door slammed shut behind them.

Once more, Ned found himself inside a prison cell, the second
time in three weeks, although this time alone. He kicked the
door in anger after it was closed behind him and shouted an
obscenity at the guard. He was fairly sure this wasn't the same
prison as before – firstly, because he'd been arrested by the
national police this time and not the Mat Vu; and secondly,
because he hadn't recognised his surroundings when he and
Arnett had finally been escorted in separate directions. Unlike
last time, he was in a cell with no window, so he couldn't even
see what was outside. He wondered if this was Chi Hoa, the
largest prison in Saigon, built by the French during the Second
World War, though not completed until ten years later in 1953.

Ned sat on the bench, a simple wooden affair consisting of
five dirty wooden slats fixed into the wall at each end. More
like solitary confinement, he mused uncomfortably, than a
conventional cell. Without a window, the room was unbelievably humid, and he felt the heaviness of the air upon him. He
took off his photographer's waistcoat, which for some reason
hadn't been confiscated, and thought of photographing the

cell; although his Nikon had been taken off him, he still had his beloved Leica. But the room was so small and plain that there was really nothing of note to photograph.

After less than twenty minutes, he was covered in sweat. He felt as if he'd walked into a sauna fully clothed, even though he was only wearing thin cotton trousers and a T-shirt. He sat and thought about Mel and Pham, hoping they'd got off the square and back to the office okay. He was thankful he'd handed all his used film to Mel, having watched the film in his Nikon being ripped out and exposed to the light, thereby ruining any pictures he'd taken on it.

Another hour passed in silence; not even a fly could be heard, which was unusual for Saigon. Ned felt drained of energy. He'd taken off his T-shirt by now to use as a flannel to wipe the sweat off his face, but it hadn't helped his mood. His throat was dry and his head pulsing; he knew he must be dehydrating. Sitting as still as possible, he wondered if they were really going to charge him with a public disorder offence or, worse still, assaulting a policeman. It was true he had struck an officer – but for good reason. He wondered what the punishment was in this increasingly authoritarian country for such an act. Did Mel know he'd been arrested? Did anyone?

The noise of a key interrupted his thoughts, and the gust of wind created by the cell door opening brought a small relief from the thick humid air in the room. Ned stood and quickly put his sodden T-shirt back on, feeling exposed without it. Three men walked in, none of them in uniform, but their close-cropped hair and dark glasses gave them away. Even when they weren't wearing black leather trench coats, Ned had become an expert in spotting one of Nhu's secret police. In fact, he was sure he'd seen one of the men here earlier at the pagoda.

The younger two walked around and positioned themselves behind Ned, leaving the older, obviously more senior officer standing by the door.

"You're a fucking idiot, you understand?" this one said in English. "You're in lot of trouble, you understand?"

Lacking enough energy to get angry, Ned stood still and stared at the man, but said nothing. For his trouble, he was punched from behind in the left kidney; the blow was uncompromising and made him shout out in pain.

"I asked you a question. In this country, it's polite to answer."

Ned stood up straight again and stared at the senior officer a while longer, before calmly replying through gritted teeth, "I understand what you're saying, but I didn't do anything wrong this morning."

Another punch from behind, this time to the right kidney.

"Not what I asked," said the senior officer.

In a flash of anger, Ned spun around and raised his fist, ready to strike the policeman who'd hit him, but a kick to the back of the knee sent him sprawling to the ground. He lay there, stunned by the speed with which he'd ended up on the floor, before being hauled up to his feet again by the junior officers.

"Where are your camera films, Mr Rivers?" demanded the interrogator.

"It was in my camera, but the policeman who confiscated it took the film out and exposed it to the light."

"And where are the other rolls of film?"

"I don't have any other rolls. I was still using my first roll of the day. There wasn't very much to photograph until you lot came bulldozing into us. I only managed to shoot about twenty pictures and now they've all been destroyed."

"I don't believe you. Where are they?"

"Search me, but you won't find any," Ned said defiantly.

At a sign from the interrogator, the man on his right quickly searched through Ned's waistcoat and found not only the Leica camera in the inside pocket but five rolls of Kodak Tri-X black-and-white film scattered around the many outer compartments.

"So what are these?"

"They're unused, there's nothing on them," said Ned, trying to double-bluff his way out of his predicament.

"You lie. Destroy them," the interrogator shouted to the one holding the films. "And the camera too."

Carefully, and with much enjoyment, the junior policeman opened each canister, removed the film and pulled the acetate out from the plastic cassette, exposing it to the light. Then, looking Ned straight in the eye, he took the little Leica and threw it violently on the floor, causing glass shards and small metal parts to spin off in every direction. He then stamped on the remains to make sure it wouldn't work again. To finish his little performance, the policeman bent down, opened what was left of the back, and drew out the acetate film from its little plastic cassette before looking back up at Ned with a victorious sneer.

Ned wasn't fussed about the films – he knew there was nothing on them – but the camera, that was different. He was distraught to see his beloved Leica smashed to pieces, his faithful companion since he'd first started working with BPA.

"It's simple, Mr Rivers. We want to know what the Buddhists are planning next, and if you don't tell us, you'll be charged with assaulting a policeman – a very serious crime in South Vietnam."

"Fuck you!" Ned spat. "That was my favourite camera. Why should I answer your fucking questions?" His outburst surprised even himself, but he regretted it a moment later when his impudence earnt him another blow to the left kidney.

"You Americans don't listen very well, do you? You talk a lot, but you never listen. I said I want to know what the Buddhists' plans are?"

"Firstly, I'm British, not American. And secondly, I haven't a clue what their plans are. I'm a photographer, not a Buddhist activist."

The senior policeman looked at Ned with anger and then nodded at his assistants. Instantly, Ned felt another blow to each of his kidneys and fell to the floor from the pain. This time, they didn't make him stand again, each instead giving him a swift kick to the back as they stepped over him and left. The interrogator remained standing by the door.

"We'll go and talk to Mr Arnett now. When we come back, it would be a good idea for you to remember what the Buddhists are planning, Mr Rivers. We've been very gentle with you so far, but we lose patience quickly." He turned on his heel and marched out the cell, closing the door behind him.

Ned let out a groan as he attempted to straighten his body on the concrete floor. He could feel something digging into his back and with a struggle managed to pull part of his Leica out from under him. He didn't want to die this way, not in a hot cell in Saigon. He'd always assumed he'd make it past nineteen but right now he felt death was quite close at hand.

Lying on the floor in a puddle of his own sweat, he tried to remain as still as possible; when he did move, shards of pain shot up his sides. He wasn't sure how long he stayed in that position before, at last, the policeman who'd originally arrested him came in and found him on the ground. He picked Ned up and told him he had a visitor, then helped him hobble out the cell to a large office opposite the main entrance, where he settled him down into a wicker tub chair.

"Water...water...can I have some water?" Ned asked hoarsely.

To his surprise, he heard the policeman order an underling to fetch some water before gently offering Ned the glass when it arrived. Was this 'good cop, bad cop' at play? He was even more confused when a wet cloth arrived for him to wash his face and hands with. He looked around – the office obviously belonged to someone important. There was a large teak desk at the far end with two chairs in front of it. On the wall above the desk hung a large portrait of President Diem dressed in a white suit.

Ned sat in the tub chair, one of four occupying the end of the office closest to the door, while above him a large wooden fan span vigorously to generate enough air movement to keep anyone below cool. He was still wiping his face when Peter Arnett arrived escorted by a policeman, who offered the New Zealander the tub chair to Ned's right. A moment later, a short, rotund Western gentleman dressed in a smart, lightweight suit and smoking a cigarette entered the room and introduced himself.

"Good afternoon, gentlemen. My name is Gordon Etherington-Smith and I'm the British Ambassador to the Republic of Vietnam. Mr Arnett, I've been asked by the New Zealand government to act on your behalf. And as a British citizen, Mr Rivers, I am of course your official representative. I'm not sure what you two have done, but the police are keen to charge you both with public disorder and assault. However, I've had a quiet word with the chief of police and we both agree that, under the circumstances, it would be best for any charges to be dropped."

"Does that mean we're free to go?" asked Ned weakly.

"Yes, Mr Rivers, you're both free to go. But the chief of police requested there be no more instances of disorder or assaulting policemen in the future."

"Really, so he didn't apologise for letting his guys kick the shit out of us?" Arnett asked angrily. "We should be asking you to issue a formal complaint on our behalf."

"Well, if you wanted me to, I could," murmured the Ambassador calmly. "But I think it probably best that the matter be laid to rest. Getting you both off assault charges was not easy." He stood, offered his hand to each of them, and departed.

The two newsmen stood slightly bewildered by the swift change in their fortunes and walked uneasily out the station, Ned being handed his Nikon as he went.

"You're right about one thing, Peter," said Ned with a groan.

"Oh yeah, what's that?"

"It'll take more than a few of Nhu's attack dogs to get me down."

11

Although the mood was convivial, there was a feeling of concern among those sat around the table on the rooftop bar. The attack on the newsmen four days previously had unnerved them and demonstrated how far Nhu's secret police would go to maintain control of what was reported in the press – even the foreign press. Each of them had individually urged their employers to make representations to the Diem government to ensure the safety of foreign correspondents in South Vietnam, but none of the news organisations had done so, believing the dangers had been exaggerated by their men on the ground.

Ned listened as David Halberstam recounted how the lack of concern shown by his bosses at the *New York Times* had incensed him so much that he'd chosen to personally write to the President of the United States to request help.

"Did the White House respond to your complaint?" asked Mel.

"Did they, hell!" Halberstam said, standing at the head of the table in front of his colleagues clutching a piece of paper. "Let me read you what I got through the wires this morning from my foreign news editor: *David, the upper floor have asked me to convey their anger at your personal complaint to President Kennedy regarding your allegation of brutality toward the news media on behalf of the Saigon government. As you know, we at the* New York Times *have to remain neutral from all political interference, so it does not help when you air your grievances directly to the President of the United States of America. If you have a complaint, it should be made straight to your employer and not to the President. You are on assignment for the* New York Times, *you are not a US Ambassador or member of the US government – act accordingly.'"*

"Ouch, and that was from your editor?" asked Ned.

"Yeah – prick. They don't give a damn about our safety, they just want their stories."

"Jesus, David! Only you would have the balls to go straight to Kennedy about all this," said Peter Arnett as he opened a cold tin of 33 Beer and emptied it into a glass on the table.

"Well, I tried talking to the press attaché at the Embassy and the little shit wasn't interested. Said there was nothing the Embassy could do. I mean, what the hell do they do there? Because, clearly, they're not interested in the welfare of their countrymen. What else was I supposed to do? Complaining to the President was the next logical option."

"Don't you think the President's got more important things to worry about than the wellbeing of Mr David Halberstam of the *New York Times*?" interjected Mel. "Who, by the way, writes almost daily about how Kennedy's strategy supporting the South Vietnamese government is a crock of shit, and how he should get over here and see for himself what a colossal mess it all is. Don't you think Mr Kennedy should be looking at the bigger picture, like how to avoid World War Three with Russia?"

"No, absolutely not. The job of the President of the United States is to look after me," said Halberstam with the curl of his lip showing just a hint of a smile.

Arnett picked up the empty can of 33 Beer and threw it at the tall New Yorker. "You arrogant bastard!" The can hit

Halberstam on his forehead, prompting all those sitting around the table to burst into laughter, including the target, the hero of the 'double seven scuffle', as the 7th July incident had become known in the American newspapers.

"Ow, that hurt," said Halberstam, rubbing his head with mock pain. "Is that the only thanks I get for rescuing your sorry little Kiwi ass the other day?" And the assembled members of the foreign press burst out laughing once more at the good-natured banter.

"You didn't rescue me," countered the Kiwi. "I had it all under control. Those little buggers turned and fled because they could see the anger in my eyes." And to reinforce his point, Arnett gave his best theatrical glare to those around the table.

"Are you saying Ned's photograph – which appeared on the front pages of the *New York Times*, the *Washington Post* and many other important newspapers – of me hauling your ass up and keeping the secret police at bay was all a fake?"

"Boys, boys, boys! Stop your bickering," interrupted Mel, trying to encourage a sensible discussion. "If you remember, we agreed to meet up to discuss what we can do to stop being harassed and bullied again. I know you're only playing around but, honestly, I feel threatened by these guys, and if nobody else is going to help us, then we need to do something for ourselves."

They were sat around a large teak table on the rooftop bar of the Rex Hotel on the corner of Le Loi and Nguyen Hue Boulevard. The hotel had only been open for eighteen months, the very first guests being four hundred members of the US 57th and 8th Transportation Companies, who'd arrived on the USS *Core* with their CH-21 'flying banana' helicopters and promptly taken over the new establishment. Most of the current guests were still US servicemen billeted here on arrival before moving on to their bases.

The bar occupied much of the top floor, with the greater part of it open to the elements. Ned, Mel, David Halberstam, Peter Arnett and Neil Sheehan were sat at a table closest to the edge with fine views up and down Nguyen Hue Boulevard. To the left was the colonial Hôtel de Ville, the city hall; across the boulevard sat the classical Saigon Opera House; and to the right, all the way down Nguyen Hue, they could just make out the muddy waters of the Saigon River as it neared the end of its journey to the South China Sea.

On the streets below, the sounds of dusk falling across Saigon created a background hum to their conversations five floors up: the scream of the two-stroke motorbikes, the deep growl of military trucks, and the constant blasting of horns as the population fought to get home at the end of another humid day. And if one cared to listen very carefully through the discord, the songbirds could just be heard chattering and calling as they danced through the warm air, feeding on insects before roosting in for the night. The evening was young – there was still light in the sky – but those around the table knew all too well how quickly night came on in the tropics. Among the potted ferns and other exotic species scattered around the bar, the staff were lighting candles and setting out lanterns to enhance the atmospheric mood.

Mel looked at each of her companions. "I've been in Saigon just over a year now, but it's changed a lot in those twelve months. It's become more intense, more explosive; the peacefulness is gone. I get the impression it's going to come to a head soon, but I'm not sure how."

Ned smiled. "I've only been in the country six weeks and already I've been shot at and arrested twice. They must really hate me!"

Mel sighed. "I saw Ba and Dai yesterday. The attack on us has them worried – they think they're next in the firing line."

"Well, they're bound to be," said Halberstam. "They're the focus of Nhu's anger. And with the failure of that joint communiqué between Diem and the head Buddhist guy, something's bound to happen between them. The monks are raising such merry hell, encouraging the whole population to join them; there's no way Diem will stand for that much longer."

Arnett agreed with a nod of his head. "But equally, Diem has to watch his back too. I met with a high-ranking ARVN officer the other day and, reading between the lines, I could tell he was pretty annoyed with how Diem's handling this Buddhist crisis. I wouldn't be surprised if he's not in the thick of any coup against Diem. I asked him why the Viet Cong were being so quiet at the moment. He thought it was because they were happy for the Buddhists to be taking the fight to the government while they sit back and enjoy it. But he did expect the VC to re-involve themselves again at some point."

"Okay, but what are we going to do to protect ourselves?" insisted Mel, who was obviously more concerned about personal safety than the others.

The group fell silent as a waiter in a traditional blue uniform with a red Chinese-style collar appeared at their table with fresh drinks. Arnett had moved onto gin and tonic, Halberstam and Sheehan were now drinking Johnnie Walker with coke, whereas Mel and Ned had chosen to stick with the longer 33 Beers.

Out of caution, Sheehan waited until the waiter had finished placing the drinks, bowed to the table and departed. "Mel, unless you buy yourself a handgun to protect yourself with, there's not a lot you can do."

"A handgun, I don't want a gun."

Sheehan grimaced. "Well, you'll just have to use your wits then, because this country just got a whole lot more unfriendly to journalists like you and me."

Mel seemed unimpressed. "I was hoping somebody was going to come up with a clever solution that involved our agencies clubbing together and forcing a concession from Diem that ensured our safety. Not having to buy freaking pistols and revolvers."

"Sure, Mel, that's really going to happen," responded Halberstam without even trying to hide his sarcasm. "Shall we ask Diem if he'd just be nice to the monks at the same time?"

Arnett swilled his gin around his glass. "David might be a sarcastic Yank, but he does have a point. This is fast becoming a warzone and shit happens. We've just got to get used to it and deal with it."

The group fell into a prolonged, sombre silence, until Ned piped up cheerfully: "Well... I am off to the White House at the end of the month to receive a photojournalism award. Why don't I just have a quiet word with John-boy while I'm there and see what he can do? Who knows – maybe I'll succeed where David failed!"

His colleagues stared at him, dumbstruck at how Ned had managed to keep such monumental news quiet. The conversation on security came to an immediate halt, and another round of drinks was promptly called for.

12

WEDNESDAY 31ˢᵀ JULY 1963

The Photojournalist Awards were an annual prizegiving ceremony and this year, not only was it being held at the White House for the first time, but the President himself had agreed to present them. The majestic East Room, recently refurbished under the knowledgeable eye of the First Lady, was playing host to the event, and President Kennedy was in a relaxed mood, knowing in two days' time he'd be escaping to his holiday house in Hyannisport, Massachusetts for a long overdue rest.

Ned had come with his boss, James Lund, BPA's irascible and long-serving foreign news editor. They'd travelled down from New York in Lund's 1957 Chevrolet Bel Air Townsman station wagon to attend the ceremony, stopping off for lunch on the banks of the Delaware River at Wilmington, just south of Philadelphia.

Ned had never been to Washington before, let alone the White House. His father had been stationed at Fort McNair after the Second World War, but Ned had already left for England by then. In fact, he'd considered meeting up with his father while he was in the States, but he didn't have an address or contact details and wasn't very bothered either way. The man had shown little interest in keeping in touch after Ned and his mother had moved back to England, so Ned wasn't overly inclined to make contact now. Knowing BPA were paying his air fare from Saigon to the US, principally so he could attend the event but also to meet his bosses in New York for the first time, Ned had decided to add some extra days onto the trip and take them as leave.

Once through security, Ned and Lund entered the White House under the front portico held aloft by its tall, sculptured white columns, and on into the Entrance Hall. Ned marvelled at the sense of history and importance around him. To think that Lincoln and Roosevelt – both Roosevelts in fact – had used this same doorway, had lived in this house, truly excited him. It inspired him to know he was standing in the entrance to probably the most important building in the world, certainly the one with more influence on international affairs than any other – to Ned, that was thrilling.

Together with all the guests arriving for the ceremony, he and Lund were ushered on through the Entrance Hall and left into the Cross Hall. They moved down the corridor, admiring their surroundings. Ned didn't care if he looked like a tourist recently arrived in a new city; he was happy to gawp. There were portraits of past Presidents hung on the walls, red upholstered antique sofas and chairs lining the corridor, and huge chandeliers illuminating the thick red carpet they were walking along.

They reached the entrance to the East Room, where once again their invitations and identities were checked by a guard before they were allowed in. Ned had expected the East Room to be huge but was pleasantly surprised to find it rather small and intimate. There was a stage at the far end with only about three hundred chairs laid out in front of it, and he realised in that moment what an honour it was to have even been nominated for the award.

He remembered back to the morning in early July when news of his nomination had first broken via a wire from head office and how proud it had made him feel. Mel had been full of enthusiasm and told him he'd regret it for the rest of his life if he didn't fly to America and accept the award in person. He sat down and watched as a motley collection of photographers and media managers took their own seats before the ceremony began.

Ned's picture of Thich Quang Duc engulfed in flames and surrounded by the monks of Xa Loi Pagoda had been entered in the 'Most Influential Photo' category. It was the final award of the evening, which had been won in previous years by such prestigious photographers as Robert Capa for his Omaha Beach landing pictures on D-Day; Dorothea Lange for her image taken during the Great Depression of the despairing *Migrant Mother* with two of her seven children; and Yousuf Karsh for his iconic photograph of a belligerent-looking Winston Churchill (who, so the story went, only looked so stroppy because Karsh had unexpectedly whipped the cigar from his mouth moments before the picture was taken). Ned was beyond proud to even be nominated in the same category as these past winners. In his view, Robert Capa was the godfather of war photojournalists, and here Ned was, his own work being considered on the same level – unbelievable.

When the time came for President Kennedy to read out the nominees, Ned, in his dazed state, failed to even hear the names of his two rivals; though he did grasp that one had taken the legendary photo of Kennedy signing the order for a naval blockade to stop the Russians transporting their nuclear bombs to Cuba; while the other had taken the famous shot of James Meredith, the first black student admitted to the University of Mississippi, being escorted to his registration by US marshals against a backdrop of white protesters, including the State Governor.

"And the award goes to…"

Ned closed his eyes in anticipation.

"…Ned Rivers for his photograph of the immolation of Thich Quang Duc in Saigon," exclaimed the President to the applauding audience.

It took a moment before Ned fully understood it was his photograph that had won the prestigious award, his photograph that had been chosen over so many others from the last twelve months, each with their own power to influence. He had to restrain himself from running down the central aisle, such was his excitement, reminding himself to play it cool and walk with his head held high, as if he'd always known the prize would be his. He bounced up onto the stage feeling taller than ever and found to his surprise that John F. Kennedy was shorter than he'd anticipated. As they shook hands, the President smiled and congratulated him.

James Lund was the first to slap Ned on the back after he returned to his seat. Kennedy remained on stage and eyed his audience a moment longer as the room slowly fell silent. Ned guessed he was drawing out the suspense and only when he had the room's undivided attention would he start talking. He admired the man's showmanship, beginning to understand his great public appeal.

"No news picture in history has generated so much emotion around the world as that one," Kennedy declared, pointing to Ned's photo, which was still being projected onto a screen behind him. "What's happening in Saigon at the moment is a crucial reminder about the importance of free speech. Without free speech, a country cannot be called a democracy. It is core to the American belief in liberty…the ability to say what you want without fear of arrest. And an important part of free speech is having a free news media: free to write what they believe, free to print photographs that highlight injustice; and free to report on events that the government of the day might prefer you didn't report." Kennedy raised an eyebrow here and left a pause for effect, waiting for the polite laughter to die down before continuing. "I congratulate you all on your role as envoys of free speech, often operating in countries that do not share our ideals. As Ned Rivers's photograph here shows, there are many parts of the world where people have to resort to extreme measures and dramatic gestures to get their message across. We must aid those who are fighting against tyranny, fighting against injustice, and fighting for the freedoms that we take for granted in this country. Our allies in this struggle may not always be perfect, but where we can influence and persuade them to allow their people the same right to free speech that we enjoy, we must make the case and help them make the change. Thank you, ladies and gentlemen, for your help in making American democracy the beacon for other less fortunate nations to follow."

He stood back to indicate the end of his speech and accepted the enthusiastic applause that followed.

"Now, ladies and gentlemen, I hope you'll stay on and join me for drinks in the State Dining Room, which is located at the other end of the Cross Hall," said the President, gesturing to his right. "I'll join you shortly but first I have to make an important appointment. An appointment I believe will help secure democracy in a nation fighting to keep its head above the water, one which occasionally lets its morals slip, but which needs our help and advice to find its feet once more and prosper." With that, Kennedy was whisked away by his advisors. The room stood as one and clapped him on his way.

Later, during the reception, Ned found himself surrounded by admirers wanting to know all about his experience of the immolation. Was it really as horrific as it looked? Did anyone try to put the fire out and save the monk? Why did he do it? Ned was re-telling the story for about the sixth time when he felt a tap on his shoulder and turned to find none other than President Kennedy himself and a second man by his side.

"Mr Rivers, I wanted to congratulate you again on your award. It really is well deserved, and I meant what I said earlier – I've never known a photo to have such a dramatic or emotional effect on such a huge number of people. Unfortunately, it hasn't done me any favours, but I can hardly blame you for that."

"Thank you, Mr President," said Ned, rather starstruck. "And thank you for inviting me into the White House today, you don't know what an honour this is for me."

"Well, I don't always agree with what you guys print in your newspapers, especially when you attack my policies, but I'll always support your right to print what you want."

As the President was speaking, Ned looked across to the man standing by his side. He was tall – about six foot one – and smartly dressed, in his early sixties with dark, slightly greying hair set with a side parting. But it was the intensity of the man's stare that Ned really noticed; his eyes seemed to be boring into his core as if searching his inner soul.

Kennedy noticed Ned's gaze. "Ned, I want to introduce you to Henry Cabot Lodge. I thought it might be interesting for the two of you to meet since you'll soon have a lot in common. You might even be useful to each other. I've just asked Henry to be the next US Ambassador to South Vietnam, and Henry has graciously accepted."

"Congratulations, sir," said Ned, putting his hand out in greeting.

"Ned," said the tall man, offering a firm handshake in return. "I just want to congratulate you as well on your photograph. It's a helluva picture."

President Kennedy cleared his throat. "One of the areas I've asked Henry to focus on when he arrives in Saigon is press relations. I'm not sure you boys over there are getting on too well with the Embassy."

"That's true, sir. The Embassy seems to view us as their enemy, which does make life rather difficult. All we're doing is reporting on what we see, it's not as if we're making it up."

Henry Cabot Lodge eyed Ned carefully and asked, "So in your opinion, have the Buddhists been infiltrated by the communists as President Diem tells us?"

Ned was appalled by the suggestion and – forgetting whom he was talking to – launched into an impassioned defence. "No, that's a crazy suggestion! The Buddhist monks are simply fighting for equal rights with the ruling Catholics. They're not putting forward a communist agenda, they just want the persecution to end. They're not communists, that's a lie put forward by Diem and Nhu to defend their strongarm tactics against the monks' peaceful demonstrations. Diem, and Nhu especially, are the problem. It was Nhu who ordered his secret police to attack us journalists earlier this month." Turning to the President, Ned continued making his point forcefully. "And when we complained to the Embassy and asked for their help, they did nothing. That's why we don't trust them, sir – we just don't feel they'd help us in a crisis. Nearly all the journalists over there are American citizens, yet the Embassy sees them as the problem and won't lift a finger to help them."

Henry Cabot Lodge stood bolt upright. "Why then does Diem keep telling us the monks have to be defeated since they're nothing but a front for the communists?"

"That couldn't be further from the truth, sir. I'm convinced that when you meet President Diem for the first time, you'll see him for the liar he is. All he's doing is using American military aid to crush his enemies and keep him and his family in power; that's why he's telling you the monks have been infiltrated by the communists – so he can crush them with your support. But they're innocent, they're religious people; they might protest, but they always do it peacefully." Ned was surprised at how vehemently he was defending the monks. But he knew what he said to be true; after all, he'd spent the last six weeks visiting their pagodas and witnessing their demonstrations. He knew many of them personally and the accusation they were communists angered him.

The President interrupted at this point, asking, "And how do you propose we can encourage President Diem to offer equal rights to the Buddhists?"

"I'd persuade Diem to remove his brother and his sister-in-law from having any positions of influence in the government, sir. Nhu and his wife are the real enemy of the Buddhists. Most of us in the press think the Nhus run the show anyway and Diem is just the face of the government."

"Well, it was good to meet you, Mr Rivers," said Lodge suddenly, putting an end to the discussion. "And when I arrive out in Saigon next month, we must meet up and continue this conversation. Oh, and well done again on your award."

"Thank you, sir," replied Ned. "It's been a pleasure meeting you. And when I get back to Saigon, can I tell the leading monks that the new US Ambassador understands their concerns and will be fighting their case for them?"

Lodge smiled inscrutably but offered no answer and turned away from Ned, ready to be introduced to someone new by the President.

"Goodness!" said James Lund, who'd been standing behind Ned listening in to the exchange. "I didn't realise you'd become chief spokesman for the South Vietnamese Buddhists, Rivers."

"Well, hardly their chief spokesman," said Ned defensively. "But I did promise I'd try and help them – and you don't get a much better opportunity than that!"

Part II: Sparks

13

With Ned's unexpected visit to America over, he was back in Saigon by the evening of Saturday 17ᵗʰ August. Although he'd only been away a short time, he found himself shocked once more by the differences between East and West, remembering the same emotion he'd felt the first time he'd set foot in the country back in May. It had taken the well-ordered streets of London with their tolerant drivers waiting patiently in queues for Ned to notice the discord and chaos of the roads here in Saigon; or the comparative cleanliness of Washington DC to be aware of the filth and rubbish strewn around the streets of the South Vietnamese capital. Extreme as the differences were, he reassured himself he'd no longer notice either the chaos or the rubbish within a matter of days. Though now he was back, he'd have to toughen up and be on his guard once more.

After landing at Tan Son Nhut Airport, Ned headed straight to Mel's house for a full debrief. Having not seen each other for more than three weeks, there was much to discuss and catch up on. But before the serious conversation about Saigon politics and the Buddhist demonstrations could begin, there were more immediate needs to address.

The moment the front door had shut behind him, Ned and Mel fell into a strong embrace, but the journey from the airport and the sticky heat had left Ned drenched in sweat and feeling very uncomfortable. Mel suggested he make use of her walk-in shower to freshen up, which he gratefully accepted. No sooner had he tilted his head back and let the cool water wash over him than he felt a pair of hands soaping his back. Turning slowly until the hands had moved to his chest, he looked down to find Mel smiling up at him. He put his arms around her waist and pulled her in tight. What followed was as passionate and intimate as the night of his departure, leaving Ned in no doubt their relationship had survived the three-week interlude.

Once satisfied and dry, with a bottle of ice-cold beer each, they went outside to sit in Mel's garden and caught up on the events of the summer.

Ned told her about the photographer awards and how he'd used the opportunity to tell Kennedy what was really happening in Saigon, revealing he'd also been introduced to the new Ambassador to South Vietnam. Mel confirmed the ineffectual Nolting had already left and a guy called William Trueheart was acting as stand-in until his successor's arrival. She explained how the situation in Saigon had deteriorated; the monks had continued to hold their weekly demonstrations, but now the police were becoming more physical in their response, with some of the protests having resulted in violent clashes. And underlining the desperate mood, there had also been more self-immolations.

"Oh, that's terrible," said Ned, remembering the dreadful day back in June when he'd witnessed Thich Quang Duc's defiant act. "How many more?"

"A twenty-year-old monk killed himself at the beginning of the month, and then three more, including a novice and a nun, all this week. The last one was yesterday in Hue. But the government's only going to crack down harder if they keep it up."

"Then I guess tomorrow's demonstration will be highly charged. Have you seen Ba and Dai since I've been away?"

Mel took a long swig of her beer until it was empty and set the bottle down on the table. "Yes, Pham's driven me over to Xa Loi a couple of times a week and I've spoken to the brothers each time. Ba still seems upbeat, but I can see Dai's getting more depressed by the events. He was very down when he heard about the novice monk killing himself."

"Poor Dai. He takes everything to heart, doesn't he?"

"Maybe you can try to cheer him up when you see him tomorrow. He clearly misses you, he kept asking about you after you left. *'Have you heard from Mr Ned, Miss Melanie?' 'Any news about Mr Ned?'* If anyone can bring him out of his gloom, it's you."

Ned chuckled at Mel's imitation. "Looks like I got back here just in time. It sounds like the whole country's about to go up in flames."

14

Ned was happy to resume the habitual Sunday-morning cyclo ride with Mel to Xa Loi Pagoda for the demonstration and protests. As usual, their behaviour reverted to complete professionalism upon arrival.

"I'll leave you to Ba and Dai," said Mel. "You guys deserve some time on your own to catch up. I'm off to find Halberstam and Sheehan. Oh, and by the way, Pham said he'd wait for you by the gatehouse." And with that, she disappeared into the crowd.

Outside the pagoda, despite the dark, ominous, rolling clouds gathering off to the south, Ba Huyen Thanh Quan Street was filling up with protesters, students, and anyone else eager to offer their support to the monks. Looking through his viewfinder on his Nikon, Ned could instantly see how many more people there were attending this morning's demonstration compared to those held earlier in the summer. And the mood had changed too. Everyone seemed more determined; the smiling faces and joviality had gone, replaced with scowls and menace.

He hurried across the street, his Nikon hanging around his neck, and found Pham at the main entrance to the pagoda, where they shook hands as old friends.

"Hello, trouble-buster, how are you? Keeping well?" asked Ned, punching Pham playfully on the shoulder.

"Ah, Mr Ned. Welcome back. How was America?"

"Not as humid as here, that's for sure. I hear you've been looking after Mel in my absence."

"Yes, I have. Very important to keep in her good books," said Pham with a broad grin. "She pays my salary."

"Good man! But remember — you're my trouble-buster, not hers," replied Ned. "Come on, let's go find those unruly brothers."

Ned could see the main pagoda gates were closed and padlocked so called on Pham to follow him around the corner to Quan Pho Street, the small alleyway Ba had once shown them that backed onto the headquarters of USAid. Although the street ran along the back of the pagoda, there were no protesters here, or indeed anyone at all, so Ned and Pham opened the little side door reserved for apprentice monks and slipped into the back corridor of the complex.

They walked along the darkened passageway until they came to a small wooden door, which they cautiously opened, the light from inside the pagoda buildings flooding through the gap and temporarily blinding them. Ned recognised the set of double doors opposite that led out to the bell tower, and the corridor of offices off to his right. These rooms were still full of banner-painting equipment, rolls of calico and paint pots strewn around haphazardly; but there were no people. He could hear chanting, however, coming from above their heads, and turned left to find the opening onto the secret stairs that led up to the great hall. He and Pham ascended, trying to make as little noise as possible. At the top, Ned nervously opened the second door leading into the hall, hoping the large screens were still in place to hide them as they entered. Fortunately, they were, allowing them to slip into the hall unseen and peer gingerly around to see what was happening.

The hall was full to capacity with chanting monks, a sea of orange with shaven heads bobbing on the surface. There were monks sitting on the floor cross-legged so as not to point their feet at anyone (a terrible insult to Buddhists, Ned had learnt). Behind them, others were standing and filling every corner of the hall. Every one of them was holding their hands together in prayer as they chanted. Ned estimated there must be well over a thousand people in the hall, more than triple the number from June, when three hundred monks had trooped out of Xa Loi for Thich Quang Duc's funeral. Among them this time were far more Buddhist nuns than Ned had seen previously, dressed in grey robes, so easy to distinguish. Ned remembered Ba had mentioned the monks and nuns coming in from the countryside to the big cities to add weight to the protests. It looked like the population of Xa Loi had increased substantially in the time he'd been away in America.

Ned was enthralled by the sound of the chanting. Around the room he could hear the *ting-ting-ting* of mini-cymbals and bells, contrasting with the deep base of the large drum that sat on the elaborately carved teak trestle base to the right of the altar, reverberating with each hit. A thick haze of joss smoke drifted up toward the ornate ceiling, adding to the occasion. The monks and nuns, seemingly in a state of suspended reality, hummed the incantations, creating a peaceful and calming effect that lifted Ned's mood and made him happy to be back at the pagoda. For long moments, he was caught up in the mesmerising feeling of tranquillity that swept over him as time became immaterial. The smells and sounds played with his mind and left him feeling helpless and immobile. Only as the chanting drew to a close did Ned come to and realise how close he'd come to falling into a hypnotic state.

Standing at the altar in front of the huge statue of Gautama Buddha was Thich Tinh Khiet himself, leader of the Buddhists in Vietnam, whom Ned had last seen on 7th July when Khiet had attempted to lead the assembled monks and crowds on a march to the Gia Long Palace, which had failed after the attack on the Western journalists by Nhu's secret police. Clearly, he was refusing to give up because, as Ned watched, the chanting ceased and the elderly monk stepped forward, leaning heavily on his stick, and started to shout at the monks, in complete contrast to the tranquil chanting of a few moments before. However, the monks responded to his speech with loud applause, illustrating their passion and enthusiasm for his message. Ned turned to Pham and asked what Khiet was saying.

"He's telling the monks that the fight is coming to a head; that Diem has broken every promise he made to the Buddhists in the joint communiqué; that he believes the government is trying to destroy Buddhism; that the situation is even worse in Hue – where he's from – because Ngo Dinh Thuc, Archbishop of Hue and Diem's brother, is attempting to forcibly convert everyone to Catholicism; he says now is not the time to give up, and only the overthrow of Diem's government will solve this crisis."

"Overthrow? Did he really say their intention is to overthrow the President?"

"Yes, Mr Ned, that's what he just said."

Ned watched at Thich Tinh Khiet stood back and allowed another monk, younger by about thirty years, to take his place. This monk spoke with even more vigour, using his arms and fists to illustrate his point. It reminded Ned of being at the theatre.

"Who's this guy?" asked Ned.

"I don't know," replied Pham. "He hasn't said his name but he's also urging the monks to protest strongly. He says that when they leave here, they must go out onto Ba Huyen Thanh Quan Street and shout their slogans loudly and encourage all the other protesters to join in. He says today should be a dress rehearsal for next Sunday's demonstration because the new

American Ambassador will be here by then. He wants next week to be the biggest and loudest they've ever held."

There were other monks at the altar standing with Thich Tinh Khiet, one of whom Ned now recognised as Dai. Although hidden from the bulk of the audience by the screens, Ned was fully visible to the senior monks looking back down the hall. When Dai appeared to be looking in his direction, Ned waved furtively to get his attention. After a few missed attempts, the monk next to Dai tapped him on the shoulder and pointed toward Ned. A smile swept across Dai's face when he recognised who it was, and he immediately made his way around to greet his old friend.

"Mr Ned, welcome back! How are you?"

"Hello, Dai. Glad to see you're still in one piece. I hear the police have been getting a bit more physical since I've been away."

Dai put his index finger to his mouth, indicating Ned should be quiet, and suggested they go downstairs.

"Before we go," said Pham, "who is that monk talking now?"

"That is Thich Tri Quang," replied Dai, furrowing his brow and narrowing his eyes, as if in disapproval. "He's responsible for organising our protests and the fight with Diem. He came from Hue with our patriarch Thich Tinh Khiet. Although Khiet is our supreme leader, he is getting too old to lead the fight, so Quang is leading our resistance against the government now."

Dai led them both back down the stairs and into an office. As Ned walked in, he spotted a page from a newspaper stuck to the wall by a desk. It was the *Washington Post* front page from late June that featured a large picture of Ba and Dai smiling as they held up the glass chalice containing Thich Quang Duc's heart – the same photograph Ned had taken on one of his visits to the pagoda.

"I recognise that picture, Dai!"

"It's good, yes? It made me and Ba famous. All the monks now call us 'the *Washington Post* brothers'. If anyone walks past me in the corridor, they shout, 'Hello, Washington!' and then burst into laughter."

"So I should call you 'Washington' from now on then?" laughed Ned. "But seriously, are you okay? I heard you've had one or two violent clashes with the police since I've been away?"

"Yes, we have. But it was the police who were violent, not us. We make it clear to all our followers that it's important we protest peacefully and without violence. We are Buddhists, we are a peaceful religion. The police are becoming more and more aggressive. Quang says it's a sign of desperation and shows we're winning the war with Diem and Nhu."

"So what happened?" asked Ned.

"We had a big demonstration on the last Sunday in July. Maybe seven or eight thousand people came; outside was very full. We prayed in the great hall as normal and then went outside to join the crowds. Thich Tri Quang spoke on a megaphone and got the crowd really angry. There was lots of shouting and cheering, especially when he said he wished it was Madame Nhu who'd set herself on fire. That was when the police charged. They came at us with their wooden batons, beating anyone in their path to the ground. The crowd started running down Ba Huyen Thanh Quan Street, but then the police attacked from that direction too. What you would call a 'pincer movement', yes?" Ned nodded. "The crowd had nowhere to run, so the students and younger protesters started fighting back. Even though we wanted it to be non-violent, they started throwing rocks at the police, and the police kept on charging into the crowds with their batons, beating people to the ground and then retreating again. The students were breaking up the pavements and walls to make smaller rocks, which they kept throwing at the police. It got very nasty. Some of the monks were able to take the more elderly protesters and the injured back into the pagoda for safety. This went on for about four hours before Thich Tri Quang called a halt to the protests and urged everyone to go home. No one died, luckily, but many monks and lots of our supporters were arrested and taken away. Not all of them have reappeared."

"Were you okay?"

"Yes, I was fine. I was helping the injured get away from the police charges. The police hit me once, but I got my hand on the baton before it struck me, so that softened the blow. Ba took a bad hit to his body though."

"Where is Ba?" asked Ned with sudden unease.

"Still upstairs, I think. But don't worry, he's fine. He has a nasty bruise, that's all. Nothing was broken."

While Ned and Dai were chatting, Pham had discovered a pile of banners laid out on a bench in the far corner of the office and was reading through their messages.

"Is this what set off a new wave of immolations? I heard three monks died last week alone." The look of concern was evident on Ned's face.

"We know we're winning, Mr Ned, but we must keep the pressure up. Some monks have chosen to martyr themselves for the cause and that is to be applauded. President Diem is now realising that the Buddhist majority are stronger than his Catholic minority, and he doesn't like it."

Ned took a step to Dai's side and put his arm around his shoulders, pulling him in tight. "On that note, my friend, I have good news for you. I met President Kennedy and, more importantly, the next US Ambassador to Saigon when I was in Washington. They both asked me about the situation here and how it could be improved, and I told them they had to persuade Diem and Nhu to make peace with the Buddhists. I even told the new Ambassador he had to find a way of getting rid of Nhu and Madame Nhu, and only then would the situation improve. I just hope I convinced him."

Dai beamed at this news and then pointed upstairs. "The speeches and morning prayers have finished. Come, let's go and join them outside for the protests."

"I get the feeling some of you are pushing for a harder, more angry response, whereas others want to keep these protests peaceful and free of violence. Is that correct?" said Ned as he walked beside Dai toward the double doors, Pham following close behind.

"You are right, Mr Ned. Even Ba and I argue on this point. Ba thinks we should be encouraging the students and other radicals who support us to rebel violently, but I cannot support that view. As Buddhists, we should always adhere to our peaceful teachings."

"What about your leaders – are they split too?" Ned held open the doors for Pham and Dai.

"Could you not tell from watching Khiet and Quang upstairs? Khiet is traditional and believes everything can and should be done peacefully; but Quang thinks we'll never win unless we motivate our supporters to more extreme acts. He thinks that if we don't win, we lose everything. And to him, that's not an option."

The three of them left the building and walked past the bell tower toward the main gates. Ned looked up to assess the light conditions; this was second nature to him now, something he did out of habit. The sun had gone and the sky was thick with brooding grey clouds, but it hadn't started to rain yet. The low light levels gave the pagoda complex an eerie, mysterious glow.

They turned the last corner to see the vast throng of monks and nuns exiting through the main gates and out into the street. Cheering greeted the Buddhists' arrival, and Ned guessed more people had arrived since he'd been inside. He prepared his Nikon, realising he'd been negligent staying in the pagoda so long when he should have been outside the gates with the protesters, taking photographs.

The crowds were dense, and Ned knew he wouldn't be able to make his way through, so Dai suggested they go up the bell tower for a better view. As they hurried over, Dai explained its features. "Xa Loi Pagoda has the tallest bell tower in all Vietnam. It's thirty-two metres high and has seven levels. You can see how the tower gets thinner as it gets taller."

Ned stopped and put his Nikon to his eye. He'd noticed how a crack in the clouds had let a spear of sunlight through, lighting the tower in a way he found appealing, and he decided to take a photograph with the dark, thunderous cumulus clouds behind the structure. Focusing his camera, he could see the Chinese-style roofs jutting out on each level, with shuttered windows facing out in each of the four cardinal directions. The shutters were latticed, allowing people on the inside to look out without being visible from the outside.

Once Ned had taken his picture, Dai rushed over to the door on the ground floor and flung it open to show them the winding wooden staircase within. Entering, Pham and Dai following behind, Ned raced up, taking the steps two at a time. He peered out the latticework shutter on the first floor but realised he still wasn't high enough, so carried on climbing, checking the view at each level. Finally, on the fifth floor, he grunted with satisfaction and, with Dai's permission, opened the shutters on the side overlooking the crowd. Sweeping his hand through his curly hair to clear it from his face, he stared down in amazement.

Ba Huyen Thanh Quan Street, wide as it was, was completely full. Ned thought back to Thich Quang Duc's funeral in June, the day he'd first been arrested by Nhu's secret police, and remembered the crowds of supporters on that occasion. But that was nothing compared to what he was looking at now; he estimated there must be four times as many today. Once more, he became aware of how the atmosphere of these demonstrations had changed. Back in June, the crowd had been celebratory, almost joyous; but now they were loud, angry and baying for blood. At the top end of Ba Huyen Thanh Quan Street, Ned could see the police lines had already formed, ten men thick, blocking the road. At the earlier protests, there had only been a handful of police present. Without a doubt, the mood has definitely shifted.

The view from the bell tower allowed Ned to focus on different aspects of the crowd, capturing the scale of the event, the sheer numbers of protesters, and the police's boxing-in tactics. He felt sure these would be the images on the front pages of tomorrow's newspapers, a fact that thrilled him. With a 200 mm lens, he was able to capture the backs of Khiet and Quang making their speeches and the horde of faces in front of them watching and listening intently to every word and command, the telephoto lens concertina-ing their faces closer together and exaggerating the density of the throng.

Even from his elevated position, the noise of the protest was loud, especially when it came to Quang's turn to speak. He worked the crowd like a professional, stoking the mood and upping the tempo of the protesters' chants, but equally ensuring he didn't push them over the top and provoke any violence or rioting, which he knew the police would counter with a heavy-handed response. It seemed Quang wanted to save the real action for next week after the new American Ambassador had arrived in town.

In anticipation of the potential for the protest to turn ugly and descend into a pitched battle, Ned remained in position high up in the bell tower. From here, he watched as the thick, rain-saturated clouds came closer. When the density of water finally became too much to defy gravity, the thunderous downpour began, drenching the crowds below, and Ned knew the demonstration was over. There would be nothing further for him to photograph today, which meant no risk of death or serious injuries. He was relieved – though, in truth, a little disappointed too.

Dai, peering through the same shuttered aperture beside him, looked out over the dispersing crowds. "Buddha knows best, yes? It's his way of telling us to wait one more week."

Two hours after the monks had first joined the protesters outside the gates of Xa Loi, Ned descended from the bell tower to find Mel and a handful of other journalists standing by the main gates debriefing together. The general consensus was Quang had successfully taken his audience to the top of the mountain but chosen to bring them back down the same way.

Along with the protesters, the journalists left the scene to return to their offices and file their reports. Pham drove Ned and Mel back to the BPA office on Rue Pasteur, where he was told he wouldn't be needed for the rest of the day and was free to go.

Inside, they found Bich, who'd ostensibly emptied another cabinet and was diligently reading each piece of paper before filing it away according to its content. Mel commended Bich on her dedication for working on a Sunday. Bich seemed to take the compliment the wrong way, however, for she hastily tidied up the few sheets left on the floor and promptly left.

Ned knew today's photographs did not need to be transmitted to New York as urgently as those of Thich Quang Duc's self-immolation and could therefore be developed in-house and wired from the local Saigon post, telegrams and telephones office. This was a slower process than having them shipped to Tokyo, but the advantage was Ned remained in control of the printing process and could examine his results.

So, while Mel typed up her report on her favourite Hermes 3000 typewriter, Ned got to work in the darkroom. This was in fact nothing more than a cupboard next to the bathroom, but it was just big enough for his needs. There were no windows and black tape had been fixed around the edge of the door to make the room lightproof. By fitting a lock on the inside, Ned had also ensured he couldn't be disturbed midway through developing a film, something which could ruin a potential 'front-pager'.

He worked quickly and confidently in the total darkness. Prising off the bottom of the canister, he removed the film and threaded it into his developing tank, making sure to work with its natural bend. Once he'd completed the task, he secured the lid on the tank tightly, knowing it was now safe to turn on the lights since the tank itself was lightproof. Next, he filled the tank with water from the tap and agitated it to pre-wash the film, thus making it more receptive to chemicals while also ensuring there were no air bubbles that could affect the development process.

He then emptied the tank of water, filled the first beaker with developer and checked its temperature to decide on the development time. He knew his black-and-white Kodak Tri-X film at 400 ASA needed six and three-quarter minutes at $20\,°C$, but only five and a quarter minutes at $22\,°C$. He prepared his stopwatch, checked the thermometer ($22\,°C$ – unsurprising, given the heat outside) and poured the developer into the tank. He'd already prepared the second beaker with stop bath, which, as the name implied, halted any further development of the film; and the third with fixer, which removed any silver halide residue and made it safe to expose the film to light.

Ned was well experienced but always concentrated on this part, knowing the slightest mistake could ruin a day's work. He agitated the tank every thirty seconds and then, exactly five minutes and fifteen seconds after starting the developing process, emptied the developer and added the stop bath. Time was no longer critical at this point. Having agitated the developer tank, he poured out the stop bath and replaced it with the fixer. After another good shake, he drained the fixer and gave the film one last rinse with water. It was now safe to open the tank, remove the film, and hang it with a clothes-peg from string stretched across the room. The final step was to squeegee the film dry.

With each of the films shot that day developed, Ned could now review the images to see if any were good enough to be wired to America. This was always his favourite part of the process. It always surprised him how the pictures he thought would be the strongest often weren't; while others he didn't hold much hope for could turn out to be real winners. In this instance, the photograph of the bell tower lit with the last of the afternoon sun looked dull and flat compared to those of the crowds, in which you could see the anger etched across the protesters' faces. But it was anyone's guess as to which ones his editors would pick.

15

The storm clouds were rolling away to the east as the two generals set off on their journey to the Gia Long Palace. Another afternoon monsoon had lashed the city, drenching yet cleansing it at the same time. The downpour had only lasted thirty minutes, less than normal, which indicated to experienced weather-watchers the monsoon season would soon be over and the humidity gone for another year.

As the generals were being driven to the palace, they didn't notice the naked children playing in the puddles or the sunlight piercing through the gap in the fragmenting rainclouds like an angel's pointing finger. They couldn't smell the sweet aroma of the frangipani or bougainvillea flowers on the cleansed air, nor did they marvel at the leftover rainwater evaporating into vapour and ascending back to the heavens.

They didn't notice because the generals were scheming.

"Ah, General Don, General Minh, come in," said Nhu, smoke escaping from his mouth as he welcomed the high-ranking officers. With the hand that held the lit Gauloise, he waved his servant away as if he was some beggar from the slums and turned to offer his guests a drink. He was sitting in his office behind his large, thickset teak desk, while the generals took their seats on a low rattan sofa across the room. Nhu liked to play power games with his visitors, especially those he had reason to distrust.

"I thought you were both in Thailand watching the military exercises. I was surprised to hear you wanted to see me," said Nhu coldly.

"Yes, *ngài*, we were in Thailand," remarked General Minh, the elder of the two. "But after ten weeks, the exercises have nearly finished, so we came back early."

Nhu tried to hide his contempt for the pair, though didn't really care if he was successful or not. He cast his mind back to the good old days when Minh and Don had worked hand in hand with him and his brother. After Diem had first come to power over the southern half of Vietnam in 1954, the country had been riddled with paramilitary groups, crime syndicates and armed religious sects, each seeking power and territory. With Minh and Don's help, both only junior colonels at the time, Diem and Nhu had been able to smash these groups and take complete control of the country for themselves. Minh and Don had been promoted to generals as a reward for their loyalty. Within five years, however, they'd been stripped of their roles as troop commanders and relegated to ceremonial titles and duties – Diem had always been nervous of those who accumulated too much power, no matter how they gained it. Minh's current official title was Presidential Military Advisor, while Don's was Chief of Staff, which effectively involved greeting incoming foreign dignitaries at the airport upon arrival. Though neither played an active military role any longer, they were both still considered high up and influential in the army's hierarchy; and to Nhu, that made them a threat.

"What do you want? Why have you asked to see me?" Although Vietnamese custom dictated the three men converse idly for a few minutes, Nhu was an impatient man and some customs bored him.

"*Ngài*," boomed Minh, quickly jumping in ahead of General Don, as was his way. "Last Sunday evening, ten members of the armed services, all of us generals, met to discuss the current state of disorder in this country. We went over possible solutions at length and eventually concluded it would be disastrous for the military to be seen to be fighting or attacking the monks, since so many members of the armed forces are Buddhists. However, we also recognised that while the cities of our great country are paralysed by these protests, it has become impossible to prosecute the war against the Viet Cong. All members present on Sunday evening agreed that General Don and myself, as your most senior generals, should communicate our solution to you and the President."

Nhu sat impassively behind his desk, searching for the trick in what was being said. When others were outlining a plan, he always assumed there must be a hidden agenda somewhere, because, in his experience, there always was. As a child, his father had taught him never to trust anyone, which was probably how Nhu had come to live in the presidential palace as South Vietnam's number two in command. Only his brother had done better, having presumably received the same lesson. Somewhere in the generals' so-called 'solution' would be some sort of manoeuvre; all Nhu had to do was spot it and then out-manoeuvre them. He lit another Gauloise, took a deep drag on the unfiltered cigarette and blew out a cloud of thick smoke in the direction of his guests.

"And what is this solution, General Don?" said Nhu, switching his attention to Minh's colleague, who hadn't said a word thus far. It never did to let one person do all the talking.

Don hesitated before replying, his brow creasing, as if taking the time to consider any unintended consequences of his answer. "*Ngài*, we want President Diem to declare martial law and order the rural monks to disperse from the cities and return to their communities. Under martial law, we can prohibit protests and gatherings of more than twenty people in one place. If the President agrees, then General Dinh can move parts of III Corps into the city to help the police control and monitor the situation with roadblocks and ensure an army presence at all main street intersections. Martial law will allow us to send the rural monks back to the countryside, temporarily close the universities, prevent gatherings of students, and within a matter of weeks, tensions will have eased."

"How many troops do you suggest should be moved into Saigon?" asked Nhu cautiously. He recognised stationing soldiers inside the capital could be the threat he'd been looking out for, the trick up the generals' sleeves. A coup would be impossible without military back-up, so any movement of troops into Saigon naturally alerted him to a range of potential dangers. And yet he strongly trusted General Dinh, notoriously one of the regime's key supporters. Indeed, Diem had personally promoted Dinh to commander of III Corps over the heads of other senior military officers rather than through normal military channels. This was a prestigious position, and one that required a faithful ally, for the occupant commanded the troops surrounding Saigon and could thus halt any coup in its tracks.

The detailed discussion between Nhu and the generals continued for a further ninety minutes before a final scheme had been agreed by all parties.

"So we're agreed that martial law should be enacted from 9.00 tomorrow morning," said Nhu as he stood from his chair and stubbed his cigarette out in an ornate jade ashtray on his desk. "In which case, I think it's about time we involved the President himself." He strode over toward the door and signalled for the generals to follow.

Nhu led the way down the corridor to the far end of the building. The three of them arrived outside the presidential office just as Diem's secretary was clearing her desk at the end of another busy day. Nhu could see through the doors into his brother's office and spotted him sitting at his desk in a smart white linen suit, reading reports. Diem welcomed the trio into his office. Once they were all seated, Nhu explained the purpose of their unannounced visit.

The conversation turned out to be quick and easy, with the President agreeing promptly to impose martial law the following morning. The generals had barely sat down before they found themselves being swiftly ushered out once more.

It was only when they were back in the car with their military chauffeur that General Minh and General Don felt free to speak plainly again.

"That seemed altogether too easy, wouldn't you say, Don?"

General Don rubbed the stubble on his cheek. "Indeed. You have to wonder what they're both up to. I've never known the President agree so readily to one of our suggestions."

General Minh looked across at his colleague. "Do you think martial law will work, or should we be actively looking to replace Diem? Now we have their agreement to station soldiers from III Corps in Saigon, it would create the ideal opportunity to organise a coup. We'd have to persuade General Dinh to join us, of course. But he's so egotistical, all we'd need to do is offer him a major government position and he'd jump at the chance."

"No," replied Don gravely. "I think on balance we should give Diem and Nhu our support and try to make a success of martial law. Morale is so low among our soldiers, we have to calm the situation peacefully and without causing further harm to the monks. Otherwise, we risk a rebellion from within our own ranks. If that happens, we'll have little chance of successfully fighting the Viet Cong and the whole game will be lost."

"Very well," said Minh as he sat back in his upholstered leather seat. "Let's continue to support the brothers. I only hope it works, for all our sakes."

Diem and Nhu stood in the outer corridor that ran around the outside of the Gia Long Palace, watching through one of the open louvers as the departing generals climbed into their waiting car. The air was still hot, though not as humid as earlier – the storm had seen to that. The sky on the eastern horizon was still light enough to contrast the menacing clouds floating in from the South China Sea but dark enough for the city street lamps to have come on, and lines of red and white car lights could be seen disappearing into the distance along the major highways. The two brothers stood for a moment, each in thought, for they were worried; they could see a trap being laid.

"Do you think they're using this crisis as an excuse to mount a coup?" asked Diem.

"I'm not sure," replied Nhu, "but I don't trust Minh or Don. You were right to remove them from command when you did. I have a plan, though, that might just solve all our problems. Kill two birds with one stone, as the Americans might say. End the Buddhist crisis dead and discredit the generals at the same time, which means they won't be in a position to stage a coup against anyone. I've been mulling the idea over in my head the last few days, but I think now is the time to put it into action before the new US Ambassador arrives. Colonel Tung is on standby."

Diem lit another cigarette as he listened to his brother, his concern gradually transforming into a smile as the plan grew clearer.

16

Madame Mai's stood on a small side street just by the quay that ran along the Saigon River, located in a three-storey building that showed signs of its age with a crumbling outer facade. This was more like a den than a club, and full of things a nineteen-year-old might enjoy.

Ned arrived at the front door in the company of a French journalist named Claude, with whom he'd been drinking that evening at the Continental Palace Hotel. His new friend – for they'd only met that night – had suggested the jaunt, though without divulging what it was, merely saying "trust me" when Ned had asked for details. Claude had expertly navigated his way there, demonstrating his familiarity with the place, before tapping on the door with three well-spaced knocks.

Madame Mai was a flirtatious lady in her forties with a big smile and a happy-go-lucky character, embracing Claude and Ned in turn as she ushered them inside. Like many Saigonese, she was an entrepreneur who'd spotted an opportunity to adapt a traditional Eastern cultural pleasure to Western tastes to appeal to the almost ten thousand stressed-out Americans now stationed in South Vietnam. Those in the know warned that this number was set to increase, as might the number returning to America housed in wooden boxes. The uptrend in deaths lately had been frightening; more Americans had been killed so far that year than in the whole of the previous one.

The establishment was neither Thai massage parlour nor Chinese opium den but something in-between. Tonight, it was full of off-duty American military advisors enjoying the relaxing and convivial atmosphere the club provided as the perfect antidote to the tensions encountered in the field. Ned could hear their laughter in the ground-floor bar, but Claude suggested they go upstairs, knowing there was another, more low-key and relaxed bar on the next floor.

They had each drunk a bottle of 33 Beer by the time two young ladies came to collect them, leading them off separately to a large room on the top floor. Ned's companion introduced herself as Phuong. He guessed she was in her early twenties. She was petite in stature and wore the customary *áo dài*, which clung tightly to her upper body, revealing her thin arms and small, rounded chest. She chose not to wear the traditional silk trousers underneath, however, so the deep side-split in the dress exposed her curved hips and long brown legs. Her straight dark hair was rolled into a small bun at the back of her neck and she had a very smooth complexion that Ned found attractive.

The room she took him to was sub-sectioned into several small cubicles, each with rush-mat walls on three sides but open on the fourth. Each space contained two rattan beds lying parallel to one another, separated by a small, low table at the head. Ned was ushered into a cubicle and told to remove his clothes and lie face-down on the right-hand bed, which was covered in a crisp white sheet. Phuong gently covered his mid-region with a small, folded cotton sheet, leaving his back and legs exposed. She knelt on the bed and began massaging his back and neck with lemongrass and coconut oil. Using both hands, she kneaded his muscles, working her fingers into his nerve sensors until she felt the knots beneath begin to unwind and straighten out. Once she'd completed his back, she moved further down his body and started on his feet. Using her thumbs to delve and prod, she stretched each toe and rubbed the feet until they glistened with oil. Next, she ran her hands up each side of his legs, reaching as far up the thigh as she could from where she knelt. After thirty minutes of gentle pummelling and stroking, with clear sighs of satisfaction from her client, it was time to move onto the next stage.

Phuong stood up and told Ned to turn onto his side before leaving the cubicle. When she reappeared, she was carrying a small black lacquered tray covered with mysterious implements, which she placed on the low table, and then lay down on the other rattan bed across from him. The only illumination came from a small opium lamp, which she carefully moved from the side table onto the tray. Slowly and meticulously, Phuong took a ball of opium the size of a pea and placed it on the end of a long metal needle to hold over the lamp's flame. The lamp was an ancient artefact, beautiful to look at, with a metal base decorated in spectacular cloisonné and a shaped glass bowl above it designed precisely for this purpose. Phuong was careful not to heat the opium too much, wanting only to sublime the alkaloids out rather than burn them altogether, which would substantially reduce the desired effect. When the substance had turned a golden colour and was beginning to soften, she used the needle to transfer it to a small bowl attached to the end of the ivory opium pipe, which was old, long and slender. She passed the apparatus to Ned and indicated he should keep the bowl close to the flame. Ned put the pipe to his lips and inhaled deeply, immediately feeling the relaxing effects coursing through his body.

Ned inhaled a second time before handing the pipe back to Phuong, who took it and re-started the process with another pill of opium. Ned watched her work in a state of blissful happiness. He couldn't believe there was anywhere better in the world right now than lying on his side before this beautiful lady. And she was beautiful. In Ned's mind, she was becoming more beautiful by the moment. And so very exotic. He peered at her carefully from under his drooping eyelids: her delicate little hands working with expertise, shaping the opium and placing it on the needle. He looked past her hands and up her willowy arms to her lithe and finely shaped neck, then back to her delicate breasts hidden behind the tight silk of the *áo dài*, before allowing his eyes to wander further down her body, which disappeared into the darkness.

Phuong handed him back the pipe and Ned breathed in deeply once more, instantly feeling the euphoria from the endorphins released into his body. The world was so beautiful, he thought. Why did people have to fight? Everyone should try smoking opium, then surely world peace would prevail. He was nodding in and out of consciousness, dreaming of his war-less utopia, when he felt Phuong climb onto the mattress behind him to gently caress his semi-naked body; long, gentle strokes starting at his neck and gliding down the sides of his abdomen as far as her arms would go, before retuning up his back. Ned tried to concentrate but was overwhelmed by warmth and joy, and as the effects of the opium grew deeper, he felt his conscious mind begin to fade, and a darkness overcame him. He passed out with Phuong beside him, enveloped in the hazy dream of his ideal, quixotic world.

The rumbling came from nowhere, quiet at first, but then more apparent. He could hear it out there in the darkness. What was it? An earthquake? No, it was a different type of rumbling, more man-made. An engine, perhaps. Yes, that was it. It was the sound of an engine. The sound of many engines, in fact; big, heavy ones. He searched for clarity, but there was only darkness. Alongside the rumbling, now growing louder, he saw lights, many lights. Headlights. And finally, out of the darkness images formed. Visions of hundreds of trucks with their headlights on full beam flooded his mind.

He awoke with a jolt and sat upright, his senses cloudy and muddled, wondering with unease what had woken him. Phuong was gone and the cotton sheet had been unfurled and placed over him, more for modesty than warmth, for the nights were still uncomfortably hot. He couldn't see much in the gloom, but this only heightened his other senses. And then he heard the noise again: the hum of heavy diesel engines. He focused on the sound and guessed it was coming from near the quay. The more he listened, the stranger he considered the situation. Trucks driving in the middle of the night were rare in Saigon, and yet he could hear many. This sounded like a convoy. And that suggested military.

With his senses now sharp, focused from a burst of adrenalin careering around his body, Ned scrambled off the rattan bed. As his vision grew accustomed to the low light, he found his clothes and was down and out of Madame Mai's within ninety seconds. He followed the sound down toward the Saigon River. Approaching the quay, he could tell the trucks were over to his right. That must mean they were on Ham Nghi Avenue heading north toward the roundabout at the bottom of Le Loi. With sudden lucidity, Ned understood the who, the what and the why of the situation. Less than a mile away in the direction the trucks were driving was Xa Loi Pagoda.

With a sickening feeling in his stomach, Ned ran furiously up Tu Do Street toward the impressive Notre Dame Cathedral on the southern side of Thong Nhat Boulevard. Before he reached the cathedral, he turned left and headed for Rue Pasteur, hoping to find a cyclo or a motorbike taxi. All day long they approached him, he thought as he ran. All bloody day they wanted his business, and now he actually wanted one – nothing, not one.

Once he'd made it to the office, he grabbed his Nikon off his desk, packed his photographer's jacket with 35 mm film and checked his Leica was still in the chest pocket. BPA had agreed to buy him a new one while he'd been in America to replace the one broken by the secret police during his arrest. As he rushed out, he noticed the clock on the wall read 12.30 am. Mercifully, he saw a familiar blue and yellow taxi passing the office as he came out. Flagging it down, he asked for Xa Loi Pagoda and, flourishing a five-dong note, urged the driver to go as fast as possible. His mind flicked back to the little club he'd just come from and he wondered if the fog had truly cleared yet.

In Saigon's congested streets during the day, the journey from the BPA offices to Xa Loi Pagoda would have taken nearly twenty minutes. But at this time of night, and with the small inducement, the taxi driver was able to reach the pagoda in just four and a half. Knowing the trucks would be approaching Xa Loi from the west, Ned asked his driver to use the smaller streets so they could arrive from the east.

As they came to Ba Huyen Thanh Quan Street, the taxi slowed. Ned could see soldiers erecting a roadblock across the street, behind which were several military trucks disgorging troops out the back. He asked the taxi driver to stop just past the roadblock and, throwing him the five-dong note, exited the car. As he slammed the door behind him, he could hear from within the pagoda the big gong reverberating loudly alongside a higher-pitched clanging – the monks were striking their metal pans as an alarm call.

An explosion on Ba Huyen Thanh Quan Street sent another shot of adrenalin coursing through him. It wasn't a huge blast, but large enough to shatter glass; he heard the distinctive sound of shards tinkling almost musically to the ground. Having already checked both his cameras were ready, he raced to the roadblock and started taking photographs.

He wasn't the first there. Even at this time of night, some local people had arrived, disturbed by the noise of engines and inquisitive to know what was happening. Ned searched for the best shot. He could see many trucks had already arrived, with soldiers rushing through the main gates into the pagoda compound. He counted fifteen two-and-a-half-ton trucks with dark green canvas canopies at the back, each carrying the distinctive ARVN logo on the doors. There was even a tracked armoured personnel carrier – or 'green dragon' as the South Vietnamese soldiers nicknamed them – parked outside the main entrance, two helmeted heads poking through the front roof hatches.

Ned had spoken at length with Ba and Dai about the possibility of the pagoda being raided. Dai had insisted it was imminent, but Ba couldn't see it happening. It would be foolish for the army to raid them, Ba had argued; why would they risk demoralising their own Buddhist troops by attacking Buddhist pagodas and monks. Dai had remained convinced the raids would come, and it would only help their cause further when they did. But had they been expecting machine guns and grenades, Ned wondered, instantly worried for the safety of his friends.

He was hardly stuck for choice as to what to photograph. Several more explosions had occurred since he'd arrived at the barrier. He could see a fire had started beside the main entrance building, illuminating the soldiers, and the noise of shooting was no longer sporadic but continuous. Ned clicked furiously, moving the film winder with professional speed onto the next frame. When the film couldn't advance anymore, he manually re-wound it back into its casing, removed it from the camera, carefully placed it in a canister and sealed it with a lid, before safely secreting it in his jacket. Since arriving in Saigon, he'd learnt that when changing a film at speed, his eyes should concentrate on what he was doing and not on what he was photographing. Misplacing and losing a completed film because you weren't watching what you were doing was a professional no-no.

From his position at the barrier, Ned could see most of the activity was taking place within the compound out of view. He reminded himself what Mel had taught him on the way back from the Mekong Delta: *You've got to be quicker if you want the good shots, and you've got to be in there among the action.* He knew he had to get inside. He looked up and identified another roadblock at the top end of Ba Huyen Thanh Quan Street, concluding it would be impossible to gain access to the pagoda through the main entrance. He was considering his options when suddenly he saw David Halberstam running up to the barrier. That confirmed it: other journalists were now arriving on the scene. But he wanted this to be his scoop. He had to get in and he knew just how.

Ned ran down the street and turned right at the end of the block, right again, and finally a third time into the little alley known as Quan Pho Street. He was relieved to find no soldiers down this dark passageway; it was deserted, as it always seemed to be. Another grenade exploded from within the pagoda grounds and Ned felt the shockwave, even protected by the eight-foot compound wall. He found the surreptitious door reserved for apprentice monks into the pagoda building, which thankfully was open. He quickly entered and shut the door again gently behind him. The corridor beyond was pitch black. He felt his way forward as swiftly as he dared to the end of the passage, which he knew led to the hallway at the end of the row of offices. His heart was beating faster than he'd ever felt before; it sounded like he'd brought along an out-of-control metronome. He wondered if the opium was still having an effect and took a deep breath to steady his racing nerves before opening the hallway door just a fraction.

The chaotic noise of the raid assaulted his ears at once: soldiers shouting, monks screaming, rifles firing, stun grenades exploding. Ned peered through the gap and saw a monk lying on the floor motionless. He raised his camera to capture the image, but before he could, a soldier strode over to the double doors from the outside courtyard, forcing Ned to lower his camera. The soldier tried the handle to find it locked, so took a step back. With a powerful kick from the flat of his army-issue boots, he smashed the door in; the noise of the wood splintering as the locks gave way crashed through the hall. Ned waited until the soldier had disappeared down the office corridor before opening the door a bit wider to get a better view around him.

There were soldiers ransacking the offices. One was busy throwing the black paint used for banners across the room and writing his own messages on the walls; another was smashing furniture with the butt of his rifle. Ned took out his small Leica and pushed it through the gap, aiming it in their direction and shooting blind. He pulled it back out of view when he saw a screaming monk being led outside by four soldiers. Each soldier held a limb, but with the monk wriggling so much to escape their clutches, the men at the back kept dropping his legs, causing him to be half-dragged. Eventually, one of the soldiers let go and smashed his rifle butt into the monk's stomach, leading the latter to cry out in pain. The other soldiers laughed and continued to haul him outside to the waiting trucks.

Ned looked through the broken double doors and saw the bell tower standing defiantly across the courtyard. He realised it could provide the ideal hiding place from which to witness what was happening at the front entrance. He checked down the office corridor and found the ransacking soldiers had moved on. He sneaked through the door, shutting it behind him, and tiptoed over to the double entranceway. He peered around the corners to see many soldiers outside, but none were looking in his direction, so he ran stealth-like to the tower, using whatever cover he could find.

The tower door had been smashed in and was hanging lopsidedly off its top hinge. He crept through and listened for any noise indicating soldiers higher up. Satisfied it was empty, he ran up the steps to his fifth-floor vantage point where he'd stood to photograph the protesting monks just three days earlier. He didn't open the shutter this time, preferring to remain hidden behind. Putting the camera lens to the largest opening in the latticework gave him enough room to shoot through without obstruction.

A building just inside the main gates was ablaze, lighting the whole scene, and the sight below was shocking. Soldiers were dragging monks out to the main entrance, where they tied their hands behind their backs before throwing them roughly into the back of the trucks. Ned watched as a monk ran out a side entrance from the great hall followed by a soldier, who lazily gave up the chase and chose instead to lift his rifle and shoot the runner in the back of the head. Ned could only stare in bewildered astonishment as the monk's head exploded before his eyes, blood, brains and bone blasted forward. He fell, dead before he even hit the ground. The soldier casually turned around and re-entered the building.

Ned was confounded by this act of brutality; this was the first time he'd witnessed such barbarism from one human being to another.

Just off the courtyard, he noticed a collection of soldiers kicking at a storeroom door. Each individual took it in turn to kick but the door held fast. After several attempts, one of the soldiers urged his comrades back and removed a pin from a hand grenade, which he placed at the threshold before darting around the side of the concrete storeroom to avoid any shrapnel from the explosion. Ned felt the shockwaves from the fifth floor of the bell tower, but as the smoke cleared, he could see the door had only been badly damaged, not destroyed altogether. The facia had blown away and the frame was in tatters, but it was enough to show Ned what the soldiers had been searching for.

Huddled together inside the storeroom, some monks were sheltering from the assault. Although the front of the storeroom was damaged, it still offered the monks a barrier of protection. An officer shouted an order and one of his men dashed forward, although he looked to Ned more like a fireman than a soldier: a large tank strapped to his back and holding a long tube attached by a pipe to the tank. Ned wasn't sure what he was looking at but felt ice crawl up his spine. He readied his finger on the shutter button. The soldier stood about twenty feet back from the front of the building and, pointing the tube at the damaged door, fired a single burst of flame. Burning fuel shot from the end and splashed all over the front of the storeroom, sending waves of fire arcing into the night sky.

What little remained of the door proved no barrier to the flamethrower and the interior of the room flared brightly with orange light. Fiery shapes could be seen dancing theatrically inside, a display that clearly amused the onlooking soldiers as they laughed with maniacal glee. Several of the figures managed to burst out and into the courtyard, but their movements eventually slowed, finally stopping altogether as their bodies were consumed. Ned was horrified to see through his lens that the bodies didn't belong to monks, but were in fact all female; it had been a group of nuns hiding in the storeroom. Despite his revulsion, he was still able to capture the scene on film.

Ned couldn't understand why soldiers of the ARVN would be this hostile and aggressive to the Buddhists of Xa Loi; they were after all the same people, in some cases members of the same families. It was rumoured many of the protesters joining the monks each Sunday morning were off-duty soldiers, so why would they act in this way now? Even under orders, Ned imagined the troops would be more caring to their spiritual leaders and fellow brethren.

The trucks were rapidly filling up now. As each reached capacity, it was driven away into the night. Ned estimated at least four hundred monks must have been carted away already and wondered if one of those included Ba and Dai. The more acts of callousness he witnessed, the greater his concern for his friends grew, and he prayed they would somehow escape this maelstrom.

He watched as another monk was dragged kicking and screaming to a waiting truck parked by the side of the armoured personnel carrier and bundled in. His eye was caught by the two people standing up through the roof hatches of the APC; one of them was clapping their hands jubilantly as if watching their favourite team win a cup game. His 400 ASA film helped him photograph at night and the light from the fire was strong enough for him to shoot with his telephoto lens. He trained it on the APC and saw that the enthusiastically clapping occupant was a woman – none other, in fact, than Madame Nhu. Ned trained the camera across to the other observer to find himself looking at Nhu himself.

How interesting, he thought. Nhu and his wife had come to watch the army raid the pagoda. This was a surprise. As far as Ned understood, Nhu didn't get involved in military matters. He fired off some more shots of these VIP observers before swapping cameras and taking a couple more on his new Leica M3, which he knew had a larger aperture and could let in more light.

Ned moved to a different window on his floor of the bell tower to give himself better views over the back of the compound. He could see a number of soldiers just below standing around watching the monks being forced onto the trucks at the main gate. At the end of the compound, behind the soldiers' backs, three monks appeared unexpectedly from a side door in the main building. Having checked no one was watching, they rushed to the eight-foot-high back wall. Ned focused in with his telephoto lens and his heart leapt as he recognised two of them. It was Ba and Dai.

The suspense of watching his friends make their escape caused Ned to start sweating and his breathing became heavier. Dai had bent his legs and put his hands together, forming an open stirrup, into which the third monk put his bare foot to use as a platform to launch himself on top of the compound wall. With help from below, he was able to pull himself up and lie along the top edge. Ned watched in a state of nervous tension, urging the three on and hoping they wouldn't be foiled by a soldier turning and exposing their bid for freedom.

Ba was next. He too was able to launch himself off Dai's cupped hands, and with the help of the other monk still lying on top of the wall, successfully reached the top. He then manoeuvred himself to face his comrade in such a way that both were able to lean down and offer their outstretched hands to Dai. Dai took a couple of steps back and then ran, putting his foot forward onto the face of the wall and thrusting himself upwards. He caught the third monk's proffered hand but missed Ba's, so was forced to hang lopsidedly, eventually losing his grip and dropping back to the ground.

Below him, Ned heard the huddle of soldiers burst into laughter. He'd forgotten about them in all the tension, but found them still watching the trucks at the front entrance. He released his breath, unaware he'd even been holding it, and looked back to the end of the compound as Dai went in for another try. Ba was urging him on silently with frantic hand movements. Dai walked back in a crouched position as far as he dared go without disturbing the soldiers, made one final check behind, and launched himself at the wall once more, leaping into the air to reach the outstretched hands.

This time, he made contact with both. From above, Ned saw a single soldier turn to look behind and prayed he wouldn't see what was happening. But when the soldier shouted a warning to his colleagues, Ned knew his friends were in trouble. Time seemed to slip into slow motion. He watched on in horror as Dai desperately scrambled to find grip on the wall with his bare feet while Ba and the other monk tried to haul him up with all their strength. Dai had got his arms over the top, Ba heaving his brother's body, when the first shots rang out. The bullets, fired from an automatic rifle, exploded in a horizontal line, chipping a dash of plaster off the rendered wall and cutting across Dai's calf muscles. Ned could see him flinch and cry out in agony, but he was too far away to hear it.

Even in the horror of the moment, Ned knew he should be capturing the scene on film. But these were his friends; he couldn't move, he was rooted to the spot. He couldn't even lift the camera to his eye. The awfulness of the situation was too much to bear.

Before Dai could regain any composure, the next burst of gunfire tore into his back, lifting his robes and flinging his body hard into the wall. He lost his grip on his brother and comrade and, to Ned's slow-motion state of mind, fell serenely to the ground, where he lay without movement. A third burst of fire exploded all around his head and Ned knew he must surely be dead.

He stared at his friend's body lying crumpled at the base of the wall and felt a wave of anger building up inside him. How dare they, how fucking dare they! In that moment, he felt a visceral hatred for the soldiers who'd shot Dai. He hadn't done them any harm, hadn't threatened them in any way. All he'd been doing was fleeing their murderous barbarity and they'd casually shot him dead like an animal. Ned had never felt such anger before – real anger, raw anger, the type that made you act uncompromisingly. He was sure the sadness would come later, but right now all he felt was rage.

Yet, from somewhere inside, he knew he couldn't let the fury become uncontrolled. He had to curb the red mist; he was in too dangerous a place to go off on some hysterical rampage of vengeance. Bringing his rage under control, Ned plotted his next move, knowing he could exact far more revenge through his photographs of those who'd ordered this raid than against any single soldier.

In his distraction, he hadn't seen what had happened to Ba and the other monk, but when he looked up from Dai's limp body, they were already gone. He knew the headquarters of USAid were on the other side of the wall, so prayed they'd survived and would find refuge and protection with the Americans.

Ned descended to the ground floor of the bell tower and peered around the corner. Many of the troops were gathered by the main gates and he could see through the darkness the way back to the smashed double doors was clear. Keeping an eye out for any stray soldiers, he ran across bent over double and through the doors into the hallway. Hearing crashing noises from above, he took the door on his right, knowing it led to the little staircase up to the great hall on the first floor. He crept upstairs, unsure as to what he'd find in there.

He quietly opened the door at the top and checked the six-foot screens were still in place. Two had been knocked over but the others remained standing. He could hear voices; one seemed familiar, but it was difficult to tell as they were talking in Vietnamese. Ned crept through the gap in the door, closing it silently behind him, and sneaked into position behind a screen. By lying flat on his stomach and pushing his head slowly around the partition, he tried to be as unobtrusive as possible while still being able to see what was happening at the altar.

The light levels in the room were low, with only two hanging lanterns in the large hall lit. The area around the altar was a wreck, the soldiers evidently having tried their best to destroy it: the ceramic vases were broken, the flowers scattered, the candlesticks looted, and the fruit pelted at the giant Buddha.

Ned could also see many of the colourful Buddhist flags had been ripped down and even the coloured glass in the windows smashed. Once more, he wondered why the average soldier would willingly destroy Buddhist artefacts when they themselves were of that faith.

The answer came to Ned as one of the disembodied voices walked into view.

Colonel Tung, his former interrogator, was making his way toward the altar, using his swagger stick to swipe at the flowers strewn across the floor and talking fast to an unknown person just out of sight. Ned blanched for a second at seeing his one-time captor, but his resolve instantly strengthened as the image of Dai's broken body crumpled at the bottom of the wall flashed through his mind. This was who he needed to get revenge against, this was the man with the monks' blood on his hands. Tung and Nhu, both as evil as each other.

In that moment, Ned realised the relevance of both men being present. Dai had once mentioned members of the secret police were mostly Catholic, not Buddhist. This wasn't an army raid; the men outside weren't soldiers – they were members of the Mat Vu dressed up as ARVN troops. And that was why they weren't showing any compassion.

But why disguise their involvement? Ned considered this new information as Tung wandered back out of view. Another man was talking now, and Ned felt he recognised the lilt of this voice too, but frustratingly couldn't see whom it belonged to. After listening a little more, he now wondered if there weren't in fact three distinct voices. A heated discussion was taking place; he knew that much, especially when he heard a familiar 'thwacking' noise, which told him someone had just been on the receiving end of that bastard Tung's stick. After one particularly loud *thwack*, Ned saw a pair of glasses come sliding across the floor. Moments later, a hand appeared, fumbling to pick them up. But Ned still couldn't catch a glimpse of their owner.

Tung reappeared by the altar. Ned was still mulling over whether this really could be a Mat Vu operation when he heard new footsteps walking across the hall. A man wearing an ARVN uniform marched into his line of sight, except Ned recognised him as the interrogator from the second time he'd been arrested. Ned knew damned well this guy was secret police and not regular army.

The man stopped a few yards short of Tung, saluted, and proceeded to speak. Knowing he needed to capture this on film, Ned was thankful he'd brought his Leica with him as it had the quietest shutter of any camera, almost silent. Choosing the largest aperture to allow as much light through the shutter in the shortest possible time, Ned framed both men in the shot and waited until Tung's booming voice was midway through a sentence before taking the picture.

The conversation ended, and the soldier saluted and retreated back through the hall. Ned remained motionless during the agonizing silence that followed, before the discussion between Tung and the other voice resumed. Ned felt sure there was a third person still in the room, but he didn't dare put his head further around the screen for fear of exposing himself. His patience was rewarded, however, when the remaining players entered the frame before him, and his assumption proved correct.

The first was Thich Tinh Khiet, the elderly Buddhist leader, leaning heavily on his walking stick, broken glasses sitting askew across the bridge of his nose with one of the arms snapped off.

But it was the other person that surprised Ned the most: appearing beside Colonel Tung, holding the glass chalice with the heart of Thich Quang Duc in his hands, was Pham.

* * *

As Pham studied the wrecked altar of the great hall, he smiled and thought back to the beginning of the evening. Driving through the dark and silent streets of Saigon had left him feeling excited and, truth be told, a little nervous. Squashed into the back of an American Willys jeep, he'd been instructed by Colonel Tung to travel with him to Xa Loi. It had felt like the high point of his career so far. He hoped by the time the sun rose in the morning, he'd have proven his worth to his boss, and promotion would surely follow.

Tung's chauffeur tasked with driving the old Second World War jeep ensured the colonel arrived at the crossroads with Ba Huyen Thanh Quan Street at exactly 12.25 am. He parked the vehicle just off the road in an unlit area to maintain their anonymity. Tung cleared his throat and hawked its contents out the side of the jeep before half-turning to Pham.

"You'll follow me tonight. I need you to identify every monk that's been instrumental in leading this revolution. I'm not interested in the foot soldiers. I want the ringleaders."

"Yes, *ngài*, I'll be able to identify them all."

Tung didn't answer, so they sat in silence, until Pham heard the heavy diesel engines labouring up Le Van Duyet Street, distant at first but growing louder as they came. All three looked down the street to see the lead vehicle's headlights appear from around the bend, closely followed by a second, and then a third. The deep growl of the 7.8 litre engines could be felt through Pham's seat as they accelerated past the jeep. He watched the convoy pass, the hairs on his neck sticking up in the excitement of the moment.

It took over five minutes before the final truck had rolled past. Tung instructed his driver to pull in behind it and follow the convoy to the pagoda entrance. The street had erupted with activity. At both ends, Pham could see barriers being erected and soldiers standing guard to prevent any unwanted attention. News of the raid would spread like wildfire through Saigon and he knew it wouldn't take long for every Western journalist and photographer in the city to descend on the scene, demanding access. After all, this was the story they'd been waiting for.

Pham stood by Tung's side as the colonel shouted orders, directing his officers to break into the pagoda and round up the monks. The noise of gunfire started immediately, quickly followed by an explosion as a grenade was used to force open the main gates. As he watched, Pham saw an APC pull up behind them, but thought nothing of it and continued to survey the assault. Moments later, a growling voice issued an instruction to Tung, addressing him by name. Pham was curious as to who would dare address his commander in such a way. He turned and was shocked to discover none other than Ngo Dinh Nhu and Madame Nhu, each standing through a roof hatch wearing a standard-issue ARVN helmet. Pham recognised them instantly and felt a sense of pride in being so close to them, and on such an important night too.

Colonel Tung moved up to stand beside Pham and saluted. Nhu nodded toward the pagoda's gates and scowled.

"I hope you've got this place sealed. I want all the ringleaders. No one can escape, you hear me, Tung?"

"Yes, *ngài*. I'll make sure we detain every last one of them."

"Do you know who they all are?"

"Yes, *ngài*. This man here is one of my best undercover officers and has infiltrated the BPA news agency. In doing so, he's managed to get close to the leaders and is confident he'll be able to identify each one."

Nhu examined Pham for a moment. "You'd better be. I want everyone locked up by morning. Is that clear?"

"Yes, *ngài*," replied Pham with confidence, proud to have been addressed personally by Nhu.

"Oh, and Tung – keep your head down. I don't want anyone to recognise you from behind the barriers and let our little secret out."

"No, *ngài*," replied Tung with a salute to Nhu and another to his wife.

Pham had already turned back to face the pagoda when he heard Madame Nhu speak. "Colonel, you will make me happy tonight, won't you?"

"Happy, madame?" asked Tung in a confused voice.

"Yes – happy. I want these treacherous orange bastards to pay for the damage they've done to us."

"Yes, madame, I see your point. I'm sure you'll be delighted by the end of the night." He turned to Pham by his side. "Come, Sergeant Pham," he said, using his spy's official rank. "It's time to go in."

"No mercy, you hear?" Pham heard Madame Nhu cackle from behind as he followed the colonel across the street to the smashed main gates and entered the pagoda compound beside him. He stood watching the attack unfolding all around. Monks were being hauled out of the building and bundled into the trucks after a quick interrogation to weed out any leaders. To his right, some soldiers were trying to batter open a large door to a storage shed, but it refused to give way.

Tung shouted at the officer leading the men, "Use a grenade. And if that fails, use a flamethrower."

From a safe distance, Pham watched as the doors were finally blasted away, allowing the flamethrower access to those hiding inside. Seeing the burning bodies come rushing out, writhing in agony before stillness and death overcame them, didn't concern Pham. After all, he reminded himself, they were Buddhists – and probably communists too. Behind him from the street, he could hear the sounds of Madame Nhu clapping her hands in pleasure and laughing.

"Where's their great hall, Sergeant Pham?" the colonel asked.

"Up those stairs, *ngài*, and through those doors."

Tung marched off up the stairs and through the double doors, Pham following closely. The hall was mostly empty;

the only person present was a single monk kneeling on the ground before the altar and praying out loud. Tung walked up behind him and stopped a few paces short. The monk continued to pray, seemingly oblivious to the intruders, until Tung knocked him forward with a shove from his right boot, causing the monk to lose balance and sprawl forward onto the floor.

"Get up!" shouted Tung.

Pham watched as the familiar figure of Thich Tinh Khiet slowly stood and faced Tung with a steadfast look of disapproval and contempt across his face.

"We've been expecting you, Colonel Tung. Eagerly awaiting you, in fact."

"Shut up, old man! I'm not interested in any of your gibbering. You're now under arrest, along with any other ringleaders when we find them."

At that moment, two soldiers burst into the hall raucously, but instantly apologised when they saw their commanding officer standing at the altar.

"Don't apologise, boys. Come in and show this piece of vermin what we like to do to Buddhist altars."

Knowing what would come next, Pham walked over to the altar and picked up the glass chalice he knew contained the heart of Thich Quang Duc, before withdrawing back into the body of the hall. Colonel Tung moved forward and swung his swagger stick at a bunch of flowers housed in a ceramic vase. With his first swipe, he took the tops off the flowers; with the reverse swing, he knocked the vase onto the floor, causing it to shatter into many pieces. The two soldiers followed his lead and proceeded to destroy everything else on the altar before tearing down the Buddhist flags and smashing the coloured glass windows. Eventually, having exhausted all options in the hall, the pair left in search of further artefacts to vandalise.

"This is what we want to do to Buddhism," remarked Tung as he looked at the leader of the monks and scrunched his foot over the flowers, squashing them flat under his boots.

"Ah, Colonel Tung, you exist in a very small universe, don't you?" commented the elderly monk serenely. "The Buddhist faith has existed considerably longer than those flowers and it will survive considerably longer than you or me."

"Survive perhaps, but it won't flourish. Not once we've finished with you. Sergeant Pham, who else do we need to round up?"

"*Ngài*, now we have Thich Tinh Khiet, we still need to locate the other key leader, Thich Tri Quang. He's been in charge of planning their uprising. We also need to find Tran Dinh Ba and Tran Dinh Dai, the two brothers who serve as liaisons with the foreign press."

Tung turned to Khiet with a scowl and, pronouncing each word carefully, asked, "Where are they?"

"You're too late, Colonel Tung. They left the pagoda earlier this evening."

"You lie!" shouted Tung, swinging his swagger stick and hitting Khiet across the side of the cheek, causing his glasses to fly off onto the floor. Dazed from the force of the blow, Khiet bent to pick them up with shaking hands, realising one of the arms had broken off. He put them back on as best he could before they were removed once more from another strike of Tung's stick.

Tung sauntered imperiously toward the altar before turning sharply and shouting at Khiet, "Tell me where they are, you orange-robed traitor!"

Khiet was saved temporarily from having to answer by the arrival of one of Tung's senior officers, dressed as a soldier of the ARVN, who marched confidently down the hall toward his commanding officer in front of the altar.

"Ah, Major Khiem. Any news on the whereabouts of the ringleaders? We're specifically looking for Thich Tri Quang and two younger monks called Tran Dinh Ba and Tran Dinh Dai."

"No, *ngài*. We're interrogating each monk before they're loaded onto the trucks, but so far none of them have revealed where their leaders are. It doesn't help that they're all dressed identically. It makes it difficult to tell who the senior ones are. But every monk is being arrested, so we can work it out back at the prison compound."

"Good," replied Tung. "Come and tell me when all of them have been rounded up."

"*Ngài*," said the major as he saluted his colonel before retreating back out the hall.

Pham, still holding the glass chalice, watched as Khiet took the opportunity to limp across to the altar and survey the damage.

Colonel Tung cleared his throat again and spat the contents on the floor. "What is that, Sergeant Pham?"

"This is the charred remains of Thich Quang Duc's heart, *ngài*. It didn't burn at his cremation. The monks collected it from his ashes and brought it back here in this chalice. They see it as a religious artefact."

"Come over here and let me have a look," said Tung.

Ned held his breath in confusion and scowled at what he was seeing. What the hell was Pham doing here with Tung? The sight of his assistant and friend standing alongside the head of the secret police just didn't compute in his mind. He could see no logical reason behind what he was witnessing.

As he watched, Pham passed the glass chalice to Tung, who inspected its contents. Only when Tung smiled at Pham and addressed him in a non-aggressive manner did Ned finally begin to suspect there was another side to his friend he knew nothing about.

With the noise of a truck revving its engines outside, Ned took the opportunity to take some shots of Tung scrutinising the chalice. As soon as Tung handed the artefact back to Pham and turned to face Khiet, his tone became more menacing. He'd clearly asked Khiet a question, but the monk stood calmly watching the head of the secret police, not saying a word. Tung repeated his question, his voice growling in anger, and when Khiet refused to answer a second time, the colonel slapped him across the face with the back of his hand. Khiet recovered his composure, straightened his back as best he could and thrust his shoulders back in defiance. Pham took a step toward the high priest and began angrily shouting at Khiet himself, confirming Ned's suspicions.

Khiet remained upright and proud despite the hostility mounted against him, prompting Tung to remove his pistol from his belt and thrust it into the elderly monk's mouth. Yet Khiet refused to be cowed by this aggression and looked calmly up to the ceiling. Ned felt sure Tung was about to pull the trigger, but a sudden commotion from the far end of the hall interrupted the scene as some soldiers entered through the double doors.

Ned could hear something scraping along the floor as they moved down toward the altar. He was still holding his little Leica camera when he heard the thud of something heavy being dropped to the ground. He could still see Khiet, now standing on his own as Tung and Pham had moved out of view, though evidently not too far judging by the frenzied discussion still in earshot.

Ned was desperate to know what was happening but didn't dare expose himself any further. He lay on the floor listening to the voices, wondering what he could do. Finally, he opted to stand up for a better view and gradually moved one limb at a time in his attempt to remain silent, until he was upright. With the conversation on the other side not losing any of its intensity, he decided now was the time to edge his Leica around the side and blind shoot in the direction of the voices. Aware there weren't many frames left on his film, he hoped for the best and took just one picture.

But he could no longer contain his curiosity and felt compelled to peer around the screen. Edging his head around so his left eye could see back up the hall, he identified Colonel Tung, Pham and a further two soldiers standing in a cluster; but it was the dead body of a monk that really caught his attention. It had been dropped on the floor at their feet, the usually bright orange robes covered in dirt with large bloodstains showing through.

Ned glanced at the face on the body and instantly recognised it as Dai's. He shuddered to see it so close and his anger flared again, but his intuition flashed a warning. He looked up from Dai's body to find Pham staring directly at him.

Ned knew he was compromised and his only means of escape was back out through the secret door and down the stairs. But even though his brain was urging him to move, his body remained frozen to the spot. It was only when he heard Pham shout a warning and all eyes turned toward him that his reflexes finally kicked into action, and he made a dash for it. He yanked the door open and pulled a screen across on his way through, trying to buy more time. He heard the door slam behind him as he took the stairs four at a time in his bid for freedom. The hallway below came into view, and he knew in that moment how best to make his escape.

Pham confirmed the dead body lying at his feet was that of Tran Dinh Dai. As Tung congratulated the two men who'd found the body and brought it to the great hall, Pham happened to look up and see movement. He studied it carefully and realised it was in fact part of Ned Rivers's head, which at that moment looked up from Dai's dead body and caught his eye. Pham was momentarily shocked at how Rivers could possibly be here, but was still quick enough to let out a warning shout to the others. The conversation stopped as everyone spun around to see what he was looking at.

Pham launched himself toward the interfering photographer, aware the others were following him. He caught sight of Rivers exiting through a door, just as one of the large screens fell, slamming and wedging it closed. Pham began pulling on the screen to move it out the way, but part of it had become lodged under the door handle. When the other two soldiers arrived, all three worked to shift the obstruction under the sharp encouragement of Colonel Tung. Soon enough, the way was cleared. Tung was first through, closely followed by Pham and the two soldiers.

As they came to the bottom of the stairs, there was no sign of the fugitive. But Pham knew exactly which way Rivers had gone and shouted for the others to follow as he set off through the door leading to the back entrance. He fumbled his way down the corridor, using his hands to guide him in the pitch darkness, desperately trying to remember how far the exit onto Quan Tho Street was. He was annoyed with himself for not having guessed Rivers might use it to gain access to the pagoda compound. He'd assumed the complex had been completely sealed off and there'd be no way for any journalists to enter. He realised now he should have warned Colonel Tung to put a guard on the back entrance, but it was too late now.

Tung would surely ask him later how he'd failed to mention this other way in. In rising panic, Pham knew his only chance of escaping his boss's anger would be to find and detain the English photographer.

Ned didn't like the dark. Never had, ever since his father had once locked him in the cellar as a little boy. He couldn't remember what he'd done to deserve this, but he recalled the punishment well enough. His father had violently pushed him down the cellar steps, making him fall in a tangle to the bottom, then flicked the light off and locked the door. Ned had lain on the floor stunned for a while, until he'd heard with growing alarm the sound of something moving around in the pitch darkness. Far away at first but shuffling closer. The young Ned's mind had filled with exaggerated images of rats the size of dogs searching for young boys to eat. Too terrified to move, he'd remained frozen on the ground until he'd felt one run across the back of his hand.

That contact was the spur he'd needed. He'd leapt up and charged up the stairs in blind panic, hitting the door with his left shoulder. The lock had splintered and broken on impact, and Ned had crashed through into the hallway. Luckily, it was mum and not dad who'd come running toward the noise, otherwise he'd have been punished further for the damage. Recognising the terror on the boy's face, his mother had taken him straight upstairs and gently put him to bed.

The horror of that night was still vivid in his memory as Ned stood silently waiting for his hunters to move on. He could feel the same sense of dread rising but knew now wasn't the time to freak out and crash through locked doors. So he remained motionless and fought to control his breathing, praying they would spread out too thinly and give him an opening to escape.

Pham continued to guide the soldiers blindly down the corridor, but it was only when one had the good sense to dig out a flashlight and shine it forward that he finally saw the door. He opened it onto Quan Tho Street, but to his horror, there was no sign of the Englishman. Fear bubbled in his stomach and began creeping up through his chest. Failure was not an option with Colonel Tung.

To think, at the start of this evening, he'd hoped this would be his big break with the secret police. Where the hell was Rivers? He couldn't possibly have run all the way to the end of Quan Tho Street in the short time it had taken them to disentangle the screen upstairs.

The soldiers were searching along the alley, but it was obvious Rivers hadn't used this back way to escape and Pham called them back. Recognising the clever trick the photographer had pulled, he turned and sprinted back along the corridor and into the hallway at the bottom of the stairs to the great hall. When the two soldiers had caught up, he ordered them to search the offices where the banners had been made. He must be down here somewhere, thought Pham, looking desperately around him.

But it was Colonel Tung, without knowing where it led, who opened the door to the cleaning cupboard.

Ned was cursing himself for taking the wrong door in his haste to escape. How could he have been so stupid? Stuck in the cleaning cupboard, he could only hope Pham and his pursuers wouldn't think to look in here. But then he heard shouting in the hall, and a moment later the door was flung open, revealing the imposing figure of Colonel Tung.

For a second, Tung looked as shocked as Ned to find him concealed in a broom closet of all places. But then he quickly issued the order for the soldiers to seize him and place him under arrest.

Ned was hauled out to the front gates of the pagoda, paraded past the green dragon – to be promptly spat on by Madame Nhu – and hoisted up into a truck, before finally being driven off into the night with the remaining monks of Xa Loi Pagoda.

17

A few hours later, President Diem, dressed in his favourite white suit, stood in the outer corridor surrounding the Gia Long Palace on the first floor watching the dawn break over the tiled roof of the Hôtel de Ville. Such a majestic building, he thought. Such a pity it was used for such a dull purpose. He made a mental note to move Saigon's administrative staff elsewhere.

Diem didn't normally waste valuable time rhapsodising about the buildings around him, but this morning he'd been ejected from his office while the radio technicians set up their equipment to allow him to make an important live radio broadcast to the nation.

What would be the best words, he pondered, to explain the need for introducing martial law. He was still suspicious as to whether General Minh and General Don's request was in fact a ruse to get soldiers onto the streets of Saigon so a coup could be mounted against him; or just a sensible solution to quell the Buddhist uprising. But he concluded that General Dinh, commander of III Corps, to whom the troops in question belonged, was a good and loyal officer, and wouldn't allow his men to be used in such a dishonourable ploy. Perhaps Minh and Don really were just concerned about the state of the country after all.

Diem hadn't seen Nhu yet that day, but if the strategy they'd discussed last night had gone according to plan, then the generals would find themselves very unpopular this morning either way. The President knew an opportunity when it presented itself and this one was not to be missed. His speech to the nation would be crucial in subtly laying the blame for the raids on the Buddhists at the army's feet. Without the support of the populace, there was no way the generals would dare mount a coup. And that, Diem decided, would be a good lesson to teach them.

From behind, he heard footsteps and turned to find Nhu walking along the corridor toward him, his face lit up by the early morning sun. Diem was surprised to see a smile on his brother's face, something he rarely witnessed.

"What news from last night?" asked the President.

"A great success, not just here in Saigon, but in every city. Colonel Tung kept me informed through the night as he received updates from around the country. Madame Nhu and myself went to Xa Loi Pagoda to observe – the most fun we've had together in years. We were there until two in the morning watching the place being systematically emptied of those rebellious, orange-robed snakes. All of them were rounded up and taken away, and the building was ransacked before Tung and his men departed. We've arrested Thich Tinh Khiet and killed one of their press liaisons while he was trying to escape. The only major player we didn't find there was Thich Tri Quang, but all in all a great success, I'd say."

The President turned and looked toward the rising sun. "And what about the rest of the country?"

Nhu took a cigarette from a packet of Gauloises and, as an afterthought, offered one to his brother, which Diem declined with a gentle shake of his head. Nhu lit his own before continuing. "From the reports we've had in, the raids faced some obstacles in Hue. Tu Dam, Thich Tri Quang's home pagoda, has been flattened and the big statue of Buddha demolished. But at the Dieu De Pagoda, crowds of people came out in protest to protect it. The Mat Vu tried blocking the access bridge with barbed wire but the crowds tore it down and then started throwing rocks at the police. I just got word a moment ago to say the Mat Vu have finally sorted out the problem by driving armoured trucks at the protesters. The report said up to thirty civilians have died as a result, but at least the bridge is cleared."

"And what have you done with those arrested?"

"Here in Saigon, we've detained about a thousand monks and nuns. Most of them are being held at Chi Hoa prison. In other cities, I don't know the numbers, but I'm reliably informed we won't be having any more problems from the Buddhists for a while."

Diem looked impatiently at his watch, aware time was running out before his live broadcast. "And there's no chance people will find out it was us who ordered the crackdown and not the generals we're about to blame?"

"No. Tung was careful to ensure all his men were dressed as ARVN soldiers. Madame Nhu and I watched the Xa Loi raid from inside an APC so no one could see us. Any members of the press were successfully held outside the cordoned area, where it would have been impossible for them to see us or tell it was a secret police operation. They did find a press photographer in the pagoda, but he was arrested, and his camera confiscated. You might remember him – Ned Rivers. He was the one who took the pictures of Thich Quang Duc killing himself. We suspect he's part of the plot to overthrow you."

The President offered a grunt of recognition at the name before putting his head through the open door to his secretary's office and demanding coffee be brought out for him and Nhu. "Well, make sure none of his photographs come to light, they could be a problem. In fact, you better make sure he never sees daylight again either."

Nhu didn't answer. Instead, he watched a small gathering of protesters being ordered away from in front of the palace by guards. Eventually, he looked back to his brother. "In a few hours, after your speech, those protesters are more likely to be found outside army headquarters than here. Just make sure you lay the blame for the raids squarely with the military. Insist we only agreed to martial law to bring a peaceful end to the crisis. Tell them we wanted to protect the monks, but last night the military took advantage of the situation to crack down on the Buddhists before martial law took full effect."

Diem was about to tell his brother he knew exactly what he planned to say when he was interrupted by the radio producer, who'd appeared from the President's office.

"Excuse me, *ngài*, but we're ready for you now."

Half a day later and half a world away, the dawn chorus of birds was still singing in the trees opposite the entrance to the Royal Hawaiian Hotel in Honolulu as Henry Cabot Lodge strode down the steps, straw hat in hand, with the poise and balance of a man half his age. He searched left and then right for his chauffeur-driven car, which before long had pulled into the drive and drawn to a stop immediately in front of him. From the rear jumped a small man, Harold Thompson, dressed in a crumpled linen suit, apologising profusely for being late.

Judging by how refreshed Lodge looked, it could well have been mid-afternoon and not five-thirty in the morning. While Thompson was still rubbing his red eyes, looking like he hadn't slept, the new Ambassador to South Vietnam was freshly shaved and ready to go.

Thompson, an official in Roger Hilsman's Far Eastern Affairs office within the State Department, permanently based in Hawaii, walked around the back of the car and greeted

Lodge with a shake of his hand. "I'm sorry to force you out of bed so early, sir," he said unconvincingly, "but your plans have changed. Secretary of State Rusk has approved Roger's idea to send you across to Saigon earlier than anticipated. Your plane leaves in two hours."

"Is that right?" said Lodge impassively, leaving the hapless official clueless as to what he really thought. "We'd better get over to the airport sharpish then. Otherwise, I'll be late for my appointment with South Vietnam, won't I? You can brief me in the car."

"Yes, sir," replied Thompson as he spotted a porter pushing a trolley loaded with suitcases toward them and shouted at the driver to help load the luggage safely into the trunk.

Before the new Ambassador could climb into the car, a young Hawaiian woman sashayed up to him and placed a lei of tropical flowers over his shoulders, draping it half down his front and half down his back, and thanking him for staying at the Royal Hawaiian Hotel. Even at that hour, Lodge remained unflappable in the face of such courtesy, smiling graciously and giving her a brief hug, as was expected.

Finally settled in the leather-upholstered rear seats, the famous pink hotel disappearing into the distance behind them, Thompson turned to Lodge and handed him a piece of paper. "First of all, sir, here's a copy of the wire from Roger Hilsman at State with your instructions to proceed at speed to Saigon. As you know from our discussion last night, twenty-four hours ago soldiers of the ARVN launched a brutal attack on the main pagodas across the length and breadth of South Vietnam. Reports from the capital have been thin on the ground and the only source of information we can rely on is President Diem's radio broadcast."

The new Ambassador tapped his fingers on his knee, suggesting he wasn't convinced by the reliability of said source. "Have we heard anything from the Embassy?"

"No, sir. Their lines were cut early in the morning after the raids and we still haven't been able to reconnect with them. The press agencies appear to be in the dark too; they've had no news from their correspondents since just after the raids either."

Lodge snorted and looked out the window. "So what do we know?"

Thompson skimmed down the notebook he was holding. "We know from Trueheart that two army generals approached Diem and asked him to declare martial law at 9.00 am local time, and that the army attacked the Buddhists in their temples during the night before it was imposed. Unfortunately, sir, that's all we know."

"My my, what are these generals up to?" mused the new Ambassador. "I thought they were the ones who understood what we're trying to achieve out there. That they understood the need to keep up the pressure on the Viet Cong. But now they've decided to attack their own civilians... Something just doesn't add up. God help us if they've gone off the rails too."

With the briefing shorter than he'd hoped, Lodge spent the remainder of the journey through the streets of Honolulu lost in thought. It was only as his car approached the newly opened John Rodgers Terminal at Honolulu International Airport that Harold Thompson broke the silence.

"I'm sorry, sir. It looks like you'll be going in blind. If we receive any more information before you arrive, we'll let you know. It's a fifteen-hour journey, and Saigon is seventeen hours ahead of us here, so you'll be landing at dusk tomorrow local time. But a lot can still happen in-between."

18

General Minh effortlessly climbed the last few steps to the top floor of army command headquarters before bursting into General Don's office. "The slimy little shit! He's really dumped on us this time."

General Don, jumping at this sudden outburst, rose from behind his desk and greeted his compatriot. Don was attired in his full dress uniform, ready for the arrival ceremony for the new American Ambassador. He looked stately and impressive, observed Minh, though in his opinion, not nearly as impressive and stately as himself. 'Big Minh' stood over six feet tall, towering head and shoulders over most other Vietnamese. He knew he cut a daunting and frightening figure when he was in a bad mood, helped in part by his two broken front teeth, a result of heavy-handed Japanese interrogation techniques during their invasion of Indochina toward the end of World War Two. And today he was in a bad mood.

"How dare he blame his crackdown on us! Did you hear his radio broadcast?"

"Of course I did," replied General Don, placing his white peaked cap on his head. "And even worse, did you hear the latest *Voice of America* broadcast? It repeated the President's line it was us who ordered it and not the government. Damned Americans, they've fallen for Diem's lies as well."

Minh harrumphed audibly and sat down in a teak and rattan tub chair before picking up a copy of the *Times of Vietnam* from his colleague's desk.

"It's only just arrived," commented Don.

Minh, wearing his most formal uniform covered in streaks of gold braid with an impressive line of medals along the right side of his chest, straightened the newspaper and perused the front page. He felt his face redden in anger as he read the headline and lead article.

MILITARY CRACKDOWN ON BUDDHISTS

In the early hours of Wednesday morning, leading Buddhist temples were raided by troops of the ARVN. The crackdown on Buddhist protests had been widely expected but government ministers were shocked at the severity. Hundreds of monks have been reported killed, with many more injured. Over a thousand have been taken into custody, including 80-year-old Buddhist leader, Thich Tinh Khiet.

Military leaders had asked President Diem to impose martial law from 9.00 on Wednesday morning to combat the growing protests against the government, but, disobeying orders to protect the monks, the generals took the opportunity to launch a crushing attack on the country's leading pagodas only hours before the law was due to come into effect.

Minh threw the paper down in disgust and stared at Don with such vehemence that the latter thought he was going to explode. "How dare they!" he finally managed to splutter again.

"Come, walk with me, we'll be late for the new Ambassador's arrival," said Don. He led his colleague out the office and down the stairs, heading out onto the driveway in front of the building to search for his chauffeur. The army command head-quarters were located at the Joint General Staff offices on the edge of the sprawling Tan Son Nhut Airport complex, so the journey to the runway to meet the incoming Ambassador took only minutes.

"There was a crowd of protesters outside the gates when I arrived this morning," Don murmured inside the car. "It never ceases to amaze me how easily people can be deceived. Do they really think the army, the most pro-Buddhist institution in the country, would attack them?"

Minh, still brooding, didn't answer. He looked out the car window at the small group of dignitaries who'd gathered at the end of a long red carpet to wait for the approaching aeroplane from Honolulu to land.

"Good God," Minh exploded suddenly, not yet able to fully control his temper. "If Diem expects us to just roll over and accept these lies, he's got another thing coming!"

The two generals took their place in the line-up of dignitaries next to William Trueheart, the acting US Ambassador, just as the aeroplane landed. As it was taxiing toward the red carpet, Trueheart turned to the two generals and scowled at them.

"I want you to know I've just come from visiting the two monks who jumped over the back wall of Xa Loi Pagoda to escape your thugs. I've told the director of the USAid mission, whose compound they fell into, that they're to be treated with respect, and under no circumstances should they to be handed over to your lot or the police. It was a damned disgrace attacking the pagodas like you did."

General Minh gave General Don a quick look and rolled his eyes before turning back toward Trueheart, just as the plane engines were cut and the doors were being opened. "When the truth emerges as to what really happened, I hope one day to receive an apology from you, Mr *Acting* Ambassador. But for the moment, I'll accept your silence instead."

William Trueheart remained staring straight ahead without another word. For at that moment, Henry Cabot Lodge Jr., the new US Ambassador to the Republic of Vietnam, appeared at the top of the aeroplane steps holding an old straw hat.

Part III: Flames

AUTUMN, 1963

19

Although the bright light was shining directly in his eyes like a scene from a Second World War movie, he knew it was Colonel Tung addressing him from the other side of the desk. He remembered the deep voice from the day he'd been arrested more than a month before. That same authoritative tone he'd grown up hating, always rebelling against and running from.

But he hadn't been able to run from it *that* night. The voice had shouted with elation when it became clear who'd been caught in the cleaning cupboard and boomed with pleasure as it ordered the fugitive to be hauled out of the pagoda and thrown into the back of a troop truck. He would recognise *that* voice anywhere, even in Vietnamese.

Except today, it was speaking English, and it wasn't shouting or booming. Today, it was purring with self-satisfaction.

Ned sat silently on his hard wooden chair, trying to be as obstinate as possible, as he'd done for the past month. A month that had felt like a decade to his free-spirited character. A month of horrors beyond his imagination. A month he didn't wish to repeat.

He was still angry with himself for having chosen the wrong door on the night of his arrest. If only he'd picked right and not left, he felt sure he'd have made his escape and experienced the joy of his photographs appearing on front pages worldwide, as he knew they surely would have. Instead, in his haste, he'd found himself in the cleaning cupboard with no chance of escape.

He remembered that night all too clearly: being bundled out of the cupboard by two soldiers; seeing the strange expression on Pham's face as he was dragged through the hallway; and the memory of Dai's body lying on the floor of the great hall.

He'd spent the last thirty-five days trying to work out what Pham's expression had meant. Had it been sorrow for his betrayal or joy at Ned's arrest?

The journey in the back of the truck was just the start of the horrors he'd encountered.

He was thrown in and landed face down on top of a monk he didn't recognise. When he tried to stand, he was knocked back down again with the butt of a soldier's rifle and shouted at in Vietnamese. It didn't take a genius to understand what the soldier meant, so Ned lay down with the others, aware that even more people were being shoved in behind him. It wasn't long before he felt the truck begin to move forward, its heavy diesel engine causing the vehicle to vibrate as it accelerated away from the pagoda.

Ned remembered from somewhere – he couldn't think where – that the best time to escape was as soon as possible after capture; the chances diminishing every second after that point. He swivelled his eyes to look around without turning his head, but could only see orange-robed bodies cramped together on the floor alongside him. He caught the eye of a young monk lying just to his right, their exchanged glance silently communicating the alarm they both felt; but he couldn't see an obvious way to escape. He tilted his eyes up at the soldiers seated over them, all smiling and laughing, euphoric at their success.

He ran through what had happened and how the bloody hell he was going to get out of this, but his mind was failing to compute efficiently. He just couldn't see a solution. He felt trapped, confused and, more than anything, worried. He hadn't done anything wrong. Surely, he'd be released when the authorities realised he wasn't a monk? But then he remembered the look of celebration on Tung's face when he'd been discovered in the cupboard.

Ned turned back to the monk on his right and they locked gazes again. The young man began communicating with his eyes, flicking them upward before focusing back on Ned to ensure he'd understood, but Ned struggled to understand the message. As the truck slowed to turn at a crossroads, the monk suddenly jumped up and flung himself at a soldier standing at the back. The surprised soldier stumbled backward and tripped over the vehicle's low tailgate, sending both him and the monk falling heavily down onto the road. The monk's fall was cushioned by the soldier and he was able to quickly stand and dart across the road in his bid for freedom.

Ned, like many of the other prisoners, was now sitting upright to better see what was happening. They were all willing their comrade on in solidarity as his daring escape looked like it might succeed. But then two soldiers standing at the back of the truck lifted their rifles to their shoulders and fired a series of single shots. Ned saw the monk hurled forward by the force of the bullets and slump to the ground, where he lay perfectly still sprawled across the pavement. One of the soldiers who'd fired jumped down and walked over to the young victim. Ned couldn't see if he was still alive, but it didn't matter. The soldier lifted his rifle once more and fired point blank into the man's head. The monk closest to Ned let out a cry of anguish, and Ned noticed with surprise it was none other than Thich Tinh Khiet, the Buddhist high priest himself.

The remaining soldiers in the truck shouted at their captives to lie flat, hitting those who didn't comply with their rifles. Ned only managed the briefest of eye contact with the high priest before he lay flat again. When the shouting had died down, there was a moment's pause before he felt something heavy being thrown into the vehicle, half-landing across his right shoulder. Ned kept his eyes closed, knowing what it must be, but eventually the pressure built within his tortured mind to open them and check. So he did...and it was. The partially blown-away face was just inches from his own, the bullet having removed part of the monk's eye socket as it exited his body, leaving a gaping hole, and forcing Ned to stare in horror into the bloodied remains of the victim's brain. The other eye was still open and stared back in frozen anguish.

The journey from Xa Loi Pagoda on the night of the raids wasn't the only incident Ned wished never to relive. For him and all the monks from Xa Loi and other pagodas in Saigon, it ended at the giant Chi Hoa prison. He'd been brought here once before with Peter Arnett by the national police after their arrest outside the Chanatareansey Pagoda back in early July. On that occasion, the British Ambassador had managed to get the charges dropped, and he hoped the same might happen again. But deep down he knew this wouldn't be the case. For a start, no one knew he'd been arrested; and secondly, Ned couldn't get the image of Colonel Tung's elation at finding him in the cupboard out of his mind. This was very much personal.

Once inside the prison, Ned was thrown into a large holding hall with hundreds of monks. From what he could tell, he was the only Westerner. There was no food or water, and he realised he hadn't eaten since lunch the day before, after which he'd gone drinking with Claude, the French journalist, at the Continental Palace Hotel before moving on to Madame Mai's. At no point had they eaten anything. As far as he knew, Claude was probably still asleep at Madame Mai's, completely unaware of Ned's predicament. Bloody Claude, he thought. Bloody French.

Every few minutes, the main door would open and two prison guards would walk in, grab a monk and haul him out. Ned had long grown bored of standing and watching this process so found himself a section of wall at the back to sit down against. He felt tired and weary, most likely the result of dehydration and overheating from so many human bodies crammed in a comparatively small space. Ned looked around the room, but apart from the set of doors through which the prison guards were extracting a single monk at a time, there were no other exits or windows, so no chance of escape.

Ned estimated a third of the monks had been escorted out before the two men walked in. These weren't normal prison guards, and as he watched them scour the hall, he recognised their pointy shoes, revealing their secret police identities. They walked further into the room than any guards had done so far and continued to scan the crowd. It didn't take long for their eyes to fall on Ned, who found himself dragged to his feet and out the hall, protesting his innocence with every step. But even Ned knew his outcry lacked confidence and authority; he was just too drained by this point.

He was taken into the outer courtyard and thrown into the back of a prison van with a caged interior. There were three more Buddhist monks in here, but none could speak English and they remained silent apart from a few mutterings. The sun had already risen so the temperature inside the van was considerable, and Ned simply didn't have the energy to interact with them. He lay on the floor beyond exhausted, his head now thumping angrily from lack of water.

Another two hours passed holed up in this airless oven before, finally, the back door opened and a fourth monk was pushed in, after which the van started up and set off. One of the monks, possibly the first to have been left in the vehicle, was in bad condition. Everyone was still but this individual hadn't moved at all for some time. Ned's concern was validated when the van finally stopped and the rear doors were opened. Everyone was able to climb out except this one monk. The guards shouted at him to begin with, before prodding him with their rifles, but there was no response. Eventually, one dragged him out by the ankle, but he slithered over the edge and slumped onto the ground. Even Ned could tell he was dead. The monk was left where he lay, and the remaining four captives were led off.

As he looked around wearily, Ned recognised this court-yard and the three-storey building surrounding it, realising with a start he'd been to this prison too. It had been after his first arrest with Pham on the day of Thich Quang Duc's funeral. This confirmed his worst fears – he was now being held by the secret police.

Over a month had passed since the night of the raids, and every day he'd been marched to this interrogation room and grilled by faceless voices hiding behind blaring lights. In the first few days of his incarceration, he'd barely understood the shouting voices demanding answers about the Buddhists. Although he'd been dragged there physically, mentally he wasn't present at all.

This cluelessness was the result of fever bought on by his maltreatment on the day of his capture. Upon arrival at the Mat Vu gaol, he'd been hauled to a large cell containing nearly thirty monks, where he'd immediately collapsed to the floor. It was only through the kindness and camaraderie of his cellmates that he recovered. They ensured he ate enough food and drank enough water from the limited amounts supplied and mopped his brow with a damp rag when he was in fever. Without their compassion and care, Ned knew he wouldn't have survived. The monks recounted later how badly dehydrated he'd been, and they'd feared his would be another name to add to the growing list of the dead from the raids.

A week into his ordeal, the fever began to subside and his senses returned. For the first time, Ned was able to comprehend what was happening around him, more aware now of his situation. The interrogations had continued, and the voice behind the bright light remained angry and demanding, persistently questioning Ned about his knowledge of the monks' activities. But with his energy returning, Ned was able to protest his innocence and even demand his release, which of course was ignored.

Ned wasn't the only one being interrogated. Each of the monks was taken at some point in the day, and they didn't always return. The number of people in the holding cell dropped from one week to the next. Nobody knew what happened to them, but each member of their group felt the loss when one of their own failed to return.

Although few of his cellmates could speak English, Ned was able to befriend one monk called Giang. Not only did *giang* mean 'river' in Vietnamese and so they shared the same name, but he could also speak enough English to converse with Ned. The hope among the monks was that, with so many arrested in the early hours of 21st August, it was taking the authorities this long to fully establish everyone's innocence, and they were being released one by one. But a few older voices had darker suggestions as to why their cellmates were not returning.

For long hours, Ned and the monks tried to piece together from their different perspectives all that had happened on that fateful night. It was Ned who broke the news about Dai's death. No one knew what had happened to Thich Tinh Khiet, or to Thich Tri Quang, the architect of the rebellion.

Ned confirmed Khiet had been arrested and taken to Chi Hoa prison along with him, while some of the monks were sure Quang had left Xa Loi Pagoda several hours before the raid. Nobody knew where either was now, however.

In the dark hours when Ned lay awake pondering his fate, his mind kept returning to the image of Dai being shot from the wall, or of his body crumpled on the floor of the great hall, and his anger would return. He held Colonel Tung personally responsible for Dai's death. As for Pham, he still couldn't fully grasp his involvement, but thinking about his former friend only served to increase his rage.

But it wasn't only the injustice of the raids that made Ned furious; he felt his professional standing had been damaged too. He was the only photographer to have made it into Xa Loi that night, and he knew in his heart his pictures would have made the front pages. What a wasted opportunity to advance his career, he scolded himself. Instead of being celebrated, he'd been incarcerated and forgotten about.

Would anyone on the outside come for him? Surely, they had to know he was here. Where was the British Ambassador demanding his release?

But then he remembered they probably had no idea where he was.

And to cap it all, he'd lost his cameras, almost as precious to Ned as water to life.

Over the last five weeks, Ned and the monks had developed a strategy of remaining silent during the interrogation sessions as there appeared to be no consequences for doing so. Today, however, was different.

Up until now, the voice questioning him from behind the light had never sounded familiar. Today, for the first time, he recognised it and knew Colonel Tung had finally come. It was the soft, calm tone that perturbed Ned, so different from the aggressive shouting that had come before. Only in the confidence of victory could a voice be this self-assured; the voice of someone who knew they'd won.

"I salute you, Mr Rivers. I think you're a very good photographer."

Ned didn't respond, determined to stick to his approach. Yet Colonel Tung's triumphant tone was testing his strategy of silence, drawing him into the conversation.

"If you were Vietnamese, you'd be exactly the kind of person I'd want in my special forces," purred the colonel.

Ned straightened and stretched his legs under the table in front of him, beginning to feel truly uncomfortable.

"Innovative, daring and dedicated. You know, you were the only photographer to get into Xa Loi Pagoda on the night of the raid?"

Ned could picture the man sitting there behind the light, his thin moustache perfectly tailored, staring at him with beady eyes like a snake before the attack. Although glad not to be on the end of more barked insults and accusations, this gentle approach was making him equally nervous.

"I think you're the only journalist who knows it was the Mat Vu who raided the pagodas. While the rest of the world still believes it was the ARVN and their stupid generals."

Ned kept his eyes closed against the bright light shining directly at him and reminded himself to keep silent.

"And now the generals are in disgrace, the Americans are confused, and the Buddhists are defeated, all because of me. I like that. I find it very amusing," Tung said. "Since you already know my little secret, we can turn this light off now, wouldn't you agree? Yes... I find it highly amusing the generals are taking all the credit for my success."

As Ned's eyes readjusted to the gloom, the glare of the light now gone, the image of Colonel Tung's face sharpened before him and he felt his rage return, his control beginning to slip away.

"I suppose you find it amusing that so many monks have died too," he fired, his temper finally snapping.

"You think I care about the monks? They're nothing but a plague of locusts that needs to be destroyed," countered the colonel with venom.

Ned bristled at the insult to his friends and his face reddened at the memory of Dai. But getting angry with Colonel Tung was unlikely to help him. He dreamt of revenge but now was not the time. It would have to wait until he was holding the ace card, though he wondered if that moment would ever come.

Tung opened a file on the table between them, revealing a pile of black and white photographs. Ned watched suspiciously as these were laid out before him. He didn't need to be told what they were of or who had taken them; he identified them instantly as his own pictures from the night of the raid.

"They're good, these photographs, wouldn't you agree, Mr Rivers? I assume you recognise them. It's difficult to hide a camera in a cleaning cupboard, isn't it? I'm afraid it didn't take us very long to find it...or your film. But really, a mop bucket – was that the best you could do?"

"It was pitch black, it was a cleaning cupboard, what else was I meant to do with it!"

"I thought this one was particularly good," said Tung, pointing to a picture of five figures, each engulfed in flames, running from the blasted storage shed. "I never knew nuns burnt so quickly. And this one of Madame Nhu clapping her hands. You caught her well, she'd like that. I think I'll keep it for her as a memento of the occasion."

"And why don't you give her this one too?" spat Ned, pointing at a photograph of a monk falling to the ground, taken at the exact moment his brains had been blown out, behind him a 'soldier' with the rifle still to his shoulder. "She'd like that one, wouldn't she? She could show it to her children and cackle like the devil woman she is."

"Be careful what you say, Mr Rivers. That kind of talk could get you in a lot of trouble," Tung said with steel menace. He picked up the remaining photographs and looked through them, making appreciative gestures every few seconds. "But I do like this one of me inside the great hall. You know, you really are very good. This one might have even made it onto the front pages. It's lucky no one else took any pictures like these, otherwise our little secret might not have been so secret."

Laughing contentedly, Tung picked up the photographs and put all but one in a metal bin he'd retrieved from near the door. He took out a box of matches, struck one theatrically and lit the corner of the picture he still had in his hand. Both men watched the flame grow and the photograph curl in the heat before the colonel dropped it into the bin with the others.

"There goes the only evidence. Except for you, of course. But for you, I have a choice. You can live or you can die."

Ned met Tung's gaze as the colonel examined him, but eventually turned away under the fierce scrutiny. No longer blinded by the light, he could see the room they were in lacked any features besides the door, the simple wooden table and chairs they were sitting at, and the bin of burning photographs. He turned back to the man opposite, who was still watching him with a sardonic grin.

"You think you're so clever, you journalists. But none of you picked up that Pham was one of mine. He reported back everything of any importance. Every discussion you had with the monks, the location of each demonstration and the names of the leaders. He did it right under your nose, but you didn't spot a thing. Maybe if you'd even bothered to learn our language, you might have had better luck. But sadly, Pham's identity is blown now, so we need someone new to spy on the foreign media and their informers. Someone in a position to hear the latest gossip, someone with access to the American Embassy, someone trusted by his companions. And, most importantly, someone happy to report back to us. Do you know anyone, Mr Rivers, who might fit that description?"

"Are you trying to recruit me?" asked Ned, sitting forward and looking incredulously at Tung. "Do you really think I'd want to spy on my colleagues for a bastard like you?"

"Well, that's your choice. But it's the choice you need to make if you want to live."

"And if I don't?"

"Then you die."

Ned considered the proposition a moment. He wondered how he'd managed to get himself into a 'tails you win, heads I lose' situation?

"What's to stop me agreeing and then revealing it was you who ordered the monks to be arrested and killed?"

"*Where's your evidence?* they'll say. *You're a photographer, where is your photographic proof?* they'll ask. And then I'd have you killed for breaching our little agreement anyway."

Ned could see his options running out very quickly. He watched the flames rising out of the bin of burning photographs for a moment, desperately seeking a solution to his predicament. But then Tung hammered the final nail into his coffin.

"Do you really think I'd trust you to spy for me? I wouldn't trust you to wipe my ass! No, the time has come for you to disappear for good, Mr Ned Rivers."

The colonel spent several seconds delighting in the look of shock on Ned's face before he stood and shouted through the door in Vietnamese. The door opened and a guard dressed in military fatigues marched in with shoulders back and eyes forward.

"Take him out to the courtyard and kill him like the others," demanded Tung, in English for Ned's benefit. Then he picked up the empty folder and strode out past the guard without another word.

Ned fully expected to be frogmarched down and out to the courtyard, but instead the guard left the cell and locked the door again behind him. Ned sat back down with his mouth hanging open and a sheen of sweat breaking out on his face. Was this it? Was this how he died? An image of his mother appeared in his mind, followed by Mel, and a sense of panic started to overtake his thought process.

The fear had almost disabled him when the door opened minutes later and two different guards appeared. The first looked slightly mad. When he grinned inanely, Ned could see he was missing most of his teeth, with only a single front one remaining in his swollen gums. He was much larger than the average Vietnamese soldier and Ned guessed he was the muscle in this pairing. The second guard was obviously the brains, and Ned shivered involuntarily at the look in his eyes – as evil a person who'd ever trod the earth. The man stared at Ned like a weasel might at its captured prey. The larger guard – the oaf, as Ned thought of him – motioned for him to leave the cell. As Ned obeyed, the weasel quickly stepped in behind him and thrust a rifle into his back, leaving the oaf to lock the cell door, pass in front of Ned and lead them down the corridor.

Whenever Ned had previously been escorted back to his holding cell from the interrogation room, they'd turned left, but this time he was taken right. At the end of the corridor, they came to an iron-grilled gate set in an iron fretwork surround, which the oaf opened with one of several keys attached to a large ring on his belt. He stood aside to let the prisoner and his colleague through, the latter still urging Ned on with the point of his rifle.

Ned walked through the gate, recalling the maxim about attack being the best form of defence – an attack he knew would have to come very soon if he was to survive the next hour. As the weasel navigated through the open gate, the oaf now behind them, Ned swung around and pulled the rifle.

Though taken aback by the sudden manoeuvre, the guard kept hold of his weapon. But Ned had pulled it sufficiently forward to reverse its direction and thrust the butt back into the man's stomach. With a second yank, he felt the guard's grip give and the rifle come away.

The oaf, having used up all his concentration to unlock the gate, watched helplessly, trapped behind his colleague, who was now doubled up in pain in the gateway. Ned thrust the rifle butt into the muscled guard's face and saw the last remaining tooth explode out his mouth through spurts of blood as his head jolted backward. To most, this would have been a disabling blow. But as the oaf straightened up, he fixed Ned with a malevolent grin and crashed through the opening like a raging bull elephant, flattening his companion to the floor in the process. Within two yards of Ned, he pulled back his right arm and threw it forward with a clenched fist. Fortunately, Ned saw this coming and pivoted backward on his right foot, allowing him to move his head out the way and simultaneously use the rifle to block the punch. The fist hit the gun with such force that it was knocked from his two-handed grip.

Once more, Ned was surprised at this giant's capacity to compartmentalise his pain and continue the fight. He squared up to Ned and launched another attack, though this time with his left fist – perhaps he was feeling the pain in his right hand after all. Taking advantage, Ned easily dodged the lazy thrust and, with the oaf off balance, kicked him hard between the legs. No time for fighting honourably – this was life or death. The oaf bent over double, offering Ned the chance to hit him hard in the face with his knee and send him tumbling to the floor.

Remembering the danger still posed by the other guard, Ned turned to pick up the rifle. To his dismay, the weasel had already retrieved it and was pointing it directly at him.

"Stop there! No move!"

Ned froze mid-stride and stared at the guard with alarm. The weasel, sensing victory, slowly started to smile, a grin of villainous anticipation. Just to the right of this evil smirk, a small movement caught Ned's eye. He focused in on the shiny metal of the gate and realised the flicker was the oaf's reflection, who'd stood back up and was charging at Ned from behind in pure anger. Ned dropped low, just catching the weasel's psychotic grin turn to shock as he did so. Instead of flattening Ned as intended, the oaf tripped over his crouching body and, fell forward with the momentum of the charge, slamming into his colleague and smashing his head on the iron fretwork surrounding the gate. The blow knocked him out, leaving the weasel pinned to the ground under his great weight.

Ned, spying his opportunity, sprang forward and retrieved the rifle. Without thinking of any consequences, he used the butt to launch a lightening attack on the two guards, leaving them both battered, bloodied and unconscious, possibly even dead. But he wasn't worried – it had been them or him.

He dragged them out the way of the gate, one with more difficulty than the other, and bent to retrieve the keyring attached to the oaf's belt. He nipped back through the way he'd come, locking the gate shut behind him as he went. He knew he didn't have long before his escape was detected – the noise of the fight would surely attract other guards – so he ran as fast as he could back down the corridor, until he reached a matching iron gate. Much to his amazement, he managed to unlock it using the same key and passed through.

He could have made his bid for freedom alone but knew he owed it to his former cellmates as well. How could he live with himself, knowing now what fate they all faced? He knew the way back to his cell intuitively. Once there, he rooted through his large collection of keys, trying to find one that looked the right size for the lock, but they were all too similar. Already, some monks had gathered at the other side of the door, aware something was different. They could see Ned through the small grilled opening and began encouraging him. Frustratingly, the first few keys fit but wouldn't rotate.

Just as he was giving up hope, he felt the catch give, and the door swung open under pressure from the monks' behind it. Ned urged his companions out, shouting, "Go! Go! Go!"

But no one really knew where. Further down, another corridor crossed theirs perpendicularly, creating four possible exits, and the monks ran haphazardly down all possible options. Ned chose one he hadn't been down before and rushed along the bare concrete floor until he came to another locked gate. The monks who'd run ahead of him had already turned back because of the obstacle. Ned urged them to follow, but they couldn't understand his English and disappeared the other way, leaving him alone. Just beyond the gate, he saw a set of stairs leading up, which he sensed would be problematic since he wanted to go down.

But as he was considering his choices, he heard a shout and assumed the guards had raised the alarm. He may have given his escape away by releasing all his Buddhist friends, but he also hoped, conversely, it would create more confusion, which might help. Knowing he wouldn't have time to retrace his steps, he quickly unlocked the door and hurried up the winding steps. As he climbed, he heard shouting from the floor below, forcing him to increase his pace. He felt guilty for not leading the monks to safety but reasoned that, with the guards alerted, it was every man for himself.

At the top of the steps, Ned found a flimsy-looking wooden door and searched for a suitable key. He heard footsteps coming up the stairs quickly behind him. With nowhere to hide, his only option was to kick the door open. Miraculously, on his first attempt, the locks splintered and the flimsy door flew open, leaving him blinded by the strong sunlight bursting through from outside. With the footsteps growing louder, Ned stepped through into the light and hid behind the door. He waited until he could tell his pursuer was just on the other side and then slammed the door shut with all his strength. The sound of the wood colliding with a body was all too audible. Ned opened the door to find a guard sprawled unconscious on the floor. Satisfied the man wasn't going to cause him any more problems, Ned paused to assess the situation.

He was on a flat roof. Peering over the sides, he quickly worked out it was the top of the main building, three storeys high. It made him feel giddy. Having never suffered from vertigo, he wondered if this was from being in the open, bathed in bright sunlight, or from being free for the first time in five weeks.

He was looking down into the courtyard below him where guards and secret policemen were running around like frenzied ants. Only when the first bullet zipped past his head did he realise he was being shot at. The second one cracked into the side of the building below his foot, but before he had a chance to react, a third caught him on his upper arm, spinning him around and throwing him to the ground.

He sat up, dazed and alarmed as a stab of pain crystallised his thoughts. He stared down at his right arm. It was bleeding, though not profusely, and he thanked God the aim hadn't been more accurate. With relief, he found he could lift the arm above his head and bend it at the elbow, suggesting it was nothing more than a superficial graze.

Come on, he urged himself. He had to find a way off this roof, and without going down into the courtyard, he added as a cautious afterthought. He stood and dashed across the roof, keeping low and out of sight. Looking beyond the large expanse of roof, Ned could see the busy streets of Saigon below him – tantalizingly close, but he still had to work out how to get there. He continued running across the top of the main building, away from the courtyard, and discovered the neighbouring property was connected rather than detached. Its roof was about six feet lower than the police headquarters, an easy jump.

As he peered down, he was disturbed by loud, animated shouts behind him. Turning, he saw four guards had emerged from the doorway, their leader pointing in Ned's direction. Another had already crouched into position and the unnerving sensation of bullets flying around him confirmed now was not the time to sit and ponder. Ned jumped down to the neighbouring property, taking shelter behind the wall while bullets smacked into the roof, causing chips of concrete and other materials to spin off at different angles. He looked around urgently, knowing time was running out. In the corner of the roof, diagonally across from where he now sat, he could see two poles sticking up. He wasn't sure what they were for, but he was closer to them than his pursuers. And a pole, whatever its purpose, offered a solution to his predicament.

He took a deep breath and ran for the two poles about thirty yards away. He hadn't got more than halfway before the guards spotted him and fired a volley of bullets. They exploded all around him, but none hit their mark, and he knew, with luck, he could cover the last fifteen yards before the next hail came. Without time to consider its function, he launched himself at the nearest pole, grabbing it and letting the momentum carry his body over the side of the building. Clinging on for dear life, he heard the crackle of gunfire just as he was going over the edge. With huge relief, he discovered the poles were part of some bamboo scaffolding erected against the side of the property. Although they swayed under his weight, they didn't break, having been tied to the building. When he'd steadied himself, he saw a platform just a few feet below him and dropped down onto it.

The Vietnamese workers seemed most surprised to witness a Western man jump down from the roof above and quickly dash along the platform before scampering down the makeshift ladder and disappearing to the platform on the level below. Ned guessed they would be no less shocked to see the four guards appear after him, rifles cocked and ready to fire.

Ned was halfway down the flimsy scaffolding when he heard authoritative shouting from above, and knew the guards weren't far behind. As he hurried down the final ladder, he looked around to find he'd landed in an enclosed courtyard. Although potentially problematic, he soon spotted a large, elaborate gate, which – thank God – was open. Beyond the impressive entranceway, Saigon traffic was swarming in every direction like wasps from a disturbed nest.

It then occurred to Ned the guards above him might have been shouting instructions to the building workers below, for at that moment he was approached by a man in ragged overalls and flipflops menacingly wielding a shovel, clearly intending to apprehend the Westerner. But as the labourer closed in, Ned could see the fear in his eyes at being forced into such a dangerous task. Evidently, this simple builder wanted nothing to do with a fleeing prisoner, which gave Ned confidence. He searched for a weapon, but all he found was a pail of water, which he picked up and threw at the trembling workman. The builder spun to avoid the dirty bucketload. This was all the gap Ned needed to sprint past him and on toward the open gateway.

He was through the gates and turning right when another volley of gunfire rang out from behind. In front of him, the side window of a passing truck disintegrated from one of the bullets. The truck veered left and smashed into a row of parked cars. Within moments, the street had filled with a crowd of shouting pedestrians. Ned was thankful for this distraction, knowing his pursuers wouldn't give up the chase so easily. He looked back up the street toward the main entrance to the police compound and was alarmed to see more guards running in his direction. But then he noticed they were chasing an orange-robed monk, whom he recognised as Giang, his English-speaking cellmate. Silently urging him on, Ned decided now was not the time to stop and shout his support or watch his flight.

Running along the main road, Ned seized the first opportunity to turn down one of the small side streets. Here, the houses and shops narrowed to a point where only bicycles and Honda Cubs could navigate through the throng of people. Many shopkeepers had returned from their afternoon naps and were busy setting out their wares in the narrow passage. Outside the houses, old ladies sat on cheap wooden chairs watching the passers-by and preparing their families' evening meals. Ned zigzagged between them, trying to maintain speed without drawing too much attention. Any time he saw a left or right turn, he took it to avoid staying on the same street for too long. He knew this maze was his friend – if he was lost, it was highly unlikely the guards would be able to follow him.

Eventually, he slowed to a walk. The afternoon heat might have been dwindling but the temperature was still high, and he hadn't exercised for over a month. Keeping a brisk pace and continuously looking over his shoulder, he tried to work out where he was going and how he would get there. But the warren of tiny streets looked the same, and without realising, he'd taken three right turns in a row. With a jolt of recognition, he arrived back on the same main road he'd been on less than ten minutes earlier. To his dismay, he'd wandered straight back toward his pursuing guards. There were more of them now; he could see at least six to his left and a few more further down the tightly compacted street to his right. Clearly, they wanted him back. Knowing what he knew, Ned could understand why Colonel Tung had thrown all resources into his recapture.

But he was equally determined not to be recaptured and killed, and moved back a pace into the shadow of the alleyway as he pondered his next move. He was considering the merits of retreating back the way he'd come when his attention shifted to a wisp of a man appearing from around the corner. It took him several seconds to realise that standing before him was none other than Ba. The last time Ned had seen him was on the night of the raid on top of the wall trying desperately to help his brother escape. Until this moment, he hadn't known if Ba had survived that dreadful night or not. Ned was utterly confused, but when he saw Ba smile, he launched himself forward and embraced his old friend with relief.

"What the hell are you doing here, Ba?"

"Trying to keep up with you, of course."

"Have you been following me?"

"Yes, along with half the guards from the prison. Quick, you need to follow me if you don't want to get caught."

Ned had a hundred and one questions but knew now was not the time, so he followed his friend. Ba pointed to a small street across from where they stood. Choosing their timing to coincide with a mass of pedestrians walking past their position, they crossed over the road full of guards and entered another small alleyway. Although hoping to remain unobserved, a cacophony of shouting behind them confirmed they'd been spotted.

"Quick, hurry!" shouted Ba.

They ran down the alleyway, jammed – like most other tightly compacted residential side streets in Saigon – with bicycles, mopeds and scooters parked outside their owners' grilled doorways. Large pots filled with ferns and bougainvillea were dotted along the way in an attempt to make the residents' environment less austere and concrete. Mangy dogs fought with each other and discarded rubbish littered the street, all obstacles Ned and Ba had to navigate carefully. From above, old men with wispy beards watched silently from their balconies, almost close enough to reach out and touch their neighbours opposite. And a confusion of electricity cables hung in a mess from one property to the next. Ned and Ba charged down this micro-habitat, avoiding children, dodging dogs and jumping over small wooden stools left haphazardly in their path.

Ned felt they'd successfully outrun the guards when the alleyway opened up onto a large square filled with street vendors preparing for the evening rush. It was a fifty-fifty choice as to which way they turned. Unfortunately, they went left and ran straight into a white-uniformed policeman, who was knocked backward into the foul-smelling gutter. As the policeman rose in a rage, Ned panicked and punched him across the cheek, sending him back into the gutter. Knowing their pursuers would soon be entering the square, Ba pointed to a Lambro – a three-wheeled Italian vehicle used as a small goods transporter across the city – parked on the side of the road.

The back was full of vegetables but it provided an instant escape route. The owner, a small middle-aged man wearing a dirty cotton shirt and flipflops, had just sat down in the driver's seat when Ba hauled him out and – apologising profusely over the man's protestations – took his place at the handlebars. He shouted across to Ned, who covered the short distance to the vehicle in three long steps and leapt into the back, just as Ba was pulling away from the curb.

The pursuing guards emerged from the alley right in front of them. Having seen Ned jump into the Lambro, they quickly squatted and prepared to fire. Without enough time to turn into the square, Ned shouted at Ba to drive straight at the crouched guards.

The first shot hit the Lambro just as it mounted the pavement. Ned wasn't sure if it was the bullet or the violent jump that caused the windscreen to shatter, but by the time he'd gathered his senses, he could see the guards had scattered to avoid being hit by the little vehicle. Ba turned the handlebars left to avoid going back down the alley, which would have been too narrow, and accelerated along the pavement surrounding the square instead, forcing mothers with their children to jump both ways. Finally managing to reposition the Lambro back on the road, Ba twisted the hand throttle as far as it would turn and sped away and off the square.

In all the action, Ned had been flung from one side of the vehicle to the other, and was now covered in vegetables. If the guards had managed to fire any more shots, he hadn't heard them over the loud whining noise of the engine, as Ba pushed the 175 cc to its limits.

"Jesus, Ba! What are you trying to do – kill me?" Ned shouted through to the cab, having successfully stabilised himself. And then, as an afterthought: "And when did you learn to drive one of these things?"

"Just learning now, Mr Ned. But don't you worry, all under control." From behind, they heard a cacophony of horns and revving engines.

"Won't they catch us in this, Ba? It's not exactly the quickest vehicle on the road."

Ba laughed. "Don't worry, Mr Ned. The secret police might be better out in the open with their fast cars but they're useless in these side streets. I'll look after you, you'll see."

For an hour, they drove through the city, avoiding the main roads and sticking to the smaller streets. Ned took the opportunity to tear up some discarded hessian fabric he'd found lying next to him and roughly bandaged up his arm. By kneeling in the back, he was able to stick his head through the rear cab window and converse with Ba. He learnt how, after seeing his brother murdered by Tung's men, Ba and his comrade had jumped off the wall into the grounds of USAid, where they'd taken refuge. They'd stayed there two weeks, despite Nhu's demands that the Americans should hand them over. Luckily, the new American Ambassador had visited them soon after his arrival in Saigon and insisted the monks were on US territory and should not be given up. Eventually, having decided the situation had calmed sufficiently, the pair had been able to leave the premises unobtrusively under false names. The first thing Ba had done was try to establish contact with any monks who'd survived and avoided capture. He knew Dai had died on the night of the raids, but he'd also heard a Western photographer was being held at the supposedly 'secret' police holding centre.

"So," Ba continued, shouting from the cab, "I went down there each day to find out if it was you. This afternoon, as I was leaving, I heard gunshots. I ran toward the shooting and I saw you appear through the gates of that building site and sprint across the road into the maze of small streets with several guards after you. I followed, trying to catch up, but I lost you. I knew you'd get lost too, so I stayed on the main street, hoping you'd re-appear at some point. You were lucky it was me who saw you first and not the guards."

"Thank you, Ba, you may have just saved my life. And Ba, I'm so sorry about Dai. He was such a good and kind person."

"Don't feel sorry for him, Mr Ned."

"Why not?"

"Because he was a good and kind person. In the Buddhist faith, if you're good and kind, when you die, you'll be reborn as something even better – maybe even a god. Can you imagine Dai as a god? He'd like that."

After an hour of driving, Ned had decided his next move. He knew he couldn't return to his own apartment, where they'd surely be waiting for him, so he asked Ba to drop him off a mile from his destination, revealing his plan and how his friend might be able to help.

The sun had now sunk fully behind the horizon and the silhouettes of the city's tallest buildings loomed against the last pinks and mauves still gracing the sky.

* * *

The house was in darkness when he arrived. It was obvious no one was inside. He waited for the private neighbourhood security guard to patrol further up the street, before slipping through the gate and waiting unobserved on a bench, hidden in the densest part of the garden. The waxing moon (or was it waning? Ned wondered, having not seen it for over a month) was rising when Mel's noisy VW Beetle pulled up outside her gates, and she emerged carrying her camouflaged jacket and helmet.

Ned waited until she'd passed through the garden gate before standing up. His movement obviously caught her eye because she stopped suddenly and stared into the gloomy depths of her garden. Her surprise as Ned walked out of the shadows was palpable.

"Hello, Mel," he said simply.

"Ned, is that you?"

They stood feet apart, looking into the other's eyes, before Mel dropped the jacket and helmet to rush over and embrace him fully. Despite the stab of pain from his arm, Ned relished the chance to hold her tightly, suddenly aware how close he'd come to never touching or seeing her again. The realisation made him well up.

They stayed in each other's arms for what seemed like an age, neither wanting to break contact. Finally, Mel pulled away and looked up into his face.

"We thought you were dead. Where have you been?"

Ned stared into her eyes. Without answering, he kissed her on the lips. The kiss was warm and soft, but quickly grew urgent and passionate. Eventually, Ned pulled back and simply held her tight once more. "My God, am I pleased to see you."

Mel was full of questions as she led him gently inside, but her curiosity turned to concern after seeing him in the light. Ned hadn't realised how much his condition had deteriorated in the five weeks he'd been locked away. Now, standing in front of a mirror, he could see how much weight he'd lost, how sallow his face had become, and how disgustingly dirty he was, still wearing the same clothes from the day of his arrest. Mel had been good enough not to mention the smell.

After a shower and a large bowl of pork noodles, they retreated to the living room sofa, where Ned explained the whole story of his capture, imprisonment and escape. It took over an hour to recount, with only the occasional interruption from Mel.

In the meantime, Mel worked on bandaging the gunshot wound in his right arm. She was shocked to discover Dai had been killed during the raids and confirmed she hadn't heard from Ba in that time. So many monks had disappeared that night that it had been impossible to find out the whereabouts or condition of each of them. She'd been worried when the brothers had gone missing and was deeply saddened at Dai's death, though reassured to hear of Ba's escape and survival.

Her anger only intensified when Ned explained how Pham had been planted as a spy in the BPA agency to observe the journalists and monks for the secret police. Mel didn't know what had happened to him either; he hadn't been seen since the raids. She'd asked Bich if she knew, but Bich was inconsolable. Her brother, a trainee monk at a pagoda in south Saigon, had been among those arrested that night and still hadn't been released.

Eventually, Ned asked the awkward question: why had nobody tried to secure his own release?

Mel explained what steps had been taken to find him. She'd alerted both the British and American Embassies but heard very little from either. Although both had confirmed they were conducting their own investigations in collaboration with the South Vietnamese government, neither had found anything conclusive about his whereabouts. Vague reports about a Westerner being held at the Chi Hoa prison had surfaced in the days following the raids, but nothing concrete had materialised, giving Mel no platform to investigate further. Their press colleagues and friends from other agencies had even written articles on his disappearance, but most editors had been reluctant to print too many stories about one of their own. What articles had been published, in Mel's opinion at least, had helped to keep the pressure on the Embassies to continue their investigations. She assured Ned she hadn't given up and was in fact waiting at that very moment for a response from HQ in New York, who'd raised the issue directly with the State Department in DC. Ned was relieved to hear that, although he'd had to escape Colonel Tung's clutches by his own means, he hadn't been completely forgotten about in his absence.

And then he asked the question that had weighed on him the most. "Does my mother know I was gone?"

Mel touched his good arm softly. "Yes, Ned, she knows. I made sure our London bureau kept her informed of everything we were doing to locate you. I can't imagine how happy she'll be to hear the good news. You should send her a telegram as soon as you can." Ned nodded silently in agreement, distraught as to how worried his poor mother must have been.

The conversation moved on to who was behind the raids. Ned asked who everyone believed had orchestrated that night's violence, and Mel confirmed his suspicions the blame had been laid at the feet of the military – just as Tung had said. She explained how not just Xa Loi had been attacked that night, but every important pagoda in all the main cities up and down South Vietnam, from Hue in the north to Can Tho in the south, resulting in thousands of monks being arrested and hundreds killed. Even though Ned had witnessed the violence first-hand, he was still shocked to hear the full scale of it.

"So the world really believes it was the military?" asked Ned in frustration.

"We all had our suspicions it was the government, but they strenuously denied it and said it was the generals. That they got carried away with power under martial law. And that's the way it's been left. We tried to tell the execs in New York we shouldn't be so quick to believe the government, but they refused to print anything without further evidence."

Ned thought about this last comment for a while. "No wonder Colonel Tung was so happy today during my interrogation. He was almost laughing when he told me the 'stupid' generals were in disgrace, the Americans were confused, and the Buddhists were defeated."

Mel stood up from the sofa and went to fetch some more beers from the kitchen. "We need evidence to nail these sons of bitches," she said angrily on her way back, handing Ned a fresh bottle.

"Well," said Ned, taking a grateful sip. "I've been thinking about that. And there's a small chance I may know where to get some."

20

Having discussed the situation, it was agreed an extra security guard should be booked to patrol Mel's house, which she'd offered to Ned as refuge. Ironically, when the guard arrived, Ned and Mel were preparing to leave. Some thirty minutes after midnight, dressed in dark clothing to better camouflage themselves, they slipped away into the streets.

A curfew was still in place under martial law, but after five weeks was no longer being strictly enforced. Mel explained they'd be unlucky to come across any patrolling soldiers away from the centre of town. They found a cyclo driver willing to take them, for a large reward, to the junction of Le Van Duyet Street and Phan Dinh Phung Boulevard, the same place where Thich Quang Duc had self-immolated. This was as close to the centre as the driver would go.

Crossing over Le Van Duyet Street on foot, Ned knew they had to be extra vigilant from this point. They walked in the shadows as much as possible, the streetlamps throwing only limited light in small patches along the road, and stopped before each junction to check for army roadblocks.

The streets were quiet, so unlike during the day, with only the noise of barking dogs to break the silence. They carried on along Phan Dinh Phung Boulevard until they came to Ba Huyen Thanh Quan Street. Xa Loi Pagoda was two hundred and fifty yards up the road, but there were still two junctions to navigate. Turning left onto Ba Huyen, they crept forward and found their first military checkpoint. Two soldiers were standing by a makeshift barrier strung across the road, quietly chatting and smoking, the noise of their conversation alerting Ned to their presence. He and Mel crouched in the shadows watching them for a few minutes, but the men didn't move, or offer any opportunity for the pair to sneak past. The only option was to go back the way they'd come and try a different route. This part of Saigon was very grid-like in layout, so there were more than two ways around the roadblock. Ned just prayed these weren't cut off as well.

It took an hour of careful skulking through the city's empty streets, but eventually they arrived at the same junction where Ned had been dropped off on the night of the raids. On that occasion, the secret police had already erected barriers across Ba Huyen Thanh Quan Street to keep unwanted visitors away from the front entrance of the pagoda. But there were no barriers tonight, not even a checkpoint. Regardless, Ned and Mel avoided the front, skirting around to the back instead, where they found the small, unlit Quan Pho Street.

Ned reached the back door first and stopped to listen. The city was as silent as he'd ever known it. Slowly and carefully, he opened the door and peered in. He'd expected to find it pitch black inside, and so it was. Switching on the torch he'd borrowed from Mel, he led her on tiptoe up the corridor, unsure what to expect at the other end. The door into the hallway was closed as usual. He turned off the torch, pushed the door open a crack and peered beyond, his eyes readjusting to the low light.

Silence. Darkness. Was anybody still living here? Mel had told him the pagoda had been emptied and closed in the days after the raid, but surely some of the monks would have returned by now. Opening the door just enough for them to slip through into the hallway, Ned made his way straight to the cleaning cupboard where he'd hidden so unsuccessfully.

"When I realised my mistake that night, going in here instead of escaping out the entrance we just used, I knew they'd find me. So I found a hiding place for my Leica, but there was no room for my Nikon or my film canisters. I dumped those in a bucket and covered them with a mop. The secret police found them, but I'm hoping they didn't find my little Leica."

Pointing the torch against the far wall where some old brushes and mop handles were leaning, Ned found the wonky air vent cover he'd spotted that fateful night, glad to see it was still able to pivot on the single remaining screw keeping it pinned to the wall. When he'd first opened the cupboard door during the raid, the reflection of the flames outside in the metal of the vent had alerted him to this potential hiding place.

Mel held the torch while Ned rotated the cover upward, revealing the darkened space behind. Putting his hand inside, he ferreted around for a moment. Had the torch been illuminating his face, Mel would have seen a broad grin spread over it. Triumphantly, Ned withdrew the small Leica camera and showed it to her.

"This is how we're going to nail those bastards."

They retreated as silently as they'd arrived back down the corridor and out onto Quan Pho Street.

"I need to get over to our offices. You'd better go home. I'll come to you in the morning once I've developed this film."

"You've got to be kidding, right? You disappear for five weeks and when you finally reappear, you want to go off on your own again? Sorry, Ned, but I'm coming with you to make sure you don't get into any more trouble!"

She leant forward and kissed him.

"Come on…"

And off she went down the road.

Ned was going to suggest developing the film in the morning as an alternative solution, but in truth, he was as eager as Mel to see what was on it. He ran to catch her, believing the reward would be greater than the risk.

It was the darkest part of the night now and the streets had become quieter still. Even the dogs had stopped barking. During daylight hours, they'd have walked down Phan Dinh Phung Boulevard until it intersected Rue Pasteur, then right and onto the BPA offices a few minutes later. Tonight, that wasn't possible, so they opted for the smaller back streets that ran parallel with the main boulevard, sneaking through the shadows, pausing at junctions to check they were safe before running across the road, and generally trying to stay as quiet as possible. Mel was still full of questions about Ned's ordeal, about the raid on Xa Loi, about what he intended to do next; but Ned just shushed her. To be honest, he didn't know what his plan was after this, but it didn't involve getting shot out here on the streets by a soldier.

Rue Pasteur cut Thong Nhat Boulevard, the main road leading to Independence Palace. The area on either side was planted with many tamarind trees, old and gnarly, with their pod-like fruit hanging heavily. Ned was particularly nervous as they found themselves forced to cross this parkland. Although the President no longer lived in this particular palace, he assumed there'd still be armed soldiers in the vicinity. But the BPA offices were just on the other side, so they crept forward, always on the lookout for checkpoints and patrols. There was one at the intersection, but Mel suggested they walk around it through the trees.

The moon was high in the sky, and when the clouds parted, complicated silhouettes took shape from the trees and their branches. It was difficult to know what was solid and what wasn't. Ned's nerves were particularly tight. Was that a person or a shadow moving?

They waited until the moon was obscured behind a cloud before sneaking across the road to Independence Palace and had just made it to the trees on the far side when a sharp crack sounded suddenly in front of them, shortly followed by another loud noise from behind. A gunshot. Ned had become an expert at recognising these – was this the third or fourth time he'd been shot at in the last twenty-four hours? The crack of the bullet hitting a tree had preceded the sound of the shot itself, meaning their assailant was still some way behind them.

Ned grabbed Mel's hand. Crouching low, they ran from tree to tree, keeping to the thickest mass of shadows. Two more shots rang out, but they didn't hang around to see where from, knowing every soldier in a square mile would have been woken. It was imperative they get to their offices as quickly as possible.

They were hiding behind one of the thicker tree trunks, hoping they'd lost their pursuers, when the noise of a twig breaking alerted them to a nearby presence. They held their breaths in silence a while, but then a small, khaki-clad soldier appeared from behind the tree, pointed his rifle at them and shouted what sounded to Ned like: "*Zer-tai-lin!*"

"He's saying 'put your hands up'," said Mel.

"How do you know? You don't speak Vietnamese!"

"Look at his rifle, I can read that!"

Sure enough, the soldier was using his weapon to indicate they should raise their hands. They both promptly obeyed. Ned knew they should never have stopped to recover their breath.

But their luck changed when the soldier made his own mistake and came too close. At over six feet tall, Ned's reach was considerably greater than the five-foot soldier's. As had become abundantly clear today, he knew attack was his best option if he wanted to avoid ending up in front of Colonel Tung again. Lightning fast, he pushed the barrel of the rifle away with his left hand and punched the soldier on the side of the face with his right. The soldier fell like a stone to the floor. Immediately, Ned grabbed his weapon and threw it off to one side.

"Have you killed him?" whispered Mel urgently.

"I'm not a murderer! But he will be a bit groggy when he wakes up. Power-to-weight ratio doesn't seem to work in these guys' favour, I've discovered. Come on, quick, let's get out of here!"

Crouching low once more, they'd reached the edge of the trees within thirty strides. Within forty more, they were back on a residential side street running parallel with Rue Pasteur. Two minutes later, they'd made it to the back entrance of the BPA offices. A quick unlock of the door and they were in. The curfew only applied to those caught out on the street, so once inside, they were safe at last.

Eager to see the images he'd captured on his Leica, Ned went straight to the darkroom and prepared his chemicals. Having not used the room for over a month, it took him a little longer than usual to start the process. But fifteen minutes later, his black and white negative film had been developed and he brought it out to show Mel. They used the bathroom to view it following Mel's sensible suggestion that the light in the main office should remain off. Knowing the secret police would be looking for Ned, it was best not to advertise their position.

As they looked through the images, their excitement mounted. The first few had been taken from the bell tower and showed the pagoda's main entrance being overrun by soldiers. More importantly, there was a sequence of Nhu and his wife watching the raid through the roof hatches of the APC. The film then cut to the great hall with images of Colonel Tung holding up the chalice containing Thich Quang Duc's heart. And finally, the harrowing picture of Dai being dragged across the floor toward Tung and Pham. It was difficult to see any detail as these were only negatives, but Ned was surprised to still see Mel looking upset. Even after getting to know her better the past few months, he still considered her a hardened professional in the field.

"These are good, Ned," she said, her voice trembling. "The world's going to be shocked – the first concrete evidence of the government's involvement in the raids."

Ned acknowledged their importance and explained how he planned to use them to help the monks achieve justice. "I owe it to Dai. I promised him and Ba I'd get their movement the worldwide publicity it needs, and these are the pictures to do that with."

Mel watched quietly as Ned set up the darkroom enlarger so he could print some of the negatives to make photographs. Once the red light was on and the chemical baths had been prepared, Ned busied himself burning the first image onto the silver halide-coated photographic paper. An hour later, the drying line was filling up with small photographs hanging innocently – except the images were explosively incriminating.

As Ned was counting down the timing on the final print, he and Mel suddenly froze in the same instant.

"There's someone out there, Ned. Did you hear that?"

Ned nodded and put his finger to his lips. Slowly, he leant across and bolted the door as quietly as possible from the inside with the lock he'd installed to ensure nobody would enter his darkroom inopportunely. They continued to listen in silence and began to make out the noise of at least two people walking around and whispering. It was difficult to deduce exactly what was happening. The intruders weren't upending furniture or trashing the office; instead, they seemed to be tiptoeing around in a controlled fashion.

Ned heard footsteps growing closer, when suddenly the door handle rattled as someone tried to open it from outside. Ned was sure he heard his name being whispered. He and Mel remained silent, their eyes locked together, not daring to move in case the floorboards beneath their feet gave them away. They waited, expecting another attempt to open the door and hoping desperately it wouldn't involve gunfire or violence – Ned had had enough of that for one day.

But nothing happened. The footsteps and soft voices seemed to retreat back to the main office at the front of the building. Mel and Ned remained completely motionless, listening intently, still not daring to move a muscle. Was that splashing they could hear? Ned couldn't be sure. But moments later, the first whiff of burning reached their nostrils, and soon the noise of flames increased from a whisper to a roar. They knew they were in trouble.

"Quick, grab the prints!" whispered Ned urgently as he hurriedly pulled his roll of negative film out of the enlarger. He placed it carefully back in its canister, which he roughly shoved in his trouser pocket.

"Are you ready?" asked Mel. "We need to run for the back exit and pray they haven't positioned anyone out there." Without waiting for an answer, she unbolted the door and ran.

The smoke was already thick and acrid as they left the darkroom. The flames were fighting their way out of the main office and Ned could feel the intense heat radiating toward him. He bent low to find the cleaner air and covered his mouth and nose to keep the smoke out of his lungs, though rationally accepted this was hopeless.

The back door was located in the kitchen. Mel was already there but had collapsed and was kneeling on the floor coughing harshly into her chest. It was obvious she was losing consciousness from lack of oxygen. Ned grabbed her under the arms with his left hand and pulled back the bolts with his right. As the door opened, air rushed in momentarily, causing the high-temperature gases in the smoke to explode outward. Ned and Mel were propelled through and landed in a heap on the road outside.

Ned lay on the tarmac, breathing deeply to replenish the oxygen in his bloodstream. Looking over to Mel, he was relieved to see her trying to sit up too, also inhaling heavily. Remembering the danger they were in, he stood and picked her up again beneath the arms. "Come on, Mel! We have to get out of here."

The sky in the east was growing lighter as he led her down the small street running parallel with Rue Pasteur. Behind them, thick smoke and flames were pouring through the open kitchen door, but Ned didn't want to wait around to watch the spectacle for fear of being caught. He continued down the street, unsure where he was going. By luck, they came across a wizened old lady opening the grill across the front of her small street café. With streaks of black soot smeared across his face, Ned looked at her imploringly. Perhaps in response to their distressed appearance, she accepted his plea, ushering them inside her small space. Ned took one last look to check no one was watching before he dragged Mel across the threshold and the little old lady shut the grills behind them.

Over the next two hours, their rescuer clucked around them, cleaning their faces with a wet cloth, making cups of tea and, to Ned's delight, appearing with a plate of fresh croissants, which were devoured instantly. He and Mel sat either side of a small metal table, holding their cups with both hands and trying to make sense of their lucky escape. Outside, they could hear the sirens of the fire brigade and police who'd descended on the BPA offices en masse, but they opted to stay hidden until after curfew had been lifted.

"What are you going to do with these then?" asked Mel, removing the photographs from inside her bra. Apparently, it had been the safest place she could think of in the heat of the moment.

"I've been thinking about that. I know you're keen to break the story about Nhu's involvement. But can you give me forty-eight hours? I know how we can help Dai and Ba. We just need to keep the secret between us a little longer."

* * *

Several hours later, Ned – sleep-deprived but energised by a new sense of purpose – took a cyclo along Ham Nghi to number thirty-nine. The American Embassy in Saigon was not a particularly impressive building, built in concrete with small windows, though Ned liked the way the front facade was one giant curve. In the short space of time he'd been in the country, counter-car bomb measures had appeared on the street out front: large, white-painted, cylindrical concrete blocks positioned strategically to prevent a vehicle being driven straight into the building. Ned found security measures had been stepped up inside too; he was subjected to a full body check before being admitted to the reception. All suggesting the US authorities didn't believe the communist threat had gone away simply because the enemy had kept a low profile over the summer.

Henry Cabot Lodge's private assistant collected Ned and ushered him into the Ambassador's office. Lodge stood from behind his desk and stepped around to shake Ned's outstretched hand.

"Mr Ambassador," said Ned. "I just want to say thank you for seeing me at such short notice."

"That's absolutely fine, Mr Rivers. Or can I call you Ned? I remember my promise to continue our conversation when we met at the White House for your award. Though I must say, I was very surprised to hear you'd requested to see me – last I heard, you'd disappeared. Your colleagues at BPA asked me to help locate you pretty much my first day in this office. They thought you might have been arrested. I put through a call on their behalf to the President's brother, Nhu, asking if his people had any information. A few days later, I was told none of the South Vietnamese authorities knew anything about your disappearance and there was no record of your arrest. So I'll admit I'm slightly intrigued – what did happen to you?"

Lodge indicated for Ned to take a seat in a formal-looking leather club chair on the other side of the large office. The Ambassador sat opposite him and they waited in silence while his private assistant poured them each a cup of coffee.

"Well, I can confirm I was arrested and being held by the secret police since the night of the pagoda raids. And I think Nhu would have known that personally."

"I did suspect Nhu wasn't telling me the whole truth. But I couldn't afford to openly call him a liar so soon into my posting. Not without building up a little credit first, you understand? I did, however, task our Embassy security team with finding out what had become of you. Every time I followed up, though, they had nothing to report. Anyway, mystery over. Here you are."

"Indeed, here I am." Ned paused, not entirely satisfied by the Ambassador's explanation. He took a sip of coffee. "You told me when we met that you'd help me any way you could, so I wanted to show you these." He retrieved the pile of hastily printed photographs from his jacket pocket. "To see if you could assist in protecting the monks."

"I'm not sure I said anything quite so explicitly, but go on," said the Ambassador as he picked up the photographs and looked through them, visibly surprised at what he found. Ned filled him in on all the details, from the night of the raids to his arrest and imprisonment, and the events of the previous day resulting in his escape. But it was the involvement of Colonel Tung and the secret police that the Ambassador was most interested in.

"You can confirm for sure, then, it was the secret police under Tung's command that led the assault on the monks —and not the ARVN?"

"Yes, sir, these photographs clearly show it. I saw with my own eyes not only Colonel Tung issuing the orders but also Nhu and Madame Nhu watching the whole affair. She loved it, she was clapping her hands with glee every time a monk was killed or thrown in the back of the trucks. There's no doubt it was the Mat Vu that attacked Xa Loi Pagoda and not the army."

Lodge, impeccably dressed as ever, fished his horn-rimmed reading glasses from the inside pocket of his suit jacket and closely inspected the photographs of Madame Nhu. Continuing through the rest, he checked each one thoroughly before looking back up at Ned. "And how can I help you help the monks?"

"Well, sir. I was hoping these photographs might be useful in exposing the truth. If they get out, the government – and Nhu and Tung in particular – will be damaged. And even though that won't bring back any of the dead monks, I'm sure it will be cheered by the ones who are still alive. I can give you twenty-four hours free use of these images before I wire them and the accompanying copy to BPA New York this time tomorrow."

The Ambassador studied Ned for a moment with his interrogating eyes, then finished his coffee and stood up.

"Listen, Ned. To be quite honest, I'm not sure what I can do with these. I'll hold onto them for now, but I reckon BPA's subscribers will use them to better effect than myself. I appreciate the proposition though, and if I can think of any other way to help, I'll be sure to let you know."

Ned was somewhat taken aback by Lodge's sudden lack of enthusiasm, having expected a much stronger response. But he knew his time was up when the man stood and held out his hand.

As he was being ushered out, the Ambassador repeated to Ned once more how relieved he was he'd shown up safely.

Shutting his office door behind Ned Rivers, Henry Cabot Lodge returned to the leather club chair to retrieve the photographs. He quickly looked through each one again and smiled to himself, before walking across to his desk and buzzing the intercom.

"Sally, I've got something that urgently needs wiring through to the State Department."

21

Roger Hilsman, Assistant Secretary of State for Far Eastern Affairs, was running late for the office. It was such a beautiful morning, not a cloud in the sky above Washington DC, and there was no inclination to rush. Being a Saturday, the Department of State's offices were virtually empty. The Department's policy was to have the minimum number of people necessary working on a weekend to cover the requirements of the world's geopolitical situation at a given time. The hoohah over the bashing of the Buddhists in South Vietnam had died down, and apart from a coup in the Dominican Republic midweek, the world was quiet.

William Averell Harriman, Under Secretary of State for Political Affairs, met Hilsman as he exited the lift on the fifth floor. "Morning, Roger."

Hilsman stopped and looked at Harriman, who was smiling, which was rare for the famously dour man. Hilsman didn't consider the man his boss, although he'd been promoted into his position when Harriman had been elevated by the President to the more important Political Affairs brief back in April. Despite this, Hilsman still had huge respect for the seventy-one-year-old because of what he'd achieved in his career: US Ambassador to the Soviet Union during the Second World War; Governor of New York; narrowly missing out on the Democratic nomination for both the 1952 and 1956 presidential elections; and now considered the elder statesman of the Democratic Party. He eyed Harriman, trying to guess why he was looking so pleased with himself.

"Okay, you've got me, what is it?"

"I think we've got them," Harriman replied, letting a sly grin appear across his face.

Hilsman knew exactly who Harriman meant by 'them'. They both held the same view, one they knew was not shared by many of their colleagues inside the Kennedy administration, and certainly not over in Defense. They both hated the ruling family of South Vietnam; Nhu in particular, though they didn't have much time for Diem either. They were both of the opinion that the Ngo Dinh brothers were dragging South Vietnam further into the mire, and the conflict with the Viet Cong would be easier to win if the country was led by someone who had the support and respect of its people. As they saw the situation, this did not represent Diem, who cared so little for the majority Buddhist peasant population that he didn't deserve to be President.

Hilsman's face lit up. "What have you got?"

"Come and have a look. Michael's looking at them in the conference room."

Hilsman followed Harriman down the corridor like an excited child, almost running to catch up, keen to see what the excitement was about.

Inside, Michael Forrestal was leant over the conference table, staring in disbelief at the overnight cables from Saigon. Forrestal was Harriman's thirty-five-year-old protégée, having served as assistant naval attaché in the Moscow Embassy just after the war and now working as a senior advisor to McGeorge Bundy, the presidential National Security Advisor. Forrestal was known as the third man in the anti-Diem triumvirate and was perfectly placed within the White House to have the President's ear. He looked up as Hilsman entered. "Roger, you've got to look at these. Conclusive proof at last. There's no doubt now – not only did Nhu know about the raids, but it was him and Colonel Tung who organised them."

Hilsman sat down and looked through the photographs that had arrived from the Saigon Embassy. They were accompanied by a short note from the Ambassador stating he'd recently come across these images, that they were top secret for now but would be released to the newspapers from tomorrow.

"Okay, so how can we use these?" asked Hilsman of his two colleagues.

Harriman, chin resting on his chest, harrumphed before turning to Hilsman. "Nhu lied to us. He said he had nothing to do with the raids and it was the generals who organised it. Can you believe the gall of the man, to blame his generals for something he did himself? He has to go, they both have to. They've lied to us and led us on a merry dance once too often. We need to use these photos to start the ball rolling for a US policy change to have them removed from office. Simple as that."

Hilsman stood up and wandered over to the window that looked out on 21st Street NW. "Simple as that, huh? How do you propose we change a key plank of US policy to overthrow our closest ally in South-East Asia on a Saturday?"

"Easy," said Harriman as he sat down at the conference table. "We draft a cable to Lodge authorising him to start exploratory talks with the generals, in which he tells them they have the green light from the President to organise a coup." He removed his favourite fountain pen from his inside pocket and began to draft the cable. "Then, all we have to do is get the President to sign it off."

Thirty minutes later, the three men studied the completed draft and signalled their approval.

"Okay, we've done the easy bit of writing it," said Hilsman. "Now, how are we going to get the President to authorise it?"

Since Kennedy was away for the weekend at his beachside home at Hyannisport, they agreed that Forrestal, being the only White House employee among them, should telephone him, a task he usually performed daily in any case to keep the President apprised of events whenever he was away from Washington.

It was close to midday when Forrestal made contact. "Good morning, Mr President. Have you received copies of the overnight cables from Saigon I sent through to you?"

"Yes, yes, I've received those. I've got them here in front of me," came the voice over a crackly line from Massachusetts. Forrestal had rung on a speakerphone to allow the others in the room to listen in.

"Very good, sir. Well, the major news from Saigon is the emergence of these photographs taken on the night of the pagoda raids, which clearly show the involvement of Nhu and his paramilitary police force. Sir, State think now is the time to issue new instructions to Lodge for him to apply pressure on President Diem to remove Nhu and Madame Nhu from government. Furthermore, Mr President, State considers that, if Diem refuses to remove his brother and sister-in-law, then Lodge should be authorised to find an alternative leader."

There was a pause at the other end of the line. Those listening to the speaker wondered if the connection had broken, but then it crackled back to life.

"Michael, that would be quite a change in our stated position on South Vietnam, don't you think?"

Forrestal looked up at Hilsman and Harriman. "Yes, sir, it would. But the Nhus have become such a liability that State deem it vital they be removed from power."

"Can't this wait until Monday when we can have a proper face-to-face discussion with the key ministers rather than rushing it through on a Saturday afternoon?" said the President, offering his opinion.

"Sir, Roger and Averell believe a cable should be sent immediately with the new instructions. They're of the opinion we cannot delay."

Once more, there was silence from Massachusetts. Forrestal looked up at his colleagues, wondering if he should say something more to help persuade the President.

But then the line crackled again. "Okay, Michael, if Roger and Averell believe these instructions can't wait until Monday, you need to get other senior ministers to agree before I'll sign it off. Come back to me when you have their collective agreement."

As the line went dead, both Hilsman and Harriman slapped Forrestal on the back in praise – and not a little excitement.

The afternoon was spent tracking down key government personnel to explain why policy had to change, and why the cable containing the new instructions had to be sent urgently to Saigon. The first senior executive they tried was their boss, Dean Rusk, who they knew shared some of their views on the futility of continued support for President Diem. The Secretary of State was at home when he received the phone call from the Under Secretary of State for Political Affairs. Harriman described the photos proving Nhu's involvement, read through the draft cable, and confirmed President Kennedy had agreed for it to be issued, pending sign-off from his Secretary of State. He thought it best not to mention this was only on the condition that other key members of the government had approved it too.

"Very well, Averell, if the President has understood the implications, then I'm happy to give the green light."

With the endorsement of the Secretary of State, the three anti-Diem policymakers were able to get verbal sign-off from most other senior government executives or their deputies.

When Forrestal called the President back at Hyannisport later that evening, he was able to confirm support from Secretary of State Dean Rusk; Deputy Secretary of Defense Roswell Gilpatric; Marine General Victor Krulak, Assistant to the Chairman of the Joint Chiefs of Staff; and CIA Deputy Director Richard Helms, in the absence of his boss John McCone.

Just after 9.30 pm, President Kennedy authorised the sending of DEPTEL 243 to Ambassador Henry Cabot Lodge at the US Embassy in Saigon:

> *It is now clear that whether military proposed martial law or whether Nhu tricked them into it, Nhu took advantage of its imposition to smash pagodas with police and Tung's Special Forces loyal to him, thus placing onus on military in eyes of world and Vietnamese people. Also clear that Nhu has maneuvered himself into commanding position.*
>
> *US Government cannot tolerate situation in which power lies in Nhu's hands. Diem must be given chance to rid himself of Nhu and his coterie and replace them with best military and political personalities available.*
>
> *If, in spite of all your efforts, Diem remains obdurate and refuses, then we must face the possibility that Diem himself cannot be preserved...*
>
> *... You may also tell appropriate military commanders we will give them direct support in any interim period of breakdown central government mechanism.*

It was several hours later, well into the next day, when Ambassador Lodge's reply to Cable 243 arrived at the Department of State:

> *Believe that chances of Diem meeting our demands are virtually nil. At the same time, by making them we give Nhu chance to forestall or block action by military.*

Risk, we believe, is not worth taking, with Nhu in control combat forces Saigon. Therefore, propose we go straight to Generals with our demands, without informing Diem. Would tell them we prepared have Diem without Nhus but it is in effect up to them whether to keep him.

Roger Hilsman departed the office late on Sunday, convinced this beautiful weekend had only improved. Not only was he confident he'd finally found a way of removing the troublesome Ngo Dinh family from office, but he also believed his cable would help South Vietnam emerge stronger and in a better position to prosecute the war more effectively under new leadership.

He whistled to himself as he took the lift down to the carpark level, trying to recall the name of the tune on his lips, though without success. Not that he cared, for he knew he'd just made the world a better place.

22

Saturday 5ᵗʰ October 1963

Mel wasn't sure what to suggest any longer. They'd been over the argument several times in the last few days. She'd tried to make him see sense and even resorted to playing the boss card, but Ned had grown in confidence since he'd first arrived in Saigon and was putting up strong resistance.

Ned understood Mel was only trying to protect him, but he was becoming fed up hiding in her house like a timid child. It was more than a week since he'd offered the Ambassador the photographs in return for his help, yet he'd heard nothing back. Now Ned wanted to go and help the monks himself, but Mel was strongly against the idea. She insisted he keep a low profile, keep his head down and stay out of the centre of town. Their new office – which had been quickly set up at the Continental Palace Hotel on Tu Do Street, near the Saigon Opera House, since the fire had destroyed the last one – was being continuously watched. Even other Western journalists had reported an increased secret police presence around them. It seemed the Mat Vu weren't even trying to be discreet anymore; they just stood on the opposite side of the road, watching.

Mid-week, Ned had been temporarily buoyed when his photographs of the Xa Loi Pagoda raid and Mel's accompanying article had been published in newspapers around the world to great acclaim. But that high had been replaced by a new low. The strength of the international press reaction in its renewed condemnation of the South Vietnamese government must have angered Nhu and Tung further, and the realisation he was now even more wanted plunged Ned deeper into despair. He didn't know what to do with himself. He paced around the living room, his mind whirring, desperately trying to persuade himself the situation wasn't as dire as it felt. Eventually, he concluded the best way forward was to get back on the metaphorical horse.

"Mel, I know you're only trying to help, but do you know what it's like being stuck here? I'm a photographer, why can't I go and photograph things?"

"Because it's too dangerous for you at the moment. You do realise Colonel Tung will string you up if he catches you, right? You'll become one of the disappeared."

After another heated discussion, they finally settled on a compromise whereby Ned would travel to Hue, the old imperial capital far to the north of Saigon, and meet up with Joseph Coleman, BPA's reporter embedded with South Vietnam's 1st Infantry Division responsible for guarding the demilitarised zone at the border areas with North Vietnam. At least there he'd be far away from Saigon's secret police until the heat had died down.

It was a great idea, which would have worked had a car not pulled up outside the house within minutes of their decision. They'd both grown acutely attuned to the comings and goings outside on the street, so were suspicious to see a young Vietnamese man in an ill-fitting suit come to the door. Mel answered once Ned had hidden in the bedroom.

"Good morning, madame," the young man said in a cheerful manner. "I have come to collect Mr Ned Rivers and take him to a meeting."

Mel studied him, assuming this was a trap. "What meeting? And what makes you think he's here?"

"So sorry, madame, but I cannot tell you the nature of the meeting. But if you tell him I have Mr Lodge in the car, then perhaps he will come."

Mel looked out onto the street to see a small, dirty, old Mercedes Benz. There was definitely someone in the back seat, but it didn't look like the type of car a dignitary would travel in, and certainly not the US Ambassador. Unsure of the veracity of what she was being told, she set off down the garden path and out the small front gate to approach the car. The occupier, seeing her coming, opened his window and looked out. He was wearing a worn-through straw hat, which he took off in greeting as he peered up.

"Good morning, Miss Johnson. I do apologise for disturbing you on a Saturday, but I was hoping to borrow Mr Rivers for a couple of hours. I was reliably informed I might find him here."

"It is you, Mr Ambassador. Forgive me, I was just checking. You can't be too careful these days."

"Indeed, you can't, Miss Johnson. But if you wouldn't mind asking Mr Rivers to accompany me, I would be most grateful." The Ambassador tipped his straw hat once more.

Duly summoned, Ned climbed into the back seat of the old Mercedes Benz next to Henry Cabot Lodge as the chauffeur in the ill-fitting suit set off toward the centre of town.

"I'm sorry for picking you up in this old thing, Mr Rivers. But you're not the only one who has to be careful. Luckily, we have a few old pool cars at the Embassy to help us move around the city without drawing any attention."

Ned looked around the car, noting the interior looked as old and threadbare as the outside.

"I hope you don't mind me calling on your help – let's just call it *quid pro quo* for my assistance with the monks. You probably think it strange for a journalist to be brought in on state business, but it does happen from time to time. You will, however, need to sign this affidavit confirming you understand the US Espionage Act of 1917 and the restrictions it places on you not to reveal anything of what you are about to see and hear."

Ned took the proffered document, wondering what help the monks had received from the Ambassador in his week of radio silence, but signed the document anyway after a cursory look through, his curiosity and restlessness having got the better of him. He noted Lodge hadn't actually expanded on the details of their meeting, nor their end destination, but Ned didn't feel the need to ask; he assumed all would be revealed in due course. Instead, they discussed Vietnam as a country and how different it was to America. It turned out the Ambassador was as impressed with the average Vietnamese worker as Ned had been on his arrival, and at how a simple bicycle could be used in so many variants, from taxi to delivery vehicle.

The car eventually stopped outside a row of shops; not the kind with display windows, as Ned was used to back home, but with grilled shutters over the facade. Being 9.30 in the morning, these grills would have been unlocked for nearly four hours already, indicating the shop was open for business. Ned recognised they were in Cholon, Saigon's Chinese district, but he wasn't sure exactly where.

The chauffeur was first out and opened the door for the Ambassador before leading him into one of the shops halfway down the row, which revealed itself to be a dental practice. Ned hurried to catch up and was shown through to the back of the 'shop', where a set of stairs led to the first floor. The chauffeur stood aside to let the Ambassador and Ned go up together.

Ned was amazed to find they'd entered a space more like a 1950s gentlemen's club than a grubby office as he'd expected to find. The walls were panelled in dark oak with original oil paintings hanging on them; the floor was covered in thick, maroon-coloured carpet; and the furnishings were Western in a traditional style. There was a small bar at one end with a range of whisky and gin bottles lined up on a shelf behind it. In the centre of the room stood two leather Chesterfield sofas and a couple of high wingback club chairs surrounding a low coffee table.

As they entered, Ned saw three men were already present, each of whom stood upon seeing the Ambassador. Two were Westerners, the other Vietnamese. The first Westerner was about forty-five years old, thickset, with his hairline forming a V-shape at the front of his head – definitely American, guessed Ned. The other was a little younger, with a pinched face that reminded Ned of a ferret. The Vietnamese man was much larger than his average countryman and dressed in military uniform. Ned noted his broken front teeth and corresponding lack of a smile.

The Ambassador shook hands with the Vietnamese officer. "Thank you, General Minh, for coming along today. May I present Ned Rivers, the photographer with the BPA news agency whom you asked to meet. You're already familiar with his latest set of photographs published this week in the world press. Ned, this is General Duong Van Minh." He then pointed to the elder American and his ferret-faced comrade in turn. "And from the American Embassy, allow me to introduce Lucien Conein and Don Peterson."

Ned shook hands with each man in turn, none of whom smiled or said a word.

"Good. Introductions done, let's get to the crux of this meeting. Ned, the general – and my colleagues too for that matter – are very interested to hear *your* story from the night of the raid on Xa Loi Pagoda."

Only too pleased to tell his version to anyone who wanted to listen, Ned spent the next hour outlining the events of the early hours of 21st August, recalling all he'd seen and heard.

And the Vietnamese general seemed equally keen to hear the details, particularly regarding Nhu and Madame Nhu's involvement. He probed Ned at length about Colonel Tung and how much of the raid he was personally responsible for.

The Ambassador and the two gentlemen from the Embassy remained quiet throughout the discussion, content to let General Minh ask the questions. For his part, Minh continued to look through Ned's prints while interrogating him, as if matching the images to the events. Eventually, he declared, "Thank you, Mr Rivers, you have been very articulate in your description of that night, but that will be all for now."

As the big Vietnamese general stood and shook his hand, Ned looked around to find the other two Americans sat quietly by the bar behind him. He'd completely forgotten about them during his discussion with Minh and wondered why they were there. As if on cue, Conein, the more bullish of the two, stood and gestured to Ned to follow him down the stairs, leaving Petersen silently watching them as they left.

At the bottom of the stairs, Conein instructed the chauffeur to drive Ned back to Mel's house. As Ned was preparing to leave the premises, Conein leant in close.

"Be careful out there, Mr Rivers. I should probably warn you – your name's been found on a hit list drawn up by Colonel Tung himself."

Ned stopped in his tracks and stared at the big American as he digested what he'd just been told. "How did you find that out, Mr Conein?"

"You don't need to know. But just trust me when I say, be careful. I mean it."

As Ned was driven home, Lucien Conein, an operations officer with the CIA, walked back up the steps and re-joined the meeting. By the time he'd sat down in his club chair, Ambassador Lodge had fetched a bottle of whisky and four glasses from the bar.

"So, General, are you now convinced of Nhu and Tung's involvement in the raids?"

"Well," replied General Minh. "I always knew it was them who'd organised it, since I knew it wasn't us. But it was still interesting to hear the details. And I'm shocked at their barbarity. I had no idea Nhu hated the Buddhists that much. I'm disgusted by how psychotic he's become."

The Ambassador carefully poured out four glasses before gently pushing the tumblers across the table in each man's direction. "The question is, what are we going to do about it? I know you've been keeping Lucien updated of any plans you might have heard for a coup against Diem, but we all know those were never going to come to anything. I think it's time to get serious, General Minh."

"What do you mean…exactly?" asked Minh, leaning forward and looking keenly at the Ambassador.

"Clearly, the American government cannot be seen to be involved in determining the leadership of a foreign country," said Lodge. "But, completely off the record, you may be interested to read a cable I've recently received from the US State Department." He casually passed across the three-page cable to the general.

Minh picked up the pieces of paper and carefully unfolded his reading glasses in order to peruse the words. When he'd finished, he put the pages down and looked questioningly at the Ambassador. "Have you already spoken to President Diem to ascertain if he'll remove his brother?"

"No, General Minh, of course I haven't. You know as well as I do that Diem would never remove his brother from his current role. And I've told the State Department that too. In fact, I've recommended we skip straight to the second part of the cable – the complete removal of the President and his brother."

Lodge paused and let the silence sit heavy in the room before continuing.

"I'm therefore confirming that the US government will offer no objection to the overthrow of the ruling family. And as you can see from the end of the cable, the US government will, furthermore, support any military personnel who subsequently assume the leadership of South Vietnam."

General Minh smiled for the first time, particularly enjoying the sound of these last words. "Thank you for organising this meeting, Ambassador Lodge, and for your candour. It's been very enlightening. But if you would excuse me, I have much work to do – and colleagues to speak to."

"Thank you, General Minh. Now that you know the US government's position, could I ask that you keep Mr Conein and Mr Peterson involved in any developments?"

On that note, the Ambassador stood up and shook the general's hand before declaring their meeting closed.

23

Except for the intriguing trip to Cholon six days previously, Ned had stayed hidden at Mel's house all week, making him feel like a songbird trapped in a cage. He had just enough room to flap his wings but couldn't really go anywhere. He felt frustrated and angry and, if truth be told, perhaps a little scared. Understanding your life was in danger was one thing; but to be told your name was on a hit list elevated the threat so much higher and made it a concrete fact.

He didn't dare leave the city, though. Not now. Not knowing what he did. It would be like an astronaut walking away from the chance to be the first to step on the moon – should that ever be possible.

Despite having signed the non-disclosure affidavit, he'd quickly told Mel what had happened and whom he'd met, but reassured himself he hadn't revealed any state secrets as such... because he didn't actually know any. After all, he was the one who'd done all the talking. But still, he and Mel had come up with a plausible explanation as to what the meeting had been about. As a result, they knew the next big move in this giant game of chess being played out by presidents, generals and ambassadors would take place in Saigon; they just didn't know when. But at least he wasn't in the demilitarised zone a thousand kilometres to the north.

Even so, Ned was not keen to stay trapped in Mel's gilded cage a minute longer than he had to. Most likely out of frustration and restlessness, he was becoming somewhat blasé about the threat to his life compared to Mel, and when he'd suggested meeting up with their friends and colleagues from the foreign press corps, she'd refused...at first. But eventually his charm and arm-twisting had worked, and Mel had reluctantly agreed to accompany him, though Ned suspected she'd only relented after he'd threatened to go on his own.

The streets seemed more subdued than normal as they walked up Le Loi toward Lucky Kim's, one of their favourite meeting places and popular with the offspring of Saigon's elite. Ned, although acting nonchalant, was still nervous at the idea of being recognised and took the precaution as they walked of bending down occasionally, as if to re-tie his shoelace, to check if anyone was following them. He'd put on a baseball cap and dark glasses, causing Mel to laugh at this attempt to disguise his six-foot, blond, Western appearance on the streets of Saigon.

Ned appreciated the new Mel. He felt she was acting differently toward him since his escape from prison. Prior to his latest arrest, she'd treated him as a colleague in public rather than a lover, even occasionally being cold and detached with him, only showing her softer, more passionate side on the few occasions they were alone in the bedroom. But since his escape, she'd become much more open and caring, allowing her emotions to become more visible and more honest. They strolled side by side down the street, happy in each other's company and chatting excitedly about what might happen. Mel linked her arm up through his and listened to his view of how a coup against President Diem could play out.

They climbed the six steps up to the veranda running along the front of Lucky Kim's, still laughing at Mel's wisecrack at how dull Ned's evening would be when no one recognised him in his brilliant disguise. The bar was on the south side of Le Loi, a wide, tree-lined avenue penetrating into the heart of Saigon. The premises were triple the width of most other shops along here, with concertina-ing doors that joined the large interior with the small outside veranda facing the street. Along the edge of this concrete terrace ran an iron railing that ensured the space felt private for their clientele.

Ned and Mel were first to arrive and chose to sit at a large table on the veranda, which was still bathed in golden light from the dying sun. Over the next thirty minutes, their friends and colleagues from the foreign press corps began to appear, creating a jovial atmosphere: David Halberstam, tall and upbeat; Neil Sheehan, the most dedicated and hardworking Western journalist stationed in Saigon; and Peter Arnett, fully recovered from his altercation with the secret police.

As they arrived, each of them greeted Ned like a long-lost friend and commented on how glad they were to see him back. They chatted as friends do with wit and humour about the events of the past five weeks, each wanting to hear about Ned's incarceration and escape, as well as his role in the pagoda raids themselves.

Like Mel, the other reporters had openly discussed the likelihood of the raids having been a secret police operation since Halberstam had spotted Tung on the night himself. So they'd felt pleased – and vindicated – when Ned's photographs finally emerged. Many of the foreign news editors back in America had originally accepted the South Vietnamese and US governments' version of the story blaming the military, despite the protestations of their own journalists on the ground. That was until Ned's incontrovertible evidence had been published, at which point the editors had been forced to make embarrassing U-turns and admit their own correspondents had been right all along. As a result, Ned was now somewhat of a hero in the eyes of his colleagues.

Inevitably, the discussion moved onto where the Buddhists protests could go from here, and if there was even any leadership left to continue their revolt.

"Did you hear what happened to Thich Tri Quang?" asked Peter Arnett.

"No," said Ned, intrigued. "None of the monks in my cell knew what happened to him."

"He learnt about the raid a few hours before and lost his nerve. I have it on good authority he ran to the American Embassy and asked for asylum. Apparently, he's still there."

"Oh, that's poor," replied Ned. "Leading your troops into battle and then doing a Houdini moments before the fighting commences." They all had a good laugh at how the monk's bark had turned out to be bigger than his bite. "And what about Thich Tinh Khiet? When I was captured, I was thrown on the same truck as him. But I haven't heard what happened to him since?"

"God, you have been in the wilderness, haven't you?" laughed Halberstam in his booming New York accent. "He's still under arrest but he's in hospital. Right now, he's too ill to effectively lead the Buddhist movement, so the secret police have left him alone to recover. I think they know they can't touch him now the Americans are watching closely."

"The only reason the Mat Vu aren't watching him is because they're watching me instead," said Arnett. "Everywhere I go, I see the bastards following me."

Ned shot Mel a worried glance.

"And me," replied Sheehan. "I think everyone in the country's a spy for them now. They're getting quite intimidating."

It turned out nearly everyone present had their own story of being watched or followed by the secret police. Halberstam was certain this increased activity presaged a crackdown on the foreign news corps by Nhu, who they guessed was furious at having been outed as the true mastermind behind the raids.

"They're tapping my phone," said Halberstam. "I can hear it *click-click-clicking* when I talk. In fact, there's probably some Mat Vu in here right now watching us." The New Yorker had been facing the road with his back to the bar so had to turn around to have a look. The others followed suit and their eyes settled on two Vietnamese gentlemen sat at a neighbouring table, both wearing white shirts and grey slacks. As soon as they noticed they were being observed, they looked away. The table of journalists burst out laughing at how easy it had proven to identify their followers. Not long afterward, the two Vietnamese gentlemen stood up and left the bar.

The talk eventually moved on – again, inevitably – to the expected coups against President Diem. Although Ned kept quiet about his meeting with the Ambassador, all the correspondents knew an attempt could occur at any time. The wires to their various contacts and spies were running red hot with gossip and rumours about who was doing what, but Ned was relieved to find General Minh's name was not one of those being bandied about.

The sun had finally moved over the roof of the veranda and was now quickly disappearing under the horizon, while the sky in the east turned a deep blue, only a shade lighter than black, forcing the cars and motorbikes rushing along Le Loi to turn on their headlights. The dusk chorus of crickets and katydids had taken over from the daytime calls of the cicadas, and the city that never rested seemed to take a moment to pause before the evening shift restored its intensity.

Mel was sat at the side of the table closest to the pavement with her back to the road, drinking whisky from a tumbler and chatting to Arnett. Ned was seated across from her holding a bottle of beer and joking with Sheehan about the joys of being able to drink again. It was then they heard a loud screeching of tyres skidding on tarmac. Looking past Mel, Ned watched as an unloved old French Renault 4 delivery van ground to a halt out on the street. The passenger door opened and a young Vietnamese man wearing a black cotton headband jumped out and ran three paces up toward the railings. Mel and Arnett were still chatting and only stopped when they became aware of the silence around the table. Before he could work out what was happening, Ned saw the young man pull something out of an object in his right hand, then throw the object up toward where the group were sitting.

Thinking back later, Ned was reminded of when he'd been ten years old and gone to a baseball game with his dad. He'd never really been into the sport, unlike his friends, so hadn't been paying full attention to the game. He'd been jerked back to reality, however, by a loud cheer and the sudden sight of the baseball coming straight for him. Somehow, and completely unexpectedly, the young Ned had caught the ball before casually throwing it back down to a player on the pitch.

The same state of bewilderment came over him as he saw the object fly through the air in his direction. Instinctively, he reached forward to catch it and recognised what it was – with the latticed outer shell, it looked identical to the ones he'd seen in Second World War movies. His jaw dropped and the blood drained from his face. The realisation he'd just caught a live grenade was more than alarming and sent a chill throughout his body. Without thinking, he threw it back hastily toward the road. Unfortunately, the grenade hit one of the iron pillars holding up the roof of the veranda and ricocheted off to land on the pavement three feet below them.

Then it exploded.

The blast was deafening, creating a rippling wave of energy radiating out in a massive burst with extraordinary speed and power, knocking Ned clean off his feet. Thrown backward, he landed several feet away on the bar floor. Moments later, he came to on his back, surrounded by dust and debris. Trying to make sense of what had just occurred, the sequence of events came back to him quickly, and he realised someone had just tried to kill him. The image of Colonel Tung floated into his mind and all became clear.

As his memory and understanding returned, silence gave way to a loud ringing in his ears, but he was able to stand and look around. The table he'd just been sitting at now lay upside down and broken on the floor. As were his friends, though they were gradually beginning to pick themselves up and dust themselves down. He crossed to Arnett, who was kneeling, and helped him up, looking out onto the road for the French delivery van as he did so. It was gone, but scanning further down Le Loi, he spotted it stationed in the middle of the road some fifty yards from Lucky Kim's. Feeling an anger take over, he ran to the entrance of the bar, jumped down the steps to the pavement and sprinted toward the vehicle.

As he approached, he could see both doors open and a body lying on the ground on the driver's side. Standing over the body were two American military advisors dressed in their fatigues. One was still holding a revolver as Ned arrived on the scene, and he realised what must have happened.

"Did you shoot him?" he asked, indicating the body lying face-down on the ground.

"Yes, sir. We heard the explosion and saw a guy jump into the van. We watched it pull away and it came straight toward us at speed. We confirmed he was VC because of the black head-band, so I opened fire. I got the driver but missed the passenger. He bolted. The driver tried to run for it too, but I got him."

Ned's ears were still ringing but he was able to hear most of what the US soldier had said. He bent down and turned the body over violently in his anger. Two things surprised him at once: the fact that the body was still alive; and whom it belonged to. His anger instantly gave way to puzzlement as he recognised the man he'd once called his friend lying mortally wounded on the ground.

"Pham, what the hell are you doing?"

He realised what a stupid question this was as he remembered the look on Pham's face when he'd been arrested during the raid, betraying his true feelings. The recollection of this treachery created a powerful new surge of rage inside Ned, and he felt like punching Pham's face.

"Why are you trying to kill me?" he shouted down at him.

A dribble of blood was beginning to flow from Pham's mouth. When he coughed, a fine mist of bloody saliva sprayed outward into the air.

"Orders...it was my orders. You're an enemy of the government and they want you dead. They want all of you dead."

He coughed again and clutched at his chest. Ned looked down and removed Pham's hands, revealing the bullet wound below. The shirt was covered in blood and Ned could see the bullet must have punctured a lung. Pham's breathing was very faint, each breath of air taken with difficulty.

"But we were friends, Pham, how could you do this to us?"

Pham looked up at Ned. "We were never friends. You try to help our enemies...so Nhu wants you dead. I was just doing what he ordered." His eyes, although dulled as his life ebbed away, still emanated the same hatred Ned remembered from the night of his arrest.

"But why are you dressed as VC?"

Pham continued to stare at Ned with silent hostility, leaving Ned to guess the answer to his own question. From the secret police's perspective, it would be much easier to blame his death on the Viet Cong – fewer questions would be asked.

A crowd of onlookers had gathered around the van, keen to see what was happening. Ned remained kneeling by Pham's side until he took his final wheezy breath. Afterward, one of the soldiers closed Pham's eyes out of respect. Ned wondered if, before long, the mounting number of deaths in this country would make soldiers immune to such little acts of decency. He stood up and walked slowly back to Lucky Kim's, confused by the hatred in Pham's eyes, not fully grasping what he'd done to deserve such animosity.

As he approached the bar, he was surprised at how little damage the explosion seemed to have caused. The veranda and its roof were still standing, although parts were hanging limply at jaunty angles and the glass in the concertina doors had shattered. The blast had mostly been contained by the concrete sides of the veranda.

He climbed the steps to find his friends grouped in a circle, some kneeling, but all studying the floor. Only then did he realise something was wrong, and he rushed the last few steps to barge his way to the front. To his shock, everyone was gathered around Mel, who was lying perfectly still on the damaged veranda. She looked asleep, except for the pool of blood that had haemorrhaged onto the floor around her head. Sheehan was kneeling at her side, having removed his T-shirt to wrap around her head as a temporary bandage to stop the flow of blood.

"Jesus, what's happened to her?" asked Ned desperately.

It was Halberstam who replied. "Something must have hit the back of her head when the grenade exploded, probably a bit of shrapnel. She's breathing – just – but she hasn't come round yet."

Ned knelt down by Sheehan's side and touched her neck. He couldn't feel a pulse, but her skin felt very clammy. Realising he didn't actually know where to hold his fingertips, he checked on his own neck to find the correct spot. When he re-positioned his fingers on Mel's neck just to the side of the windpipe under her jawbone, he felt a light beat. "She's got a pulse, not very strong, but it seems to be beating very fast."

"Okay, that's not good," said Halberstam. "It means her heart's having to work harder than normal to keep the right amount of oxygen circulating."

Ned looked at him blankly.

"It means she's lost a lot of blood, Ned," Halberstam explained softly.

For the next few minutes, there was a rush of activity as they waited for the ambulance to arrive, which Arnett had already called. Sheehan was sent off to find a blanket to keep her warm, even though it was still twenty-six degrees, while Ned stayed by her side to ensure she was comfortable. He found a shard of broken glass about the size of a playing card and held it to her mouth to see if it steamed up. He'd heard this was the best way to check someone was still breathing in an emergency and was relieved to find it worked. But the amount of blood soaking into Sheehan's T-shirt concerned him; it clearly hadn't stemmed the flow, and the pool on the floor was getting bigger around her head. He wasn't sure what to do and could feel his dread rising. He felt sure she might go into some sort of shock at any moment. She still hadn't come around and was now looking very pale.

Ned tried hard to keep a lid on his panic. He was close to erupting like a volcano, so was relieved when Arnett reappeared with the two Vietnamese military medics who'd been called to the scene. They too checked Mel's pulse and then fetched a stretcher, which they positioned alongside her before lifting her carefully on. Her head lolled sideways alarmingly, so one of the medics checked her blood pressure. Quickly, a mobile intravenous drip was set up and hung from a pole attached to the stretcher.

Once her blood pressure had stabilised, she was lifted up and carried out of the bar to the military ambulance. Desperate with worry, Ned asked the ambulance crew where she was going. As a Westerner, she'd be taken straight to the American field hospital at Tan Son Nhut Airbase. Ned was allowed to travel with her, but the Vietnamese police who'd since arrived at the scene refused to let any other members of the group go, as they were required to give statements.

As the ambulance set off, Ned felt numb with guilt about the evening's events. What had seemed like a good idea to relieve the boredom of being cooped up in Mel's house had descended into tragedy. Not only was Mel badly injured, but it had been at the hands of a man he'd once considered a friend. He understood why *he* was a target for Nhu and Tung but was furious at their wider vendetta against the foreign press corps. Once more, he could feel the rage rising, but as he looked across at Mel and saw the consequences of his crusade, the feeling abated to be replaced by concern for her wellbeing. He realised it was dangerous to get so worked up. He needed to remain calm and focused. For Mel.

The US military hospital was located in an adapted aircraft storage hanger at the Tan Son Nhut Airbase. Within seconds of the ambulance arriving, the front doors flung open and nurses and porters were rushing Mel inside. In the whirlwind of commotion, she was propelled through the doors marked *Theatre*. As soon as they had shut behind her, calmness befell the space outside.

Ned was left in the makeshift reception area, which consisted of a few rattan chairs lined up along a back wall. False internal partitions had been constructed to subdivide the huge hangar into smaller rooms, but these were only eight feet tall with cotton muslin 'ceilings', and the noise from the patients reverberated around the vast space.

Ned sat down on a chair and waited...and listened. Each time a doctor or nurse appeared, he jumped up to ask for news. Each time, he was told to be patient; he'd be given more information when there was some to report.

The minutes turned into hours.

Just before midnight, an American doctor appeared with an update. "She's still in a coma and her pulse is weak, but she's fighting. It looks like a piece of shrapnel cut into the side of her neck just below the skull, badly damaging her left vertebral artery, causing a great loss of blood, which resulted in her suffering an ischaemic stroke. To make matters worse, she's also suffered an intracranial bleed in the brain, either from the explosion itself or a piece of flying debris."

"But will she live, Doctor?"

"We've stemmed the bleeding and now we're trying to release the pressure on her brain. It's not something I can predict...but we're hopeful."

The doctor disappeared, leaving Ned alone again with his head full of further questions. He returned to his chair, feeling marginally more optimistic than five minutes before. Time seemed to slow as he waited. He kept checking a clock hanging on the far wall but was shocked to discover how little the minute-hand had advanced each time. He tried to sleep but his brain was too wired, the pace of thoughts racing through his mind too fast. Most of these began: '*What if...*' or '*If only...*'.

At 12.50 am, the front doors to the hospital opened. Although his eyes were closed, Ned was still wide awake, and he opened them to see Ba standing alongside a smartly dressed American guard.

"What are you doing here?" Ned said in surprise as he stood and went over to meet him.

Before Ba could answer, his American escort asked Ned if he could vouch for the monk's identity. Ned confirmed Ba was his friend, and the guard allowed Ba to proceed into the reception before taking his leave.

Ba came closer. "I heard about Miss Johnson. I was so worried about her."

Ned was touched and sat back down in his chair. "Thank you, my friend, she'll appreciate that. How did you know she was here?"

"Saigon is a small city and news travels fast. How is she?"

"She's in theatre now. She's still unconscious but the doctors think she'll pull through."

Dressed in his orange robes as ever, Ba looked out of place in the sterile white environment of the hospital. He looked around at the set-up before letting his eyes fall back on Ned. "And how are you, Mr Ned?"

"Me? I'm fine. It's Mel we need to be concerned about."

"I'm concerned for you both. I know how fond you are of Miss Johnson."

"Yes," replied Ned quietly. "I am fond of Miss Johnson. She's come to mean a lot to me. It's a pity it took such a horrible accident for me to realise that."

"Then make sure you tell her when she's better."

Ned didn't answer. He didn't mean to be rude, but his mind was full of thoughts and he was trying to find the right words for when she awoke to tell her how much he cared for her. Regaining focus a few moments later, he glanced up at Ba, who was still standing, looking ill at ease.

"Sit, Ba, you're making me feel even more guilty staring down at me like that."

"It's me who feels guilty. I'm the one who got you involved in our fight with President Diem. If I hadn't approached you, you wouldn't be sitting here now, and Miss Johnson wouldn't be in there."

"Nonsense, Ba. You can't think like that. We chose to get involved, we were chasing a story. That's why all of us Western journalists are here in Saigon. Don't blame this on yourself. It's Nhu and Tung who are responsible."

Ba sat down on a neighbouring chair and nodded his head in solemn agreement. Ned returned to staring at the floor and was soon back in his own world of thoughts, barely aware of his friend by his side.

Finally, at 2.50 am, the door from the theatre opened and the same doctor who'd spoken to Ned several hours earlier appeared. Ned leapt up and rushed over in his eagerness to hear an update. The doctor's face remained blank and Ned was unable to determine whether he carried good news or bad.

"How is she, Doctor?"

"We've had a few scares, but I think she'll pull through. She'll have to return to America as soon as possible given how badly wounded she is. Her blood loss was severe, and we're not sure we've been able to stem it completely. From the amount she lost, we were lucky she didn't go into hypovolemic shock, which would have caused her internal organs to shut down. But for now, she's..."

He hadn't even finished his sentence before alarms sounded from the room behind him.

"Doctor, come quick! She's relapsed," shouted a nurse in a blue surgical facemask through the open doorway. The doctor rushed back in and the theatre door swung shut after him.

Ned looked at Ba, who'd stood up and joined him in the middle of the reception. Both their faces exhibited a look of bewilderment, shifting quickly to anxiety. From beyond the walls, they could hear shouting and panicked commands as the surgeons fought for control. They could do nothing but pace the floor and wait for news. The urgent voices from the other side slowly calmed and the alarm bells eventually ceased their piercing intrusion. Ned was left wondering what was going on, the suspense becoming unbearable.

Finally, the theatre door opened once more and the same doctor emerged. This time, Ned could read his facial expression all too clearly.

The doctor stopped just in front of them and put his hand on Ned's upper arm. Ned stared back in horror and disbelief. The doctor took a deep breath and said, "I'm sorry. We couldn't save her. We thought she was through the worst, but suddenly her heart stopped." He paused to let the news sink in. "We tried to revive her, but she didn't respond. We just couldn't get her heart started again."

Ned stared blankly, the colour having drained from his face. He turned to Ba and began to speak, but no words came out. At a loss, he went and sat back down on the rattan chair and covered his face with his hands. Even Ba wasn't allowed to see his tears.

24

The death of Mel hit Ned hard.

It wasn't only the guilt he felt at having persuaded her, against her better judgement, to go out that night. She'd also become his rock of stability, one he'd leant on heavily. Not that he'd realised this before she'd been taken away. The sense of security she'd provided – physically, by letting him live at her guarded house; mentally, as his professional guide; and of course emotionally – was now gone, leaving him badly adrift.

Luckily, Ba had recognised Ned's vulnerable situation and offered his own house as a refuge. At first, Ned had refused. But Ba insisted – the Mat Vu had flexed their muscles and proven they were willing to kill. Finally, with Ba's house buried away deep in a tight-knit Buddhist neighbourhood, Ned saw the rationale of the offer and accepted.

Ba's family made him feel more than welcome. As Buddhists, they understood the danger he was in, so considered his safety their primary concern. The house was no more than two miles from the wide boulevards of the town centre but might have been a million miles for all the differences. It was small and simple, spread over two floors and tightly tucked in among a mass of other houses. The street outside was just wide enough for a bicycle, like all the streets in this rabbit warren of a community. The nearest road large enough for a vehicle was almost half a mile away. At night, the space outside became an extension of each house; once the kerosene lanterns were lit, it sprang to life with neighbours gossiping, mothers cooking, children playing and dogs rutting. Ned welcomed the sanctuary and knew he was safe inside the strongly pro-Buddhist community.

In the aftermath of Mel's murder – as her death was viewed by the American community – Henry Cabot Lodge had sought Ned out to offer his condolences. The Ambassador was furious an American citizen had been killed in this way on the streets of Saigon, and he made no bones as to whom he thought was to blame. He reassured Ned he'd spoken to President Diem and told him in very undiplomatic language that no more journalists, including Ned, were to be targeted by the South Vietnamese authorities. Diem had tried arguing the Viet Cong were responsible for Miss Johnson's death, but had ultimately agreed to ensure the journalists' safety, meaning Ned was essentially exonerated, relatively free to live and work again openly.

What was more, Lodge had invited Ned to act as the official pool photographer when Admiral Harry D. Felt, commander of all US forces in the Pacific region, arrived in Saigon in ten days' time for an official visit. This included an audience with President Diem at the Gia Long Palace. Relieved, Ned had thanked the Ambassador for ensuring his security and that of his colleagues, and graciously accepted the offer to photograph the meeting, eager for both the opportunity and the distraction.

With the threat to his safety diminished, Ned now had work to do. He'd been tasked by his editor, James Lund, with keeping the Saigon bureau operating while they waited for Harry Roberts, who'd been recalled from Vientiane to take over Mel's role. The civil war in Laos was losing importance to events in Vietnam, so Harry had been more than happy to make the change.

Throughout this period, Ba and his confidantes from Xa Loi kept an eye on Ned to ensure he wasn't followed as he made his way back each night to the safe haven of the Buddhist community. Ba fretted constantly about his friend, particularly when Ned told him of Lodge's offer. Ba felt the Ambassador was sending him into the hornet's nest, but Ned reassured him such a public event meant he'd be perfectly safe, even inside the home of his enemy. Nonetheless, Ba remained concerned.

Every evening, the two of them spoke together about what the future held for Buddhists and the monks in this country. Sitting on a small balcony overlooking the street below, with only a single candle to illuminate their faces, the pair chatted for hours. Ba tried to explain how the Buddhists mistrusted anyone in power; even if there were a military coup, his people would still feel vulnerable. He did concede, however, that a military government would be marginally better than Diem and Nhu – but only marginally.

Both Dai and Mel came up frequently, for both were terribly missed. Ba spoke often of his love for his brother and the keen sense of responsibility he felt for his death. Ned talked about Mel and how, despite the short time they'd known each other, he felt as if he'd lost a soulmate. How aloof she'd been when he'd first arrived. But as they'd worked closer together, their relationship had grown stronger. And without even realising it, they'd fallen for each other.

One night, Ned announced he was going to Tan Son Nhut Airport. Mel's coffin was due to be flown out of Saigon, and he asked if Ba would accompany him to say a final farewell.

A few days later, Ned stood silently on the concourse, waiting to pay his last respects. The airport was considerably busier than when he'd first arrived five months earlier. He thought back to his optimism and excitement on that occasion; so different to the emotional cacophony he was now feeling.

He watched as a fresh batch of American military advisors unloaded from a huge transport plane before lining up and marching off at double quick time, heavy packs bouncing on their backs, confidence oozing with every step. Ned wondered how many of them would return to America in the same condition.

Beside him stood Ba, a man he now considered his close friend and on whom he'd come to rely so much in the period since Mel's death. They watched solemnly as her coffin was rolled out onto the concourse toward them by a young American solider, one of the wheels on the trolley squeaking intermittently as it turned. The coffin was plain and uncluttered, made from soft wood finished in a dull, dark varnish. It saddened Ned to see Mel in something so ordinary, reducing her to just another number rather than reflecting her individuality and achievements. He guessed all Americans who died in this foreign land would make their final journey home in something similar.

As if to confirm his thoughts, nine more identical coffins on identical trolleys appeared from the main building, all being wheeled in the direction of the transport plane.

The young soldier escorting Mel's coffin rolled it just in front of Ned and Ba before taking a step backward to allow the men space to say some last words. But Ned had none to say, and simply placed a yellow Da Lat rose on the lid, letting his hand slide slowly over the wood to the modest metal plate bearing her name, where he left the flower in silent tribute and closed his eyes. He remembered the words he'd chosen back in the hospital, the words he was hoping to use once she'd recovered, words to describe how much she meant to him. But now all he could do was whisper them and hope, wherever she was, she'd hear.

He stayed there with his hand on her coffin for almost a minute. When he opened his eyes, they were moist, and he wiped the tears away surreptitiously before taking a step back. Ba took the opportunity to move forward and quietly uttered a gentle chant to support Mel's peaceful transition. After a minute, the young soldier came to wheel the trolley away.

Ned and Ba watched silently as Mel's coffin joined the loading queue by the aircraft ramp alongside the others. For a long while, nothing seemed to happen, and Ba used the moment to offer some words of comfort.

"She was a good person, Mr Ned. I'm sure she'll move easily into the next life."

"Yes," said Ned softly. "She's probably already been reincarnated as a queen bee, busy bossing her workers around, exhorting them on to ever greater lengths to find pollen." He gave Ba a sad smile. "There'll be a pollen shortage soon, you watch. Bee colonies everywhere will be short – except for hers."

In spite of themselves, the two friends laughed out loud, piercing the melancholic atmosphere for just a moment, before silence descended once more.

After fifteen more minutes, the row of coffins had been loaded into the aircraft, Mel's among them. The ramp was lifted, and the huge Douglas Cargomaster taxied to the end of the runway, from where it began its lumbering charge into the sky, leaving Ned and Ba small specks in the hostile city below.

25

Lucien Conein, operations officer for the CIA, closed his front door, walked down the garden path, and spotted them before he'd even set foot on the pavement. He was so certain they'd be there that he'd have gambled his grandmother on the probability. However, this was the one morning he couldn't afford to be followed – he'd have to lose them. From previous experience, Conein knew this wouldn't be a difficult task. Too much thought had already gone into these plans for them to be jeopardised, even ruined, by lack of care and not allowing enough time to shrug off his tail.

He walked casually along the pavement as if out for a stroll, full in the knowledge the wide boulevard made the task of trailing him very simple. He wanted to put his Mat Vu observers at ease, less prepared for his tricks. Turning onto a smaller street filled with overhead balconies, Conein kept the same casual pace, hoping the less busy area would force his followers to drop back. Not wanting to alert them to his awareness of their presence, he avoided the urge to look behind him and continued walking.

The street was only wide enough for a single vehicle to travel up or down. On that morning, however, even a small car would have struggled with the amount of portable food stalls and fruit sellers set up along its length; it was mostly bicycles and the odd Vespa scooter (carrying up to six members of the same family) that passed him. Halfway down, he stopped and bought some deep-fried chicken from a wizened old lady with thinning grey hair standing behind her portable wok. She gave him a broad grin as she returned the change, revealing her betel nut-stained mouth and rotting teeth. Conein smiled back graciously.

As he walked on to the intersection with another street, he slowed his pace, pretending to be engrossed in his food. He turned the corner oh so casually, making sure to look relaxed. But as soon as he felt out of sight, he sprinted across the narrow street to a small café with wooden tables and chairs scattered on the pavement in front of its open grilled entrance. He darted inside, hoping his followers hadn't seen him from so far away, and threaded his way through the tables out to the back, where he knew an exit led onto an old wooden jetty protruding into a small tributary of the Saigon River.

The water was dark and foul-smelling with slicks of oil and other noxious substances floating on its surface, indicative of a shanty town further upstream. Moored alongside the jetty bobbed a small sampan with a low, curved rattan roof covering the central section of the boat. He quickly jumped on board, acknowledged the boatman and ducked under the roof, where he concealed himself beneath a dirty blanket. Moments later, he felt a bicycle being placed on top of him to screen the tell-tale human-shaped lumps showing through. Sampans with bicycles onboard were a common sight on the waterways of Saigon and wouldn't seem out of place to anyone on the lookout for something abnormal.

The boatman pushed off and had already drifted a hundred yards when he saw members of the secret police walk out the back of the café and search around the jetty. By then, however, his was just one of many similar sampans out on the water, and they paid him no attention.

Conein only had to hide under the blanket for twenty minutes as the sampan was propelled upstream along the tributary toward the shanty town. The distance covered was enough for the boatman – a paid helper of the American Embassy – to be sure they hadn't been followed and it was safe for his charge to emerge. Minutes later, he moored his craft alongside a wooden wharf just below the sprawling area of discarded corrugated iron and plastic sheeting that housed some of the city's dispossessed and poor.

Conein came out from under the blanket and dusted himself down before disembarking with a nod to the boatman. A member of the Embassy staff was waiting on the road next to the wharf in a small, unobtrusive Renault 4CV painted in the same blue and yellow colours as Saigon's taxis. Conein climbed in and was driven without incident to the dental practice in Cholon.

General Don and General Minh were already sat waiting for him upstairs in the Chesterfields, drinking coffee and smoking cigarettes. They greeted him with genuine warmth as he entered, for these three men had a long and chequered association. Lucien Conein had been born in France but moved to America a few years later. Despite this, he'd always maintained his affiliation to his mother country and had joined the French army at the outbreak of the Second World War, where he'd met Tran Van Don as a junior officer. They became lifelong friends. Nearly twenty-five years later, long after Conein had transferred back to the American military and the OSS (precursor to the CIA), Don had told the US Ambassador the only American he'd confide in was Lucien Conein – or 'Lulu', as the general affectionately called him, certainly the only man alive who'd ever dare to.

Greetings and small talk concluded, the three men got down to business.

"Lulu," said Don. "I have some good news for you. Our coup will commence within two weeks."

Conein looked up in surprise. "Two weeks! Will you be ready?" And then a devious smile of understanding spread across his face. "Does that mean you've managed to recruit Dinh?"

During their previous meetings, the biggest hurdle to the coup's success had been General Dinh, commander of III Corps, whose troops were stationed in bases surrounding Saigon, especially to the north and west. His support was essential; without it, his troops could put down any coup almost instantly. He was, however, a big supporter of President Diem and, other than Colonel Tung, the only military officer to take his orders straight from the Gia Long Palace. His allegiance to the President and the ruling family was strong and well-established, as evidenced by the use of his troops in Saigon during martial law. Until he could be persuaded to turn, there was no chance the coup could work.

Conein lit a cigarette. As he blew the smoke out, he asked how they'd managed to convince General Dinh to jump ship.

General Minh answered. "In the end, Dinh was easy to recruit. We just had to work on his huge ego. Don and I kept telling him how good a leader he was and repeated that message over and over. Given how vain he is, he lapped up our praise. We even bribed his soothsayer to tell him he was going to be promoted soon to an important role in the government. Haven't you noticed how much taller he's been walking lately? He's been insufferable, telling anyone who'll listen he's the greatest general in the ARVN. He already thinks he's the most important person in the country. We started telling him he should be the next Interior Minister and ask Diem to promote him into the cabinet. Well, our hard work paid off last week. At the chief of staff meeting with the President, which we all attend as generals, Dinh asked outright to be made Interior

Minister. But the President slapped him down instantly: '*You know I won't have military personnel in my cabinet. Of course you can't be interior minister, don't be so stupid!*' You should have seen Dinh's face afterward – he was so angry. After that, it didn't take much to convince him Diem was a fool who'd lost the support of the people, and what we needed now was new leadership – with people like him in high positions. He was soon on our side."

Conein laughed at how easy it had been indeed to win the general over. "So now you have Saigon surrounded with troops friendly to the coup."

"Well, parts of it. But the plans get a bit more complicated from here," said General Don. "We still haven't recruited General Cao, commander of IV Corps in the Mekong Delta, so we have to find a way to have his 7th Division in My Tho, the closest one to Saigon, reassigned to Dinh's III Corps. Only then will we have the whole of Saigon encircled with friendly troops, impenetrable to any Diem loyalists outside the ring."

Conein was puzzled as to how this crucial next step could be accomplished. Without the 7th Division, it left both the front and back doors wide open for General Cao, another well-known Diem loyalist, to repeat what he'd done during the 1960 coup attempt and surge up with his men from the Mekong Delta. The plotters would be wiped out within hours of launching their own takeover.

But Minh, ever confident, enlightened him. "It seems this is being take care of for us. We heard from our spy inside the Gia Long Palace that Nhu's discovered a coup is being planned – although he doesn't know the details. Especially not the fact that Dinh has switched sides. Apparently, Nhu's solution is to fake a coup of his own, and when we come out to support it publicly – as he suspects we would – his men will swoop in and arrest us all. They've called it Operation Bravo. Dinh says Nhu's asked him to lead the loyal troops responsible for the arrests. And to do that effectively, Dinh told Nhu he'd need control of the 7th Division. Luckily for us, Nhu agreed. So as of next week, Dinh's second-in-command, Colonel Co, will take over the 7th Division, and we'll have completed our impenetrable ring around Saigon. III Corps should be big enough to both defend the perimeter against loyalist forces on the outside and overcome any resistance inside the city."

Conein stood up and walked over to the pot of coffee left on the bar, taking the opportunity to consider any flaws in the plans as he poured himself a cup. He added a splash of milk before returning to his seat in one of the leather wing chairs. "So you've worked out how to keep any Diem loyalists on the wrong side of your ring. But how are you going to overcome the ultra-loyalists within it, like Colonel Tung's special forces and the presidential guard?"

"Easy," replied Minh, uncrossing his arms and using his free hands to gesticulate as he answered. "Dinh has said that some of his troops, including an armoured brigade, can be used during Operation Bravo to mount the fake coup. This allows them to come into central Saigon without ringing any alarm bells in the Gia Long Palace. The only trouble is that the Americans won't be happy to see these brigades in Saigon rather than fighting the VC in the countryside. So as a sop to them, Nhu's agreed to send four companies from Colonel Tung's special forces out of the city to replace them. They're due to leave Saigon next week on 29th October, and Nhu's decided to launch his fake coup on 1st November."

"All Saints Day," chimed Don, raising an eyebrow. "An auspicious day in the Roman Catholic calendar."

"Let me guess," said Conein with a smirk. "You're going to launch your real coup on 1st November as well?"

Don grinned back at his friend and confidante. "Exactly! Friday 1st November is the last day of Admiral Felt's visit to South Vietnam before he goes back to America. He has a meeting at the palace with President Diem in the morning and then a ceremonial send-off from the airport at midday. And we plan to mount our coup immediately after he's left. Most of the special forces will be in the countryside. The 7th Division to the south will be under our control. Several of Dinh's III Corps brigades will be in town. And all we have to do is defeat the presidential guard. What could possibly go wrong?"

Conein smiled to see his usually understated friend so full of *joie de vivre*. He only hoped his optimism was well placed.

"Just so you know, Ambassador Lodge will be attending the meeting between Felt and Diem too, and he's asked our friend Ned Rivers to be the official pool photographer for the occasion. I think he's trying to repay Rivers for allowing us to use his pictures against Nhu. But between you and me, I also think the Ambassador finds it funny he can bring Nhu's most hated newsman straight into the heart of Diem's government without any repercussions!"

26

FRIDAY 1ST NOVEMBER 1963

9.30 am

The journey to the Gia Long Palace from the US Embassy was short and quick, especially with the outriders clearing a path for the convoy. Sitting in the back of a car next to John Mecklin, the Embassy's press affairs director, Ned's mood flittered between nerves and careless recklessness. One moment, he felt like Daniel entering the lion's den, praying he'd be safe alongside Lodge; the next, the thought of Mel's murder burst into his mind, leaving him angry and rash, and eager to meet the perpetrators head-on.

He wasn't sure why the Ambassador had selected him as 'pool' photographer in the meeting between President Diem and Admiral Felt but he was pleased to have been asked. Better to be involved than not, he'd decided, although the thought of crossing paths with Nhu made him shudder, and his nerves resurfaced.

The convoy raced down Gia Long Street, creating a cloud of swirling dust behind it, and swept through the raised barrier into the palace grounds. From here, the gleaming black limousine at its lead continued on alone and drew up in front of the large portico while Ned's car pulled off and stopped twenty yards to the side, leaving him to scramble out and rush to catch up to the dignitaries' vehicle. He had the lens cap off and his Nikon primed as he ran to capture the scene of the American VIPs climbing out the Plymouth Coronado, with President Diem waiting to greet them. Opposite the portico, facing the building, two lines of presidential guards dressed in their finest ceremonial military uniforms stood to attention, the noise of their boots sounding as one as they struck the ground together.

First out, from the front passenger seat, stepped a US marine acting as security, who rushed around to smartly open the rear door facing the palace. Ambassador Lodge emerged and stood erect, running his hand through his hair to smooth down some wayward strands as he waited for Admiral Felt and General Harkins, commander of all US troops in Vietnam, to appear beside him. Ned pulled the focus on his Nikon a little tighter, capturing Lodge in his simple beige double-breasted linen suit; behind him, the general and the admiral in their finest full dress white uniforms bedecked with medals, ribbons and ample gold braid to display their authority and seniority within the US military hierarchy.

President Diem, wearing his own favourite white double-breasted cotton suit, stepped forward to meet them. Hands were shaken, greetings made, and the President led his guests through the portico and up the stairs to the front doors of the palace. Ned captured the whole scene on film, including each handshake, before following the dignitaries inside.

He looked on as the three Americans, each towering several inches over the diminutive President, were escorted through the entrance hall and into one of the state rooms. Following behind, Ned was taken aback by the grandeur of the space. Even compared to the White House, it was lavish and opulent: the floor covered in thick red carpet with yellow detailing; the high ceiling with ornate coving, a large cut-glass chandelier hanging pendulously at its centre; the walls interspersed with large windows, each shrouded with large drops of deep blue silk curtains tied back to allow daylight to flood the interior. The room itself was sparsely furnished. Toward the back stood a single large, ornate chair covered in velvet, across from which three rather more simple dining-style chairs had been arranged.

Once the dignitaries were seated, Diem facing the three Americans, Ned was ushered forward to photograph the scene, then asked to step away to let the meeting begin. He watched from a distance, where it was impossible to make out what was being said, though he did notice Diem was doing all the talking, forcing the Americans to sit forward to hear.

Unsure how long the meeting would go on, Ned chose to go for a wander around the palace. However, members of the presidential guard had taken up strategic positions at the foot of the grand French colonial staircase that swept up to the first floor in two partitions; while others were stationed outside the surrounding rooms, limiting Ned from venturing much further than the entrance hall.

Every ten minutes, he quietly re-entered the state room to see how the meeting was progressing, surprised each time to find the President still speaking. The only time Diem appeared to stop was to light another cigarette. Even after an hour, the situation hadn't changed – just the President talking...and smoking.

Finally, ninety minutes after they'd sat down, all four stood up, indicating the meeting was over. Ned thought the admiral looked as if he'd been asleep; his eyelids were drooping, and he slyly stole a yawn when his back was turned to Diem. As the party moved toward the entrance hall, Ned stood aside to allow the two officers past him, but noticed the President had put his hand on the Ambassador's arm to stop him leaving the room.

With a voice so quiet Ned could only just hear, the desolate-looking Diem spoke to Lodge. "Please tell President

Kennedy I am a good and frank ally; and I would rather be frank and settle questions now than discuss them after we've lost everything."

The Ambassador nodded in agreement and looked away. On seeing Ned, however, he turned back to the President. "Have you met, Mr Rivers, President Diem? He's the photographer I told you about from the BPA agency based here in Saigon. You might have seen some of his pictures in the newspapers."

Diem gave Lodge a contemptuous look but shook Ned's hand begrudgingly without making eye contact, then quickly strode off after Admiral Felt and General Harkins to say goodbye.

Ned was amused to see the Ambassador give him a covert wink before following on.

11.30 am

As the convoy departed the Gia Long Palace, it turned right onto Le Van Duyet Street, rushed through the crossroads where Thich Quang Duc had self-immolated, and continued north through the tense city to Tan Son Nhut Airport. Even Admiral Felt, freshly arrived, commented to his companions how quiet the city seemed that morning.

At the airport, the Plymouth Coronado pulled up alongside the American aircraft that would take Felt and his staff back to their headquarters in Honolulu. General Don and General Minh were already there to meet him. As the two highest-ranking generals in the ARVN, they were responsible for overseeing the official arrival and departure of all American VIPs.

Ned leapt out the trailing car in time to photograph the admiral and General Harkins in a final conversation with the two Vietnamese officers at the bottom of the aircraft steps. He was authorised to get in close and noticed through the camera's viewfinder General Don looked uneasy, frantically chewing gum and checking his watch, as if anxious for the visitors to leave. But neither Harkins nor Felt seemed to notice, apparently happy to continue discussing strategy and how America could further help the South Vietnamese army in the war against the communists. Eventually – much to General Don's relief, it seemed – Admiral Felt put out his hand for a final shake before bounding up the aircraft steps two at a time.

Fifteen minutes after the planned midday departure, the aircraft taxied to the end of the tarmac, received permission for take-off from the tower, and set off down the runway with its engines at maximum throttle before lifting into the air and disappearing into the cloudless blue sky.

Those left on the concourse below had already turned their backs and were climbing into their cars for the return journey when four M24 tanks appeared at the far end of the runway. Each machine moved to one corner of the tarmac and parked up with its barrel facing outward.

Only General Minh witnessed the manoeuvre, since he was the one who'd ordered it.

12.45 pm

Thirty minutes later, General Minh was waiting for his guests in the antechamber to the officers' mess dining room attached to the Joint General Staff Headquarters, just one hundred yards from Tan Son Nhut Airport. His guests had been invited for one o'clock. By twenty past, all had arrived and were drinking gin and tonics, chatting animatedly. The occasion didn't seem unusual. After all, they'd all attended briefing lunches here before, and today's seemed no different.

"Gentlemen, shall we go through?" Minh shouted rhetorically above the hullabaloo generated by twenty senior officers, between them representing all major branches of the ARVN.

The general led the way into the dining room, stopping past the door to stand and shake each man's hand as they entered. Minh enjoyed these weekly lunches but today even he was feeling a touch apprehensive. Not that those present would have noticed. The general looked his usual self: controlled, in command of the situation, bullish – even when the formidable Colonel Tung appeared.

The officers located their places at the immaculately laid table according to their name cards, with General Minh at one end and General Don at the other. Beside the twenty-two officers, four spotlessly dressed waiters drawn from the junior ranks of the catering corps were present, drawing back chairs and helping the luncheon guests take their seats.

Only after he'd checked his watch to confirm the time was a moment past one-thirty did Minh stand and clear his throat loudly to garner everyone's attention. As the room fell silent, the general spoke.

"Fellow officers. It has become quite clear we are not winning this war as we should be. Where we should be victorious, we are defeated. Where we should be succeeding, we are failing. There is a reason for this, however. In the last six months, we, the army of South Vietnam, have not been clear in our objectives. The distraction with the Buddhists has diverted our attention from the communists…or so we tell ourselves. But, as you and I all know, this is nothing but an excuse. The actual reason is that we are fighting this war with our arms tied behind our backs, our legs shackled. As soon as we get close to the Viet Cong, we pull back and let them escape into the countryside. In reality, the army of South Vietnam is being used to protect the President and his family, for he knows as well as we do that he has lost the confidence of the people of this country. Not only the Buddhists, but also the students, and now the army. Gentlemen, I can confirm that, as of a few minutes ago, a coup has been launched with the aim of removing Ngo Dinh

Diem as President of this great country. And I need to know from those seated before me who will support…and who will oppose us."

He paused to mark the end of his speech and the room fell completely silent. Then, the doors at each end of the dining room burst open. Ten soldiers entered carrying their standard-issue M1 rifles. They were led by Minh's personal bodyguard, Captain Nhung, distinctive in his black eyepatch that hid a gaping hole where his right eye had been removed following an explosion. He instructed the troops to spread out around the room, their guns pointing inward on the shocked officers.

"Stand if you are with us," commanded General Minh. "But remain seated if you disagree with our intentions."

The tension in the room was palpable, the pause longer than the general had expected. But then, in quick succession, seventeen senior officers stood and clapped enthusiastically. Minh scanned the room for those who'd remained seated. To his left, Colonel Khang of the 22nd Division. Further down the table, Brigadier General Nam, one-star general and commander of the Civilian Irregular Defence Group. But it was the officer to his right that least surprised him. Colonel Tung stared back at the general with pure hatred and fury in his eyes.

Minh glanced at each of the three men in their seats but addressed only Colonel Khang and General Nam, ignoring Tung. He knew no amount of cajoling could persuade this lapdog to turn against his master, Nhu.

"You have no reason to fear. This time, Diem and Nhu are finished. General Dinh is with us. His III Corps is encircling Saigon as we speak. So General Cao and IV Corps won't be coming to the rescue as they did three years ago. The only threats within the city are Colonel Tung's special forces and the presidential guard. For your information, three companies of Tung's men were relocated out of Saigon earlier this week, and their leader is sitting here – I don't think they'll be causing us too many problems today. Which leaves III Corps free to face the presidential guard. Perhaps, in light of this, you'd like to reconsider your position?"

The three seated men exchanged glances as if they were in the middle of a high-stakes poker game. Only Colonel Tung let his true feelings show on his face. The first to stand was General Nam. Colonel Khang followed suit soon after, throwing his white napkin down on the table as he rose to his feet.

"Thank you, gentlemen, for your support," smiled Minh. "Captain Nhung, since Colonel Tung appears to be the only officer unwilling to join us, please take him down to the cells and lock him up. As for the rest of you…" Minh held up a microphone and recorder in his right hand. "I want you to confirm your loyalty by speaking into this device and declaring your name, your rank, and finally your support for the overthrow of President Diem."

1.00 pm

Ned climbed into the cyclo and asked the driver to take him to the new BPA office. The old fire-damaged office on Rue Pasteur was still undergoing renovations, and before her death, Mel had secured the lease on a new space within the Continental Palace Hotel. Ned closed his eyes and let the wind gently caress his face as he travelled back into central Saigon, wondering where Mel would be today if she were still alive. He missed her greatly and often found himself thinking about what she'd have thought and done in a given situation. He let out an audible chuckle imagining the delight she'd have felt at Diem's expression after the Ambassador had made a point of introducing Ned to him that morning.

The sun beat down and Ned basked in its warmth, pleased with how the meeting had gone. He was still alive, he reasoned, and he hadn't been arrested. Furthermore, he'd had the chance to photograph some of the key players in one of the most important news stories in the world right now. For the first time in many weeks, he began to relax. Maybe he would find a way to remain in Saigon, if only he could neutralise the threat posed by his nemesis, Colonel Tung.

As he sat back and mulled his dilemma, he was interrupted by the cyclo driver, keen to start a conversation, remarking Le Van Duyet Street appeared quieter than normal for this time of day. As one of the main highways in the city centre and the arterial route to the airport, it usually remained busy, even during the midday siesta. But as Ned looked around, he understood what the cyclo driver was referring to. There was definitely less traffic on the road and even the pavements were empty of people. The hairs on his neck began to stand on end and he felt a tingling sensation in his stomach. Something was up, this wasn't usual. Could this mean what he thought?

No, not possible – he'd just left General Don and General Minh at the airport, and neither seemed particularly apprehensive... But then he remembered how Don had been nervously chewing gum and constantly looking at his watch.

"Bloody hell!" he cursed out loud. "How can I have been so blind!" He felt his blood pressure rise as a shot of adrenalin hit his system. The coup, the bloody coup had begun.

His hunch was reinforced as the cyclo approached the bottom of Le Van Duyet Street near the entrance to Camp Le Van Duyet, headquarters of General Dinh's III Corps. Emerging from the main gates Ned could see a procession of military jeeps and two-and-a-half-ton troop trucks filled to the brim with soldiers.

"Follow the trucks!" Ned shouted to the driver with excitement and certainty. The young man smiled at his fare and increased his cadence, attempting to keep up with the rear truck in the convoy. Meanwhile, Ned was busy taking photographs of the long line of military vehicles as they turned off the Le Loi roundabout onto Ham Nghi Road before turning right onto another tree-lined street. As the chase grew longer, the poor cyclo driver began blowing furiously, the veins on his muscular arms and legs sticking out from the increased pressure of his circulating blood.

They finally caught the convoy as it slowed to a halt outside the National Police Headquarters. Immediately, the tailgate of each truck dropped down and a rush of soldiers disembarked, each carrying an M1 rifle. Ned instructed his driver to pull in behind the last vehicle. Even before the cyclo had fully stopped, he'd jumped off with his Nikon at the ready. He followed as the soldiers rushed up the steps into the police HQ, capturing the moment the lead officer burst through the doors with his troops. Two young soldiers bearing 5th Infantry insignia had just been posted at the entrance and stopped Ned from going inside. Before long, however, he was able to photograph a high-ranking military officer escorting a collection of senior policemen out the building and loading them into one of the trucks.

Ned ran up beside the officer. "Is this the start of a coup against President Diem? Have you taken control of the national police?"

His questions were ignored, and he found himself forcibly pushed out the way by the officer's aide. Ned watched as orders were issued and troops began climbing back into the trucks. The officer, now standing in the lead Willys jeep, indicated for the convoy to follow, but only half the vehicles pulled into formation and moved off after him. The other half remained empty, as the remaining soldiers stayed behind to guard the police HQ.

Not wanting to lose the smaller convoy, Ned ran back to his cyclo driver, who luckily had hung around to wait for payment. He urged him on after the trucks. The driver didn't have as far to peddle this time. The convoy only travelled half a mile or so before stopping once more, and Ned realised they were now outside the Interior Ministry. Again, he was in time to photograph the same senior officer and a smaller band of troops barge their way into the building. But again, Ned was stopped from entering and so waited outside. He didn't anticipate any resistance from civil servants, however, and when he didn't hear any shots, he decided there must be other more interesting photo opportunities occurring elsewhere in the city. He knew he had to get back to the office at some point to alert Harry Roberts, who'd now arrived back in Saigon as Mel's replacement.

He was still calculating what to do next when from above came the unmistakable *swooshing* sound of two jets shooting over the city. The noise had seemingly come from nowhere and he ducked involuntarily at how low they were flying. Moments later, two more aircraft appeared in the clear blue sky overhead, though not moving as fast. Ned watched them turn one hundred and eighty degrees and dive steeply toward the river just two blocks from where he was standing. As the jets dropped down, they began strafing their target, then disappeared out of sight behind the buildings on the other side of the street, only to pull out of their dive a moment later and sweep back up into the sky.

Ned knew he had to get to whatever had just been targeted and hastily waved over his cyclo driver, still patiently awaiting payment. "What's over there?" Ned asked, pointing in the direction of the river to where the aircraft had been firing.

"They attack naval barracks," said the driver calmly. "You want go?"

"Yes, we go fast?"

The cyclo driver nodded. Ned jumped in the front and they set off for the naval barracks on the quayside along the Saigon River just past the end of Ham Nghi Road. Central Saigon being so small, moving from one place to another proved quick. As they passed the familiar American Embassy, the tallest building by far on Ham Nghi, Ned looked up to see some of the staff gathered on the roof watching events unfold. Since the aircraft had appeared in the sky, there was even less traffic on the streets now, and the journey to the river took just a few minutes.

Ned recognised he was close when they came to a road-block across the street. A company of soldiers from an airborne brigade were manning it and stopped the cyclo from travel-ling any further. Beyond the roadblock were more troops from the same brigade, but they were milling around looking very relaxed. Emerging from the main gates were some naval officers under armed guard. Like the senior policemen before them, they were calmly loaded onto a troop truck, which departed a few minutes later. The aircraft had disappeared from the sky and Ned was left with the overriding impression this coup was a very low-key and well-mannered affair. After weeks and months as the main point of conversation within the foreign press corps, the actual event was failing to live up to the hype. If anything, it was all a bit of an anti-climax.

On the other side of the roadblock, Ned caught sight of Danny O'Connell, the photographer he'd come to blows with at Mel's party earlier in the summer. He knew he'd just started freelancing for AP, the largest news agency in town. O'Connell caught sight of Ned and came across to the roadblock.

"I think you're a bit late, Mr BPA hotshot," he said sarcas-tically. "The naval commanders already surrendered. Oh dear, did you miss the fight?" He didn't wait for Ned to respond and simply turned and walked away, laughing to himself as he went.

Ned kicked the roadblock in anger, knowing the gobshite had stolen a march on him. Where he'd captured soldiers 'fighting' civil servants, the bastard had managed to get soldiers fighting soldiers. He remembered Mel's advice from their trip down to the Mekong Delta: *You've got to be quicker if you want to get the good shots, and you've got to be in there among the action.*

Recognising the naval barracks could now be added to the growing list of strategically important institutions that had surrendered to the plotters without resistance, Ned knew it was time to get back to the office and assess the situation with Harry.

The Continental Palace Hotel sat on the corner of Tu Do Street and Lam Son Square, next to the Opera House, in the very heart of Saigon, and had been popular with Western correspondents throughout Vietnam's recent troubles. During the Indochina War, the hotel had been nicknamed Radio Catinat, in reference to the old name for Tu Do Street during the French era. It was the accepted meeting place for anyone involved in Vietnam's affairs, from journalists and politicians to businessmen and spies; to meet, to drink and to discuss the day's events. It was no surprise, then, that many news organisations had chosen it as their base of operations, among them *Newsweek*, *Time Magazine*, and now BPA.

Ned made it back to the hotel just before 3.00 pm and immediately ran up to the roof, where he assumed Harry would be. Four storeys high, the building offered partial views around the city. As he reached the rooftop, Ned found some twenty people peering out over the edge watching the coup unfold, though none of them his boss. Almost all non-military traffic had disappeared from the streets, so any movement now was likely to be soldiers from one side or the other. In the centre of the crowd, Ned found the hotel manager, with whom he'd become acquainted, and asked for an update.

"It's very quiet at the moment, nothing much seems to be happening. The only shots we've heard came from over there toward the special forces compound, but they're only very intermittent. It's almost as if the soldiers don't want to fire at each other."

Ned had a quick look out over the city for himself and was surprised to find how very few soldiers there were surrounding the Gia Long Palace off to his right. He decided to go down to the office to check for Harry. He wasn't there, but Bich was and greeted Ned with excitement. Ned had never seen her this animated, having normally found her so quiet and introspective. The thought of Diem being deposed appeared to have enlivened her. Her green eyes flashed quick and bright as she asked Ned what was happening on the streets. Ned gave her a hasty update and asked after Harry. Bich said he'd left the office twenty minutes earlier but had left Ned a note:

> *General Minh's office rang and asked if you could visit him at the JGS offices asap. He didn't say why. Harry, 2.30 pm.*

Ned breathed in heavily and let out a low whistle. Why would General Minh want to see him? But if a coup leader wanted him to visit said coup's headquarters, he'd be a fool to decline the offer. He told Bich where he was going and rushed out the hotel onto the square, where he soon located a taxi driver prepared to drive him back to Tan Son Nhut Airport.

Within fifteen minutes, he was being escorted into the coup's central command centre.

4.00 pm

The French doors leading out onto the colonnaded corridor surrounding the Gia Long Palace were still open, allowing President Diem and his brother to listen to the noises of their fake coup. From their vantage point in the office on the first floor, they'd been able to see troop trucks driving along the roads and occasionally hear the distinctive sound of tracked vehicles moving on tarmac. But it was the roar of two air force jets strafing the river that had Nhu rushing to the balcony.

"At what point do you think General Dinh will launch the second part of Operation Bravo?" the President asked.

Nhu, one foot in his brother's office and the other in the colonnaded corridor, was trying to work out what was happening and lit another cigarette before replying. "It should be soon. It all depends on whether those vipers at the JGS have come out against us yet."

Diem could tell Nhu was pleased with his operation and had no doubts about its success. But he also knew they needed many others to play their parts – both for and against him. The plan relied on the treacherous generals declaring themselves openly against him, which he felt certain they would. And seeing the military out on the streets and the air force in the sky would surely be enough to persuade them to support the sham, without suspecting it was all part of Nhu's grand strategy.

Diem hoped there might be other casualties in the ensuing chaos – Henry Cabot Lodge for one, and that bloody photographer Ned Rivers, despite his pledge to the US Ambassador that no more journalists would come to harm. He was still fuming at the so-called diplomat's audacity in choosing Rivers to photograph the morning's ceremony. And then he had the gall to introduce the man to him directly!

The President was finally pulled out of his thoughts by his secretary announcing from the outer office that General Minh was on the phone.

"He's bitten," shouted Nhu in triumph, running back to his brother's desk to overhear the conversation.

Diem picked up the handset to the black Bakelite telephone sitting on his desk. "General Minh, I assume you are responsible for organising this rebellion. It will not succeed. You know that, don't you? And when it fails, I'll have you shot for treason."

Nhu stretched closer to the handset to hear the general's reply.

"Mr President, we have you surrounded. We've already taken the Interior Ministry, the National Police Headquarters, Navy Command and both radio stations. Our intention is not to kill you but simply remove you from power. If you give up now, we can offer you a dignified resignation and safe passage to a location of your choosing. However, if you continue to hold out, I shall have no hesitation in attacking the Gia Long Palace. You have one hour to make up your mind and contact me at the JGS Headquarters." Minh's voice cut out abruptly to be replaced by the dial tone.

The President looked at the handset in disgust before replacing it in the cradle. He fumbled in his jacket pocket for his packet of Gauloises, took one out and lit it in agitation. "Are you sure everything is going to plan, Nhu? Why did he say they'd already taken control of the radio stations, Navy Command and the police? Has our plot become real?"

"It has to appear real, Diem, that's the beauty of my plan. Only by appearing to have a chance of success will the traitors come out of hiding and pin their colours to the fake coup's mast. That's what they're doing now. I promise you, it won't be long before General Dinh sweeps into Saigon with III Corps, takes back control and rounds all these vipers up. Why don't you ring him for an update?"

Diem considered his younger brother's reasoning and agreed to contact General Dinh for reassurance. He shouted through to the outer office to get the man on the line. Moments later, his secretary appeared to say the general was not available at present to take his call.

"Just be patient, Diem, everything will be fine," said Nhu confidently.

Diem watched the smoke twisting up from his cigarette, deep in thought, before replying. "We haven't got that much time though. Minh said he'd order troops to open fire on us within an hour."

Nhu laughed delightedly. "Brother, you seem to have forgotten that General Minh doesn't command any troops. The men out there are Dinh's and he's not going to let them fire at us. Just because we want Minh and Don to believe it's real, it doesn't mean you have to too!"

The pair sat listening to the sounds of heavy diesel engines manoeuvring around outside the windows accompanied by the occasional burst of machine gun fire. Diem hoped his brother's plan was working but wondered, after twenty minutes of silence, why Dinh hadn't called them back. He shouted to his secretary to try again, but she came back with the same response. A few minutes later, the tension was broken by one of the President's bodyguards rushing into the office carrying a portable radio.

"*Ngài*, sorry to interrupt, but the rebels are broadcasting."

Nhu indicated to the bodyguard to set the device down on the President's desk and turn it on.

"*After nine years of the hated Diem regime, the army has today come to the rescue of the people and deposed him. The new administration, to be led by the army, will be run for the people of the Republic of Vietnam. It is important that we now unite after the divisive, corrupt years of the Ngo Dinh family. The change of leadership is supported by the following members of the military...*" Statements from senior officers announcing their support followed one by one. Diem and Nhu listened to the full list, relieved not to hear the names of General Dinh or Colonel Tung.

Nhu looked up at his brother. "Don't worry, Diem, it means nothing. It just makes our fake coup seem even more plausible." But Diem could hear a change of tone in Nhu's voice, not quite so confident as before.

A particularly heavy and sustained amount of gunfire suddenly erupted from outside. Nhu hurried to the French doors and looked out to identify its provenance.

"Where's that fighting coming from?" asked the President anxiously as he rushed around the desk to join his brother.

"Over there," Nhu said, pointing. "It looks like it's near Tung's special forces compound."

Together, they watched as a plume of smoke began curling up into the sky no more than five blocks from their palace. The President took another long drag of his cigarette, feeling the reassuring effects of the smoke deep in his lungs.

"Nhu," he said nervously. "If General Minh doesn't command any troops, then who's ordering those troops to fire on the special forces?"

Nhu remained silent. Diem watched the conviction fall away from his face. He'd never envisaged Operation Bravo would involve a full-on firefight and wondered who could possibly be shooting at whom. A while passed before he was finally able to catch Nhu's eye. In that single moment, his brother's poker face folded to reveal panic and rage.

"Where is General Dinh?" shouted Nhu, rushing to the outer office and demanding the secretary get him on the line immediately.

Time appeared to move slower than normal for the two brothers, but finally General Dinh was tracked down and a line established through to him.

"General Dinh," said President Diem, attempting to sound calm. Once more, Nhu stuck his head close to the receiver so he could hear the general's reply for himself. "There's a lot of firing down in the streets, what is happening? Have you commenced your sweep into the city to round up the rebels yet?"

The line crackled and burst into life. "You're finished, you despotic little arsehole! You and your psychopathic brother, you're both finished. All you care about is yourselves! Well, let me tell you, there are more important things to worry about than saving you. I've supported you loyally these past few years, but the moment I ask to be included in your government, you reject me as if I were some rancid lunatic. And now you're going to pay the price. I'm done shielding you from rebellions and coups – no more. Today, I am the rebel, and there's no one left to protect you."

As the shock of their former ally's tirade sunk in, Nhu slumped back into his chair. Diem slowly put the phone down without a word, finally realising his brother's plans had gone seriously awry, and wondered what could be done to correct the problem.

"Ring the Ambassador," Nhu suddenly blurted out in dismay. "He'll be able to stop it."

Diem snorted in derision. "You fool! Don't you see? The rebels would never have started this without the Americans' support. The Ambassador isn't going to do a thing to stop it."

But Diem knew hope was disappearing fast and agreed to put in a call to try their luck.

"Ambassador Lodge, good afternoon," said the President as calmly and politely as possible in the circumstances. "You may have noticed some units from my army have rebelled and I would like to know your government's position on the matter."

"Yes, Mr President, I have heard the shooting," replied Henry Cabot Lodge, who, having returned from his meeting with Diem earlier that day, had chosen to take lunch on the roof of his Embassy and wait for the fireworks to begin. "Unfortunately, I'm not acquainted with all the facts. Furthermore, it's four-thirty in the morning in Washington, and the US government cannot possibly have a view yet."

"But you must have some general idea. After all, I am a chief of state and you represent our closest ally."

"As I told you only this morning, Mr President, I admire your courage and the great contributions you've made to your country. But now my concern is for your physical safety. I have intelligence those in charge of this uprising have offered you and your brother safe conduct out of the country if you resign. Have you heard this?"

"No," replied the President tartly, knowing for sure Lodge was not going to help him.

"Well, if I can do anything to ensure your safety, please don't hesitate to call me."

"I am trying to re-establish order!" finished Diem abruptly, slamming down the phone. He sat back in his chair and looked at Nhu across his desk. "We're finished. Dinh has turned against us and the United States isn't coming to our rescue."

The sense of loneliness and rejection was intense, the silence cutting. The two brothers had schemed and conspired all their political lives, but now it seemed others had beaten them at their own game.

"Oh, come now, all's not lost," enthused Nhu suddenly in one last effort to regain control of the situation. "There are many loyalist troops still out there – the presidential guard, Tung's special forces. Cao's IV Corps are only two hours away in the Mekong Delta, and they saved us last time. You remember how we called the plotters' bluff by asking them here to negotiate. That gave Cao enough time to arrive from the south. Let's do it again. Ring Minh and invite him here to discuss a deal. You watch – before a settlement can be reached, our allies will have arrived and the rebellion will be over."

In light of their desperate situation, Diem knew such a call to the rebels at the Joint General Staff Headquarters was probably their last chance to head off the impending disaster. Nhu was right – his own guard, with Tung's forces and IV Corps, just two hours to the south, would all remain loyal. But the question playing over in his mind was whether they could beat Dinh's III Corps – and would they get here fast enough? A delay tactic was probably his final throw of the die.

He picked up the phone, dialled the number for the JGS Headquarters and waited for the generals to answer. When General Minh picked up, the conversation that followed was fraught and expletive-laden. In no uncertain terms, Minh told the President it was the people's wish to have a different government and it was time for him to go. Diem defended himself aggressively in turn: even if the people did want change, it was not for the military to take actions into their own hands – a democratic election was the correct course.

Eventually, recalling the point of the call, the President looked up from the phone at his brother, listening in as ever, composed himself, and then cast his fly.

"General Minh. Why don't you and General Don come over to the palace so we can negotiate a ceasefire and agree a timetable ending in free, democratic elections for a new government?"

Diem hoped to God the fish would bite.

4.00 pm

The command centre at the Joint General Staff Headquarters was a considerable space with walls covered in plans and maps showing troop movements and their locations. The largest map showed Saigon's District One, the central area where government institutions were based, on which coloured stickers had been stuck with the name of each battalion and its commander. On a different map displaying Greater Saigon and the surrounding area, Ned noticed a series of blue stickers encircling the city, all positioned on main arterial roads leading into the centre. The room was frenetic, abuzz with excitement, with uniformed officers shouting instructions while soldiers answered a bank of phones and repositioned the map stickers as troop positions changed. Most present were diligently hard at work, though some senior officers looked a little more pensive and nervous.

General Minh was busy studying the Central Saigon map with General Don when Ned was escorted in. On seeing him, Minh immediately gave an order in Vietnamese to a subordinate before striding across the room to greet the photographer. "Thank you for coming Mr Rivers. I expect you're wondering why I asked you?"

"I am a little curious as to why I'm here, but I'm glad you invited me."

"Today is a monumental day," said the general, motioning with his arm to indicate all the maps and plans around them. "And you may not know it but your photographs of Nhu and Colonel Tung at the Xa Loi Pagoda raids played an important part. They were the final proof we needed to persuade the Americans they could no longer trust Diem and Nhu, and a change of leadership was required."

"So the Americans organised today's coup attempt?"

"No, of course not. Today's coup – and by the way, it's not an attempt. It will succeed – has been organised by the South Vietnamese military, but for the greater good of the country. As a way of saying thank you for your contribution, I thought you might like to photograph my command centre and perhaps take some pictures of myself and General Don."

Ned had never attended a coup before, but he was fairly sure this was an opportunity even more established photographers were rarely offered. He didn't care if he was only there because its leader wanted his own picture splashed across the world's news.

"Thank you, General Minh, that's very generous of you. Are you winning then?"

"Everything is on schedule. The only pocket of resistance is coming from the special forces," said the general. Before he could continue, he was interrupted by a shout of protest coming from a side door leading into the command centre. Ned looked around to see what the commotion was about and the hairs on the back of his neck prickled as he recognised the imposing figure of Colonel Tung walking through the door. It was only when he realised his nemesis was under armed guard that he quickly relaxed again.

Minh strode back to General Don's side as Colonel Tung was brought to them, whereupon a vicious argument broke out in Vietnamese. Ned watched the three men shouting, enjoying the sight of Tung now under the cosh himself. Suddenly, without warning, General Minh removed his personal revolver from its hip holster and thrust it into Tung's temple. The argument came to an abrupt halt. A telephone was placed in front of the colonel and the receiver shoved firmly into his hand. The despondent delivery of Tung's instruction down the line told Ned all he needed to know: the special forces had been stood down and instructed to surrender to the rebels.

Remembering why he was there, Ned took out his new Leica camera from the inside pocket of his sleeveless jacket and captured the moment of Colonel Tung's capitulation.

He was shocked, however, that Tung had acquiesced so easily. The authoritarian figure with his sharp, pencil-thin moustache now looked bitter, ready to explode in anger. Only then did he look across the room to see Ned for the first time. His face registered shock to find his downfall being witnessed not just by a member of the foreign press, but by the one he despised most. Ned nodded his head in greeting. Like a small terrier barking aggressively at a bigger dog from the other side of a secure fence, he gave the colonel his widest smile. Tung returned a look of such contempt that Ned thought he might melt under the onslaught.

General Minh gave a sharp order to his one-eyed bodyguard, who issued a further instruction to the two soldiers accompanying him. They sprang toward Tung and marched him back out the room, rifles pointed at his back. Observing the gleeful expression on Ned's face, Minh promptly shouted, "Captain Nhung, why don't you take Mr Rivers with you?"

Though framed as a question, Captain Nhung knew better than to contest this order. With his one good eye, he looked over to the photographer and indicated for Ned to follow. Without hesitation, Ned rushed over and followed the captain down an austere corridor with a concrete floor leading outside onto a tarmacked area, where a number of small jeeps were parked.

Colonel Tung was ordered to sit in the front passenger seat of a Willys jeep while the two soldiers escorting him jumped in the back, their rifles still aimed at the prisoner. With no room left inside the vehicle, Captain Nhung suggested Ned stand on the rear footplate. As Ned got in position, Nhung jumped behind the wheel. The jeep moved off toward a compound exit guarded by four soldiers, who immediately raised the barrier on recognising the one-eyed driver. Nhung drove out into the airbase grounds along one of the many tarmacked service roads surrounding the runway to a patch of rough grass on the far side of the strip, Ned clinging on tight as the captain swung the little jeep around the tight corners. As soon as the vehicle came to a standstill, Ned dismounted, while Nhung and the two soldiers hopped out, shouting at Colonel Tung to do the same.

The light outside was beginning to fade as the colonel was marched into the rough grass, though still strong enough for Ned to use his Nikon F with his preferred 50 mm fixed lens to photograph the event unfolding before him. Nobody had explained what was about to happen. Ned hadn't really stopped to think about it until he raced forward to capture the scene from the front and nearly fell into a large trough dug into the grass – six feet long and just as deep.

Finally understanding why they were all here, Ned stood in front of the hole as Colonel Tung was ordered to kneel at the far end. He expected more of a reaction from the man now stooped before him. But beside a continuing look of pure hatred aimed in his direction, there was no other discernible emotion.

Ned found it hard to reconcile his own feelings, however. He wanted to shout out at his nemesis, recalling his anger when Dai had been killed by Tung's own troops. He wanted to celebrate the fact that the man responsible for Mel's murder was finally beaten. He wanted to cheer to the sky that the soldier behind the deaths of so many innocent monks was about to receive his punishment. He wanted to taunt Tung about being alive while the man – still dressed in his military best from the day's lunch – was kneeling beside his own grave.

But he couldn't. He remained silent and looked on through the viewfinder in dumbfounded shock. It was only when Captain Nhung drew his service pistol and unceremoniously shot the colonel through the back of the head that the trance was broken. The bullet went straight through Tung's skull, exiting beneath the jaw in an explosion of blood that splattered across his jacket.

Ned flinched as he heard the shot, but continued taking photographs as the man who'd caused him so many problems in the short time he'd been in Vietnam toppled forward into his grave. The sight of someone being executed before his eyes failed to shock Ned, and he recognised how desensitised he'd become since the immolation of a monk just five months earlier.

General Minh watched his loyal bodyguard stroll back into the command centre as if he'd done nothing more than nip out for a newspaper. Seeing Ned Rivers behind Nhung, the general issued an order for a taxi to drive the photographer back into town. The key pictures had already been taken.

A junior officer attracted Minh's attention to inform him President Diem was on the line. The general walked to the phone and picked it up.

"Good afternoon, President Diem. Are you calling to surrender?"

The room was silent.

All the rebels hoped the call presaged an early end to the coup, though the hostile, shouted exchange that followed showed little promise of a quick capitulation.

Eventually, however, the voice coming through the receiver softened and the tenor changed. "General Minh. Why don't you and General Don come over to the palace so we can negotiate a ceasefire and agree a timetable ending in free, democratic elections for a new government?"

"Mr President," replied Minh. "I seem to remember you trying that tactic the last time you were in this situation back in 1960. And on that occasion, you delayed long enough for General Cao and Colonel Tung to save your skin. Well, let me tell you, not only is the 7th Division under our command; it's also stopped Cao and the remainder of IV corps from coming to your aid by seizing all the ferries along the Mekong River and holding them on the Saigon side. Furthermore, you may not be aware yet that Colonel Tung is dead. And before he died, he ordered his special forces to stand down. The only thing keeping our troops out of your palace right now is your presidential guard. We will not be negotiating. You will surrender unconditionally right now, or else we will flatten the palace with you and your brother inside."

There was silence on the line and Minh started to wonder if the connection had been lost. But after a short pause, he heard the President's voice once more.

"General Minh. You may think you've been very clever, but I have no doubt my guards will stand by me until any one of my loyal units can break back into Saigon to crush you. Time is on my side, not yours. They are already coming. And I shall look forward to seeing you shot for treason."

Minh tried to interject, but the line was already dead.

5.30 pm
As Ned sped back down Le Van Duyet Street in the back of a taxi for the second time that day, the city in front of him glowed a warm orange. The western sky off to his right was

aflame with waves of different hues weaving in and out of each other. And in the centre, a bright orb the colour of dark amber dropped toward the horizon, unaware of the momentous day it was bringing to an end.

Ned harried his taxi driver to ever greater speeds as they raced on toward the city centre, the streets still eerily quiet with very little traffic about. He instructed the driver to take a left turn onto Gia Long Street, perusing the area surrounding the palace as they passed. He was surprised to find no sign of rebel troops, having assumed it would be the main focus of the generals' attention. What didn't surprise him was the sight of Diem's presidential guard erecting barbed-wire defences around the perimeter, clearly preparing for the inevitable battle. Where the convoy of cars had parked for Diem's meeting with Admiral Felt only a few hours earlier, there now stood two tanks guarding the main entrance.

Ned asked to be left at the Continental Palace Hotel. He guessed he had a small window of time in which to find Harry and drop off his used film since it seemed there would be no further fighting until darkness descended on the city. Harry was still nowhere to be found but he'd left another note stating he was at the public telegraph office attempting to wire his updates on the coup to New York. Good luck with that, thought Ned, knowing the lines were bound to be down. But at least his report would be front of the queue when they were working again. With Mel gone, he understood it was even more vital for Harry and himself to gather the news as efficiently as possible and get it across to New York in double quick time to beat their competitors. He knew what they were up against. Their rivals were armed and ready to report on every detail of the coup, especially Associated Press, the largest of the news agencies, who'd accurately foreseen the event and brought in several extra reporters and photographers – including that arsehole Danny O'Connell.

With a long night ahead of him, Ned took the chance to refuel and collect additional supplies of film before heading outside to assess the situation. Evening had now fully descended upon the city, with the sitting moon low in the sky just above the tallest buildings, its strong glow illuminating the unlit streets. Keen to ensure he took the best photographs of the night, Ned set off for the Gia Long Palace to check if rebel troops had surrounded it yet. Before he could get there, however, he saw a flare launched into the sky east of the palace. A moment later, a loud explosion shattered the silence of the city. He stopped to listen. As he tried to comprehend what was happening, a machine gun opened up in reply, confirming the fighting had resumed.

Ned guessed it must be coming from the presidential guard compound to the east of Independence Palace. He checked his watch to find it was just after 8.00 pm. Holding his Nikon tightly to stop it banging against his chest, he ran in the direction of the noise. Another flare spiralled into the sky and he realised he was close to the action. Turning a corner, he came across a company of M113 armoured personnel carriers parked along the street. He slowed his pace and tried to get his breath back as he sought out the commander in the lead APC, whom he found standing at the front talking to one of his NCOs.

"Are you a loyalist or a rebel?" asked Ned, thinking it might be wise to check before further inquiries.

"I am loyal to my country but a rebel against Ngo Dinh Diem," the soldier told him bluntly without a hint of friendliness.

Ned was taken aback by this haughty attitude, especially from someone he guessed was only a few years older than him. He tried again. "What unit are you?"

"We are 1st Armoured Cavalry Regiment, part of Colonel Thieu's 5th Division in General Dinh's III Corps."

Ned didn't know anything about Colonel Thieu or his 5th Division, but did at least recognise General Dinh as the man who'd turned on his old mentor, the President.

"Are you attacking the presidential guard?"

"Yes, very soon we hope, but we are being held back in reserve. The barracks are around the next corner. But you can't go up there. No journalists near the siege," said the young officer harshly.

"That's okay, I'm a photographer, not a journalist," shouted Ned, having already set off up the street at a sprint toward the guard compound, hoping the officer wouldn't bother to chase him. As the street ended in a T-junction, Ned looked left and found what he'd been looking for. Positioned along the road in front of him stood a tank and four APCs, all pointing in toward the barracks on the right-hand side. The compound was protected by a high brick wall built around the main entrance in the middle. This was guarded by thick steel gates, which were firmly shut.

Ned crept up the street, hiding behind one APC, then sprinting to the next and taking cover behind that. He peeked around the side of the vehicle, searching for a soldier, but there was no one; just the APCs and the single M24 tank. As he was wondering where everyone was, he found himself startled by the sound of heavy machine guns opening up behind him. He ducked instinctively and crouched low to the ground. Looking up, he saw a battalion of paratroopers – identifiable from their maroon berets – running down the left-hand side of the street along the low concrete row of shops. They'd taken cover in the shops and on the rooftops, and it was on the roof directly behind him he saw a group of three surrounding a heavy machine gun on a tripod firing directly into the compound.

Ned realised he'd managed to get himself right in the middle of the fighting. But at least that allowed him to photograph the soldiers from in front, which he hoped would provide a more intimate feel of the action. He watched the tracer bullets flying above him in the direction of the compound. As he scanned along the row of shops, he saw a paratrooper waving him over from a doorway. First checking it was safe, Ned ran and took shelter alongside him.

The front grill of the shop had been pulled open and a number of soldiers were crouching in the darkness. Ned asked what unit they were from. A young junior officer wearing his beret at a jaunty angle confirmed they were paratroopers, also from Thieu's 5th Division, tasked with clearing the presidential guard compound with the help of the 1st Armoured Cavalry Regiment.

As they were talking, the turret of the tank began to move. A moment later, it fired at the main entrance, blowing a hole in the brickwork securing the top hinge to the left-hand gate. The heavy steel gate sagged sideways. Ned watched the tank lower its barrel and fire again, this time at the bottom. The projectile smashed into the side of the gatehouse and knocked the remaining hinge clean away. Slowly, with nothing left to support it, the gate crashed forward onto the pavement.

The junior lieutenant whom Ned had been talking to issued a command to the platoon of soldiers nearest him. When he gave the 'go' signal, some twenty men scrambled from their cover and followed him toward the opening. Ned was in two minds whether to follow. Should he climb up to the roof and join the men up there – certainly the safer option – or go in with the attacking paratroopers?

You've got to be quicker if you want to get the good shots, and you've got to be in there among the action.

Ned quickly chose the latter and gave chase, not wanting to be left behind. He was catching up to the paratroopers when another heavy machine gun started firing. He'd assumed it was the one positioned on the roof behind him, but seeing the lead paratroopers collapse to the ground before him, he realised they'd been shot at from in front. He watched another six men go down before his brain sent an urgent message to his body: *Abort, take cover!* Passing the open doorway into the guardhouse overseeing the main entrance, he jumped through and fell heavily to the floor. Moments later, several other like-minded paratroopers scrambled in behind him.

The guardhouse had windows looking out onto the barracks. Immediately in front was an open parade ground, beyond which stood several long, low wooden buildings. Only the gable ends of the barracks were visible to Ned and the group taking shelter alongside him. With the sky cloudless and the moon full, he could clearly make out the dead paratroopers lying still on the parade ground. Among the fallen was the young lieutenant who'd beckoned him over and offered him protection.

From behind came the sound of the heavy machine gun firing. Only when the soldiers inside looked out the window all the way down the parade ground to their left could they see what their comrades were shooting at. Emerging from behind the end barrack was another M24 tank, this time belonging to the loyal presidential guard. Ned watched its turret swing around toward the row of shops across the street. Moments later, it fired. In the darkness, the explosion emanating from the end of its barrel lit up the surrounding area, temporarily blinding Ned. From behind, he heard the shell crash into the shops with a mighty roar. He was unsure if it was a direct hit, but the ensuing silence confirmed the paratrooper machine gunners were no longer in the fight.

As Ned's eyes started to regain focus, he could make out the presidential guards' battle tank slowly grinding its way along the front of the barracks toward the guardhouse. With increasing alarm, he watched as the turret slowly started to traverse and swing around to face them. As the inevitability dawned on those taking shelter that they were next in the firing line, each man leapt to his feet and made for the door, fighting not to be the last one out. They were still acutely aware of the danger from the machine gun sitting atop the tank; they didn't want to meet the same fate as their comrades out on the parade ground. Fortunately, having seen the enemy shell burst into the shop, their own M24 tank had moved forward, crunching its way through the shattered gates to find and destroy its loyalist counterpart.

Ned's only option was to take cover on the far side of the rebel tank, its two-inch-thick steel armour offering the cover he needed. Recognising, however, that he'd be blown to dust if the guards' tank chose to fire toward him, Ned peeked around from his position to check how much trouble he was in. In the light of the full moon, he was relieved to see the loyalist tank still aiming at the guardhouse, having seemingly not yet spotted the approaching threat. Ned pulled his Nikon close to his face, choosing the lowest aperture setting to account for the low light levels, and moved the viewfinder to his eye. Focusing as best he could in the given conditions, he clicked. And as he did so, the guards' tank fired.

The noise shattered the silence, but he didn't witness the flame bursting from the end of the barrel, indicating the viewing prism mirror in his camera had been lifted at the exact moment the tank had fired. The subsequent shockwave from the shell exploding and demolishing the guardhouse was enough to make him duck back behind the rebel tank, his heart racing. Feeling a shared affinity with the paratroopers, he hoped to God they'd all made it out in time.

He was busy studying the smoke and dust rising from the collapsed building when the turret of the tank he was sheltering behind started moving around to its left. Ned guessed what was about to happen. Still shaking from the previous, relatively distant blast, he was anxious not to be standing so close to the rebel tank when it fired. He took several paces back and held his hands over his ears for protection. The noise, when it came, was incredible. Ned watched the area light up. When the smoke had cleared, he saw the loyalist tank on fire. Not only were flames bursting out in every direction; the turret had been blown off its fixings and was now hanging half-off the side of at a peculiar angle.

Cheering erupted from behind the main compound wall. Looking over his shoulder, Ned saw the remaining paratroopers storming through the open gates and spreading out across the parade ground. They used whatever cover they could, including the shadows cast by the strong moon, but they met no resistance. Following close behind were the four M113 APCs, tracks rattling as they manoeuvred onto the parade ground to add supporting firepower.

Ned expected the presidential guards, presumably secreted throughout the barrack buildings, to start defending their positions at any moment; but there was no defensive attack. He ran with the paratroopers toward the wooden buildings, managing to capture an image of a soldier with a bulky M60 machine gun thrust out in front of him as he moved. When the soldiers reached the barracks, they discovered a door on the side of each building. With practised training, the first soldier checked the route was clear and the rest filed in through the doorway to spread out across the barracks. But there were no guards inside, only silence.

Twenty minutes later, Ned was standing alongside an officer, who reported that the entire compound was empty. The only defence the presidential guards had left behind was the single M24 tank, now destroyed. The officer's name was Major Hau, commander of 3 Company from an airborne battalion. As well as an English speaker, Ned found him to be friendly and informative.

"Was that as easy as you expected, Major?" asked Ned as they walked back outside.

Hau looked across to the six dead bodies lined up in a row on the edge of the parade ground. "We expected the fight against the presidential guard to last several hours; they're an elite force after all. But, as we've discovered, they're not here. If not for the lieutenant's bravado, we could have taken the barracks without any loss of life."

"Where do you think they went then?"

Before the major had a chance to reply, the now familiar sound of machine gun fire exploded from the centre of town. Hau looked past Ned in the direction of the Gia Long Palace and shrugged his shoulders, as if to say: *There's your answer.*

27

Midnight

Ned felt sick when he realised he'd positioned himself in the wrong place once again and castigated himself for the error. He should have thought more logically. Obviously, the world's newspapers would want to feature photographs showing the fall of the Diem government and not the defeat of the presidential guards. Why would they use a picture of an army barracks takeover when they could show the capture of the presidential palace itself? If there was going to be one iconic image of today's events splashed across the front pages, it was important it should be one of his – not anybody else's, and certainly not Danny O'Connell's. He couldn't bear the thought of that. He couldn't be happy with an 'almost ran' on page two.

He was relieved, therefore, when he returned to the town centre to discover the assault on the Gia Long Palace hadn't yet taken place. No sign of fighting, arrests or resigning presidents. The defining shots of the coup were still up for grabs; and to get them, he'd have to follow Mel's advice.

Having accepted a lift from Major Hau in the back of a cramped APC to the area surrounding the Gia Long Palace, he set out to explore the streets, trying to identify the rebel generals' next move. It was surprising to think the coup had been running for twelve hours already, and except for the odd skirmish, very little had happened. Ned suspected the generals were trying to avoid too much bloodshed while hoping President Diem would see the futility of resisting any longer and offer his resignation. But so far that hadn't happened. And the longer Diem held out, the more chance he had of being rescued by his loyalist officers outside the city. Given it was already past midnight, Ned was surprised Minh and Don still hadn't ordered the final assault.

As he scampered around the neighbouring streets to the palace, he discovered pockets of soldiers waiting for their final instructions. The airborne troops who'd 'liberated' the presidential guard barracks were now resting in among the trees either side of Thong Nhat Boulevard, just to the west of Notre Dame Cathedral, along with their comrades from the 1st Armoured Cavalry Regiment who'd been in reserve for the siege. Behind the Opera House on Lan Son Square, he found a company of marines, and along Le Loi he learnt Colonel Thieu had positioned two infantry battalions, from the 7th and 9th Regiments respectively, with back-up from an armoured regiment, all bearing the insignia of his 5th Division.

Ned decided that, if he were in charge of planning an assault on a well-defended building, he would choose the marines to lead it. Half-walking, half-trotting to ensure he didn't miss them, he returned to the Opera House. He found the company of marines sitting in small groups of five or six men perched on their packs, resting and joking among themselves as they awaited further orders. Around them were gathered inquisitive children who'd escaped the clutches of their mothers and come out onto the moonlit streets in search of excitement.

As Mel had taught him that day in the Mekong Delta, seemingly so long ago now, he went in search of the company commander to ask to join their mission, and was directed toward a squat man sitting on his own. When the officer stood up, Ned sensed his authority and understood why he'd been chosen to lead this group of one hundred and twenty men. Barrel-chested in comparison to most Vietnamese men, he eyed Ned as if this were a distraction he could do without.

"Are you the company commander?" asked Ned, trying his luck nonetheless.

The officer stood bolt upright. "Yes, I'm Captain Quan. What do you want?" His reply was bullish in tone, spoken in a deep voice.

Ned introduced himself and asked permission to accompany the marines if they were called up to assault the palace.

"What do you mean, 'if we're called up'? Of course we'll be called up, we're marines!" he boomed. "I'm not going to sit here all night scratching my arse."

Ned paused to consider his answer, leaving the captain free to continue his tirade as to why the marines were best placed to carry out the attack. Having given him enough time to express his fierce pride in his regiment, Ned finally interrupted as tactfully as possible. "Captain Quan, I've come because I agree. That's why I'm asking to join you."

The captain stood silenced, fixing Ned with an analytical stare, before a big grin spread across his face. "You're a good talker — I like you. If you promise to photograph my men as brave and heroic, you can join us." As he spoke, he clapped Ned on the upper arm with enough power to almost knock him off his feet.

Before the conversation could continue, a young soldier carrying the company's radio on his back, its long antenna arcing through the air, bounced up to his commander and held out the handset. Captain Quan took it and spoke into the receiver in Vietnamese, then passed it back to his operator and called for silence. There followed an impassioned and rousing speech.

As soon as he'd finished talking, the men stood up eagerly, slung their rucksacks on their backs and picked up their rifles.

"What's happening?" asked Ned.

"You were right!" exclaimed Quan. "I got the instruction – take up position on the corner of Gia Long Street and Rue Pasteur ready for the assault on the palace." His huge smile and sudden bonhomie exposed his excitement.

Quan formed his men into several columns and marched them up Tu Do Street, then left onto Gia Long Street, Ned bringing up the rear with his camera primed. The captain stopped his men one street back from the palace to brief them. After they'd moved off again, Ned asked what the plan was. Through a mix of verbal and physical demonstration, Quan explained his men were to move forward in small numbers and take up positions in any building facing the palace within their arc of responsibility. He'd authorised them to knock down any door that stood in the way of their mission. Once in place, they were authorised to shoot any defender they saw within the palace grounds. He'd also allocated a third of his sector to each of his three non-commissioned officers, instructing them to spread their men evenly across their respective areas.

Clear now on what to expect, Ned opted to follow a high-calibre heavy machine gun team, hoping they'd make an interesting subject to photograph. The moon, now high in the sky, provided plenty of light as the three-man crew started forward. One carried the Browning machine gun, the second the heavy tripod, and the third the ammunition.

Ned followed as the soldiers slipped down an alleyway and emerged onto Rue Pasteur. In front of them across the road stood the palace compound wall. Well over six feet high, it was topped with strands of barbed wire strung taut from one post to the next. As Ned looked down Rue Pasteur, he could see other soldiers creeping along the street in the moonlit gloom to take up their positions. No more than ten yards down the street, his team of marines came to a security grill pulled tight across the entrance to a shop.

The first marine called as quietly as he could through the grill until an elderly man appeared from within. Ned listened as an argument developed in angry whispers, until the shop owner finally drew the grill aside and allowed the three soldiers plus Ned to enter. The old man led the party up to the second floor and showed them into a bedroom. Ned deduced he and his family must live on the floors above the shop. The bedroom contained two small single beds, neither of which was occupied. Ned guessed the family had moved out earlier that day when it had become apparent what was happening, leaving only the old man to protect their property.

The soldiers entered the bedroom to discover a pair of French doors that opened out onto a small balcony with sculpted iron guardrails. Crucially, the balcony looked out across the palace gardens onto the palace itself. The old man retreated, and the soldiers turned off the lights in the corridor to ensure they weren't backlit in any way, then opened the doors and mounted the machine gun onto its tripod.

Crouching down on the balcony beside them, Ned had a clear view of the palace and its grounds. He could see two presidential guard tanks parked in front of the portico facing out through the main entrance onto Gia Long Street. On the roof of the palace, people – presumably soldiers – were moving around stealthily, preparing their defence. Occasionally, he heard a burst of machine gun fire, but he had no visibility on the back of the palace, so couldn't tell if it was coming from rebels or loyalists.

Surveying the two warring sides, the anticipation of witnessing the final assault in this coup filled Ned with excitement, but he could also feel his stomach clench with tension. As a child, he'd heard his father talk about his battle experiences in Europe; now it was his turn to face the violence of war. He reassured himself these were professional nerves rather than outright fear, knowing he had to be here on the front line if he wanted to take better, more immediate pictures and beat his competitors.

Rumbling down Gia Long Street from the opposite direction to where he was crouched, an M24 tank inched its way toward the main palace gates followed by three tracked APCs. The gates were as tall as the wall on either side and made of solid timber, blocking the tank commander's view into the compound. Ned tried to focus his camera on the scene, but it was too dark, so he watched instead as the tank turned on its right track, coming around to face the gates, and then drove straight through them. The wooden bar slung across the inside of the barriers creaked and groaned before finally splitting apart under the intense force. The gates burst open, allowing the rebel tank to barge its way into the palace grounds.

It was barely halfway through when both defending tanks fired simultaneously. Both shells appeared to pierce the advancing tank's armour before exploding from the inside, causing it to shudder visibly. When the smoke cleared, Ned could see through the darkness that the tank had been horribly disfigured, a huge hole punching out from one side and both tracks blown off. No one inside could possibly have survived such a blast.

The defending tanks' attack on the rebels had acted like a starting pistol; after a small pause, all hell broke loose. The machine gunners alongside Ned on the balcony opened fire at the loyalist troops on the palace roof, joined by many others hidden among the shops and houses on Gia Long Street and Rue Pasteur. Coloured tracer bullets flew through the night sky, many deflecting up into the darkness after striking a physical object on the palace roof. Ned was mesmerised by the light show they created. Most of the tracers flew toward the roof; when a defending machine gun could be seen returning fire, the attackers shifted aim onto that spot. Ned didn't fancy being one of the men on top of the palace, and certainly not those highlighting their position by having the temerity to shoot back. At times, the array of tracer bullets flying through the sky became so thick it became difficult to distinguish one side's from the other's.

Ned soon learnt giving away one's position through the ejection of red-hot gases from the end of a firing barrel worked both ways. He was happily watching the tracers speed in toward the palace roof when he heard the concrete below his balcony being struck by bullets. He ducked instinctively, then looked up to see a line of tracers flying in his direction. The balcony had almost certainly saved his life and the lives of the soldiers lying next to him. The machine gunner had ducked down too, releasing the trigger, thereby discontinuing the tell-tale sign of their position. The next burst of bullets struck their building higher up and off to the left, confirming their assailant had lost track of their precise location. From then on, the marine on the machine gun fired in short bursts with longer intervals in-between. More bullets and tracer fire did come at them, though not so tightly now, and the threat seemed diminished.

Ned stayed with his marine machine gunners for what felt like the whole night. When he looked at his watch, however, it turned out to have only been ninety minutes. A lot of fire was still coming from the defenders, both from the roof and now from within the garden too, but there was an equal amount of returned fire from the rebel positions. No one side seemed to be making progress. Ned had tried capturing a series of slow shutter speed pictures with various different apertures to show the intensity of the fire and tracers, all centred on the palace, but he wasn't hopeful of getting the shot he needed. During a small interlude in the firing, therefore, he chose to leave the gunners and go find Captain Quan for an update.

Before he could locate him, however, he came across Danny O'Connell one street back from Rue Pasteur photographing the airborne troops who'd captured the presidential guard barracks earlier in the evening. They'd now moved forward and were awaiting their final orders. O'Connell looked up from photographing a particularly grizzled-looking soldier and grimaced when he saw Ned.

"Come to trespass on my territory again, Rivers?"

"Don't worry, O'Connell," Ned replied. "I've already been into battle with these guys. But if you want to shoot them resting, that's fine by me!"

As if to back up his statement, one of the paratroopers waved enthusiastically and shouted across: "Hey, you join us again for next fight?" Ned gave a little wave back.

O'Connell stood up straight, bristling at the insult. "Don't talk crap, Rivers! You missed the navy compound being overrun, you're such a wuss. I bet you never saw a bullet fired in anger in your life."

Ned stood his ground, holding back the urge to punch O'Connell in the face. "Says the man hiding one street back from the action. I didn't see you on Rue Pasteur just now. And where were you when Colonel Tung was executed?" He regretted giving away this last bit of information, though he did enjoy the look of shock on O'Connell's face. The man obviously hadn't heard the news. Ned covered his mistake with a smug laugh as he turned away and continued on, hoping his rival would be just as riled up as he'd felt on the receiving end earlier that day.

There was now as much activity in the streets surrounding the palace at three in the morning as there normally would be at three in the afternoon. More soldiers and armour had arrived, and some local people had ventured out to see how it would all end. Ned didn't want to stray too far from the palace, knowing the grand finale could happen at any moment. He was amazed Diem still hadn't offered his resignation. Maybe he thought help was on the way. Regardless, the climax of this eventful day felt close. But Ned knew he still hadn't taken his front-page photograph – that picture was still out there.

The siege of the Gia Long Palace continued through the early hours of the morning. Machine guns rattled, tracer bullets flew, and as the sky's inky blackness began to assume a hint of grey in the east, the loyalist defenders launched a series of mortar bombs against the attacking positions, causing serious damage to the buildings along Rue Pasteur and Gia Long Street.

Ned continued his search for Captain Quan, convinced the marines still had an important part to play in the final assault. He found the man standing in the open on Gia Long Street with his back to the palace wall talking to his three NCOs.

"Have you received new orders?" shouted Ned, once the latter had received their briefing and moved off.

"Yes, we're going in," answered Quan with satisfaction. "I just ordered my NCOs to gather the men here. There's a rumour General Cao has broken through Saigon's perimeter and is on his way with IV Corps to rescue the President, so General Minh has ordered the assault on the palace to start now... And yes, you can come too."

Ned felt a flutter of excitement in the pit of his stomach. To be the one to photograph the downfall of President Diem and his brother! Now, *that* would be the iconic photo he was after. Such a pity Madame Nhu was away in America trying to drum up support for her brother-in-law's government – she'd have been the icing on the cake.

His thoughts were interrupted by the returning marines. Within minutes, all one hundred and twenty of their number were lined up along the street. The squat bulldog of an officer turned to shout more instructions at his men, who in response began checking their weapons were fully loaded and ready for action.

Ned took the opportunity to change the film in his Nikon. He'd only used ten images so far on his current roll of twenty-four, but he wanted a fresh one for the big assault. By the time he looked up again, he was surprised to find dawn had already arrived.

5.00 am

At five o'clock exactly, a tank from the 1st Armoured Cavalry Regiment drove down Gia Long Street from the direction of Tu Do Street and stopped just past the crossroads with Rue Pasteur. The marines, taking shelter in the lee of the protective wall surrounding the President's compound, were ordered to move in behind the tank and prepare for the final assault.

Ned photographed the scene as the soldiers lined up, the light levels now high enough for the camera to capture the nerves showing through their forced smiles. Rifle, ammo, grenades and helmet straps checked, a final shout of encouragement from their captain, and then, without warning, the tank fired. The shockwaves coursed through Ned's body, but he was undeterred and ready with his camera, successfully capturing the tank as it accelerated forward, emitting great clouds of black diesel smoke, and smashed through the hole it had created. As it passed into the compound, a ten-foot section of what remained of the wall collapsed, leaving strands of barbed wire hanging loosely in the void. Within seconds, Captain Quan was leading his company of marines through the gap and into the palace gardens. The two M24 tanks belonging to the presidential guard, still pointing toward the main entrance gates, were unprepared for the incursion from this quarter, and the grounds were soon overrun by the rebels.

As he photographed the soldiers charging through the breach, Ned began to fret he'd be left behind and quickly followed the last marine into the gardens. Beyond, he could see the rebels charging forward toward the protective shelter of the portico and the front entrance. All too aware of the presidential guards on the roof spraying the area wildly with bullets, Ned still found time to ponder how much the scene had changed since he'd last been here less than twenty-four hours ago. Miraculously, no marines had been hit by the defending fire. Captain Quan ordered his men to join the rest of their comrades under the portico as they arrived from their sprint across the lawn, though away from the main doors. Ned was busy shooting the breathless soldiers with his camera. Now the sun had made an appearance above the horizon, each man was lit perfectly in warm tones.

Captain Quan briefed his marines bunched together along the front of the building to the left of the main doors. Two came forward, one of whom Ned recognised from the machine gun team he'd accompanied during the night. Quan held the two men in check with his right hand balled and raised aloft. Then, as soon as he chopped his hand downwards, the three of them burst forward toward the front door. Ned realised in a flash that this was his chance to be at the heart of the action, and he ran in behind the soldiers.

Quan and his two men fired a defensive burst as they moved in, but it soon became apparent there was no return fire. The front entrance was shut and locked, but undefended. Using the sole of his boot, the captain aimed in the small gap between the two doors and smashed them open. Confidently, he strode into President Diem's final bastion, the last building in the city to hold out against the rebels. And Ned followed immediately after.

The entrance hall – where Ned had been just the previous morning – was clear. He followed the soldiers left into the ornate state room that had hosted the meeting with Admiral Felt, but this too was empty. Having exhausted the only two rooms in the palace he'd visited, he was unsure where to go next. He could hear shouts of joy from the rest of the marines as they stormed into the building through the main doors, the last defence now clearly breached. Ned opted to explore the first floor, taking the steps up the French colonial staircase two at a time in his rush to keep up with the men as they filtered out to track down the residents.

At the top of the stairs, he found a corridor leading off in each direction and a room directly in front of him. As he opened the doors straight ahead, he was blinded by the sun, still low on the horizon, streaming in through the large windows. The room itself was little more than an office. He walked to the window that looked out from the back of the palace: disappearing across the lawns and out through the back gates was a line of presidential guards. It seemed they knew the fight was lost. Ned felt reassured – there was unlikely to be any defenders left in the palace to take a shot at him.

Eager to avoid being fired on accidentally by a nervous marine, however, he re-emerged slowly into the corridor and observed as they continued their sweep around him. He chose to turn right down the thick-carpeted passageway and entered a room at the end that looked like it could well be Diem's personal office. But the President himself was nowhere to be seen. The room was very orderly and uncluttered, the desk entirely cleared of papers. Ned had a good look around, but there was nothing to hold his interest. He snapped a few routine photographs and was returning along the corridor when suddenly he heard shouting.

Thinking the soldiers might have found Diem or Nhu – or both – Ned rushed toward the noise and eventually found himself inside a private apartment. The front hall was long with several doors leading off into different rooms. Along the corridor stood antique oriental side tables covered in fine *objets d'art*. Expensive artworks hung from the walls, mostly depicting scenes from the Catholic religion. On one side table, he found a pair of portrait photographs in matching frames, one of Nhu, the other of Madame Nhu, revealing whose apartment he'd wandered into.

The shouting had come from the couple's bedroom, where some soldiers had discovered Madame Nhu's lingerie. The chamber was large and ornate and well laid out, with a neatly made four-poster bed covered in an expensive-looking silk throw. In the corner stood a chest with the drawers pulled open, while a collection of marines were gathered in the middle throwing lingerie about, some even trying it on and impersonating Madame Nhu, much to the amusement of their comrades.

Ned photographed the soldiers frolicking. The need to release tension, having lived on their nerves for most of the night, was all too apparent. Hearing a loud cheer from the room opposite, he went across to Nhu's dining room, where another group had discovered a crate of whisky. The cheering grew louder as the men opened each bottle one by one, took a swig of the fiery liquid and passed it on. Their good humour and obvious enjoyment made for great pictures, but Ned knew they wouldn't make the front pages. He had to find President Diem if he wanted that newsworthy shot.

Retracing his steps down to the ground floor, he came across one of the marine NCOs setting up guards at the main entrance.

"Do you know where Captain Quan is?" Ned asked.

The non-commissioned officer stared blankly at him, and then his face burst into a huge smile. "Ah, Captain Quan?" He indicated for Ned to follow him through to the back quarters of the palace where the kitchens were, showing him to a plain wooden door with a small stairway behind it. The NCO looked very pleased with himself as he pointed down the stairs. "Ah, Captain Quan."

Ned thanked him and made his way down the simple, utilitarian concrete steps, with barely enough headroom for him to stand up straight – nothing like the grand colonial staircase he'd just taken to the first floor. The walls were covered in dirty white paint peeling off in patches. Every ten steps, the way down double-backed around. Ned was wondering where he was heading when he heard voices from below. Having descended what must have been sixty feet, he rounded a corner to find two familiar faces.

"Major Hau, Captain Quan," Ned said in greeting. "This is interesting. What happens down here?"

"I didn't think it would take you long to find us down here," replied the marine captain with a smile. "There have been stories for some time that President Diem had a tunnel built under the palace, but no one was sure...until now. Come, have a look."

Quan led the major and Ned further along the corridor until they came to a plain-looking wooden door set in a frame that blocked the corridor, with a handle and a very large key sticking out.

"Open it," said the captain.

Ned leant forward to turn the handle. Finding the door unlocked, he pushed. It was heavier than he'd anticipated, but it swung open, revealing the rumoured tunnel behind it. This was an extension of the corridor they were standing in, except the walls beyond the partition were bare concrete, plain bulbs hanging down every few yards to light its length.

"Have you been down there to see where it goes?" asked Ned in surprise, peering into the gloom.

"I haven't, but I sent two of my men to find out," said Captain Quan.

"I assume the President and Nhu escaped down here sometime in the night?"

Captain Quan raised his hands up. "When, who knows? But Major Hau and I are sure this is *where* they went. My men have searched every room in the palace and no one has found them."

As he finished speaking, they heard footsteps coming down the stairs. The marines' radio operator appeared a moment later, still carrying his apparatus on his back. He saluted the two officers and addressed them hurriedly in Vietnamese, which sparked an urgent-sounding discussion. After less than a minute, the operator saluted again and disappeared back up the steps.

"We've just been informed that Generals Minh and Don are on their way here to collect the President and escort him back to Joint General Staff Headquarters for the formal handover of power," Captain Quan told Ned with a wry smile, before turning to Major Hau. "Do you want to tell them the good news or shall I?

Ned understood why the captain looked so concerned. Not only had Diem and his brother escaped, but they could be anywhere in Saigon now, or beyond. Even for a tough marine, the thought of telling the fearsome General Minh that the transition from Ngo Dinh Diem to himself would not go ahead as scheduled was clearly a source of some trepidation.

7.00 am

The air in the courtyard remained cool and fresh although the sun had already risen above the horizon. The shadows were able to linger a little longer thanks to the banyan trees surrounding the space, their gentle rustling in the morning breeze the only sound to break the peaceful silence. The brothers hurried through this oasis of tranquillity to find sanctuary in the building at the end of the courtyard.

Just the sight of the church's pastel yellow exterior inspired a sense of calm and reassurance in the beleaguered President. Everything would be fine, he resolved as he entered the Catholic Church of Saint Francis Xavier alongside his brother, praying they'd find refuge from the maelstrom of events enveloping them.

Diem looked to the altar at the far end to see the body of Christ hanging from the cross and was immediately overcome with a sense of empathy with his Saviour. He suddenly understood how the man must have felt in the hours before his capture. But unlike Jesus Christ, Diem had no ambition to die for his people.

The church was empty. Finding a pew, the brothers sat down together and sighed in unison. Diem tilted his head back and studied the ribbed vaulted ceiling and mint green detailing on the walls, appreciating the soothing effect of the interior. The last twenty-four hours had not panned out as he and Nhu had anticipated, and he relished any interlude that might afford him some peace.

Where had it started to go wrong? He couldn't pinpoint the precise moment when the plan had started to derail, but the exact time at which they'd given up hope of recovering the situation was clear in his mind. At 10.10 pm the previous night, he'd put down the phone after talking to General Cao, commander of IV Corps in the Mekong Delta and his last loyal general, who'd confirmed he would not be able to fight his way through and rescue them.

No sooner was the handset back in its cradle, Nhu had taken the decision to leave the palace, believing the assault would start imminently. Within fifteen minutes, they had descended to their secret tunnel, taking only one bodyguard for protection, and hurried along the passage to the spiral staircase and freedom at the other end, half a kilometre away. Here, the bodyguard had opened the heavy steel door onto Le Loi, but shut it again quickly after casting a look around.

"We can't go outside," he'd said. "The street is full of rebel soldiers, hundreds of them."

Diem remembered with a small smile – although he hadn't found it amusing then – how they'd been forced to return to the palace for a disguise. Luckily, after a quick search, the bodyguard had found them each an ARVN infantry uniform to ensure they would blend in as they walked through the ranks of soldiers resting on Le Loi.

Once more back along the tunnel, where this time they'd actually exited through the heavy steel door and stepped out into the open. With their protective helmets pulled low over their foreheads, Diem and Nhu had followed the bodyguard through the densely packed scrum of soldiers camped out on the street and walked up Le Loi away from the centre of town.

Nobody had raised the alarm or got in their way. The only heart-stopping moment had come as they'd had to make way for a staff car driving slowly through the throng. Unable to help himself, Diem had stolen a glance inside and caught the eye of its occupant. General Dinh, commander of III Corps, whose troops were all around them on Le Loi, had stared back belligerently. For one heart-stopping moment, the general had seemed to recognise the small, older soldier in a private's uniform; but then he'd turned his head and looked elsewhere.

The pre-arranged pick-up by a palace Land Rover had gone smoothly. Forty minutes later, having driven through the back streets of Saigon to avoid rebel checkpoints, the car had delivered them to Ma Tuyen's house in Cholon. Ma Tuyen was a Chinese merchant and friend of Nhu's. Diem didn't approve of the man, but he'd realised now was not the time to vocalise this. He suspected Ma ran the opium trade through criminal gangs on Nhu's behalf, and this was probably the source of his brother's personal wealth, though he'd never raised these concerns. Either way, Ma Tuyen was the one now offering him refuge and protection.

Nhu had had the foresight to install an extension of the palace's telephone network at the house, so any calls appeared to be coming from within the Gia Long Palace. After a broken and interrupted sleep, Diem had woken early, the next steps clear in his mind. At 5.00 am, he'd called the rebel generals at the JGS Headquarters and offered his resignation. It was agreed General Minh would come to the palace and escort him back to the command centre, where a formal handover of power would take place in front of a television crew and members of the national and international press. Diem had been perfectly happy to agree to everything, since he didn't plan on honouring any of it; so long as Minh was sufficiently duped to give him the breathing space he needed to escape.

Next, with Nhu sitting subdued and unshaven in the corner of the room, Diem had called Henry Cabot Lodge at his residence.

"Good morning, Ambassador Lodge. I hope I'm not disturbing you?"

"Of course not, Mr President, I'm glad you feel able to call me. Our conversation yesterday afternoon didn't end how I'd have liked."

"I agree, Ambassador, but let's put that behind us. Things were tense yesterday afternoon."

"Indeed they were. And I'm afraid you've caught me on the hop this morning. I haven't had my briefing yet as regards the current situation. Have you managed to quell your rebelling units yet?"

The President had had to take a deep breath, knowing the Ambassador was fully aware of the current situation. "Ambassador, I would like to accept the offer you made yesterday afternoon – of an aeroplane out of the country for me and my brother."

There'd been a pause on the other end of the line before the Ambassador had responded. "Of course, Mr President. I can arrange that. But if I send my driver over to the palace to pick you up, how's he going to get access?"

"I am not at the palace, I am in Cholon. Can your driver get to Cholon?"

"Of course."

"Good. Send him to the Catholic Church of Saint Francis Xavier on Hoc Lac Street. We'll meet him there at 8.00 am.

"Fine, I'll get that arranged," Lodge had said, before pausing again briefly. "I just want to add, President Diem, you've been a good and loyal ally to the United States. I'll do everything in my power to get you and your brother out of the country safely."

Secure in the knowledge he and Nhu would soon be rescued, Diem had put the phone down and asked Ma Tuyen to drive them to the church. Being All Souls Day, he was keen to take holy communion before the Americans arrived. The nearby Saint Francis Xavier held a special place in his heart as the site of his first communion in Saigon following his move from the north.

Diem knelt forward in his pew and offered a prayer to his God. He gave thanks that the US Ambassador was coming to save them and apologised to his Maker for not being stronger and defeating his enemies.

By the time he'd finished, a priest had arrived to offer the brothers communion. They moved to the altar and knelt solemnly behind the communion rail. Heads bowed and hands clasped, they listened as the priest, fully robed in cassock and stole, incanted the words and prayers of the Holy Eucharist. He'd already lit the largest of the candles on the altar's higher candle bench in recognition of the importance of his small congregation and was now preparing the sacrament. This completed, he turned to face the altar and with both hands lifted the small silver paten holding the Eucharist bread.

"Blessed are you, Lord, God of all creation. Through your goodness, we have this bread to offer, which earth has given and human hands have made. It will become for us the bread of life."

The President and his brother replied in unison, "Blessed be God forever."

The priest then turned and picked up the chalice, which he cleaned with the purifier, a white cotton cloth marked with a red cross. He poured a small amount of wine into the chalice, followed by some water. Then, with his right hand around the node and left hand at the base, he offered it up once more to Christ above the altar.

"By the mystery of this water and wine may we come to share in the divinity of Christ, who humbled himself to share in our humanity. Blessed are you, Lord, God of all creation. Through your goodness, we have this wine to offer, fruit of the vine and work of human hands. It will become our spiritual drink."

"Blessed be God forever."

The priest continued through the rituals, washing his hands in a bowl to the right of the altar before returning to the centre to incant his prayers further. All the while, Diem and Nhu listened in silence. Kneeling at the altar rail, Diem felt a serenity he hadn't known for a long time, certainly not in the last couple of days. If truth be told, probably not since before the incident in Hue back in May that had started this whole long ordeal with the Buddhists. It was an inner peace, an affinity with Jesus Christ that he always felt during communion. In that calm, he wondered what he could have done differently. Where exactly had he lost the support of the people? He couldn't be sure, but he knew it was too late to change things now.

Only when the priest came forward with the paten and the sacrament did he realise he hadn't been paying attention to the Eucharist prayers, and scolded himself for the sin he considered this to be.

Holy communion over, the brothers thanked the priest and returned to their pew...and waited. At exactly 8.00 am, they heard the door to the church creak open behind them. Diem looked across to Nhu and quietly whispered, "Are you ready?" Nhu, his spirit evidently shattered by the events of the last twenty-four hours, nodded in resignation, and they both stood up.

They were halfway down the nave when the church door opened fully, and Diem saw for the first time who the American

Embassy had sent to pick them up. He stopped abruptly and realised his worst nightmare was confirmed.

Ambassador Lodge could not be trusted.

7.00 am

With the sun climbing in the sky, evidence of the night's battle could be seen strewn across the grounds of the Gia Long Palace and the surrounding streets. The M24 tank that had only made it halfway through the main gates was still smouldering; rubble from the mortar explosions lay in heaps on the ground; and the palace itself was pockmarked and badly scarred from the high-calibre machine gun bullets that had struck it continuously through the night. Airborne, marine and ranger soldiers continued to pour into the building through the broken front doors, many exiting later carrying a keepsake, a trophy to remember the occasion by.

News of the rebel victory spread like wildfire. Out on the streets, the soldiers manning the checkpoints and sitting on the turrets of their tanks were receiving the adulation of the crowds and being showered with French baguettes and other foods as the grateful civilians cheered the downfall of President Diem and his hated brother, Nhu.

In the midst of this merry chaos, a military convoy escorting two staff cars drove at speed toward the palace, forcing those in the road to jump aside as it passed. The procession stopped on Gia Long Street, unable to turn right into the palace grounds because of the destroyed tank blocking the entrance. Generals Minh and Don climbed out of their cars, closely followed by Captain Nhung, and strode undeterred around the still smoking tank, across the forecourt and into the palace. Inside, they were met by Major Hau and Captain Quan, who stood to attention and saluted before showing their superior officers into the empty state room.

"So where are they?" General Minh demanded.

Both Captain Quan and Major Hau hesitated a moment, unsure how to break the news. Hau, being the senior of the two, spoke first.

"*Ngài*, it appears the President and his brother have escaped."

"Escaped!" the general bellowed, spittle escaping past his broken front teeth. "What do you mean, escaped?"

"*Ngài*, they've gone, they're not in the palace. They've… escaped."

"But I took a call from Diem less than two hours ago offering his surrender and resignation. He agreed to meet me here at 7.00 am."

"I'm sorry, *ngài*, but I think he deceived you. He's definitely not in the palace."

Noticing his comrade's face reddening and wanting to avoid a scene, Don turned to Captain Quan. "Do you have any idea where they've gone?"

"Yes, *ngài*. We found a tunnel in the basement. I sent two of my men to investigate and they reported back just before you arrived. They said it runs half a kilometre south-east. At the end, there's a metal spiral staircase leading up to a door at ground level. When they opened it, they found themselves on Le Loi. The area is still packed with soldiers from Colonel Thieu's 5th Division, so Diem and Nhu must have escaped before the troops arrived."

Minh removed his white uniform gloves and slapped them across the palm of his left hand. "Those double-crossing bastards! You can't even trust them to turn up to their own capitulation."

Don started pacing the room. "How are we going to find them, Minh? Where would they have gone?"

"Your guess is as good as mine. They could have any number of secret locations to hide away in." Minh strode toward the chairs at the end of the hall, still laid out from the previous morning's meeting. Suddenly, he kicked the one nearest to him before picking up a second and hurling it across the room. "We have to find them!" he roared.

Having temporarily discharged his fury, he turned to face the other three men, unsure what to suggest. He and Don had prepared for many scenarios over the last twenty-four hours, but they hadn't considered this one.

Behind his colleagues, the door to the hall opened. Captain Quan's radio operator stood there staring at the enraged general like a rabbit caught in headlights. After a moment, he remembered himself and cleared his throat. "Excuse me, *ngài*. I have a Colonel Truc here from JGS wanting to talk to you urgently."

"Come here, man, pass me the handset."

The radio operator scurried into the room and handed General Minh the handset with a look of terror.

"Colonel Truc, General Minh here. Go ahead."

"*Ngài*, we've just taken a call from the American Embassy with information on the President's location."

The news of Diem and Nhu's whereabouts lifted both the generals' spirits. Their shoulders took on a new rigidity and they allowed themselves a confident smile. With a sense of relief that his victory had been recovered, Minh briefed a junior officer to gather all the journalists who'd found their way into the palace grounds and relay the message that President Diem and his brother had been captured. The official handover ceremony would go ahead as planned at the Joint General Staff Headquarters at Tan Son Nhut Airport at 10.00 am. All members of the press were invited, and they would have a chance to ask questions afterward.

As the metaphorical grey clouds lifted from above the generals, Don stepped across to Minh and shook him vigorously by the hand. "I knew we could do it, old friend. Ours is the victory."

"Indeed it is, General," replied Minh earnestly. "Today is the day that future historians will declare the fortunes of the Republic changed – mark my words."

Ned felt smothered by the arrival of so many members of the Western press at the palace and decided to move away from the pack to seek out original scenes no other photographer would capture. He and Harry Roberts had bumped into each other at last, and the pair had moved upstairs to investigate what was left of Diem's private apartment. Consequently, they were unaware of the press briefing taking place downstairs.

Diem's apartment on the first floor overlooked the grounds to the back of the palace. It was clear the soldiers had already rampaged through his quarters; the place was a mess, what remained of the contents of the cupboards and drawers scattered across the floor.

As Ned was exploring the President's spacious bedroom, he happened to look out the window and noticed an M113 armoured personnel carrier and two Willys jeeps parked up on some hardstanding close to the building. A collection of senior officers alongside the vehicles were being briefed by none other than General Minh himself.

Ned had no idea what they were discussing but decided to photograph the furtive gathering all the same. He captured the officers jumping into the jeeps as the APC started up, sending a plume of black smoke high into the air. The last officer Minh spoke to was his own bodyguard, Captain Nhung. The general indicated for Nhung to follow him around the back of the APC, where he appeared to give him an additional, private briefing. Nhung then climbed into the lead jeep, and the convoy set off.

Curious as to what he'd just witnessed, Ned watched the vehicles leave down the back driveway, before wandering across to re-join Harry in Diem's living room. Harry mentioned he was nipping back downstairs to see if there were any updates on the brothers' whereabouts, and left Ned on his own.

Ned was photographing Diem's book collection, which mostly consisted of large French hardbacks now strewn across the floor, when Harry returned.

"What did you find out?" asked Ned, kneeling on one leg as he tried to capture the scene from a low angle.

Harry stood and watched with his notepad in one hand and a half-chewed pencil in the other. "Apparently, they've captured Diem and Nhu."

"Really! Where?"

"I'm not sure, but the handover ceremony's still taking place at 10.00 am."

Ned looked up from his camera. "Oh yeah, where?"

"Here. It's being held downstairs now. Apparently, the generals are concerned they might lose the President a second time," he replied with a chuckle.

Ned checked his watch. "Still a couple of hours to go. Shall we see if we can find anything of interest in Nhu's office while we wait?" He wound a completed film back into its canister, popped the back off his Nikon, removed the canister and secreted it in his jacket pocket.

8.00 am

President Diem's stomach dropped as he saw the outline of a smartly dressed military figure standing in the church entrance. Sunlight was streaming in, silhouetting the man against the open doorway, but Diem could still tell this was no American officer.

The sense of hope he'd enjoyed in his sanctuary was shattered. The knowledge his cover and location were blown felt like life itself had been expunged. Despite this, Diem, followed by his dejected brother, walked toward his foe in an upright and honourable manner. Now was not the time to show weakness. He was still the President. He had to retain a dignified demeanour.

Approaching the figure, still trying to determine his identity, he was shocked to find he didn't recognise him. They hadn't even had the good grace to send a high-ranking officer, he bemoaned silently.

"Ngo Dinh Diem and Ngo Dinh Nhu," said the officer with authority. "You are both under arrest. Please follow me." He indicated they should proceed through the open door of the church, and Diem and Nhu did as instructed. As they stepped into the courtyard, they were met by several other officers of the ARVN, none of whom Diem could identify. They were ordered to turn around for their hands to be tied behind their backs, before being prodded forward toward the back of an armoured personnel carrier standing by.

Grasping the manner in which they were about to be transported, Nhu suddenly came alive. "This is the vehicle you send to carry your President?" he asked in disgust.

The officer explained General Don had requested that the President wear a clean white suit for the handover ceremony, which meant they had to return to the Gia Long Palace. The APC would offer them protection on the dangerous streets.

His head bowed in resignation, the President watched as the steel door at the back of the vehicle opened with a loud screech, and he and his brother were pushed gracelessly inside. As the door shut with a thud behind them, he looked up in surprise to find an ARVN officer with an eyepatch sitting motionless in the corner, watching them intently with his one beady eye.

Within twenty minutes of its arrival, the convoy departed, leaving the church courtyard as peaceful and tranquil as before. Only the banyan trees broke the silence with the gentle rustling of their leaves.

9.00 am

Ned and Harry walked out of Nhu's office, having failed in their methodical search for any interesting or incriminating documents, primarily due to the language barrier. The palace was quieter than before, a sense of emptiness having settled about it. The physical structure hadn't changed, but already it felt *flatter*, almost as if the power invested in the building were slowly escaping like air from a punctured tyre. Ned could sense it as he walked down the stairs. The soldiers who'd assaulted the building four hours earlier had been rounded up and marched off – along with their souvenirs – back to barracks, leaving just a few of their number behind to keep the general population out.

Ned halted at the bottom of the grand staircase and wondered where everyone was. Surely, if the handover ceremony was due to take place in an hour, the place would be buzzing with activity. The generals would be setting the stage for their historic announcement; the television crews assembling their lights and fixing their cameras on tripods; and the remaining journalists preparing their questions to ask at the concluding press conference. But there was none of that – no generals, no television crews and, crucially, no journalists.

The panic started in Ned's stomach as a kind of hollowness. The more he searched for his colleagues, the sicker he began to feel. He and Harry walked through the empty state rooms on the ground floor and were checking outside by the back entrance when Ned stopped to look at his boss. His forehead furrowed, his eyes narrowed, and finally he voiced the question that had been running through his head.

"Who told you the handover ceremony was taking place here at the palace?"

"Danny O'Connell did," said Harry. "I ran into him at the bottom of the main stairs in the entrance hall."

Ned looked up to the sky as if asking for guidance, then back to Harry. "He's had us for fools. That bloody arse! The ceremony hasn't been moved here. It must still be happening at JGS Headquarters."

Harry looked aghast at his mistake, and Ned began to pace the gravelled parking area in ever-decreasing circles as he considered how they could get to Tan Son Nhut Airport in time for the ceremony. Suddenly, his thoughts were interrupted by the familiar guttural noise of a tracked vehicle approaching. Up the back drive, an M113 armoured personnel carrier was trundling toward them followed by two Willys jeeps. Ned glanced around, but there was no one else near them – just Harry and himself.

The three vehicles stopped by the back entrance to the palace, a yard or two past where Ned and Harry stood. The senior officer, whom Ned recognised from the convoy earlier that morning, jumped down and walked to the back of the APC, scowling at the presence of these Western journalists. He continued to eye Ned with suspicion as he pushed the lever down and pulled the heavy door open.

From where he was standing, Ned was best placed to see into the back of the vehicle. For what felt like an age, he stared in disbelief at the scene before him. Then, remembering what he was there to do, he raised his camera to his right eye and started clicking away.

Instinct took over. His only job now was to capture the image in focus and at the correct exposure. As he looked through the viewfinder, he knew this was the iconic shot he'd been waiting for; the shot that would surely make it onto the front page of every newspaper in the world. This was his reputation right before his eyes.

Slumped across the floor of the vehicle lay the bloodied and unmistakeably dead body of the President of the Republic of Vietnam, hands tied behind his back, face caked in blood, the one visible eye bloodshot and swollen. His white shirt was soaked red, his dark suit stained with dark patches. Behind him lay his brother Nhu in the exact same condition. Looking unconcerned by the events that had very evidently taken place, a blood-splattered Captain Nhung climbed impassively over the bodies, emerged from the vehicle beside Ned, and re-holstered his revolver.

The senior officer who'd opened the hatch had been slow to look inside, distracted by this photographer who'd evidently come to record their capture of President Diem. When he finally did so, his face turned quickly to shock. He grabbed Captain Nhung and shoved him back inside, pushed the journalists out the way, slammed the hatch shut, and ordered the convoy to move out. With the photographer chasing after it down the drive, still snapping away, the procession took off down Le Thanh Ton Street and disappeared into the morning traffic.

Ned returned to Harry in the parking area and they looked at each other in amazement.

"Holy shit, Harry! Are we the only journalists in the world who know Diem and Nhu's fate?"

"I think we are," said Harry, still stunned. But then he pulled himself together and fixed Ned with a determined stare. "Come on, we've got work to do."

Epilogue

Ned lowered the head of the enlarger, allowing him to zoom in on just a small part of his picture. Using the focus knob, he ensured the projected image was as clear as possible on the paper. When he was ready, he clicked the 'on' button and counted down. *Five, four, three, two, one* – and 'off'. Carefully removing the photographic paper from the enlarger, he transferred it to the developing dish, where he swilled it around, having made up the necessary chemicals in advance. Slowly, the white paper started to fade. Not everywhere – only where the light had penetrated through the negative film. An image began to appear, and as the seconds ticked by, his memories of the last six days gradually took form before his eyes.

What a six days it had been.

By early afternoon on Saturday 2ⁿᵈ November, the public telegraph office had reopened, allowing cables to be sent once more, and both Ned and Harry had taken full advantage. While other agencies were still floundering for the truth as to the fate of President Diem and his brother, BPA were busy dispatching the real story, accompanied by photographic evidence. Ned heard later from a fellow journalist that the APC with the bodies inside had driven to JGS Headquarters, and on discovering what had happened, many of the rebel generals had been truly shocked. The journalists waiting for the press conference were told an accident had occurred and the handover ceremony would not be taking place. It was only later that afternoon that the official story was released: the brothers had committed suicide. For the first few hours, most news outlets, including Saigon Radio, had reported that the brothers had grabbed a gun from the soldier escorting them and used it to shoot themselves.

But Ned knew the truth. He'd seen the bloodied bodies with their hands tied behind their backs.

The President of the United States was told of Diem and Nhu's deaths during a meeting – coincidentally – about Vietnam late on Friday night (Eastern Standard Time) at the White House. By all accounts, he'd gone very pale and left the room for a few moments.

In Saigon itself, the news of the brothers' demise had been greeted with jubilation and the population had come out onto the streets to celebrate. Buddhist monks flew their flags openly and the city became a sea of orange. The only violence occurred against institutions that had been run by Nhu, including the offices of the *Times of Vietnam*, which were burnt to the ground, while other buildings had their windows smashed and were looted.

The real truth behind the killings didn't break until Ned's photographs, which showed the bodies slumped in the back of the APC with their hands bound, had worked their way back along the undersea cables to San Francisco and onto New York, before being wired to all of BPA's subscribers. As the world woke on Sunday morning, many of the most influential newspapers, not just in America but around the world, had published the story of the coup, including news of the murders. Ned's image of the blood-drenched President and his brother, clear evidence of their violent end, was splashed across the front pages, and any newspaper not subscribed to BPA had to play catch up. The President's assassination had now become the focal point of the story.

Using only his safety light for illumination, Ned stopped agitating the print in the developer bath. With a pair of tongs, he placed it in the second dish with the stop bath, ensuring the developing process came to a halt. It was funny, he reflected, how keen he'd been to beat Danny O'Connell to the front pages, but it was his rival's duplicity that had put him in the right place at the right time. Ned hadn't seen O'Connell since that night, but he would take great pleasure in thanking him next time he did.

Even after the photographs had been widely published, many on the rebels' side had continued to assert that the brothers had committed suicide, including US Ambassador Henry Cabot Lodge, who'd stated in Monday's papers that he believed the official version of events to be true and accurate. By Tuesday, however, the rebel generals and Lodge had changed their tune, and assassination became the accepted reality. The *Washington Post* had led with a story in which General Don claimed he hadn't wanted the President dead; the intention had always been to let him and his brother seek asylum abroad.

Ned placed the print in the fixer solution, which stopped any further chemical reactions and made it safe to expose to daylight. Finally, he washed it in clean water to remove any lingering chemicals and hung the picture up to dry on his little washing line.

By Wednesday, all the papers in America had been asking the same question: who had authorised the murder of President Diem? Thursday's papers had reported on General Minh's assertion, during a press conference the previous day attended by every member of Vietnam's growing foreign press corps, that he didn't know who was behind the assassination or why it had happened.

Ned walked over to the darkroom door and switched on the light before wandering back to his drying print. He held the photograph close to his face to get a good look. There before him was proof of what he thought he'd seen on that historic morning six days earlier.

He remembered standing at Diem's bedroom window looking down on General Minh as the man had ordered his officers to go and arrest the President at the church in Cholon – not that Ned had known this at the time. He recalled how Minh had given one last briefing to Captain Nhung around the back of the APC, out of sight of the other officers, and gestured in a way that hadn't made sense to Ned in the moment, mainly because he'd been too far away to see it clearly.

But looking closely at the blown-up, zoomed-in photograph of Minh talking to his one-eyed bodyguard, Ned could now see the hand signal in vivid detail. The unmistakable image of the general with his right hand pointing to his head: two fingers extended toward the temple, the bottom two curled back into the palm, thumb raised upward. The universal sign for 'shoot'.

Ned looked up and handed the black and white photograph to the orange-robed figure standing beside him, who'd watched the entire developing process with fascination.

"There you are, Ba – a present for you. Call it insurance if you like. But with this, you can guarantee Minh and his junta won't ever persecute the Buddhists like Diem did before them."

Recognising the significance of the photograph before him, Ba's face broke into a huge smile. In that instant, Ned understood that the Buddhists hadn't just survived the horrors of the last year; they would also likely emerge as a powerful force in the nation's future. One Ned knew he wanted to stay and witness, and help record.